THE BOOK

This edition of *The Odyssey* employs the vigorous and renowned prose translation of Samuel Butler, revised by Malcolm M. Willcock of Cambridge University. Supplementary material has been provided by Walter James Miller, noted critic, author, and translator. The supervising editor of this edition was Harry Shefter. An up-to-date bibliography has been added to this new Enriched Classic.

THE AUTHOR

Born in the 8th century B.C., Homer has been the national poet of Greece for nearly three thousand years. Beyond his obvious far-reaching effect on literature, his influence on the conception of deities was enormous and his authority was almost unquestioned. Tradition represents him as blind and poor in his old age.

TITLES AVAILABLE IN THE ENRICHED CLASSICS SERIES

The Odyssey

HOMER

Translated by
SAMUEL BUTLER

POCKET BOOKS

New York   London   Toronto   Sydney   Singapore

For information regarding special discounts for bulk purchases,
please contact Simon & Schuster Special Sales at
1-800-456-6798 or business@simonandschuster.com

POCKET BOOKS, a division of Simon & Schuster, Inc.
1230 Avenue of the Americas, New York, NY 10020

ISBN: 0-671-01548-6

First Pocket Books printing September 1969

30 29 28 27 26 25 24 23

POCKET and colophon are registered trademarks of
Simon & Schuster, Inc.

Front cover illustration by Rafal Olbinski

Printed in the U.S.A.

CONTENTS

INTRODUCTION

❦

A. Homer's Life and Reputation

After many decades of historical "detective work," we now
know that *The Odyssey* was composed in Asia Minor in or
very close to the year 720 B.C. We know that both *The Iliad*
and *The Odyssey* are based on historic events that occurred
about 1230 B.C. We know, also, that these first great works of
Western literature were composed by an artist who used
complex materials and techniques developed by his predecessors. True, we still know frustratingly little—of a *personal*
nature—about the artist himself. But we are now able to re-
construct much of the *public* and *professional* side of his
life.

1. Homer and the Greeks

Homer, as he was known to the ancients, was born in the
restless Greek world of the early eighth century B.C. At least
seven cities later claimed the honor of being his birthplace.
Significantly, the seven places are widely scattered—Smyrna
and Colophon on the west coast of Asia Minor; island cities
on Chios, Rhodes, Cyprus; Argos and Athens on the Greek
mainland. Another Greek island, Ios, was supposed to be
the place of his death. Obviously, Homer was an extremely
popular poet who traveled wherever Greek was spoken. In

many places, he stopped long and often enough for the proud natives to consider him as one of themselves.

As a professional poet, he was a member of a privileged group, a sort of semireligious brotherhood with a well-organized craft knowledge. Doubtless, he served an apprenticeship to an established bard. While performing the kinds of tasks that would be assigned to a young assistant—like stringing the master's lyre with twisted gut (p. 281)—he also learned how to tune and play the instrument. He had to commit to memory a vast repertory of traditional lays and hymns based on myths passed on orally from many generations back: wondrous stories about the sun-god Helios, Prometheus the Fire-Bringer, Theseus and the Minotaur, Heracles and the Twelve Labors. And he had to practice the art of improvisation, putting together on demand a poem suitable for a special occasion, accompanying himself on the lyre as he recited the long, flexible lines of Greek heroic poetry.

At last a journeyman, out on his own, he tucked his instrument under his rough goat-wool cloak and took to the road and the sea-lane. Traveling alone was dangerous in those days, but as a bard supposed to be under the protection of the divine Muses (p. 103), he enjoyed relative safety. And he was welcome everywhere because, in addition to being an entertainer, he filled what would today be the roles of journalist, historian, genealogist, and teacher of tradition and custom. He performed at religious festivals, at poetry contests, at banquets given by rich noblemen; he sang for dinner on land and for passage at sea.

We have a fair idea of what he might have looked like— and how he may have felt—from representations of performers in later Greek art and literature. On a fragment of a fifth-century-B.C. amphora (a two-handled jar) we have a painting of a bard or *rhapsode*. He wears a long, graceful cloak. Standing on a platform, he is "projecting" with chin and beard pointing toward his audience, probably an outdoor audience. And in Plato's *Ion,* the rhapsode Ion says: "During the tale of pity my eyes are filled with tears, and when I speak of horrors, my hair stands on end and my heart throbs. . . . When I look down upon the spectators from the stage, and behold the emotions of pity, wonder, sternness on their faces . . . I feel obliged to give my whole attention to them. For if I make them cry, then I shall laugh over the receipts; but if I make them laugh, then it is I that shall cry—when the time of payment arrives!"

For an indoor performance, Homer would have occupied a seat of honor covered with a soft, thick rug. Servants would place tables with food and drink at his side (pp. 92–93). Noble guests might share choice morsels with him and call upon him to sing about some great event, hero, or god (p. 103). The noble host, especially, would expect to hear the praises of those divine—or, at the very least, semidivine—figures from whom he himself claimed descent: maybe Heracles (p. 150), Jason (p. 154), or even Zeus himself! For Homer lived in a day when the ruling class justified its position by its blood ties, real or alleged, with great names of the past. One of the bard's main jobs was to glorify both great ancestor and great descendant (pp. 39–40).

To meet the needs of any particular occasion, Homer might select standard lays from the repertory of his profession, but for the sake of prestige, he surely would, whenever possible, play an original composition. "I make all my lays myself," Phemius says when offering his services to Odysseus (p. 291), and we can be sure the man who put that speech in Phemius' mouth used a similar boast when seeking patrons for himself.

If the noble host liked the poet's performance—considering not only his originality but also his tact in genealogy—then Homer could expect to be retained indefinitely. Indeed, sometimes he might have been "held over" against his will (p. 291). Tradition has it that a cruel noble, determined to keep a talented bard in his service, might even blind him to reduce his chances of running away. Notice that Demodocus, another bard in *The Odyssey* (p. 92), is blind; and it was widely believed in the ancient world that Homer became blind in his latter years.

Late in life Homer composed and performed a *Hymn to Delian Apollo*. In this work, which is similar in style to *The Iliad* and *The Odyssey,* the author appeals to his audience, the maids of Delos, to remember him as a good poet and "a blind old man of craggy Chios."

During an extended engagement, Homer could work on an epic—a long narrative poem about a great national hero—which he might recite in nightly instalments, taking maybe two to three weeks to complete the tale. It is more likely, however, that he composed such full-length works— up to 15,000 lines—for a religious festival like the Panionia (All-Ionia) in Mykale. On such occasions, rhapsodes working in relays could easily perform an epic in two or three days. Many ancient stories about Homer suggest that he even directed a team of rhapsodes.

We believe Homer composed *The Iliad* first. This is the more youthful, exuberant, passionate of the two epics extant. Perhaps he chose to write about the Trojan War (*Iliad* means "of Ilium," and *Ilium* was a Greek name for Troy) because he knew the terrain well. That famous war had been fought in the northwest corner of Asia Minor, north of Chios and Smyrna, two cities often mentioned in connection with Homer. Also, he probably reasoned that since every Mediterranean Greek community had been represented in the Trojan War, a poem about that conflict would appeal to audiences wherever he traveled. And the Ionians—among whom he was probably born and raised—were a mixture of migrants from all parts of Greece who would have a natural interest in a war that had involved all their ancestors.

Drawing on the treasure of traditional stories at his command, he focused on a seven-week period in the tenth year of the war. He dramatized a quarrel between two Greek generals, Agamemnon and Achilles, and the effect of this schism on the morale and fortunes of both Greeks and Trojans. The work is famous for its magnificent descriptions of the ebb and flow of heroic combat, its tender scenes such as Hector's farewell to his infant son; and the dramatic portraits of Helen on the walls of Troy, of her abductor Paris; of the great fighters Ajax (p. 149), Odysseus, Achilles (pp. 147–49), and Diomedes (p. 29).

We assume *The Odyssey* is the later poem because its author is more seasoned in his craft, more mature in his interests. Some scholars believe the two poems were composed as much as fifty years apart. This seems plausible since we have learned how many creative Greeks lived well into their seventies or eighties. But recent researchers date *The Odyssey* close to 720 B.C., or about thirty years after *The Iliad*.

For this latter work, Homer chose the story of Odysseus' return from Troy—a fascinating series of ordeals and triumphs from which Odysseus emerges as the ideal blend of brain and brawn probably required for survival in a heroic age. Here Homer emphasizes not youthful abandonment to war and glory but mature concern with war's aftermath, with family and civic responsibility. Even the gods behave more thoughtfully, more spiritually in *The Odyssey* than they do in *The Iliad*.

For his description of some of his outdoor scenes—like a whirlpool in the Straits of Messina (p. 154) and meadows of parsley near the Straits of Gibraltar (p. 149)—Homer probably drew on information supplied him by Phoenician sailors, whom he doubtless met in every port (p. 200). And the monsters certainly he had heard about from the Phoenicians; cannibals (p. 124) and octopuses (p. 154) that they had encountered were magnified, of course, in the retelling, especially since such tales helped keep the Greeks out of western waters which Phoenicians then controlled.

But many settings and situations are based on Homer's first-hand observation and experience. He was all too familiar with the stowing away of goods in the hold of a ship (p. 164), and he himself had probably traveled the road that Telemachus takes from Pylus to Lacedaemon (p. 38) and had noted the difference in terrain between mainland and island (p. 53). Many nights, en route from one noble's abode to the next, he had settled for a bed in a swineherd's hut (p. 189). From countless slow approaches on foot, he could describe in detail the outer grounds of many splendid palaces (pp. 84–85).

The vivid indoor scenes in *The Odyssey* are clearly drawn from the vantage point of Homer's own seat as bard—he had seen queens spinning (p. 41) and receiving unexpected guests (pp. 85–86) and the young lords making passes at the serving girls (p. 284). The two minstrels in *The Odyssey*—Phemius and Demodocus—are probably closer to the real Homer than we can even speculate. For example, how could Homer, in all those years of playing for wine-drinking warriors, have avoided bloody indoor brawls? The Western world's first great poet surely knew what it was like to hide under a bench and live to describe the experience (p. 292).

His major works—*The Iliad, The Odyssey,* and *Delian Hymn*—made him famous in his lifetime. But was the spectacular difference between Homer's appeal and that of his contemporaries and predecessors due only to Homer's superiority as poet and storyteller? Perhaps other poets composed only shorter works, like the lays so often mentioned or recited in *The Iliad* and *The Odyssey* (pp. 11, 75). If so, then Homer actually would be the inventor of the longer poem. Perhaps he was the first poet to develop full characterization, or first to exploit the literary possibilities in the *alphabetic writing* that had been introduced about 850 B.C. Maybe he was the inventor of the long simile so prominent in his work, the value of which we will discuss later.

In any event, judging strictly from truths implicit in his

work, we may safely add that: (1) his own personal philosophy was an asset to him: he belived in the rationale of the social order in which he lived; like Shakespeare, he could glorify his patrons and give artistic sanction to their right to rule, without compromising his artistic integrity; (2) he was, in spite of this aristocratic social view, a man of broad, deep human sympathies; and (3) he was a "consummate genius," a man, like Shakespeare or Beethoven, who can take over forms created by his predecessors and carry them to their highest, fullest development. These inferences become clearer when we study his style and characterizations.

Poets who lived during and after Homer's day extended his stories with at least six other epics, telling of the Trojan War before and after the period covered in *The Iliad,* of the return from Troy of heroes other than Odysseus, and of the last years of Odysseus' life. Significantly enough, while all eight epics—known as the Epic Cycle—were widely quoted in later Greek writings, only the oldest have survived in their entirety—Homer's two.

Within three centuries after Homer's death (roughly the same time period that separates us from Shakespeare), Homer had become a sacred institution in the Greek world. By now the epics had been committed to writing, and each city had its official manuscript copies of *The Iliad* and *The Odyssey.* Every schoolboy studied, memorized, recited Homer not only for his religious and historical content, but also as models for proper writing and speaking (pp. 25–26, 97, 165). Writers in other media drew on these epics for materials, metaphors, and themes: Aeschylus the playwright, for example, modestly referred to his own masterpieces as "slices from the Homeric banquet." To be compared with Homer meant that one had achieved success. Sophocles became known as the Homer of Tragedy, Plato as the Homer of Philosophy, Sappho, the lyric poet, as "the female Homer."

Greeks, meanwhile, had become history-conscious and

tried to construct a coherent picture of their own political and cultural past and of great personalities like Homer. This was difficult because Homer had lived in a time and place where records were not kept. In epic poetry he had worked in an impersonal, anonymous medium; even in his hymns it was inappropriate for him to refer to himself except, as we have seen, in passing, and then he would refer to himself not as Homer but as "me."

Herodotus, Father of History (about 485–425 B.C.), counted the generations between himself and Homer and speculated that the poet had lived "but 400 years before my time, no more." In our dating system, that would have been about 850 B.C. But we realize now that Herodotus reckoned three generations to a hundred years whereas modern historians find it more accurate to reckon four generations per century. When thus adjusted, Herodotus' calculations coincide neatly with the dates established by today's experts: Homer flourished about 750 B.C.

Thucydides, the Greek historian who followed Herodotus by one generation (as we count a generation!), had to take great pains in his writing to establish the simple fact that festivals had been held on Delos in earlier times. It was he who identified the Delian hymn as Homer's, an identification supported by modern linguistic studies.

Homer was discussed by the earliest literary critics: Plato condemned his "irreverence" for the gods, Aristotle spoke of *The Iliad* as the first great tragedy. Scholars became concerned that most manuscripts of the epics varied tremendously, as was indeed inevitable, since Homer and his team doubtless freely adapted the poems, condensing or expanding as occasion demanded. About 150 B.C., Aristarchus of Samothrace, Alexandrian scholar, collated numerous versions of both works and published a standard text. It was he who divided each epic into twenty-four books, one for each letter in the Greek alphabet. Notice that we do not know what mistakes Aristarchus may have made, what he may have omitted, or whether he included more than Homer would have approved (the repetitious passages, for example).

2. Homer and Western Culture

During the Golden Age of Latin culture, Roman poets imitated Homer's style and Romanized his materials. For example, Virgil's *Aeneid* is based on Homer's Aeneas in *The Iliad*. Virgil was especially inspired by the Achilles' Shield concept in *The Iliad* and by the world-of-the-dead scene in *The Odyssey* (Book XI). After Rome fell, Greek literature was virtually unknown in Europe. But medieval minstrels knew of the "matter of Troy" through Latin poets, and Dante based his *Divine Comedy* not on Homer but on Virgil. Happily, the mid-East scholars had kept Homer, Plato, Aristotle, and other classical authors alive, and, in Florence in 1488, upon the revival of learning in Europe, *The Iliad* and *The Odyssey* were reprinted. They set literary standards for the Renaissance: as one critic has said, "The Renaissance *was* Homer." Reading Homer in Greek became part of every cultured person's education. Homer served as model, guide, or inspiration for major English writers from Shakespeare to Tennyson, and strongly conditioned even the literature of our own day.

Ezra Pound and James Joyce, for example, two giants of twentieth-century literature, have used Homeric themes and materials prominently in their works. Homer's pervasive influence is evident in our use of his storytelling techniques—the "flashback" in novels and short stories, the "cliffhanger" in movies and television. In all literary forms, narrative and dramatic, we are constantly concerned with what is for us Homer's greatest innovation—the character.

But Homer's influence on our times goes far beyond literature—Homer is part of our everyday language. In our personal relations, we refer to a trusted adviser as a *mentor* (pp. 20–21), to a talkative person as a *windbag* (p. 122). We call an alluring woman a *Siren* (p. 153), and if she brings out only the worst in men, a *Circe* (p. 129). In some predicaments we say we are *tantalized* (p. 150), or, worse yet, *caught between Scylla and Charybdis* (pp. 154–55). In politics, we suspect our enemies of *Trojan Horse* tactics (p. 45), while we consider our own unheeded predictions as *Cassandra*-like (p. 146). In psychology, we talk of *protean* personalities (pp. 48–51), of neurotics trapped in the *oedipal* situation (p. 142). And in search of terms that will be universally understood, our scientists go back to Homer for names for elements and organs, like *helium* and the *nectary* (p. 64). Hence, we are not being idolatrous but fact-minded when we speak of Homer as "the fountainhead of Western civilization."

3. The "Homeric Question"

During the Romantic revolution in thought and the arts (roughly, beginning in 1795), writers and critics tended to idealize the common man to the extent that they questioned the existence of uncommon geniuses. They tried to prove that some of the great works of the past were the output not of single authorship but of communal collaboration. While this attitude produced much valuable evidence about the development of folk ballads and some books of the Bible, it played havoc when it raised the "Homeric Question."

The "higher critics" exploited the fact that the Greeks had themselves been puzzled about Homer's identity; of course, as we have seen, the classical Greeks had difficulty reconstructing the details of their unrecorded history, political and literary. For much of the nineteenth century, it was skeptically assumed that *The Iliad* and *The Odyssey* were really collections of separate lays, all fictitious in nature, written at different times by different bards, and then loosely pieced together, with much overlapping and repetition, by some editors and scholars. Homer as a single writer vanished.

But then in the late nineteenth century, Heinrich Schlie-mann, taking his cues from Homer himself, went to Turkey and, digging at Hissarlik (Castle Hill), unearthed Troy; then he went on to Greece and excavated golden Mycenae (p. 32) and the Palace of Tiryns. Structures, weapons, cups, tripods (p. 245), and brooches (p. 250) found in these "digs" corre-sponded to many described in *The Iliad* and *The Odyssey*. It was obvious that these epics had been inspired not by dif-fuse fancies but from traditional knowledge of historical events and places. Every subsequent archaeological expedi-tion in the Mediterranean has given us new insights into Homer's world, from Nestor's Pylos (p. 25) to Idomeneus' Crete (p. 30) to Hector's Troy (pp. 3, 27).

Meanwhile, scientific linguists have studied Homer's lan-guage. They have established that *The Iliad*, *The Odyssey*, and *Delian Hymn* are different in style from the poems of Hesiod, the cyclic epics, and other hymns extant. The Ameri-can scholar Milman Parry and others have gone into the field to observe techniques still used by "oral" poets who improvise heroic songs for public performance in modern Yugoslavia. In 1961 a doctoral candidate at Columbia ran the 15,693 lines of *The Iliad* through computers to check the characteristic sub-tleties of the metric patterns. His findings are clear from a front-page headline in *The New York Times*:

Iliad One-Man Job, Computer Indicates

and from the "jump head" that continued the story on an in-side page:

COMPUTER GIVES HOMER HIS OWN

As a consequence of studies like these, most Greek scholars now believe—as the classical Greeks themselves believed—that *The Iliad* and *The Odyssey* were composed by one man.

True, like Shakespeare, he borrowed from other writers; both before and after his epics were committed to writing, some passages were tampered with; but the milieu that the works reflect, their style, attitude, metrical contours, and structural techniques all indicate unity of authorship.

Definitive studies on Homer's dates have been made by T. B. L. Webster who has correlated overall patterns and themes in Homer with eighth-century-B.C. trends in Greek pottery; Homer's Shield of Achilles (*The Iliad*) with eighth-century shields found in Crete; Homer's athletic contests (pp. 94–97) with historical evidence of the Greek Olympics; and Homer's vocabulary and grammar with what we know about the growth of the Greek language. From these and similar studies, he concludes that ". . . *The Odyssey* was not composed in isolation from *The Iliad*. It is likely . . . that they were composed for two different festivals. Of their dates, we can only say that *The Iliad* was not composed long if at all before 750 and *The Odyssey* was not composed long if at all after 720. Thus a maximum gap of thirty years between the completion of the two poems is possible."

4. Translations of Homer

Homer's continuous popularity with today's readers is evident in the steady stream of translations into modern languages. About thirty-five English versions of *The Odyssey* alone have appeared in the last 350 years, for an average of one every decade. The translators include some of the leading names in English literature, each of whom has emphasized a different side of Homer's nature. The Renaissance poet and playwright George Chapman (about whose translation Keats wrote his famous sonnet "On First Looking into Chapman's Homer") saw Homer as a Renaissance man. The great "Augustan" poet Alexander Pope saw Homer as an Augustan. And to Colonel T. E. Lawrence—"Lawrence of Arabia," who translated *The Odyssey* under the pen name of

T. E. Shaw—Homer was a bookworm, but still a decent chap, for all that. And to Samuel Butler, author of *Erewhon* and *The Way of All Flesh,* Homer was really a young Sicilian girl. Typical of Butler's arguments to be found in his book *The Authoress of the Odyssey* was that only a woman writer would think that timber is seasoned *before* it's cut down (pp. 65–66). Again, archaeology has come to Homer's rescue: man or woman, Homer was right about the order in which the Greeks seasoned and cut their wood.

In spite of his eccentric views about Homer's sex, Butler has given us one of the best translations. What the modern reader wants, M. M. Willcock has pointed out, "is simple, natural, modern English so that he can read the . . . *Odyssey* as if it were a novel. And a good natural translation will bring the reader nearer to the original, because the simplicity of the translation will correspond to the simple language and thought of Homer." And it is Butler's version—as edited and corrected by Mr. Willcock, assistant lecturer in classics at Cambridge University—that we shall be studying here.

B. Historical Background

The Odyssey is not only the greatest adventure story of all time; it is also a major document in the growth of the West. While its literary charm is hard to miss, its broader cultural value can be lost to us unless we see it against a background of Greek life and thought.

1. Ancient Greek Wars and Migrations

The Trojan War, the curiosity of Odysseus, the strange monsters he encountered, are all related to one great historical phenomenon:

Before Odysseus' time in the thirteenth century B.C., until well after Homer in the eighth century B.C., the peoples of Greece were expanding restlessly, first toward the southeast and east, then toward the west. These migrations reached such proportions that, historically speaking, they are surpassed only by the colonization of the New World.

Achaeans, Argives, Danaans—as Homer usually calls his Greeks—were a mixture of Mediterranean and northern peoples who by 1500 B.C. had become a major power in and around the Aegean Sea. Their rulers lived in massive walled fortresses built on high ground (p. 37). Their most powerful overlord reigned at Mycenae (p. 32) on low hills above the Argive plain, six miles northeast of Argos (p. 33), where the stone fortifications, "beehive tombs," and famous Lion Gate, all recently unearthed by archaeologists, are still standing.

About 1450 B.C., the Mycenaeans were powerful enough to subdue the Minoan Empire based on "wide Crete," largest island to the south of the Greek mainland (p. 249). They occupied Cnossus, the Cretan capital, and sacked the magnificent palace of King Minos (pp. 230, 248), which, with its many rooms, halls, and corridors, had come to be known to the Achaeans as "the labyrinth of the Minotaur." Viewed from the air, its ground-plan still resembles a maze.

Mycenaean and Minoan cultures merged; we find the heroes from Crete's "hundred cities" highly regarded in *The Iliad.* And thousands of clay tablets found recently at Cnossus, Pylos, and Mycenae reveal that these societies truly had much in common. They all kept records in a *syllabic script* recently deciphered as an early form of Greek. Speaking for the moment, about military matters only, these records reveal a world organized for war-making. Scores of tablets indicate that bronze, from which virtually all weapons were made, was rationed to smiths who worked under government control. A typical Cnossus tablet notes storage of a lot of 6,010 arrows, and another of 2,530; a typical Pylos tablet reports that wood-cutters were delivering 150 axles to the chariot factory. Military rosters, records of personnel transfers, "orders of battle," all indicate careful and constant control over resources and manpower. These records resemble Hittite tablets of the same period in which, incidentally, a minor Achaean leader is described as commanding 100 charioteers and 1,000 infantrymen.

Expanding eastward across scores of islands scattered through the Aegean Sea, the Mycenaeans established trading posts in Asia Minor. While most of the area was held by Hittites, the northwest corner was controlled by the Trojans. The latter had built, three miles from the Hellespont (straits now known as Dardanelles), one of the most beautiful fortress-cities in the ancient world. Troy rose on broad terraces on which the city's expert architects had constructed freestanding houses of polished stone. In rich settlements near this citadel, the Trojans spun yarns and wove textiles. On their fruitful plains, they raised crops and tamed horses. Trojan boats brought home not only great catches of fish but loads of shell food. Surplus grain and horses they traded for Mycenaean pottery, Cretan bronze, and Asiatic gold.

Imagine how this wealthy, productive, proud city tempted the warlike Mycenaeans. True, they enjoyed cordial trade relations with Troy, but they also competed with Troy for international trade. And Troy stood as a barrier to the East. Troy controlled both the Dardanelles water route and the land route across northern Asia Minor. Apparently, the Mycenaeans simply waited their chance. First there was an earthquake in Asia Minor about 1275 B.C., which the Greeks doubtless knew had weakened the Trojan citadel. Then the Hittite empire, east of Troy, began to disintegrate, making it even more attractive for the Mycenaeans to penetrate into that area. And they finally found a suitable provocation for war. According to Greek tradition, this came when Paris, son of King Priam of Troy, visited King Menelaus of Sparta, fell in love with his wife Helen, and with her full consent, carried her off to Troy (pp. 43–45, 146, 178).

Menelaus appealed to his elder brother, King Agamemnon of Mycenae, who summoned the Greek lords from all the islands and city-states to unite in war against the Trojans. The Mycenaean armada of more than a thousand vessels included, according to *The Iliad*, "twelve ships with red-painted bows," manned by "high-hearted men" from Dulichium, Zacynthus, Ithaca (p. 106), and Elis (p. 53), all led by King Odysseus (p. 178), famed for his wisdom in council.

For nine years, as Greek writers tell us, the Achaeans kept the Trojans on the defensive. Under the leadership of their great warrior Achilles (pp. 147–49), whose very name made the strongest enemy tremble, the Greeks destroyed eleven inland and twelve seacoast towns (p. 28), but they could not take Troy proper. In the tenth year, according to Homer, Agamemnon offended Achilles, and that moody, prideful commander withdrew his own troops from the fighting and sulked in his tent. As a result, the balance of power shifted; the Trojans found themselves on the offensive. Under the lead of Hector, one of Paris' brothers, they almost drove the Greeks into the sea. Returning to combat only to avenge the death of his beloved friend, Achilles slew Hector and incidentally saved the Greeks.

But later Achilles too was killed (p. 67), and now the Greeks resorted to stratagem to get inside Troy and take it by night. They burned their camp and pretended to be sailing home, leaving on the beach a gigantic wooden horse: probably an armored tower on wheels such as was often used for storming high fortifications. Inside its hollow belly were hidden, in full war array, fighters like Odysseus, Menelaus, Diomedes, Anticlus, and others (p. 45). On the outside of the horse was inscribed: A THANK-OFFERING TO ATHENE, FROM THE GREEKS. Some Trojans suspected a trick, but most were unwilling to offend the goddess Athene by inspecting her property, or even by neglecting it, and so they dragged the horse intact inside the city gates. That night,

while the Trojans celebrated their supposed delivery from
siege, the heroes slipped out of the horse and opened the
gates for the Greek army which had returned under cover of
darkness. Tall Troy was put to the torch, males to the sword,
females into chains (pp. 103–04).

After the spoils were divided, according to Greek tradition, most of the leaders—like King Nestor of Pylos—
reached home safely (p. 30). But when Agamemnon
returned, he was slain by his wife and her lover (pp. 32–33),
and some of the heroes ran into storms and other difficulties
(pp. 32–33). Long before the last heroes had gotten home,
their exploits had become a staple subject in every minstrel's
repertory (pp. 10–11, 102–04).

Ironically, though, Mycenaeans returned home to enjoy
only a very brief period of glory as Troy's conquerors: within
a generation they themselves were under siege. Dorians,
northern migrants armed with iron, hacked their way down
into Bronze-Age Greece. Pylos was destroyed about 1200
B.C., Mycenae fell about 1100 B.C., and only Athens survived
Dorian assaults. Hence, refugees from all over Greece—but
mainly from Pylos—poured into Athens. Elsewhere, Dorian
invaders and Mycenaean survivors blended into one popula-
tion. But the entire Greek world—exhausted, fragmented,
isolated—collapsed into economic and cultural depression.

In their Dark Age, the Greeks looked back upon their
Mycenaean past with nostalgia and wonderment. Whenever
a tomb of a Mycenaean hero was rediscovered, it was made
into a shrine. Hero-worship cults sprang up with yearly cele-
brations of Nestor in Pylos, Agamemnon near Mycenae, and
Odysseus in Ithaca.

Record-keeping was discontinued. So far as the populace
and even the rulers were concerned, the old *syllabic writing*
became a traditional memory, a magic thing mentioned
vaguely by poets in their heroic tales of the great past. And if
the poets themselves used the *syllabic notation* (not likely

because it was a slow process), they kept it a closely guarded craft secret. Probably, they did not record their poetry at all until after the innovation of *alphabetic writing* about 850 B.C.

Rallying in the ninth century B.C., the new Greeks established colonies in the western Mediterranean, until then almost entirely unknown to them (pp. 71–72, 73–74, 108–09). And a new strain of Pylian-Athenians settled in Asia Minor, mainly in Ionia, the region south of Troy that included mainland cities like Smyrna and islands like Chios.

As we shall see in our discussion of characterization, the eastward expansion helped determine the personality that Homer created for his beloved Odysseus, while the westward movement provided the trials that Odysseus had to face. In Ionia the bards flourished anew, developing their traditional materials and the metric patterns known as Ionic hexameters. While still looking back to the Golden Age of Mycenae, Homer and his colleagues miraculously revitalized their own.

With new restless energy and a fresh viewpoint, the Ionians began that speculation into the nature of reality that later Greeks were to call philosophy. The colonies naturally continued their relations with the home cities, and Ionian developments in arts and science took root and flowered into a new Golden Age in Athens. It was in that city that the Panathenaean festival was held, at which Homer was recited—by relays of rhapsodes—from about 555 B.C. on. Athens became the center of Greek drama based largely on Homeric literature.

2. *Greek Society and Government*

The Mycenaean world was highly centralized, politically as well as militarily. At the top was a king, guardian of the decrees of heaven. He bestowed lands, gifts, and privileges on his nobles—his captains, governors, administrators of factories and estates—in return for which they owed him full mil-

itary and civic support. The nobles controlled the large bodies of craftsmen, commoners, land serfs, and slaves. All
grades in the social pyramid were held together by dues and
services paid upward (p. 164), and by gifts and rewards
passed downward (pp. 251–52, 275–76).

Hence, it is no poetic exaggeration that in *The Odyssey*
Menelaus has thought of making Odysseus an outright gift
of an entire subject city (pp. 42–43); in *The Iliad*, Agamemnon offers Achilles seven cities in which the "people will re-
vere him as a god." And notice that Homer has the
"stranger" tell Penelope (pp. 246–47) what a ruler of such a
city would owe to his people in return for their loyalty: a
healthy economy and an honest administration (p. 247).

The Mycenaean kingship—as Homer understood it—
was not necessarily hereditary. Odysseus has succeeded his
father to the kingship, apparently because he had demon-
strated his right to the succession, but Telemachus might
not succeed Odysseus (pp. 12–13). For one thing, he has not
yet proved himself (p. 10); for another, his mother is still
alive and the noble who marries a king's widow might
thereby claim the throne himself. Oedipus, for example, already an established hero, had strengthened his claim to the
throne of Thebes by marrying the dowager queen (p. 142).

Clay tablets thus far found do not indicate clearly
whether the thirteenth-century-B.C. king had absolute or
limited powers. But we do know that early in Greek history
the assembly—an incipient form of legislature and court—
had very definite rights. In any event, by the time Homer
recreated the Mycenaean social order in *The Iliad* and *The
Odyssey*, he assigned to the assembly an important part in
public and even military affairs.

Although it comprised all free males, the assembly apparently could be convoked only by a nobleman and only for important matters: during Odysseus' nineteen-year absence,
there has been no meeting of these councillors (pp. 14–15);

and Telemachus now calls them together on a problem affecting the royal house. They could not, apparently, initiate action: they were convoked to hear announcements and to discuss problems and cases put to them (pp. 8–9). Once they had been consulted, however, their advice and opinion, being matters of public knowledge, could not easily be flouted. Notice that even in a military assembly, Odysseus feels he must go along with the majority (pp. 158–59). And the suitors, powerful enough to risk the displeasure of the queen and the king's son, nevertheless fear Penelope and Telemachus if they gain support of the assembly (pp. 213–14).

In a formal assembly, when a man asked for permission to speak, a herald would lend him a staff or baton that indicated that he "had the floor" (pp. 14–15). Augurs, members of the priestly class, would watch for signs in the heavens that might indicate how the gods felt on the subject (pp. 17–18). Since the king was also usually the high priest, he and the augur, as ancient history makes abundantly clear, often found it possible to outwit the majority by "receiving" only those signs favorable to their own view.

There was no written law, simply custom and the king's will as modified by public opinion. One important custom was the *lex talionis,* the "law of retaliation." If a man's family had been wronged, and he had tested the reaction of the assembly and gotten sufficiently strong sanction, he could assume his right to seek revenge by direct action (pp. 261–62, 316–17, 318). In certain cases he would be expected to seek revenge as a duty, as when all Greece waited for Orestes to grow up and avenge his father's death (pp. 4, 29–31). But a man hesitated to take direct personal action even when in the right because he might then have to go into exile (pp. 196–97, 261–62, 299–300, 316–17).

Exile was feared because a man alone, away from the protection of his family and community, had to throw himself upon the mercy of strangers, and he would very likely be seized and sold into slavery (pp. 183, 184, 199, 223) to join that lowest class of unfortunates (p. 105). In the ancient world, a man could be a prince one day, a slave the next. Cassandra, Princess of Troy, went captive to Greece as Agamemnon's concubine (p. 146). The slave's fate was a matter of the master's whim: Eumaeus could not marry unless his master assigned him a bride (pp. 177, 276). King Laertes had every right to use Eurycleia sexually (pp. 13, 180). Although Odysseus feared reprisal for killing the suitors, he executed the slave girls with absolute impunity (pp. 293–95).

Socially and politically, heroic Greek society was patriarchal; that is, male-dominated. Queens may have taken part in official occasions (p. 85), may even have acted in a custodial capacity during a king's absence, but, generally, women were conspicuously missing from the banquet and place of assembly. A woman had only two concerns: marriage and home, and marriage was arranged for her by her father (p. 9). In both her parents' house and her husband's, her world was limited to the kitchen, loom, washing cisterns (pp. 74–75), and servants' quarters. "Speech," Telemachus tells his mother, "is man's matter" (p. 11), and she accepts his dismissal of her as proof that now he is a man and she must relinquish her custodianship. She does have, however, the protection and dignity afforded her by the system of dowry (p. 17).

Marriage was generally exogamous—that is, outside one's own family—but there are hints in *The Odyssey* that this was relatively new. The rationale for exogamy—to increase the numbers of one's close and brave allies—is explicitly stressed (pp. 105–06), while instances of incestuous marriage are mentioned often (pp. 83, 121).

Best evidences of patriarchy are the ancient habit of blaming the world's woe on women (pp. 146–47) and the practice of the "double standard." Great Homeric heroes tend to be promiscuous in their own sexual relations but scandalized at the thought of a "faithless" woman. But the Greek woman was not mere chattel; a good personal relationship between man and wife was highly valued (p. 77).

Notice that everyone, man or woman, commoner or king, was expected to lead an active life, and that this meant—to an extraordinary degree, according to our experience—an *outdoor* life. Nausicaa, a princess, not only supervises the laundering, she treads the clothes herself (pp. 74–75). Helen, a queen of divine descent, brings her sewing box into a social situation (p. 41). Odysseus has not only engaged in glorious tasks like hunting and warring, but has tended the vines (p. 314), built stone walls, hung doors, inlaid furniture (pp. 300–01). One of the main proofs of the worthlessness of the suitors is that they are unproductive idlers.

The splendid Mediterranean climate, with clear skies and fresh dry air most of the time, encouraged the Greeks to conduct most of their daytime business and social activities in the open. Men built their living quarters around open courtyards, judged legal matters in the roofless marketplace (p. 134), held their political assemblies under the blue sky (pp. 17–18), and congregated on the beaches by the thousands for religious festivals (pp. 25–26). Along with this zest for nature went pride in athletic talents (pp. 94–95) and constant cleanliness—the clean body was idolized in almost ritual bathing (pp. 36–37, 75, 78–79, 101–02, 132, 193, 254, 300).

3. Greek Mythology and Religion

Ancient Greeks tried to understand the unknown in terms of what was already known. What causes the sun to rise and set, vegetation to die and return, men to submit helplessly to the passions of love and war? One way to account for these phenomena—and to deal with them—was to personify them.

A simple but important example, for readers of *The*

Odyssey, is the Greeks' attitude toward the sea. They depended on fishing for much of their food, on communication with the islands for their trade. But they were terrified by the open water; they hugged the coasts (p. 29), rarely venturing so far from home as the western end of the Mediterranean. Without charts, logs, or compass, they could rely on only the simplest kind of "dead reckoning." Any unknown current, unseen rock, or mild storm was a catastrophe.

Watching with dread as dark clouds gathered, as calm waters suddenly grew furious, as massive waves began to pound them and fierce winds drive them to nowhere, they were appalled at the *malevolence* of the sea. They could not help seeing it in terms of themselves: this was vindictive wrath directed toward them by some great superhuman power. How had they displeased him? Not certain perhaps of specific offenses, puny men could make only a general appeal, acknowledging the sea god's greater power, asking for his blessing, mercy, cooperation. If they survived—and surely, before they went aboard ship again!—they would make elaborate sacrifices to Poseidon, as they called him, hoping to flatter him, to get into his good graces (pp. 25–26, 29, 33–34, 68–70, 138, 168).

This conception of a natural force as a supernatural being gave rise to many myths or stories about him, his feats and personality; these myths became the basis for rituals that his worshippers performed in an effort to make contact with him (pp. 3, 25–26, 34, 161–62). Mythology, then, is the essence of ancient religion. It is now seriously studied by anthropologists, psychoanalysts, and historians because it gives us major clues to man's dark origins and slow growth.

Many interpretations of Nature, of course, required more elaborate myths. Trying to account for the sun and its movement, the Greeks resorted to the most awe-inspiring movement in their own experience: they concluded that the sun was a dazzling chariot pulled by powerful white horses controlled by a strong driver. Of course, those would have to be superhorses and he a superman, and such a strong creature would enjoy immortality. The *super* part was frightening. Suppose Helios the sun god, son of Hyperion, as they called him (p. 156), became displeased with what he saw on earth? But the *-man* part was reassuring. His feelings could be understood; he could be appealed to; some bargain was possible (pp. 160–61).

The most important myths were those connected with fertility. Ancient man everywhere lived in fear that when vegetation decayed, it would never return. So eager were they to influence Nature in this regard that they included human sacrifice in their rituals. When the plants died, a priest-king had to die too; they saturated the ground with his blood to fertilize it. But they perceived the tenderer emotions also at work in the universe. Thus, after a field had been plowed three times, Demeter, the goddess of vegetation, or her priestess, would lie in the field in a man's embrace: their love would fertilize the ground (p. 63)!

Some Greeks, trying to explain the cycle of growth and death, offered this story: Persephone, radiant daughter of Demeter (p. 63), was gathering flowers in a meadow when suddenly the earth opened and Hades, god of the underworld, rode up in a chariot pulled by black horses, and carried her below as his bride. He made her queen of the nether regions, of the shadows of the dead (pp. 133, 137, 151).

Demeter, grief-stricken, refused to allow vegetation to grow on earth until her daughter was returned to her. Now without barley and wheat, men would starve and, of course, be unable to perform ritual sacrifices. So Zeus intervened. He agreed that Persephone could return to her mother if she had not yet eaten of the food of the underworld. Hades, eager to keep his bride, had anticipated this; he had fed

Persephone on pomegranate seeds. Zeus could only offer a compromise, which Demeter had to accept. For part of each year, Persephone returned to the earth, and Demeter (the word means "Grain Mother") allowed grain to sprout, flowers to bloom. For the rest of the year, Persephone returned to Hades; then grain was buried under the soil; all earth was barren.

Probably this fertility myth gained wide acceptance because it is charged with basic emotions: grief over a young girl's loss of innocence; conflict between a mother's demands and a husband's demands; association of growing up with inevitable death. The story has appeal too because of its hidden symbols: Persephone's eating the pomegranate—like Eve's eating the apple—signifies her partaking of physical love. And the whole problem of fertility involves man's yearning for immortality: like the grain, he too would like to be resurrected. (The Eleusinian mysteries, secret immortality rituals performed by later Greeks, involved worship of the Grain Mother: at a crucial moment in the ceremonies, the worshipper was shown a stalk of wheat that had been "reaped in silence.")

Not only mysterious *outer* forces but also mysterious *inner* forces were explained as part of man's involvement in supernatural drama. Overwhelmed by inspiration that seemed to come from outside himself, the poet said it came from his Muse: she merely used him as a medium; she spoke *through* him (p. 3). Struck by an idea, as if out of nowhere, a Greek believed that wisdom—that is, Athene—had come to him (pp. 70, 73, 271). Driven to irrational behavior by a romantic infatuation, a lover would blame his loss of self-control on Aphrodite, whose power no one could resist (pp. 44, 302). Tormented by a guilty conscience, a remorseful wrongdoer felt as if harassed by the Erinyes, those furies who haunted criminals even to insanity (pp. 17, 196). Ancient Greeks were especially likely to explain mass behavior in some such manner: they referred to man-made wars, to the irresponsible martial spirit in themselves, as "the rage of Ares" (p. 149). Of course, putting these psychological forces outside themselves gave the Greeks a way of coming to terms with these traits.

Before there were written records, myths served the additional purpose of commemorating historical events. Consider the story of Theseus, the Athenian hero who tracked down and slew the Minotaur in his labyrinth. Since the unearthing of the Cretan ruins, we know this is not a quaint fairy tale but a metaphoric account of the Mycenaean overthrow of Minoan culture. King Minos, the Cretan lawgiver, wore a bull-mask as his sign of office: *taurus* means bull; hence *Minos-taur!* He lived, as we have seen, in a very complex and sprawling structure. Apparently he met an ignominious death. At the end of the siege of Cnossus, he was chased through the corridors of his own palace.

Reinterpreted by modern science, the myth of Perseus beheading the Gorgon is also discovered to be historical in nature. The Gorgons were queen-priestesses in a matriarchal society—that is, a female-dominated society. These priestesses wore hideous masks; any man who dared approach a Gorgon was supposed to be turned into stone at first sight of that hideous head (p. 151). Perseus apparently was leader of a patriarchal society that overthrew the matriarchs and unmasked—perhaps beheaded—Medusa, a Gorgon leader.

Such historic struggles account for many myths hitherto not properly understood. Why did Zeus have so many "love affairs"? Not, as the Victorians claimed, because pagans were immoral! Rather, because he was the god of a patriarchal society which gradually extended its influence over numerous matriarchal communities. When Zeus-worshippers conquered Themis-worshippers, the priests of Zeus demanded that the local religion be merged with their own: in

short, that the goddess Themis be allied with the god Zeus
(p. 15). And similar reorganization of power took place in
communities that originally had revered Antiope (p. 142),
Alcmene (p. 142), Leto (p. 150), and countless others.

But the most popular Mother Goddess in the Aegean
area was Hera, who ultimately was the one most frequently
identified as Zeus' wife (p. 192). Other religious cults were
forced to relate their gods to Zeus as blood relatives: worshippers of Poseidon had to accept Zeus as the sea god's
smarter brother; worshippers of Athene had to acknowledge
Zeus as her father. In many communities, Hera was regarded as Zeus' sister.

These two factors in myth-making—that there were no
written records, and that the gods could make new al-
liances—made it possible for the ruling nobles to tamper
with the myths for their own benefit. Heroes and kings like
Heracles and Minos could always describe themselves as descended from gods (pp. 142, 149), as favored by direct association with gods (pp. 34, 319), destined at the very least to
enjoy special status hereafter (pp. 149, 150–51).

Mythopoeia—the making and remaking of myths—made
it possible for the Greeks to alter their religion as they themselves changed. Early Greeks, as we have seen, thought of
their deities as all-powerful brute forces, amoral bullies like
Cronus, who expected tribute and got it—or else. Those
early Greeks made crude bargains: they flattered those su-
perbullies with savory sacrifices and loud praise, and they
expected special considerations in return (pp. 34–35, 52).

More civilized Greeks, repelled by the savage Cronus,
preferred to believe he had been overthrown by his children, led by Zeus, and that these younger, more enlightened
gods were interested less and less in vengeance and sacrifice
of thighbones and more and more in mercy and justice.

Naturally, simple minds continued to coexist with subtle
intellects. In *The Odyssey* we find many mortals who want

to impress gods like Poseidon with massive sacrifices (pp. 46, 52), and a few who wish to impress Athene with their ingenuity. The Greeks, obviously, used their gods as their ideals.

Rituals and myths varied from place to place. A god supreme in one city might be just an exotic rumor in the next town. The power of love might be represented in adjacent seaports by vividly different goddesses. The appearance of these deities, as revealed in statues, cave murals, and gold jewelry and coins, would depend on the talent of the local wood-carver, stonecutter, and metalworker. No one objected to such diversity of religious notions. Everybody wanted a local patron god as his own special protector, and polytheism—belief in many independent gods—was the only type of religion that made sense in an apparently disorganized, chaotic world.

And here Homer exerted immeasurable influence in shaping the Greek notion of godhead. In all this apparent diversity of cosmic forces, Homer saw actual unity. In his *The Odyssey* especially, he portrays the gods as organized into a well-defined hierarchy.

Yes, there might be a local spirit or nymph for each river (pp. 70–71), cave (pp. 106, 166) or fountain (p. 222). And superior to them were powerful physical forces like Atlas who held sky and earth apart. But absolutely above all there were the Olympian gods, so-called because they lived on Greece's highest peak, Mount Olympus, where they—like all beings, divine and mortal—were ruled by one supreme being, Zeus the King (pp. 62, 63).

In other words, from hordes of deities whom he had heard about in his travels—gods local, vague, and various—Homer selected and glorified those that seemed to represent man's spiritual needs and ideals. And he depicted all of them as really different aspects of the same father-god, Zeus. He invested these majestic creatures with memorable personalities, and he gave them distinctive attributes so that each could be visualized by a listening audience: for example, Poseidon carried a three-pronged spear. Most important of all, Homer depicted the Olympians as devoted to the civilizing virtues and customs: proper removal of the dead (pp. 32, 137, 152, 310–11); hospitality to travelers and strangers (pp. 38–39, 85–86, 186–87); respect for life and property; a sense of balance (pp. 191–92, 278, 293–94), proportion (pp. 50–51, 86–87, 90), and good principles (pp. 185–86, 228–29).

Homer favored the more spiritual gods in every possible way. His characters, for example, often swear "by Father Zeus, Athene, and Apollo," the gods of justice, light, and wisdom (pp. 220, 239). He represented this Olympian trio as offering man a series of choices, a way of life by which he could prove and ennoble himself. In his emphasis on a hierarchy of values, from the lowest physical to the highest spiritual, he paved the way for Platonic philosophy. And long after Homer's gods lost their religious significance, they continued to have artistic meaning because of their beautiful symbolism.

C. Homer's Techniques and Style

Homer's enduring fame lies in his consummate artistry in story design; in his narrative, descriptive, and lyric style; and in his deep understanding of man's behavior and condition.

It is Homer's mastery of plot construction that makes it safe for us to assume that he was descended from generations of storytellers. No one artist working alone could have spontaneously developed all the yarn-spinning devices he employs with such perfect ease.

Let us consider the way he handles his action. The events in *The Odyssey* occur over a ten-year period. Homer could have related them chronologically, much as the Hebrew author of the Joseph story or the Anglo-Saxon writer of *Beowulf* handled their materials.

Thus, he would begin *at the beginning*, with the fall of Troy, when Odysseus and his fleet sail for home. Then he would describe in detail the storms, monsters, troubles with the crew, and designs of seductive women that keep Odysseus among the missing for ten years. Finally, the gods would decide Odysseus has suffered enough for his mistakes, that now the goddess Calypso must release him, and he would be thrown up on the beach of Scheria and carried by the Phaeacians to his native Ithaca. There he would meet secretly with his son Telemachus, who has just made a name for himself by undertaking a search for his father. Together they would plot the destruction of the hundred-odd suitors who—while urging Queen Penelope to give King Odysseus up for lost, to choose one of them as her new husband—have been scandalously exploiting Odysseus' wealth.

Handling his material in this simple, step-by-step fashion would have produced an interesting chronicle, epic in tone, but probably diffuse, episodic, and uneven in dramatic tension. Instead, Homer used two master devices to heighten and complicate his action.

First of all, he begins his story *in medias res*, in the middle of things, at a point in the tenth year when all the characters are already deeply involved in circumstances that have thrown them off balance, circumstances now rushing toward a crisis. In this way our poet creates *two-way suspense*. We are eager to see what happens *next*, but we also want to know what has gone *before*, how our characters have fallen into their present predicaments. The future is a mystery, but so is the past. Our author proceeds then to unfold his story in two directions, to build up our excitement by *moving back and forth across time*. Still, he produces not a sprawling story, but a tight yarn, for the events of ten years

are recounted in the course of the last forty-one days of continuous action!

As his second trick, Homer develops this action not in a
single story line but as a *double plot*. Instead of waiting for
Odysseus' arrival in Ithaca to acquaint the reader with the
situation there, Homer develops the Ithaca situation as a
separate story, a subplot. He alternates, then, from story to
story, providing variety and greater suspense by *moving
back and forth* across space. Of course, the two plots gradually converge, so *meshing* that we experience not one climax
but a series of related crises.

Now see how Homer, the master storyteller, combines
various other devices with these two main tricks to guarantee fast-paced action and self-renewing excitement.

The Odyssey opens with a council of the gods, which
serves two narrative purposes: it outlines both plots for us,
and it introduces another important family situation that
Homer uses for *contrast*. Young Orestes, contemporary of
Telemachus, has avenged his father, a fact which Telemachus
will be reminded of regularly (pp. 10, 30–31, 50–51).

Then, to foster suspense, Homer pushes the major plot
into the background while he develops the subplot. Thus, by
his 331st line of verse (pp. 11–12), he has introduced all the
main characters but one, the hero, and for purposes of
buildup, he keeps his hero in the background for some 2,000
lines! Meanwhile, open warfare has been declared between
Telemachus and the suitors (pp. 11–12), and the young son
has assumed command in his father's house (pp. 11–12), so
that actual *characterization*, or significant development in
personality, is under way.

At the assembly, Homer gives us our first *flashback*, a little
story within a big story, our first *shift across time* to fill in some
preceding action: the famous story of Penelope's stratagems
(pp. 16–17). Thus, while the Ithaca characters have been in
action for only two days, they have already sketched out for us

a period of "three years past, and close on four." Book II ends with Telemachus embarking on a little *odyssey* of his own, a kind of preliminary statement of the major theme.

In Books III and IV, Homer begins to fill in the background of the Trojan War as Telemachus hears from Nestor, Menelaus, and Helen stories that take us back ten years and more (pp. 28–31, 43–44) and, of course, build up our appreciation of the hero-to-come. Also, Homer not only continues the family contrast (pp. 30–33), but introduces another *parallel situation:* Menelaus' own return was delayed for eight years (pp. 40–42, 46–52). Again, we have another minor odyssey, a *variation* on the major theme. Then, with the background of his story fairly complete, with suspense mounting, Homer makes his first *shift across space:* "Meanwhile the suitors" (p. 53) have mounted their counteroffensive, and Book IV ends on what modern storytellers call a *cliffhanger.* The suitors are lying in ambush for Telemachus, but our author lets that situation hang while he shifts attention again, this time to the main plot.

Through another council of the gods, Homer outlines the coming events, a mere *foreshadowing*, actually, since we are still interested in the details of Odysseus' ordeal. Finally, after some of the greatest heroes and divinities of the Greek world have expressed concern for him, we meet the hero (p. 62).

After Odysseus is released from Calypso's isle and spends nineteen days at sea, Homer shifts the scene again for one of the best of his many *contrasts in mood:* he takes us from the dark fury of storm and sea (Book V) to the sweetness of Nausicaa's life in palace and sunshine (Book VI). The contrast is summed up in a magnificent touch of *irony*, as Odysseus comes out like a lion (p. 76) to face the tender maids.

Homer now exploits a Greek custom—a stranger had the right to full hospitality before he had to identify himself—to achieve a sustained passage of *dramatic irony:* that is, a situation in which the audience knows something that some of the characters do not. In Books VII and VIII, we watch with rising interest as our anonymous hero gains the admiration of his hosts purely on the basis of personality, manner, and prowess.

With hosts and readers equally impatient, Odysseus at last identifies himself and gives us the full account of his nine years' wanderings that we have waited nine books to hear. As his adventures take him away from the known Greek world to the west Mediterranean, Homer makes use of *symbolism*. The nine fairyland adventures in the unknown world stand—as we shall see in our discussion of characterization—for types of problems the maturing man must learn to face in his journey through life. While each adventure is a story in its own right, it carries also the full emotional significance of a fundamental, archetypal conflict, so that these nine ordeals add up to an *allegory*, a sustained comparison between real events and overall life conditions that they represent.

Homer has used four books to develop his subplot, eight to develop the main plot. Now he merges the two plots for the last twelve books. He continues to use the flashback and to shift scenes from one part of Ithaca to another, gradually narrowing the scope of the shifts down to just room-to-room in the palace.

For narrative tension Homer now relies on one main trick: Odysseus is in *disguise*. He may be recognized prematurely; he may fail even at that point at which he chooses to drop his disguise. Thus Homer maintains interest through six successive *revelations*, as Odysseus first deliberately declares himself to his son (pp. 209–11), is accidentally recognized by someone he is not yet ready to confide in (pp. 255–57), takes the risk of declaring himself to two servants whose courage could fail (pp. 275–77), finally takes the fatal plunge and identifies himself to the enemy (p. 284). The main crisis is past, but two touching revelations, filled more with pathos than with drama, remain: proof of identity to his wife (pp. 301–02) and father (p. 314).

The final denouement or resolution is one that a modern audience can understand only historically. To the Greeks there was nothing unusual in the idea that inevitable mass vengeance could be stopped by a thunderbolt from the gods (pp. 318–19). In any event, the main emotional tensions have already been resolved, for ancient and modern alike.

Only when we analyze it like this do we realize that Homer's plot is so intricately woven. On the surface the story seems to flow naturally and artlessly. This is the highest form of art: simplicity that conceals art.

Homer is also artistically simple in his descriptions. He never bores us with description for description's sake, with "set pieces." Rather he weaves description into the action. It is not the author who describes the beauties surrounding Calypso's cave or the wonders of Alcinous' palace—it is rather Hermes, a character, who stands still and admires (p. 62), and Odysseus, the hero, who pauses and ponders (p. 84). Each scene is brought to life by economical use of realistic, sensuous detail. Homer is careful to note, when Odysseus crawls between two olive shoots, that one has been grafted (p. 71). Homer is aware that an audience reconstructs a scene with the aid not only of *sight* clues—how oil runs off newly woven linen (p. 84)—but also of *smell* clues: how distressing to lie among seals (pp. 48–49); *touch* clues: how soft the air in Scheria (p. 84); and *sound* clues: how the Cyclops' eye hisses when it is poked out (pp. 115–16).

Accurate detailing is one component of artistic description; another equally important element is good *metaphor*. Like symbolism and allegory, which we have discussed as techniques of story design, metaphor is also an expression of a comparison or a similarity; but unlike the others, metaphor is largely a matter of language style. Here, too, Homer is famous, especially for his use of *simile,* a metaphor in which the comparison is stated openly with a big "equal sign," a *like* or an *as* or an *even so.*

Sometimes Homer uses a swift simile: "The sea took the raft and tossed it about *as* autumn winds whirl thistledown round and round upon a road" (p. 67); the wave tore "his hands *as* the suckers of a polypus are torn when someone plucks it from its bed . . ." (p. 70). But often he luxuriates in a longer, fuller comparison: "Then, *as* children rejoice when their dear father begins to get better after having for a long time borne sore affliction sent him by some angry spirit, but the gods deliver him from evil, *so* was Odysseus thankful when he again saw land and trees . . ." (p. 69).

Occasionally, the Homeric simile goes way off on a tangent (p. 104): "He wept as a woman weeps when she throws herself on the body of her husband who has fallen before his own city and people, fighting bravely in defense of his home and children. She screams aloud and flings her arms about him as he lies gasping for breath and dying, but her enemies beat her from behind about the back and shoulders, and carry her off into slavery, to a life of labor and sorrow, and the beauty fades from her cheeks—*even so* piteously did Odysseus weep. . . ."

In such an extended simile, Homer takes us almost entirely out of the immediate situation into the comparable one, until the analogous emotion is well developed—*only then* does he direct the emotion back to the story proper. In such comparisons, Homer's success results largely from his skill in explaining the story situation in terms of some experience common to all: a species of explanation of the unknown in terms of the known.

The storytelling techniques and stylistic devices we have discussed so far are those that reach us across barriers of language and time. We should mention in passing at least some of those Homeric qualities that can be appreciated only in the original Greek and in terms of his relation with his *listening* audience.

Homer's musical qualities of course are not translatable. In Greek he composed in *dactylic hexameters:* lines of six feet each, a typical foot being a *dactyl,* or a long syllable followed by two short ones (— uu), and the last foot usually a *spondee,* two long syllables (— —), with spondees also permissible in any other foot. The maximum number of syllables to the line, then, was seventeen, and the minimum, twelve.

Such classical meter depended on quantity, or length of syllable, whereas modern meter depends on quality, or accent. Therefore it is difficult to illustrate a Homeric line in English. The general idea, though, if we substitute accents for long syllables, can be gotten from Longfellow's *Evangeline:*

> *This* is the *forest* prim*ev*al, the *mur*muring *pines* and the *hemlock*.

Using standard meter made it easier for the poet to recall thousands of lines that he had to commit to memory. It also made it easier to improvise new poems on the spot because he could adapt scores of stock lines to almost any context. Thus he could always use prefabricated epithets like:

> Father, son of Cronus, king of kings (p. 4)

and:

> the child of morning, rosy-fingered Dawn (p. 65)

as well as cliché descriptions for common occurrences like:

> . . . offered me many good things of what there was in the house . . . (p. 130)

and:

> . . . his armor rang rattling round him as he fell heav-
> ily to the ground . . . (p. 319).

Homer also found it advisable to use frequent synopses and repetitions, partly to ease his own task of composition, partly to make it easier for the audience to follow the action and descriptions: they had to absorb the story by ear, and they heard it in installments. Hence, whenever he picked up the story, he would use an introductory summary in his "invocation to the muse" (p. 3), and repeatedly during the evening, he would summarize the action (pp. 62, 303–04, 309–10). Whenever possible, he would repeat a whole passage verbatim (as on pp. 211–12 and 244–45, 46 and 219–20, 162–63 and 183–84). It should not surprise us, then, that almost one third of *The Odyssey* is repetition.

The performing situation explains also the long catalogues of names and the formal speeches. Since the audience liked to hear their own families mentioned, Homer doubtless had a list ready for each community, neatly cast in dactylic hexameters (p. 93–94). And since one voice performing alone cannot recite rapid dialogue without utter confusion, the characters had to make long, full-blown statements (pp. 26–28, 105–06, 310–11).

Notice, though, that in spite of these literary conventions peculiar to a bygone day, despite the fact that the musical charm and power of the original Greek poetry are lost in translation, enough of Homer comes across, even in English prose, so that he is still read with fascination by all who love a good story with real people in it.

D. Character Analysis

"A good story with real people in it" means—for Homer as for most serious literary artists—that plot does more than just keep the audience on tiptoe. Plot must also provide the main characters with a chance to grow or, at least, to change. And it must provide the reader with insights into man's nature and condition.

Given a certain situation, certain pressures and problems, how do the characters respond? As they struggle, suffer, and learn, they precipitate new situations with which they must also interact. Plot actually is character study, and character study is plot.

Now by "main characters" we mean those persons in a story whom the author chooses to observe most thoroughly, "in the round." We follow them from their public actions into their private doubts and even into their dreams (pp. 73–74). Of course, an author cannot develop every character so fully. Just as in real life, so in art, we identify closely with only a few people at a time. We must be content with a mere passing acquaintance with multitudes of others. And so the author uses large numbers of minor characters and "walk-ons."

For our purposes, to appreciate Homer's genius in human portraiture it may be best to start with these minor figures, for with them he must achieve his effects with a few swift and simple strokes. Then we can observe how he combines these techniques with others to develop his major characters, and how he finally works out a complete theory of personality, an explanation of man's fate in relation to his conduct.

1. Treatment of Minor Characters

One of Homer's favorite devices is the *select, vivid detail* that swiftly suggests a whole dimension of personality. Notice how he introduces Alcinous. We know he is a great king of a great nation, on his way to a council meeting, but we still know nothing of him as a *person*. Then he pauses to hear his daughter's request. He understands what is really behind it—"She did not say a word" about that, "for she did not like to" (p. 74)—but he keeps that understanding to himself and acts out the situation in Nausicaa's terms. Gently, economically, Homer has sketched Alcinous as a man of quiet insight.

With the goddess Calypso, Homer uses this subtle technique to suggest not a strength but a frailty. We know she has no choice except to set Odysseus free, since the gods have so ordered. But because she loves him, she will try anything to gain his gratitude and respect. She actually takes credit for the gods' decision! "I am going to send you away *of my own free will*," she tells him (pp. 63–64). This poignant phrase does more than anything else in the scene to depict the complexity of her feelings.

Similarly, a group of suitors, who could be a mere crowd of shadowy figures at the other end of the hall, take on depth as human beings when they fail momentarily to grasp the real situation: they think the "beggar" has killed Antinous by mistake (p. 284). Later, in Hades, they are tagged again with man's inability to see the simple truth: now they think Penelope must have been privy to the plot to kill her suitors (p. 311).

By using such suggestive details, Homer also manages to avoid making his minor characters all black or all white. Consider the villains. Leiodes takes the stage for a mere minute, but that's all Homer needs to picture him as a man impotent with shame and guilt (p. 274). Amphinomus actually listens to the beggar's advice (p. 236) and on occasion even says the decent thing (pp. 213–15, 254). Even the monster Polyphemus is revealed as capable of tenderness (pp. 116–18).

Often Homer introduces a character with the exact opposite of the significant detail: *the broad stroke*. When first mentioned, Elpenor is described by his commander as a certain youth not very strong in mind and not very valiant in war (p. 135). This capsule biography contributes to the fact that Elpenor (not so much a walk-on as a walk-off) is actually a very memorable character.

Another of Homer's favorite tricks is to concentrate sometimes on *interplay* between characters rather than on the characters as individuals. Thus we know less about Menelaus, less about Helen, than we know about them as a couple. Menelaus alone is a stiff, formalistic man, given to pious abstract morality (pp. 338–39, 191–92). Helen is glamorous but manipulating and cold. Both are rather placid except when they interact with each other. Then we get fierce undertones of sarcasm and cynicism. Helen tells a story calculated to show that before the fall of Troy she was already hoping for a Greek victory (pp. 43–45). Menelaus politely responds with a story that throws suspicion on his wife's claim of a change of heart (p. 45). Moreover, he craftily uses her own excuse for a very ironic thrust: if it was not Helen's own free will but Aphrodite who had driven Helen to desert her husband (p. 45), then again it must have been not Helen but some god who prompted her to try to trap them in the wooden horse (p. 45). Why does Menelaus, a great king, endure such a destructive relationship with such an opportunistic woman? When we finally realize his real reason, we are appalled by *his* opportunism. He will not die but be retired to the Elysian fields *if* he can keep Helen as his wife and so remain as son-in-law to Zeus (p. 52)! Quietly, in his usual objective way, Homer intends that we appreciate the contrast between Menelaus and Odysseus, who refuses immortality with someone he appreciates (pp. 64–65).

2. Development of Main Characters

Combining significant details with memorable generalizations; mixing shades to avoid extremes of black and white; catching telltale qualities of a relationship as well as of the people in it—Homer naturally uses these tricks in his portrayal of major characters too. But with them he also has time and opportunity to use more complex and elaborate techniques.

Notice that Homer includes among his main characters representatives of all ages and conditions, each one at some crisis peculiar to his or her sex and stage of development. This guarantees a broad spectrum of emotions and universal audience appeal. Then, he exposes them to repeated tests and trials so that we get to know them well from different angles. And he involves them not only in *outer conflict* with circumstances and other people, but also in *inner conflict* with themselves.

We first meet Nausicaa on that morning when she becomes aware of womanhood stirring within her (p. 73). She yearns sweetly for courtship and a husband, but she signals this to the world by volunteering to manage a household enterprise. Indeed, on this day she proves to have a woman's courage and curiosity, as she alone of all the maidens has the temerity to face the shipwrecked Odysseus (p. 76). She is arch and artful, too, as she manages to hint that she is marriageable (p. 64) but not interested in any *local* man (p. 80). When she realizes that Odysseus cannot stay on her account, she asks only that he remember her for having saved his life (p. 102), leaving unsaid that she will remember him as the man who first evoked in her the power to love. She can let him go not with bitterness but with gratitude because she knows that that power is in *her*.

Like Nausicaa, Telemachus feels for the first time the urge to gain a good name (pp. 12–13, 73–74), a sure sign in Homeric society of the desire to put away childish things. He tries out his new manhood first by publicly asserting himself independent of his mother (pp. 11–12), and, when she accepts him as master of the house, he goes on to declare his new role to the suitors (pp. 11–12) and the assembly (pp. 15–16). He appears in the first two books to be cautious and indecisive (pp. 20–21), but we must remember that while his society demanded that he grow up to be a hero, it also demanded that he be modest, even self-effacing, especially in dealing with his elders (pp. 15, 25–26). He has, in the suitors, numerous examples of how untried manhood can go to extremes, betraying its insecurity and inexperience in bluster and vaunting arrogance. Telemachus is walking a tightrope in a situation in which he can hardly help looking awkward.

Homer chooses a small but significant detail of conduct to show that Telemachus is making progress in his development as an adult. He is able to turn down a gift of a chariot and horses in a manner that shows that he wants to be respected for what and who he is (p. 53). Even Menelaus can admire Telemachus' *self-respect* in this situation (p. 53). On the other hand, Telemachus gains plenty of experience in the exercise of *self-restraint,* not allowing himself to be carried away by vain hopes that the beggar is really his father (p. 210) and expressing honest doubt whether he can prove as effective as Odysseus when facing superior numbers (pp. 210–12).

Homer uses the stringing of Odysseus' bow as the crucial moment in Telemachus' maturation. On his fourth try it is clear Telemachus can string it, yet he discreetly forgoes the glory when he gets a cautious signal from his father (pp. 273–74). Telemachus has come a long way from that not too distant day when his mother could call him "a foolish boy who has never been used to roughing it" (p. 58). In the vengeance scene he fights valiantly, openly confesses his mistakes (p. 287), and in the raging tumult remembers to be fair to the minstrel and the herald (p. 292). At the end Laertes is able to see his grandson Telemachus fighting beside his son Odysseus, man beside man (pp. 318–19).

Homer sees Penelope as a far more complex and mysterious character. In some respects she is developed with greater psychological depth than any of the others. For years she has ingeniously been "playing it safe" in a situation that is hair-raising. Her lawful husband, whom she loves with a haunting passion, is long overdue and presumed lost. Men bringing her news of him are probably telling cock-and-bull stories in order to get a free meal and a cloak; indeed, if someone arrived and announced himself as Odysseus, she would suspect him of being an impostor (pp. 300–02). She cannot be sure of the real motives of the suitors; one of them at least wants to be her husband only to increase his chances of becoming chief (p. 284); many of them are willing to murder her son into the bargain (pp. 57–58). And even Telemachus is becoming impatient with her, actually willing now to lose her in order to save his property (p. 257).

She dreads the prospect of becoming bedmate to a man inferior to Odysseus (pp. 240, 263), yet she does not publicly renounce the possibility of a second marriage. According to the suitors, she has encouraged now one, now another of them (p. 16), keeping them all "on the tiptoe of expectation" (p. 19). We know that she enjoys the company of at least one of them (p. 214), and we see her baiting them all into bringing more gifts (p. 240).

Homer very cleverly has her betray her conflict when she relates a dream in which she has seen an eagle kill her twenty geese. The eagle identified himself as Odysseus and the geese as her suitors. But Penelope has already said unequivocally that she is "exceedingly fond" of seeing her "geese about the house" (p. 257), and in the dream she has lamented their death! It takes no psychoanalyst to infer from her own account of her dream that—at the very least—she secretly enjoys the suitors' attentions (p. 18). And why does Odysseus' mother find it better to omit all mention of the suitors when telling Odysseus about the situation back home (pp. 140–41)?

Yet notice that Penelope seems to sense something marvelous about the stranger to whom she confides her dream. The next morning she feels she has slept near Odysseus (p.

262), which is closer to the truth than she can establish at the moment. And Homer clearly intends us to believe that there is psychic rapport between Penelope and her husband-in-disguise for, on awakening, Odysseus too has a momentary sensation of having been with Penelope (p. 262). Again, it takes no analyst to infer that Homer sees Penelope as picking up subliminal cues about the beggar's real identity. In any event, Homer attributes it to Athene (p. 271) that now Penelope can proceed to hold the tournament in confidence that it will bring matters to a crisis.

Homer resolves Penelope's conflict by using two powerful symbolic devices: she makes the suitors humiliate themselves by measuring their manhood with Odysseus' bow (pp. 272–73); she makes Odysseus identify himself by telling the secret of their marriage bed (pp. 300–01). We feel great love for Penelope when she finally melts and says, "Do not be angry with me, . . . you, who are the wisest of mankind" (p. 301). Her conflict has been a human conflict; Homer has made her more credible by not making her perfect.

"The wisest of mankind" is of course the central character on whose development Homer is able to lavish all his combined talents and techniques, including many tricks he could not afford to use on the "supporting cast."

For example, as we have seen, Homer keeps his hero offstage until many prominent persons and gods have had a chance to discuss his plight and personality. Before we actually meet him, we have heard so much about him that we have come to wonder: How has such a prodigy come to be? How will he function in the present situation? Perhaps then it might be best for us to consider Odysseus from these three points of view: his reputation; his growth as described by himself; and his present, matured personality as we observe it ourselves in current action.

Ten years after he was last seen by any of them, Odysseus is remembered by the veteran Menelaus for his courage and endurance (p. 45), by the sagacious Nestor for his subtlety (p. 28), by the clever Helen for his cunning (p. 44), and by his people for his kindness and justice (pp. 15, 20, 55–56, 60). He is, in short, best described by his wife who says he has "every good quality under heaven" (p. 56).

Now, assuming he has not simply been destroyed in some remote place, how and why has such a superior creature been prevented from getting home? And if he was already such a paragon of intelligence and valor, in what ways has he grown as a result of his odyssey?

Leaving Troy, Odysseus and his men have two experiences in the eastern Mediterranean, in which many lose their lives because of overconfidence (p. 108), while others succumb to the temptation to become lotus-addicts (p. 108). Homer uses this "drugged sailor" episode as a transition from the real, known world to the terrifying, unknown, western Mediterranean, the fantasy world. But in all their nine succeeding fairyland adventures, they face symbolic variations of the same basic situations: in every case, man must face his problems realistically and avoid distractions if he would survive and progress.

In his adventure among the Cyclopes, Odysseus allows his passionate curiosity to cloud his better judgment, so that he is actually trapped wide-eyed in the cave before he is shocked back into his normal caution and cunning (pp. 112–14). What follows is a superb demonstration of foresight, strategy, tactics, physical aptitude, all against overwhelming odds, all too late to prevent terrific losses. And then, absolutely hysterical with his success in escaping with a few survivors from a trap he should never have walked into, he makes another colossal error. He vaunts his triumph, he taunts the god Poseidon himself (p. 119), both actions offensive to the Greek sense of decorum and self-preservation (p. 118).

For Odysseus, this narrow escape apparently serves as a warning never to be caught off-balance again; when hereafter he meets Cyclops-like situations in new disguises, he performs with greater discretion. His men fall by the way as they pay the price for distrusting their leader (p. 122), sailing into an ambush (pp. 123–24), letting their curiosity and bestiality get the better of them (pp. 126–28), and trespassing on divine property (pp. 160–161). But Odysseus refuses to allow Circe to degrade and unman him (p. 128); he prudently checks his curiosity and leaves the Hades gate before the Gorgon head can ascend and petrify him (p. 151); and he has taken proper measures to outwit his own curiosity when the Sirens offer him the bait of omniscience (p. 156). Faced with the great dilemma—whether to pass closer to Charybdis and risk possible loss of all hands, or closer to Scylla and suffer certain but limited loss of life—he avoids the classic human error—that is, trying to escape both alternatives—and he passes the test: he makes and carries out a definite decision (pp. 157–58). Finally, serving penance on Calypso's isle, he resists the temptation to be immortal, preferring to work out his destiny within his limits as a human (pp. 64–65).

Odysseus has survived a series of ordeals that symbolize the main conflicts man must resolve in his lifetime. These ordeals have refined and ennobled his personality. He has suffered disproportionately when he has acted on blind impulse; he has succeeded gloriously when he has acted on cool insight. Great as he had seemed as the young king of Ithaca and as the wily strategist at Troy, he is greater now, more experienced, more responsible, much humbler, gentler, wiser.

How appropriate, then, that when we first meet him the great hero is weeping (p. 63)! He is still paying for his overweening arrogance in gloating over his maiming of Polyphemus. And how appropriate that his first words should be words of wariness: "Now, goddess, there is something behind all this . . ." (p. 64). And at every step, he carefully formulates the alternatives and then acts as logic dictates (pp. 68, 69–71). Should he fling himself at the girl's feet or beseech her from a distance (p. 76)? Should he kill Irus outright or pull his punches (p. 235)? The decision always comes from a study of Nature and human nature. He answers a taunt first with a superb analysis of the human condition—"the gods do not grace all men alike in speech, person, and understanding" (p. 95)—and then with honorable action (p. 96). He is equally aware of such abstract concepts as the economic basis of war (p. 224) and of such practical tricks as how to meet the attack of a hostile dog (p. 177). He studies every person he encounters, and his judgment is accurate: the one suitor he offers an "out" is the one generally conceded to be basically a good man (pp. 214, 236).

Above all, Odysseus never again allows his emotions to get the better of his reason. He manages to suppress his joy at seeing his wife and his anger at the suitors, for spontaneous reactions would betray his identity; he controls his emotions until he can do something practical about them, and he expresses them only when it is safe to do so.

Figuratively speaking, he is never again trapped in a cave. When he faces 108 suitors in a room—a greater enemy than Polyphemus—it is they who are trapped. And when they are vanquished, he makes it a point to prohibit gloating. "It is an unholy thing to vaunt over dead men," he tells Eurycleia. "Rejoice in silence" (p. 293). He has come a long way since he crowed over the defeat of the Cyclops.

3. Homer's Theory of Personality

From the way he motivates and develops his characters, it is clear that Homer worked from a definite theory of personality, a set of concepts that clearly defined what a hero must do and how his action would influence his fate.

What made a man a *person,* in Homer's eyes, was his

struggle for recognition (pp. 10, 27, 73–74, 113–14). He fulfilled himself by striving at the highest level of performance possible for his peculiar talents, earning at least a good name, perhaps also renown or glory (*kudos*).

But he could succeed repeatedly—that is, survive—only if he clearly understood his limitations both as an individual and as a member of the human race. This knowledge of limits Homer associated with fate (*moira*). Losing one's sense of proportion, especially in regard to one's own right, power, and place in the scheme of things, was to Homer a calamitous violation of self. His characters caution each other and themselves to do "nothing to excess," "to be reasonable," to strive for "moderation in all things" (pp. 90, 191). To overreach oneself in the search for *kudos* was to be guilty of overweening pride (*hubris*).

And just as modern man's error in touching a high-tension wire is automatically and pitilessly punished by the laws of electricity, so the Greeks' *hubris* was automatically corrected by *moira* (pp. 49–51).

Homer's gods kept accurate score (p. 229) and administered sure justice to every man. "Aegisthus," Zeus notes at the beginning, "has paid for everything in full" (p. 4). And at the end, we can reckon that every character's fate is simply the sum total of his conduct.

WALTER JAMES MILLER,
New York University

SYNOPSES OF THE
TWENTY-FOUR BOOKS OF
THE ODYSSEY

❦

BOOK I. The poet "invokes the Muse," asking her to begin, at whatever point she chooses, the story of that ingenious hero who has traveled far and wide after the sack of Troy. . . .

During the absence of Poseidon, who has persecuted Odysseus for many years, the gods agree the time has come for Odysseus to return home. Athene, disguised as King Mentes, descends to Ithaca to visit Telemachus, Odysseus' son. His house is full of rowdy young men. Telemachus explains that they are wasting his property under the pretext of courting his mother, Penelope, who has delayed making a decision about remarrying. Mentes predicts Odysseus' return, urges Telemachus to give up boyhood, act like a man, present his case to the assembly, and take strong steps to ascertain his father's whereabouts. When Penelope descends

Forms of the Lyre

from her quarters to bid the bard Phemius to cease singing
sad tales of Troy, Telemachus seizes the chance to assert
himself: he tells her to leave such matters to him; he is master of the house.

BOOK II. Telemachus convokes an assembly, the first held
since Odysseus' departure twenty years before; he complains of the suitors' wasting of his substance and demands
they leave his palace. Antinous and Eurymachus, speaking
for the suitors, put the blame on Penelope herself: she can
end the problem simply by choosing one of them as her new
husband. Taking no action on Telemachus' request for a ship
to enable him to go in search of news of his father, the assembly breaks up. Telemachus prays to Athene for help; she

Penelope

appears now in the guise of Mentor, an old friend of his father's, borrows a ship for him, collects a crew of volunteers.

BOOK III. Next morning, the ship arives at Pylos on the
mainland; Telemachus and "Mentor" join in a hecatomb in

A Greek Ship

honor of Poseidon! In a long-winded speech, King Nestor tells of the return of other heroes from Troy, but has no specific information about Odysseus' fate. Athene miraculously vanishes. Impressed that Telemachus has been escorted by a god, Nestor arranges to send his own son Peisistratus to accompany Telemachus on a visit to King Menelaus in Sparta.

BOOK IV. Telemachus and Peisistratus are entertained at Sparta by King Menelaus and Queen Helen, who reminisce over their Trojan War experiences with Odysseus. Next morning, Menelaus tells how the god Proteus has revealed that Odysseus is held captive by Calypso. Meanwhile, back in

Menelaus Bearing the Body of Patroclus

Ithaca, the suitors, informed of Telemachus' journey, plan to ambush him on his return and murder him. Penelope is prostrate with terror at hearing these developments, but she is considerably reassured by a dream sent her by Athene.

Hermes

BOOK V. At a second council of the gods, Zeus sends Hermes to tell the nymph Calypso to release Odysseus. Certain the gods have made this decision because they are jealous of her having such a great hero as a lover, she must nevertheless obey their orders. Finding Odysseus weeping on the beach, longing for homeland and hearth, she helps him construct a raft. After seventeen days at sea, he sights land, but then Poseidon sights *him* and rouses a terrible storm which wrecks the raft. Battling waves for two days, Odysseus is helped by a sea nymph, finally reaches the shore of Scheria, kisses the earth, crawls among some olive trees, and falls asleep.

BOOK VI. In a dream, Athene visits the Princess Nausicaa, urging her to accept womanly responsibilities now that she is of marriageable age. Nausicaa asks her father, King Alcinous of Scheria, for a wagon in which to take the laundry to the washing-cisterns. Nausicaa and her young friends wash clothes by the shore and then, playing ball, wake up Odysseus. In a tactful speech, he praises Nausicaa's beauty and asks for help. The girls wash, feed, and clothe him. Nausicaa, impressed by his manliness, tells him how to get into town and appeal to her mother for hospitality.

A Greek Woman

BOOK VII. Athene, disguised as a Phaeacian, or resident of Scheria, guides Odysseus to the palace of Alcinous, where he throws himself on the mercy of Queen Arete. Noting that Odysseus is wearing clothing she has made herself,

Arete asks him about the trip that has brought him to Scheria. He tells her about his captivity on Calypso's isle, his recent release, the storm, Nausicaa's help. So impressed is King Alcinous that he offers Odysseus his daughter's hand in marriage; Alcinous promises him help in getting home if he prefers that alternative.

Athene

BOOK VIII. Next day, Alcinous orders a feast and athletic contests in honor of the stranger. Taunted by a young Phaeacian, who possibly mistakes him for a merchant incapable of physical exertion, Odysseus amazes the Phaeacians by establishing a record in discus-throwing. The blind Demodocus sings a comic tale about how Hephaestus trapped Ares and Aphrodite in their illicit love. The chieftains bestow numerous gifts on Odysseus; Nausicaa begs him to remember he owes his safety to her. At the feast, Odysseus asks Demodocus to sing of the Trojan Horse; seeing the stranger weep over the tale, Alcinous asks that he tell all about himself.

A Greek Discus-Thrower

BOOK IX. Odysseus reveals his identity and begins the story of his three-year odyssey, starting with the fall of Troy, ending with his shipwreck on Calypso's isle. Sailing from Troy in twelve ships, Odysseus' army landed in Thrace and sacked the Ciconian city of Ismarus. Driven then by tempests past Cape Malea, they visited Lotophagi land, where some of the men yielded to temptation, ate of the lotus, forgot their homeland, and had to be dragged back to duty. Thence they landed on an island of the Cyclopes. Intent on studying these barbaric, one-eyed giants, determined to collect the gifts traditionally due a visitor, Odysseus took twelve men and waited for a Cyclops in his cave. Polyphemus drove his flocks inside, sealed the cave with a huge rock, and ate two of Odysseus' men for supper. Next morning, he ate two more, then left with his flocks. On his return, Odysseus and six other survivors carried out a carefully laid scheme: they got Polyphemus drunk, blinded him by drilling out his eye with a heated stake, tricked his neighbors into thinking he was sick, and escaped hidden under the shaggy bellies of the goats and sheep when they were let out to pasture. Rowing away, Odysseus could not resist the temptation to taunt the Cyclops and tell him his real name; whereupon Polyphemus prayed to Poseidon, his father, for revenge on Odysseus.

Odysseus Offering Wine to the Cyclops

BOOK X. Guests for a month on the isle of Aeolus, who is captain of the winds, Odysseus leaves with a special gift: all the winds tied in a bag except the one he needs to get home. In sight of Ithaca, Odysseus falls into exhausted sleep; his men, suspecting that the bag contains treasure, open it and hence are driven off again. Dropping anchor in a strange harbor, eleven ships are sunk and their men devoured by the Laestrygonians; only Odysseus and his immediate crew escape. Wearily taking shelter in the isle of Aeaea, Odysseus sends half his men to reconnoiter; they are bewitched by Circe, who changes them to pigs. Aided by Hermes, who arms him with the magic herb moly, Odysseus overpowers

Circe, forces her to restore his men to human shape, remains as her guest for a year. Circe instructs him how to get to Hades, underworld of the dead, to learn about his future

Queen Persephone and King Hades, Rulers of the Dead

from the prophet Teiresias. When the crew are summoned, Elpenor wakes up on the roof and steps off to his death.

BOOK XI. Reaching the gates of Hades, Odysseus evokes the spirits of the dead. First Elpenor's ghost urges Odysseus to return to Aeaea to give Elpenor's body proper burial. Teiresias outlines the rest of Odysseus' life. His mother, Anticleia, tells him how she had died of a broken heart waiting for his return. After recalling the ghosts of many famous women, Odysseus interrupts his story, reminds his hosts of the lateness of the hour, elicits further promises of gifts and an escort. At their urging, he goes on to tell of his interview with Agamemnon and Achilles, and of seeing other great heroes.

BOOK XII. Returning to bury Elpenor, Odysseus gets instructions from Circe on how to handle the problems ahead of him. Stopping his men's ears with wax, having himself lashed to the mast, he gets safely past the alluring Sirens. Next they make the perilous passage through the straits of a

A Siren

dilemma, losing six men to Scylla in preference to risking total destruction by Charybdis. Landing on the isle of the sun god, Odysseus' men disregard his warnings and eat the sacred cattle. When they set sail, Zeus punishes them by destroying their ship with a thunderbolt; Odysseus alone escapes alive, thrown up on the shore of Ogygia, where Calypso keeps him for seven years.

BOOK XIII. Next day, the Phaeacians take Odysseus and his gifts in one of their swift ships to Ithaca. They set him ashore asleep. As they return to Scheria, Poseidon, angry at their helping Odysseus, turns their ship into a rock. When Odysseus awakens, he is unaware he is in Ithaca; Athene orients him, counsels him on how to handle the suitors, disguises him as an old beggar.

BOOK XIV. Odysseus goes to the hut of Eumaeus, the swineherd, who receives him hospitably and tells him about the local situation. Without revealing his identity, Odysseus

Colossal Statue of Poseidon

tells a long cock-and-bull story that includes a report of Odysseus' impending return. Odysseus sleeps comfortably in the swineherd's hut, but the swineherd sleeps with the pigs.

Poseidon, Apollo (or Dionysus), Pertho (or Demeter), Aphrodite, Eros

Sandals of Various Kinds

BOOK XV. In Sparta, meanwhile, Athene appears to Telemachus (in a dream?), urges him to return to Ithaca, warns him of the suitors' ambush. Bearing gifts from Menelaus and Helen, Telemachus returns to his ship at Pylos and embarks for home. While Eumaeus and Odysseus continue to swap yarns, Telemachus slips past the would-be ambushers and goes directly to Eumaeus' hut.

BOOK XVI. While Odysseus (still disguised as a beggar) and Eumaeus are preparing breakfast, Telemachus returns. He sends the swineherd into town to notify Penelope of his safe arrival. Athene restores Odysseus to his own form; he

War-Chariot

reveals himself to his son; reunited after twenty years, father and son plan vengeance on Penelope's wooers. The latter, meanwhile, are astonished to discover their plot has failed; they are rebuked by Penelope for attempting to silence her son.

Greek Swords and Scabbards

BOOK XVII. Next morning, Telemachus returns to the palace and tells Penelope what he has learned from Menelaus. Again disguised, Odysseus sets out for town in the company of Eumaeus. On the way they are insulted by Melanthius, the goatherd, who kicks Odysseus. As they reach the courtyard of the palace, Odysseus is recognized by his old hunting dog Argus, who makes a weak effort to greet

Tables

him and then dies happy. Indoors, Odysseus begs from the suitors; Antinous flings a tripod at him. Penelope expresses a desire to hear the beggar's tale.

BOOK XVIII. Irus, a tramp who always begs at Odysseus' house, resents the new beggar's presence, challenges him to a fight. Trying to avoid suspicion of his real identity, Odysseus taps Irus gently, but breaks his jaw. Penelope,

Greek Plow

made more beautiful by Athene, appears in the hall, scolds
Telemachus for allowing the stranger to be mistreated, and
evokes the admiration of the wooers. Odysseus rebukes one
of the servants for her shameless behavior with the suitors;
Eurymachus flings a stool at him. Telemachus rebukes them
and sends them away for the night.

Greek Shields

BOOK XIX. Father and son remove the armor from the
hall. Penelope talks with the "beggar," who gives her a fictitious account of his adventures with her husband, including, however, a true description of what Odysseus was once
wearing. Deeply moved, Penelope orders Eurycleia to wash
the beggar's feet. Eurycleia recognizes a scar on his leg; she
almost gives him away, but he extracts from her a promise
of secrecy. Penelope tells of a dream she has had; they discuss its significance. Penelope decides she will hold a shoot-

ing contest the following day to determine who will win her hand.

BOOK XX. Unable to sleep, Odysseus tosses and turns, but in the morning he asks for signs from Zeus and is heartened by two good omens. He is well treated by Philoetius, the stockman, but again he is abused at the banquet table. The soothsayer-in-exile, Theoclymenus, sees signs of impending disaster, leaves amid derisive laughter.

Greek Chairs

BOOK XXI. Penelope announces she will marry the man who can most easily string Odysseus' bow and shoot an arrow through twelve axe heads. Telemachus plants the axes in the earth, playfully tries to string the bow himself, is about to succeed when Odysseus stops him with a signal. Seeing the fateful moment at hand, Odysseus declares himself to Eumaeus and Philoetius, promising rewards for their assistance. They close the outer gates and send the female servants to their quarters. Dismayed by their patent inferiority to Odysseus, the suitors are horrified at the suggestion that the beggar try the bow. Telemachus takes over, sends his mother out, permits the beggar to shoot. Odysseus strings his bow, easily sends an arrow straight through the twelve axe-head rings.

BOOK XXII. Telemachus arms himself as Odysseus aims his next arrow at Antinous. Realizing now what the situation

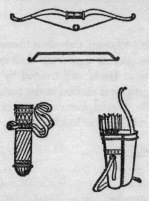

Bows and Quivers

is, Eurymachus puts all the blame on the dead Antinous, suggests that all the suitors pay heavy fines to compensate Odysseus for his losses. Odysseus shoots him next. Melanthius raids the storeroom to arm the suitors and is caught by Eumaeus. Odysseus' small group finally kills all the wooers, sparing only Medon the herald and Phemius the bard. Eurycleia identifies the twelve serving women who have been traitorous; they are forced to carry out the dead and clean the hall. They are hanged while Melanthius is mutilated to death.

BOOK XXIII. Eurycleia tells Penelope that the beggar who has rid her house of the plague is really her husband Odysseus. Cautious, unwilling to be victim of a gross deception, Penelope questions him. When he explodes with the secret of their marriage bed, she is convinced, and they embrace and talk most of the night. Just before dawn, Odysseus, Telemachus, and two faithful herdsmen leave for the country to see Laertes.

Greek Helmets

BOOK XXIV. Hermes leads the ghosts of the suitors down into Hades, where they tell their sad tale to Agamemnon and Achilles. Odysseus meanwhile proves himself to his father; Laertes is overjoyed that on this day son and grandson will compete for glory in arms, for the relatives of some of the suitors are on their way to avenge themselves on Odysseus and his men. A second bloody battle has begun

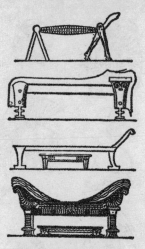

Greek Bedsteads

before Athene, with Zeus' help, declares a truce, during which both parties will make a covenant of peace.

Zeus

Homer's World

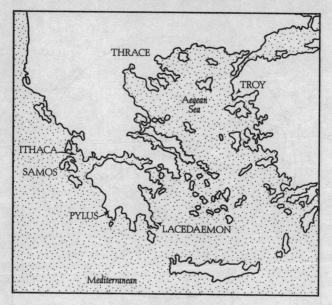

Telemachus' World

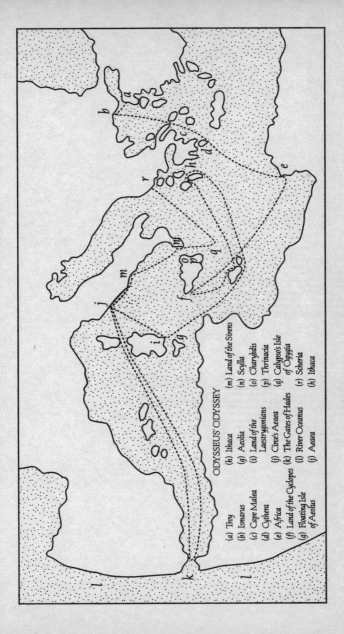

ODYSSEUS' ODYSSEY

(a) Troy
(b) Ismarus
(c) Cape Malea
(d) Cythera
(e) Africa
(f) Land of the Cyclopes
(g) Floating Isle
of Aeolus
(h) Ithaca
(g) Aeolia
(t) Land of the
Laestrygonians
(f) Circe's Aeaea
(k) The Gates of Hades
(l) River Oceanus
(j) Aeaea
(m) Land of the Sirens
(n) Scylla
(o) Charybdis
(p) Thrinacia
(q) Calypso's Isle
of Ogygia
(r) Scheria
(h) Ithaca

The Odyssey

BOOK I

The Gods in Council—Athene's Visit to Ithaca—The Challenge from Telemachus to the Suitors

TELL ME, O Muse, of that ingenious hero who travelled far and wide after he had sacked the famous town of Troy. Many cities did he visit, and many were the nations with whose manners and customs he was acquainted; moreover, he suffered much by the sea while trying to save his own life and bring his men safely home; but do what he might, he could not save his men, for they perished through their own sheer folly in eating the cattle of the sun god, Hyperion; so the god prevented them from ever reaching home. Tell me about all these things, O daughter of Zeus, beginning the tale at whatever point you choose.

So now all who escaped death in battle or by shipwreck had got safely home except Odysseus, and he, though he was longing to return to his wife and country, was detained by the goddess Calypso, who had got him into a large cave and wanted to marry him. But as years went by, there came a time when the gods settled that he should go back to Ithaca; even then, however, when he was among his own people, his troubles were not yet over; nevertheless all the gods had now begun to pity him except Poseidon, who still persecuted him without ceasing and would not let him get home.

Now, Poseidon had gone off to the Ethiopians, who are at the world's ends, and lie in two halves, the one in the west and the other in the east. He had gone there to accept a hecatomb of sheep and oxen, and was enjoying himself at his festival; but the other gods met in the house of Olympian Zeus, and the father of gods and men spoke first. At that moment he was thinking of Aegisthus, who had been killed by Agamemnon's son, Orestes; so he said to the other gods:

"See now, how men lay blame upon us gods for what is after all nothing but their own folly. Look at Aegisthus: he must needs make love to Agamemnon's wife unrighteously and then kill Agamemnon, though he knew it would be the death of him; for I sent Hermes to warn him not to do either of these things, inasmuch as Orestes would be sure to take his revenge when he grew up and wanted to return home. Hermes told him this in all good will but he would not listen, and now he has paid for everything in full."

Then Athene said, "Father, son of Cronus, king of kings, it served Aegisthus right, and so it would anyone else who does as he did; but Aegisthus is neither here nor there; it is for Odysseus that my heart bleeds, when I think of his sufferings in that lonely sea-girt island, far away, poor man, from all his friends. It is an island covered with forest, in the very middle of the sea, and a goddess lives there, daughter of the magician Atlas, who looks after the bottom of the ocean, and carries the great columns that keep heaven and earth asunder. This daughter of Atlas has got hold of poor unhappy Odysseus, and keeps trying by every kind of blandishment to make him forget his home, so that he is tired of life, and thinks of nothing but how he may once more see the smoke of his own chimneys. You, sir, take no heed of this, and yet when Odysseus was before Troy did he not propitiate you with many a burnt sacrifice? Why then should you keep on being so angry with him?"

And Zeus said, "My child, what are you talking about? How can I forget Odysseus, than whom there is no more capable man on earth, nor more liberal in his offerings to the immortal gods that live in heaven? Bear in mind, however, that Poseidon is still furious with Odysseus for having blinded the eye of Polyphemus, king of the Cyclopes. Polyphemus is son of Poseidon by the nymph Thoösa; she is the daughter of the sea king Phorcys, and she slept with Poseidon in a cave; therefore, though he does not kill Odysseus outright, he torments him by preventing him from getting home. Still, let us lay our heads together and see how we can help him to return; Poseidon will then be pacified, for if we are all of a mind he can hardly stand out against us."

And Athene said, "Father, son of Cronus, king of kings, if, then, the gods now mean that Odysseus should get home, we should first send Hermes to the Ogygian island to tell Calypso that we have made up our minds and that he is to return. In the meantime I will go to Ithaca, to put heart into Odysseus' son, Telemachus; I will embolden him to call the Achaeans in assembly, and speak out to the suitors of his mother, Penelope, who persist in eating up any number of his sheep and oxen; I will also conduct him to Sparta and to Pylos, to see if he can hear anything about the return of his dear father—for this will make people speak well of him."

So saying, she bound on her glittering golden sandals, imperishable, with which she can fly like the wind over land or sea; she grasped the redoubtable bronze-tipped spear, so stout and sturdy and strong, wherewith she quells the ranks of heroes who have displeased her, and down she darted from the topmost summits of Olympus, whereon forthwith she was in Ithaca, at the gateway of Odysseus' house, disguised as a visitor, Mentes, chief of the Taphians, and she held a bronze spear in her hand. There she found the lordly suitors seated on hides of the oxen which they had killed and eaten, and playing draughts in front of the house. Menservants were bustling about to wait upon them, some mixing wine with water in the mixing bowls, some cleaning down the tables with wet sponges and laying them out again, and some cutting up great quantities of meat.

Telemachus saw her long before anyone else did. He was

sitting moodily among the suitors, thinking about his brave father, and how he would send them flying out of the house, if he were to come to his own again and be honoured as in days gone by. Thus brooding as he sat among them, he caught sight of Athene and went straight to the gate, for he was vexed that a stranger should be kept waiting for admittance. He took her right hand in his own, and bade her give him her spear. "Welcome," said he, "to our house, and when you have partaken of food you shall tell us what you have come for."

He led the way as he spoke, and Athene followed him. When they were within, he took her spear and set it in the spear-stand against a high pillar, along with the many other spears of his unhappy father, and he conducted her to a richly decorated seat under which he threw a cloth of damask. There was a footstool also for her feet, and he set another seat near her for himself, away from the suitors, that she might not be annoyed while eating by their noise and insolence, and that he might ask her more freely about his father.

A maidservant then brought them water in a beautiful golden ewer and poured it over a silver basin for them to wash their hands, and she drew a clean table beside them. A housekeeper brought them bread, and offered them many good things of what there was in the house, the carver fetched them plates of all manner of meats and set cups of gold by their side, and a manservant brought them wine and poured it out for them.

Then the suitors came in and took their places on the benches and seats. Forthwith menservants poured water over their hands, maids went round with the bread baskets, pages filled the mixing bowls with wine and water, and they laid their hands upon the good things that were before them. As soon as they had had enough to eat and drink, they wanted music and dancing, which are the crowning embellishment of a banquet, so a servant brought a lyre to Phemius, whom they compelled perforce to sing to them. As soon as he touched his lyre and began to sing, Telemachus spoke low to Athene, with his head close to hers that no man might hear.

"I hope, sir," said he, "that you will not be offended with what I am going to say. Singing comes cheap to those who do not pay for it, and all this is done at the cost of one whose bones lie rotting in some wilderness or grinding to powder in the surf. If these men were to see my father come back to Ithaca, they would pray for longer legs rather than a longer purse, for money would not serve them; but he, alas, has fallen on an ill fate, and even when people do sometimes say that he is coming, we no longer heed them; we shall never see him again. And now, sir, tell me, and tell me true, who you are and where you come from. Tell me of your town and parents, what manner of ship you came in, how your crew brought you to Ithaca, and of what nation they declared themselves to be—for you cannot have come by land. Tell me also truly, for I want to know, are you a stranger to this house, or have you been here in my father's time? In the old days we had many visitors, for my father went about much himself."

And Athene answered, "I will tell you truly and particularly all about it. I am Mentes, son of Anchialus, and I am king of the Taphians. I have come here with my ship and crew, on a voyage to men of a foreign tongue, being bound for Temesa with a cargo of iron, and I shall bring back copper. As for my ship, it lies over yonder off the open country away from the town, in the harbour Rheithron under the wooded mountain Neïon. Our fathers were friends before us, as old Laertes will tell you, if you will go and ask him. They say, however, that he never comes to town now, and lives by himself in the country, faring hardly, with an old woman to look after him and get his dinner for him, when he comes in tired from pottering about his vineyard. They told me your father was at home again, and that was why I came, but it seems the gods are still keeping him back, for he is not dead yet—not on the mainland. It is more likely he is on some sea-girt island in midocean, a prisoner among savages who are detaining him against his will. I am no prophet, and know very little about omens, but I speak as it is borne in upon me from heaven, and assure you that he will not be away much longer; for he is a man of such resource that even though he were in chains of iron he would find some means of getting home again. But tell me, and tell me true, can Odysseus really have such a fine-looking fellow for a son? You are indeed wonderfully like him about the head and eyes, for we were close friends before he set sail for Troy, where the flower of all the Argives went also. Since that time we have never either of us seen the other."

"My mother," answered Telemachus, "tells me I am the son of Odysseus, but it is a wise child that knows his own father. Would that I were son to one who had grown old upon his own estates, for, since you ask me, there is no more ill-starred man under heaven than he who they tell me is my father."

And Athene said, "There is no fear of your race dying out yet, while Penelope has such a fine son as you are. But tell me, and tell me true, what is the meaning of all this feasting, and who are these people? What is it all about? Have you some banquet, or is there a wedding in the family?—for no one seems to be bringing any provisions of his own. And the guests—how atrociously they are behaving; what riot they make over the whole house; it is enough to disgust any respectable person who comes near them."

"Sir," said Telemachus, "as regards your question, so long as my father was here it was well with us and with the house, but the gods in their displeasure have willed it otherwise, and have hidden him away more closely than mortal man was ever yet hidden. I could have borne it better even though he were dead, if he had fallen with his men before Troy, or had died with friends around him when the days of his fighting were done; for then the Achaeans would have built a mound over his ashes, and I should myself have been heir to his renown; but now the storm winds have spirited him away we know not where; he is gone without leaving so much as a trace behind him, and I inherit nothing but dismay. Nor does the matter end simply with grief for the loss of my father; heaven has laid sorrows upon me of yet another kind; for the chiefs from all our islands, Dulichium, Same, and the woodland island of Zacynthus, as also all the principal men of Ithaca itself, are eating up my house under the pretext of paying their court to my mother, who will neither point-blank say that she will not marry, nor yet bring matters to an end; so they are making havoc of my estate, and before long will do so also with myself."

"Is that so," exclaimed Athene. "Then you do indeed want Odysseus home again. Give him his helmet, shield, and a couple of lances, and if he is the man he was when I first knew him in our house, drinking and making merry, he would soon lay his hands about these rascally suitors were he to stand once more upon his own threshold. He was then coming from Ephyra, where he had been to beg poison for his arrows from Ilus, son of Mermerus. Ilus feared the ever-living gods and would not give him any, but my father let him have some, for he was very fond of him. If Odysseus is the man he then was, these suitors will have a short shrift and a sorry wedding.

"But there! It rests with heaven to determine whether he is to return, and take his revenge in his own house or no; I would, however, urge you to set about trying to get rid of these suitors at once. Take my advice, call the Achaean heroes in assembly tomorrow morning—lay your case before them, and call heaven to bear you witness. Bid the suitors take themselves off, each to his own place, and if your mother's mind is set on marrying again, let her go back to her father, who will find her a husband and provide her with all the marriage gifts that so dear a daughter may expect. As for yourself, let me prevail upon you to take the best ship you can get, with a crew of twenty men, and go in quest of your father who has so long been missing. Someone may tell you something, or (and people often hear things in this way) some heaven-sent message may direct you. First go to Pylos and ask Nestor; thence go on to Sparta and visit Menelaus, for he got home last of all the Achaeans; if you hear that your father is alive and on his way home, you can put up with the waste these suitors will make for yet another twelve months. If on the other hand you hear of his death, come home at once, celebrate his funeral rites with all due pomp, build a barrow to his memory, and make your mother marry again. Then, having done all this, think it well over in your mind how, by fair means or foul, you may kill these suitors in your own house. You are too old to plead infancy any longer; have you not heard how people are singing Orestes' praises for having killed his father's murderer, Aegisthus? You are a fine, smart-looking fellow; show your mettle, then, and make yourself a name in story. Now, however, I must go back to my ship and to my crew, who will be impatient if I keep them waiting longer; think the matter over for yourself, and remember what I have said to you."

"Sir," answered Telemachus, "it has been very kind of you to talk to me in this way, as though I were your own son, and I will do all you tell me; I know you want to be getting on with your voyage, but stay a little longer till you have taken a bath and refreshed yourself. I will then give you a present, and you shall go on your way rejoicing; I will give you one of great beauty and value—a keepsake such as only dear friends give to one another."

Athene answered, "Do not try to keep me, for I would be on my way at once. As for any present you may be disposed to make me, keep it till I come again, and I will take it home with me. You shall give me a very good one, and I will give you one of no less value in return."

With these words she flew away like a bird into the air, but she had given Telemachus courage, and had made him think more than ever about his father. He felt the change, wondered at it, and knew that the stranger had been a god, so he went straight to where the suitors were sitting.

Phemius was still singing, and his hearers sat rapt in silence as he told the sad tale of the return from Troy, and the ills Athene had laid upon the Achaeans. Penelope, daughter of Icarius, heard his song from her room upstairs, and came down by the great staircase, not alone, but attended by two of her handmaids. When she reached the suitors, she stood by one of the pillars that supported the roof of the hall, with a maidservant on either side of her. She held a veil, moreover, before her face, and was weeping bitterly.

"Phemius," she cried, "you know many another feat of gods and heroes, such as poets love to celebrate. Sing the suitors some one of these, and let them drink their wine in silence, but cease this sad tale, for it breaks my sorrowful heart, and reminds me of my lost husband, whom I mourn ever without ceasing, and whose name was great throughout Hellas and Argos."

"Mother," answered Telemachus, "let the bard sing what he has a mind to; bards do not make the ills they sing of; it is Zeus, not they, who makes them, and who sends weal or woe upon mankind according to his own good pleasure. This fellow means no harm by singing the ill-fated return of the Danaans, for people always applaud the latest songs most warmly. Make up your mind to it and bear it; Odysseus is not the only man who never came back from Troy, but many another went down as well as he. Go, then, within the house and busy yourselves with your daily duties, your loom, your distaff, and the ordering of your servants; for speech is man's matter, and mine above all others—for it is I who am master here."

She went wondering back into the house, and laid her son's saying in her heart. Then, going upstairs with her handmaids into her room, she mourned her dear husband till Athene shed sweet sleep over her eyes. But the suitors made a great uproar throughout the dark hall, and prayed each one that he might be her bedfellow.

Then Telemachus spoke. "Shameless," he cried, "and insolent suitors, let us feast at our pleasure now, and let there be no brawling, for it is a rare thing to hear a man with such a divine voice as Phemius has; but in the morning meet me in full assembly that I may give you formal notice to depart, and feast at one another's houses, turn and turn about, at your own cost. If on the other hand you choose to persist in sponging upon one man, heaven help me, but Zeus shall reckon with you in full, and when you fall in my father's house there shall be no man to avenge you."

The suitors bit their lips as they heard him, and marvelled at the boldness of his speech. Then Antinous, son of Eupeithes, said, "The gods seem to have given you lessons in bluster and tall talking; may Zeus never grant you to be chief in Ithaca as your father was before you."

Telemachus answered, "Antinous, do not chide me, but, God willing, I will be chief too if I can. Is this the worst fate you can think of for me? It is no bad thing to be a chief, for it brings both riches and honour. Still, now that Odysseus is dead there are many great men in Ithaca both old and young, and some other may take the lead among them; nevertheless, I will be chief in my own house, and will rule those whom Odysseus has won for me."

Then Eurymachus, son of Polybus, answered, "It rests with heaven to decide who shall be chief among us, but you shall be master in your own house and over your own possessions; no one while there is a man in Ithaca shall do you violence nor rob you. And now, my good fellow, I want to know about this stranger. What country does he come from? Of what family is he, and where is his estate? Has he brought you news about the return of your father, or was he on business of his own? He seemed a well-to-do man, but he hurried off so suddenly that he was gone in a moment before we could get to know him."

"My father is dead and gone," answered Telemachus, "and even if some rumour reaches me I put no more faith in it now. My mother does indeed sometimes send for a soothsayer and question him, but I give his prophecies no heed. As for the stranger, he was Mentes, son of Anchialus, chief of the Taphians, an old friend of my father's." But in his heart he knew that it had been the goddess.

The suitors then returned to their singing and dancing until the evening; but when night fell upon their merrymaking they went home to bed, each in his own abode. Telemachus' room was high up in a tower that looked onto the outer court; hither, then, he went, brooding and full of thought. A good old woman, Eurycleia, daughter of Ops, the son of Pisenor, went before him with a couple of blazing torches. Laertes had bought her with his own money when she was quite young; he gave the worth of twenty oxen for her, and showed as much respect to her in his household as he did to his own wedded wife, but he did not take her to his bed for he feared his wife's resentment. She it was who now lighted Telemachus to his room, and she loved him better than any of the other women in the house did, for she had nursed him when he was a baby. He opened the door of his bedroom and sat down upon the bed; as he took off his tunic, he gave it to the good old woman, who folded it tidily up, and hung it for him over a peg by his bedside, after which she went out, pulled the door to by a silver catch, and drew the bolt home by means of the strap. But Telemachus, as he lay covered with a woollen fleece, kept thinking all night through of his intended voyage and of the counsel that Athene had given him.

BOOK II

※

*Assembly of the People of Ithaca—Speeches of
Telemachus and of the Suitors—Telemachus Makes
His Preparations and Starts for Pylos with Athene
Disguised as Mentor*

NOW, WHEN the child of morning, rosy-fingered Dawn, appeared, Telemachus rose and dressed himself. He bound his
sandals onto his feet, girded his sword about his shoulder, and
left his room looking like an immortal god. He at once sent
the heralds round to call the people to assembly, so they
called them and the people gathered quickly; then, when
they were got together, he went to the place of assembly,
spear in hand—not alone, for his two hounds went with him.
Athene endowed him with a presence of such grace that all
marvelled at him as he went by, and when he took his place in
his father's seat even the oldest councillors made way for him.

Aegyptius, a man bent double with age, and of infinite experience, was the first to speak. His son Antiphus had gone
with Odysseus to Ilium, land of noble steeds, but the savage
Cyclops had killed him when they were all shut up in the
cave, and had cooked his last dinner of him. He had three
sons left, of whom two still worked on their father's land,
while the third, Eurynomus, was one of the suitors; nevertheless, their father could not get over the loss of Antiphus,
and was still weeping for him when he began his speech.

"Men of Ithaca," he said, "hear my words. From the day
Odysseus left us there has been no meeting of our council-

lors until now; who then can it be, whether old or young, that finds it so necessary to convene us? Has he got wind of some host approaching, and does he wish to warn us, or would he speak upon some other matter of public moment? I am sure he is an excellent person, and I hope Zeus will grant him his heart's desire."

Telemachus took this speech as of good omen and rose at once, for he was bursting with what he had to say. He stood in the middle of the assembly and the good herald Pisenor brought him his staff. Then, turning to Aegyptius, "Sir," said he, "it is I, as you will shortly learn, who have convened you, for it is I who am the most aggrieved. I have not got wind of any host approaching about which I would warn you, nor is there any matter of public moment on which I would speak. My grievance is purely personal, and turns on two great misfortunes which have fallen upon my house. The first of these is the loss of my excellent father who was chief among all you here present, and was like a father to every one of you; the second is much more serious, and ere long will be the utter ruin of my estate. The sons of all the chief men among you are pestering my mother to marry them against her will. They are afraid to go to her father, Icarius, asking him to choose the one he likes best, and to provide marriage gifts for his daughter, but day by day they keep hanging about my father's house, sacrificing our oxen, sheep, and fat goats for their banquets, and never giving so much as a thought to the quantity of wine they drink. No estate can stand such recklessness; we have now no Odysseus to keep harm from our doors, and I cannot hold my own against them. I shall never all my days be as good a man as he was, still I would indeed defend myself if I had power to do so, for I cannot stand such treatment any longer; my house is being disgraced and ruined. Have respect, therefore, to your own consciences and to public opinion. Fear, too, the wrath of heaven, lest the gods should be displeased and turn upon you. I pray you by Zeus and Themis, who is the beginning and the end of councils, stop this, my friends, and let me endure my grief alone—unless it be that my brave father Odysseus did some wrong to the Achaeans which you would now avenge on me, by aiding and abetting these suitors. If I am to be eaten out of house and home at all, I had rather you did the eating yourselves, for I could then take action against you to some purpose, and demand repayment from house to house till I got paid in full, whereas now I have no remedy."

With this, Telemachus dashed his staff to the ground and burst into tears. Everyone was very sorry for him, but they all sat still and no one ventured to make him an angry answer, save only Antinous, who spoke thus:

"Telemachus, insolent braggart that you are, how dare you try to throw the blame upon us suitors? It is your mother's fault, not ours, for she is a very artful woman. This three years past, and close on four, she has been driving us out of our minds, by encouraging each one of us, and sending him messages without meaning one word of what she says. And then there was that other trick she played us. She set up a great tambour frame in her room, and began to work on an enormous piece of fine needlework. 'Young men, my suitors,' said she, 'Odysseus is indeed dead. Still, do not press me to marry again immediately; wait—for I would not have my threads perish unused—till I have completed a pall for the hero Laertes, to be in readiness against the time when death shall take him. He is very rich, and the women of the place will talk if he is laid out without a pall.'

"This was what she said, and we assented; whereon we could see her working on her great web all day long, but at night she would unpick the stitches again by torchlight. She fooled us in this way for three years and we never found her out, but as time wore on and she was now in her fourth year, one of her maids, who knew what she was doing, told us, and we caught her in the act of undoing her work, so she had to finish it whether she would or no. The suitors, therefore, make you this answer, that both you and the Achaeans may understand:—'Send your mother away, and bid her marry the man of her own and of her father's choice'; for I do not know what will happen if she goes on plaguing us much longer with the airs she gives herself on the score of the accomplishments Athene has taught her, and because she is so clever. We never yet heard of such a woman; we know all about Tyro, Alcmene, Mycene, and the famous women of old, but they were nothing to your mother any one of them. It was not fair of her to treat us in that way, and as long as she continues in the mind with which heaven has now endowed her, so long shall we go on eating up your estate, and I do not see why she should change, for she gets all the honour and glory, and it is you who pay for it, not she. Understand, then, that we will not go back to our lands, neither here nor elsewhere, till she has made her choice and married some one or other of us."

Telemachus answered, "Antinous, how can I drive the mother who bore me from my father's house? My father is abroad and we do not know whether he is alive or dead. It will be hard on me if I have to pay Icarius the large sum which I must give him if I insist on sending his daughter back to him. Not only will he deal rigorously with me, but heaven will also punish me; for my mother when she leaves the house will call on the Erinyes to avenge her; besides, it would not be a creditable thing to do, and I will not tell her to go. If you choose to take offence at this, leave the house and feast elsewhere at one another's houses at your own cost, turn and turn about. If, on the other hand, you elect to persist in sponging upon one man, heaven help me, but Zeus shall reckon with you in full, and when you fall in my father's house there shall be no man to avenge you."

As he spoke Zeus sent two eagles from the top of the mountain, and they flew on and on with the wind, sailing side by side in their lordly flight. When they were right over the middle of the assembly, they wheeled and circled about, beating the air with their wings and glaring death into the eyes of them that were below; then, fighting fiercely and tearing at one another, they flew off towards the right over the town. The people wondered as they saw them, and asked each other what all this might be; whereon Halitherses, who was the best prophet and reader of omens among them, spoke to them plainly and in all honesty, saying:

"Hear me, men of Ithaca, and I speak more particularly to the suitors, for I see mischief brewing for them. Odysseus is not going to be away much longer; indeed he is close at hand to deal out death and destruction on them, and punish many another of us who live in Ithaca. Let us then be wise in time, and put a stop to this wickedness before he comes. Let the suitors do so of their own accord; it will be better for them, for I am not prophesying without due knowledge; everything has happened to Odysseus as I foretold when the Argives set out for Troy, and he with them. I said that after going through much hardship and losing all his men he should come home again in the twentieth year and that no one would know him; and now all this is coming true."

Eurymachus, son of Polybus, then said, "Go home, old man, and prophesy to your own children, to save them from trouble in the future. I can read these omens myself much better than you can; birds are always flying about in the sunshine somewhere or other, but they seldom mean anything. Odysseus has died in a far country, and it is a pity you are not dead along with him, instead of prating here about omens and adding fuel to the anger of Telemachus, which is fierce enough as it is. I suppose you think he will give you something for your family, but I tell you—and it shall surely be—when an old man like you, who should know better, talks a younger one over till he becomes troublesome, in the first place his young friend will only fare so much the worse—he will gain nothing by it—and in the next, we will lay a heavier fine, sir, upon yourself, than you will at all like paying, for it will bear hardly upon you. As for Telemachus, I warn him in the presence of you all to send his mother back to her father, who will find her a husband and provide her with all the marriage gifts so dear a daughter may expect. Till then we shall go on harassing him with our suit; for we fear no man, and care neither for him, with all his fine speeches, nor for any fortune-telling of yours. You may preach as much as you please, but we shall only hate you the more. We shall go back and continue to eat up Telemachus' estate without paying him, till such time as his mother leaves off tormenting us by keeping us day after day on the tiptoe of expectation, each vying with the other in his suit for a prize of such rare perfection. Besides, we cannot go after the other women, whom we should marry but for the way in which she treats us."

Then Telemachus said, "Eurymachus, and you other suitors, I shall say no more, and entreat you no further, for the gods and the people of Ithaca now know my story. Give me, then, a ship and a crew of twenty men to take me, and I will go to Sparta and to Pylos in quest of my father, who has so long been missing. Someone may tell me something, or (and people often hear things in this way) some heaven-sent message may direct me. If I can hear of him as alive and on his way home, I will put up with the waste you suitors will make for yet another twelve months. If on the other hand I hear of his death, I will return at once, celebrate his funeral rites with all due pomp, build a barrow to his memory, and make my mother marry again."

With these words he sat down, and Mentor, who had been the friend of Odysseus, and had been left in charge of his house with full authority over the servants, rose to speak. He then, plainly and in all honesty, addressed them thus:

"Hear me, men of Ithaca. May you never have a kind and well-disposed ruler any more, nor one who will govern you equitably; may all your chiefs henceforward be cruel and unjust, for there is not one of you but has forgotten

Odysseus, who was your king and was as kind as a father. I am not half so angry with the suitors, for if they choose to do violence in the wickedness of their hearts, and risk their lives in the belief that Odysseus will not return, they can take the high hand and eat up his estate; but as for you others, I am shocked at the way in which you all sit still without even trying to stop such scandalous goings-on—which you could do if you chose, for you are many and they are few."

Leiocritus, son of Evenor, answered him. "Mentor, what folly is all this, that you should set the people to stop us? It is a hard thing for one man to fight with many about the eating up of his estate. Even though Odysseus himself were to set upon us while we are feasting in his house, and do his best to oust us, his wife, who wants him back so very badly, would have small cause for rejoicing, and his blood would be upon his own head if he fought against such great odds. There is no sense in what you have been saying. Now, therefore, do you people go about your business, and let his father's old friends, Mentor and Halitherses, speed this boy on his journey, if he goes at all—which I do not think he will, for he is more likely to stay where he is till someone comes and tells him something."

On this he broke up the assembly, and every man went back to his own abode, while the suitors returned to the house of Odysseus.

Then Telemachus went all alone by the seaside, washed his hands in the grey waves, and prayed to Athene.

"Hear me," he cried, "you god who visited me yesterday, and bade me sail the seas in search of my father, who has so long been missing. I would obey you, but the Achaeans, and more particularly the wicked suitors, are hindering me that I cannot do so."

As he thus prayed, Athene came close up to him in the likeness and with the voice of Mentor. "Telemachus," said she, "if you are made of the same stuff as your father you will be neither fool nor coward henceforward, for Odysseus never broke his word nor left his work half done. If, then, you take after him, your voyage will not be fruitless, but unless you have the blood of Odysseus and of Penelope in your veins I see no likelihood of your succeeding. Sons are seldom as good men as their fathers; they are generally worse, not better; still, as you are not going to be either fool or coward henceforward, and are not entirely without some share of your father's wise discernment, I look with hope upon your undertaking. But pay no attention to those foolish suitors, for they have neither sense nor virtue, and give no thought to death and to the doom that will shortly fall on one and all of them, so that they shall perish on the same day. As for your voyage, it shall not be long delayed; your father was such an old friend of mine that I will find you a ship, and will come with you myself. Now, however, return home, and go about among the suitors; begin getting provisions ready for your voyage; see everything well stowed, the wine in jars, and the barley meal, which is the staff of life, in leathern bags, while I go round the town and collect volunteers at once. There are many ships in Ithaca both old and new; I will run my eye over them for you and will choose the best; we will get her ready and will put out to sea without delay."

Thus spoke Athene, daughter of Zeus, and Telemachus lost no time in doing as the goddess told him. He went moodily home, and found the suitors flaying goats and singeing pigs in the outer court. Antinous came up to him at once and laughed as he took his hand in his own, saying, "Telemachus, my fine fire-eater, bear no more ill blood neither in word nor deed, but eat and drink with us as you used to do. The Achaeans will find you everything—a ship and a picked crew—so that you can set sail for Pylos at once and get news of your noble father."

"Antinous," answered Telemachus, "I cannot eat in peace, nor take pleasure of any kind with such men as you are. Was it not enough that you should waste so much good property of mine while I was yet a boy? Now that I am older and know more about it, I am also stronger, and whether here among this people, or by going to Pylos, I will do you all the harm I can. I shall go, and my going will not be in vain—though, thanks to you suitors, I have neither ship nor crew of my own, and must be passenger, not captain."

As he spoke he snatched his hand from that of Antinous. Meanwhile the others went on getting dinner ready about the house, jeering at him tauntingly as they did so.

"Telemachus," said one youngster, "means to be the death of us; I suppose he thinks he can bring friends to help him from Pylos, or again from Sparta, where he seems bent on going. Or will he go to Ephyra as well, for poison to put in our wine and kill us?"

Another said, "Perhaps if Telemachus goes on board ship, he will be like his father and perish far from his friends. In this case we should have plenty to do, for we could then divide up his property amongst us: as for the house, we can let his mother and the man who marries her have that."

This was how they talked. But Telemachus went down into the lofty and spacious storeroom where his father's treasure of gold and bronze lay heaped up upon the floor, and where the linen and spare clothes were kept in oaken chests. Here, too, there was a store of fragrant olive oil, while casks of old well-ripened wine, unblended and fit for a god to drink, were ranged against the wall in case Odysseus should come home again after all. The room was closed with well-made doors opening in the middle; moreover, the faithful old housekeeper Eurycleia, daughter of Ops, the son of Pisenor, was in charge of everything both night and day. Telemachus called her to the storeroom and said:

"Nurse, draw me off some of the best wine you have, after what you are keeping for my father's own drinking, in case, poor man, he should escape death, and find his way home again after all. Let me have twelve jars, and see that they all have lids; also fill me some well-sewn leathern bags with barley meal—about twenty measures in all. Get these things put together at once, and say nothing about it. I will take everything away this evening as soon as my mother has gone upstairs for the night. I am going to Sparta and to Pylos to see if I can hear anything about the return of my dear father."

When Eurycleia heard this she began to cry, and spoke sorrowfully to him, saying, "My dear child, whatever can have put such a notion as that into your head? Where in the world do you want to go to—you, who are the one hope of the house? Your poor father is dead and gone in some foreign country nobody knows where, and as soon as your back is turned these wicked ones here will be scheming to get you put out of the way, and will share all your possessions among themselves; stay where you are among your own people, and do not go wandering and worrying your life out on the barren ocean."

"Fear not, nurse," answered Telemachus. "My scheme is not without heaven's sanction; but swear that you will say nothing about all this to my mother, till I have been away some eleven or twelve days, unless she hears of my having gone, and asks you; for I do not want her to spoil her beauty by crying."

The old woman swore most solemnly that she would not, and when she had completed her oath, she began drawing off the wine into jars, and getting the barley meal into the bags, while Telemachus went back to the suitors.

Then Athene turned to other thoughts. She took his shape, and went round the town to each one of the crew, telling them to meet at the ship by sundown. She went also to Noëmon, son of Phronius, and asked him to let her have a ship—which he was very ready to do. When the sun had set and darkness was over all the land, she got the ship into the water, put all the tackle on board her that ships generally carry, and stationed her at the end of the harbour. Presently the crew came up, and the goddess spoke encouragingly to each of them.

Furthermore she went to the house of Odysseus, and put the suitors into a deep slumber. She caused their drink to fuddle them, and made them drop their cups from their hands, so that instead of sitting over their wine, they went back into the town to sleep, with their eyes heavy and full of drowsiness. Then she took the form and voice of Mentor, and called Telemachus to come outside.

"Telemachus," said she, "the men are on board and at their oars, waiting for you to give your orders, so make haste and let us be off."

On this she led the way, while Telemachus followed in her steps. When they got to the ship they found the crew waiting by the waterside, and Telemachus said, "Now, my friends, help me to get the stores on board; they are all put together in the house, and my mother does not know anything about it, nor any of the maidservants except one."

With these words he led the way and the others went with him. When they had brought the things as he told them, Telemachus went on board, Athene going before him and taking her seat in the stern of the vessel, while Telemachus sat beside her. Then the men loosed the hawsers and took their places on the benches. Athene sent them a fair wind from the west that whistled over the deep blue waves, whereon Telemachus told them to catch hold of the ropes and hoist sail, and they did as he told them. They set the mast in its socket in the cross plank, raised it, and made it fast with the forestays; then they hoisted their white sails aloft with ropes of twisted oxhide. As the sail bellied out with the wind, the ship flew through the deep blue water, and the foam hissed against her bows as she sped onward. Then they made all fast throughout the ship, filled the mixing bowls to the brim, and made drink offerings to the immortal gods that live forever, but more particularly to the grey-eyed daughter of Zeus.

Thus, then, the ship sped on her way through the watches of the night from dark till dawn.

BOOK III

❧

Telemachus Visits Nestor at Pylos

BUT AS the sun was rising from the fair sea into the firmament of heaven to shed light on mortals and immortals, they reached Pylos, the city of Neleus. Now, the people of Pylos were gathered on the seashore to offer sacrifice of black bulls to Poseidon, lord of the earthquake. There were nine companies with five hundred men in each, and there were nine bulls to each company. As they were eating the inner parts° and offering the thigh bones as a burnt sacrifice to the god, Telemachus and his crew arrived, furled their sails, brought their ship to anchor, and went ashore.

Athene led the way and Telemachus followed her. Presently she said, "Telemachus, you must not be in the least shy or nervous; you have taken this voyage to try and find out where your father is buried and how he came by his end; so go straight up to Nestor that we may see what he has got to tell us. Beg him to speak the truth, and he will tell no lies, for he is an excellent person."

"But how, Mentor," replied Telemachus, "dare I go up to Nestor, and how am I to address him? I have never yet been used to holding long conversations with people, and am ashamed to begin questioning one who is so much older than myself."

°The heart, liver, lights, kidneys, &c., were taken out from the inside and eaten first as being more readily cooked; the outer flesh, or bone meat, was cooking while the inner parts were being eaten.

"Some things, Telemachus," answered Athene, "will be suggested to you by your own instinct, and heaven will prompt you further; for I am assured that the gods have been with you from the time of your birth until now."

She then went quickly on, and Telemachus followed in her steps till they reached the place where the companies of the Pylian people were assembled. There they found Nestor sitting with his sons, while his company round him were busy getting dinner ready, and putting pieces of meat onto the spits while other pieces were cooking. When they saw the strangers they crowded round them, took them by the hand and bade them take their places. Nestor's son Peisistratus at once offered his hand to each of them, and seated them on some soft sheepskins that were lying on the sands near his father and his brother Thrasymedes. Then he gave them their portions of the inner parts and poured wine for them into a golden cup, handing it to Athene first, and welcoming her at the same time.

"Offer a prayer, sir," said he, "to King Poseidon, for it is his feast that you are joining; when you have duly prayed and made your drink offering, pass the cup to your friend that he may do so also. I doubt not that he too prays to the gods, for man cannot live without God in the world. Still he is younger than you are, and is much of an age with myself, so I will give you the precedence."

As he spoke he handed her the cup. Athene thought it very right and proper of him to have given it to herself first; she accordingly began praying heartily to Poseidon. "O thou," she prayed, "that encirclest the earth, grant the fulfilment of our prayers. More especially we pray thee to give honour to Nestor and his sons; thereafter also make the rest of the Pylian people some handsome return for the goodly hecatomb they are offering you. Lastly, grant Telemachus and myself a successful voyage, in respect of the matter that has brought us in our ship to Pylos."

When she had thus prayed (and she herself fulfilled her prayer), she handed the cup to Telemachus and he prayed likewise. By and by, when the outer flesh was roasted and had been taken off the spits, the carvers gave every man his portion and they all made an excellent dinner. As soon as they had had enough to eat and drink, Nestor, knight of Gerene, began to speak.

"Now," said he, "that our guests have done their dinner, it will be best to ask them who they are. Who, then, strangers, are you, and from what port have you sailed? Are you traders, or do you sail the seas as pirates with your hand against every man, and every man's hand against you?"

Telemachus answered boldly, for Athene had given him courage to ask about his father and get himself a good name.

"Nestor," said he, "son of Neleus, honour to the Achaean name, you ask whence we come, and I will tell you. We come from Ithaca under Neïon, and the matter about which I would speak is of private, not public, import. I seek news of my unhappy father, Odysseus, who is said to have sacked the town of Troy in company with yourself. We know what fate befell each one of the other heroes who fought at Troy, but as regards Odysseus heaven has hidden from us the knowledge even that he is dead at all, for no one can tell us in what place he perished, nor say whether he fell in battle on the mainland, or was lost at sea amid the waves of Amphitrite. Therefore I have come to beseech you to tell me of his melancholy end, if you saw it with your own eyes, or heard it from some other traveller, for he was a man born to trouble. Do not soften things out of any pity for me, but tell me in all plainness exactly what you saw. If my brave father, Odysseus, ever did you loyal service, either by word or deed when you Achaeans suffered hardship among the Trojans, bear it in mind now as in my favour and tell me truly all."

"My friend," answered Nestor, "you recall a time of much sorrow to my mind, for the brave Achaeans suffered much both at sea, while privateering under Achilles, and when fighting before the great city of King Priam. Our best men all of them fell there—Ajax, Achilles, Patroclus, equal of gods in counsel, and my own dear son Antilochus, a man very fleet of foot and in fight valiant. But we suffered much more than this; what mortal tongue indeed could tell the whole story? Though you were to stay here and question me for five years, or even six, I could not tell you all that the Achaeans suffered, and you would turn homeward weary of my tale before it ended. Nine long years did we try every kind of stratagem, but the hand of heaven was against us; during all this time there was no one who could compare with your father in subtlety— if indeed you are his son—I can hardly believe my eyes—and you talk just like him too—no one would say that people of such different ages could speak so much alike. He and I never had any kind of difference from first to last neither in camp nor council, but in singleness of heart and purpose we advised the Argives how all might be ordered for the best.

"When, however, we had sacked the city of Priam, and were setting sail in our ships, heaven dispersed us, and Zeus saw fit to harass the Argives on their homeward voyage; for they had not all been either wise or understanding, and hence many came to a bad end through the displeasure of Zeus's daughter Athene, who brought about a quarrel between the two sons of Atreus.

"The sons of Atreus called a meeting, which was not as it should be, for it was sunset and the Achaeans were heavy with wine. When they explained why they had called the people together, it seemed that Menelaus was for sailing homeward at once, and this displeased Agamemnon, who thought that we should wait till we had offered hecatombs to appease the anger of Athene. Fool that he was, he might have known that he would not prevail with her, for when the gods have made up their minds they do not change them lightly. So the two stood bandying hard words, whereon the

Achaeans sprang to their feet with shouts that rent the air, and were of two minds as to what they should do.

"That night we rested and nursed our anger, for Zeus was hatching mischief against us. But in the morning some of us drew our ships into the water and put our goods with our women on board, while the rest, about half in number, stayed behind with Agamemnon. We—the other half—embarked and sailed; and the ships went well, for a god had calmed the sea. When we reached Tenedos we offered sacrifices to the gods, for we were longing to get home; cruel Zeus, however, did not yet mean that we should do so, and raised a second quarrel, in the course of which some among us turned their ships back again, and sailed away under Odysseus to make their peace with Agamemnon; but I and all the ships that were with me pressed forward, for I saw that mischief was brewing. Diomedes went on also with me, and his crews with him. Later on, Menelaus joined us at Lesbos, and found us making up our minds about our course—for we did not know whether to go outside Chios by the island of Psyra, keeping this to our left, or inside Chios, past the stormy headland of Mimas. So we asked heaven for a sign, and were shown one to the effect that we should be soonest out of danger if we headed our ships across the open sea to Euboea. This we therefore did, and a fair wind sprang up, which gave us a quick passage during the night to Geraestus, where we offered many sacrifices to Poseidon for having helped us so far on our way. Four days later Diomedes and his men anchored their ships in Argos, but I held on for Pylos, and the wind never fell light from the day when heaven first made it fair for me.

"Therefore, my dear young friend, I returned without hearing anything about the others. I know neither who got home safely nor who were lost but, as in duty bound, I will give you without reserve the reports that have reached me since I have been here in my own house. They say the Myrmidons returned home safely under Achilles' son

Neoptolemus; so also did the valiant son of Poias,
Philoctetes. Idomeneus, again, lost no men at sea, and all
his followers who escaped death in the field got safe home
with him to Crete. No matter how far out of the world you
live, you will have heard of Agamemnon and the bad end
he came to at the hands of Aegisthus—and a fearful reckoning did Aegisthus presently pay. See what a good thing it
is for a man to leave a son behind him to do as Orestes did,
who killed false Aegisthus, the murderer of his noble father. You, too, then—for you are a tall, smart-looking fellow—show your mettle and make yourself a name in
story."

"Nestor, son of Neleus," answered Telemachus, "honour
to the Achaean name, the Achaeans applaud Orestes and his
name will live through all time, for he has avenged his father
nobly. Would that heaven might grant me to do like
vengeance on the insolence of the wicked suitors, who are
ill-treating me and plotting my ruin; but the gods have no
such happiness in store for me and for my father, so we must
bear it as best we may."

"My friend," said Nestor, "now that you remind me, I remember to have heard that your mother has many suitors,
who are ill disposed towards you and are making havoc of
your estate. Do you submit to this tamely, or are public feeling and the voice of heaven against you? Who knows but
that Odysseus may come back after all, and pay these
scoundrels in full, either single-handed or with a force of
Achaeans behind him? If Athene were to take as great a liking to you as she did to Odysseus when we were fighting before Troy (for I never yet saw the gods so openly fond of
anyone as Athene then was of your father), if she would take
as good care of you as she did of him, these wooers would
soon some of them forget their wooing."

Telemachus answered, "I can expect nothing of the kind;
it would be far too much to hope for. I dare not let myself

think of it. Even though the gods themselves willed it, no such good fortune could befall me."

On this Athene said, "Telemachus, what are you talking about? Heaven has a long arm if it is minded to save a man; and if it were me, I should not care how much I suffered before getting home, provided I could be safe when I was once there. I would rather this, than get home quickly and then be killed in my own house as Agamemnon was by the treachery of Aegisthus and his wife. Still, death is certain, and when a man's hour is come, not even the gods can save him, no matter how fond they are of him."

"Mentor," answered Telemachus, "do not let us talk about it any more. There is no chance of my father's ever coming back; the gods long ago planned his destruction. There is something else, however, about which I should like to ask Nestor, for he knows much more than anyone else does. They say he has reigned for three generations, so that it is like talking to an immortal. Tell me, therefore, Nestor, and tell me true: How did Agamemnon come to die in that way? What was Menelaus doing? And how came false Aegisthus to kill so much better a man than himself? Was Menelaus away from Achaean Argos, voyaging elsewhere among mankind, that Aegisthus took heart and killed Agamemnon?"

"I will tell you truly," answered Nestor, "and indeed you have yourself divined how it all happened. If Menelaus when he got back from Troy had found Aegisthus still alive in his house, there would have been no barrow heaped up for him when he was dead, but he would have been thrown outside the city to dogs and vultures, and not a woman would have mourned him, for he had done a deed of great wickedness; but we were over there, fighting hard at Troy, and Aegisthus, who was taking his ease quietly in the heart of Argos, cajoled Agamemnon's wife, Clytemnestra, with incessant flattery.

"At first she would have nothing to do with his wicked scheme, for she was of a good natural disposition; moreover, there was a bard with her, to whom Agamemnon had given strict orders on setting out for Troy, that he was to keep guard over his wife; but when heaven had counselled her destruction, Aegisthus carried this bard off to a desert island, and left him there for crows and seagulls to feed upon—after which she went willingly enough to the house of Aegisthus. Then he offered many burnt sacrifices to the gods, and decorated many temples with tapestries and gilding, for he had succeeded far beyond his expectations.

"Meanwhile Menelaus and I were on our way home from Troy, on good terms with one another. When we got to Sunium, which is the headland of Athens, Apollo with his painless shafts killed Phrontis, the steersman of Menelaus' ship (and never man knew better how to handle a vessel in rough weather), so that he died then and there with the helm in his hand, and Menelaus, though very anxious to press forward, had to wait in order to bury his comrade and give him his due funeral rites. Presently, when he, too, could put to sea again, and had sailed on as far as the high promontory of Malea, Zeus planned evil against him and made it blow hard till the waves ran mountains high. Here he divided his fleet and took the one half towards Crete, where the Cydonians live round about the waters of the river Iardanus. There is a high headland hereabouts stretching out into the sea from a place called Gortyn, and all along this part of the coast as far as Phaestus the sea runs high when there is a south wind blowing, but after Phaestus the coast is more protected, for a small headland can make a great shelter. Here this part of the fleet was driven onto the rocks and wrecked; but the crews just managed to save themselves. As for the other five ships, they were taken by winds and seas to Egypt, where Menelaus gathered much gold and substance among people of an alien speech. Meanwhile Aegisthus here at home plotted his evil deed. For seven years after he had killed Agamemnon he ruled in Mycenae, and the people were obedient under him, but in the eighth year Orestes came back from Athens, and killed the murderer of his father. Then he celebrated the funeral rites of his mother and of false Aegisthus by a banquet to the people of Argos, and on that very day Menelaus came home, with as much treasure as his ships could carry.

"Take my advice then, and do not go travelling about for long so far from home, leaving your property with such dangerous people in your house; they will eat up everything you have among them, and you will have been on a fool's errand. Still, I should advise you by all means to go and visit Menelaus, who has lately come from a voyage among such distant peoples as no man could ever hope to get back from, when the winds had once carried him so far out of his way; even birds cannot fly the distance in a twelvemonth, so vast and terrible are the seas that they must cross. Go to him, therefore, by sea, and take your own men with you; or if you would rather travel by land, you can have a chariot, you can have horses, and here are my sons, who can escort you to Lacedaemon, where Menelaus lives. Beg him to speak the truth and he will tell you no lies, for he is an excellent person."

As he spoke the sun set and it became dark, whereon Athene said, "Sir, all that you have said is well; now, however, order the tongues of the victims to be cut, and mix wine that we may make drink offerings to Poseidon, and the other immortals, and then go to bed, for it is bedtime. The sun has set, and people should go away early and not keep late hours at a religious festival."

Thus spoke the daughter of Zeus, and they obeyed her. Menservants poured water over the hands of the guests, while pages filled the mixing bowls with wine and water, and handed it round after giving every man his drink offering; they threw the tongues of the victims into the fire, and stood up to make their drink offerings. When they had made their offerings and had drunk each as much as he wished, Athene and Telemachus were for going on board their ship, but Nestor held them back.

"Heaven and the immortal gods," he exclaimed, "forbid that you should leave my house to go on board a ship. Do you think I am so poor and short of clothes, or that I have so few cloaks and rugs, as to be unable to find comfortable beds for myself and my guests? Let me tell you I have both rugs and cloaks, and shall not permit the son of my old friend Odysseus to camp out on the deck of a ship—not while I live—nor yet will my sons after me, but they will keep open house as I have done."

Then Athene answered, "Sir, you have spoken well, and it will be much better that Telemachus should do as you have said; he, therefore, shall return with you and sleep at your house, but I must go back to give orders to my crew, and keep them in good heart. I am the only older person among them; the rest are all young men of Telemachus' own age, who have undertaken this voyage out of friendship; so I must return to the ship and sleep there. Moreover, tomorrow I must go to the Cauconians, where I have a large sum of money long owing to me. As for Telemachus, now that he is your guest, send him to Lacedaemon in a chariot, and let one of your sons go with him. Be pleased also to provide him with your best and fleetest horses."

When she had thus spoken, she flew away in the form of an eagle, and all marvelled as they beheld it. Nestor was astonished, and took Telemachus by the hand. "My friend," said he, "I see that you are going to be a great hero some day, since the gods accompany you thus while you are still so young. This can have been none other of those who dwell in heaven than Zeus's redoubtable daughter, the Trito-born, who showed such favour towards your brave father among the Argives. Holy queen," he continued, "send down thy grace upon myself, my good wife, and my children. In return, I will offer you in sacrifice a broad-browed heifer of a year old, unbroken, and never yet brought by man under the yoke. I will gild her horns, and will offer her up to you in sacrifice."

Thus did he pray, and Athene heard his prayer. He then led the way to his own house, followed by his sons and sons-in-law. When they had got there and had taken their places on the benches and seats, he mixed them a bowl of sweet wine that was eleven years old when the housekeeper took the lid off the jar that held it. As he mixed the wine, he prayed much and made drink offerings to Athene, daughter of aegis-bearing Zeus. Then, when they had made their drink offerings and had drunk each as much as he wished, the others went home to bed, each in his own abode; but Nestor put Telemachus to sleep in the room that was under the echoing porch, along with Peisistratus, who was the only unmarried son now left him. As for himself, he slept in an inner room of the house, with the queen, his wife, by his side.

Now, when the child of morning, rosy-fingered Dawn, appeared, Nestor left his couch and took his seat on the benches of white and polished marble that stood in front of his house. Here aforetime sat Neleus, equal of gods in counsel, but he was now dead, and had gone to the house of Hades; so Nestor sat in his seat, sceptre in hand, as guardian of the public weal. His sons as they left their rooms gathered round him, Echephron, Stratius, Perseus, Aretus, and Thrasymedes; the sixth son was Peisistratus, and when Telemachus joined them they made him sit with them. Nestor then addressed them.

"My sons," said he, "make haste to do as I shall bid you. I wish first and foremost to propitiate the great goddess Athene, who manifested herself visibly to me during yesterday's festivities. Go then, one or other of you, to the plain, tell the stockman to look me out a heifer, and come on here with it at once. Another must go to Telemachus' ship, and invite all the crew, leaving two men only in charge of the vessel. Let someone else run and fetch Laerceus, the goldsmith, to gild the horns of the heifer. The rest, stay all of you where you are; tell the maids in the house to prepare an excellent dinner, and to fetch seats, and logs of wood. Tell them also to bring me some clear spring water."

On this they hurried off on their several errands. The heifer was brought in from the plain, and Telemachus' crew came from the ship; the goldsmith brought the anvil, hammer, and tongs, with which he worked his gold, and Athene herself came to accept the sacrifice. Nestor gave out the gold, and the smith gilded the horns of the heifer that the goddess might have pleasure in their beauty. Then Stratius and Echephron brought the heifer in by the horns; Aretus fetched water from the house in a ewer that had a flower pattern on it, and in his other hand he held a basket of barley meal; sturdy Thrasymedes stood by with a sharp axe, ready to strike the heifer, while Perseus held a bucket. Then Nestor began with washing his hands and sprinkling the barley meal, and he offered many a prayer to Athene as he threw a lock from the heifer's head upon the fire.

When they had done praying and sprinkling the barley meal, Thrasymedes dealt his blow, and brought the heifer down with a stroke that cut through the tendons at the base of her neck, whereon the daughters and daughters-in-law of Nestor, and his venerable wife, Eurydice (she was eldest daughter to Clymenus), cried aloud. Then they lifted the heifer's head from off the ground, and Peisistratus cut her throat. When she had done bleeding and was quite dead, they cut her up. They cut out the thigh bones in the customary way, wrapped them round in two layers of fat, and set some pieces of raw meat on the top of them; then Nestor laid them upon the wood fire and poured wine over them, while the young men stood near him with five-pronged spits in their hands. When the thighs were burned and they had tasted the inner parts, they cut the rest of the meat up small, put the pieces on the spits and roasted them over the fire.

Meanwhile lovely Polycaste, Nestor's youngest daughter,

washed Telemachus. When she had washed him and anointed him with oil, she brought him a fair mantle and tunic, and he looked like a god as he came from the bath and took his seat by the side of Nestor. When the outer flesh was done they drew it off the spits and sat down to dinner, where they were waited upon by some worthy henchmen, who kept pouring them out their wine in cups of gold. As soon as they had had enough to eat and drink, Nestor said, "Sons, put Telemachus' horses to the chariot that he may start at once."

Thus did he speak, and they did as he had said, and yoked the swift horses to the chariot. The housekeeper packed them up provisions of bread, wine, and cooked meats fit for the sons of princes. Then Telemachus got into the chariot, while Peisistratus gathered up the reins and took his seat beside him. He lashed the horses on and they flew forward nothing loth into the open country, leaving the high citadel of Pylos behind them. All that day did they travel, swaying the yoke upon their necks till the sun went down and darkness was over all the land. Then they reached Pherae, where Diocles lived, who was son of Ortilochus and grandson of Alpheus. Here they passed the night and Diocles entertained them hospitably. When the child of morning, rosyfingered Dawn, appeared, they again yoked their horses and drove out through the gateway under the echoing gatehouse. Peisistratus lashed the horses on and they flew forward nothing loth; presently they came to the corn lands of the open country, and in the course of time completed their journey, so well did their steeds take them.

The sun set and darkness covered the land.

BOOK IV

———————— ❧ ————————

The Visit to King Menelaus, Who Tells His Story—
Meanwhile the Suitors in Ithaca Plot Against
Telemachus

THEY REACHED the low-lying city of Lacedaemon, where they drove straight to the abode of Menelaus and found him in his own house, feasting with his many kinsmen in honour of the wedding of his son, and also of his daughter, whom he was marrying to the son of that valiant warrior Achilles. He had given his consent and promised her to him while he was still at Troy, and now the gods were bringing the marriage about; so he was sending her with chariots and horses to the city of the Myrmidons, over whom Achilles' son was reigning. For his only son he had found a bride from Sparta, the daughter of Alector. This son, Megapenthes, was born to him of a bondwoman, for heaven vouchsafed Helen no more children after she had borne Hermione, who was fair as golden Aphrodite herself.

So the neighbours and kinsmen of Menelaus were feasting and making merry in his house. There was a bard also to sing to them and play his lyre, while two tumblers went about performing in the midst of them when the man struck up with his tune.

Telemachus and the son of Nestor stopped their horses at the gate, whereon Eteoneus, servant to Menelaus, came out, and as soon as he saw them ran hurrying back into the house to tell his master. He went close up to him and said, "Menelaus, there are some strangers come here, two men, who look like sons of Zeus. What are we to do? Shall we take their horses out, or tell them to find friends elsewhere as they best can?"

Menelaus was very angry and said, "Eteoneus, son of Boëthous, you never used to be a fool, but now you talk like a simpleton. Take their horses out, of course, and show the strangers in that they may have supper; you and I have stayed often enough at other people's houses before we got back here, where heaven grant that we may rest in peace henceforward."

So Eteoneus bustled back and bade the other servants come with him. They took their sweating steeds from under the yoke, made them fast to their mangers, and gave them a feed of oats and barley mixed. Then they leaned the chariot against the end wall of the courtyard, and led the way into the house. Telemachus and Peisistratus were astonished when they saw it, for its splendour was as that of the sun and moon; then, when they had admired everything to their heart's content, they went into the bath room and washed themselves.

When the maidservants had washed them and anointed them with oil, they brought them woollen cloaks and tunics, and the two took their seats by the side of Menelaus. A maid-servant brought them water in a beautiful golden ewer, and poured it over a silver basin for them to wash their hands; and she drew a clean table beside them. A housekeeper brought them bread, and offered them many good things of what there was in the house, while the carver fetched them plates of all manner of meats and set cups of gold by their side.

Menelaus then greeted them, saying, "Fall to, and welcome; when you have done supper I shall ask who you are, for the lineage of such men as you cannot have been lost. You must be descended from a line of sceptre-bearing kings, for poor people do not have such sons as you are."

On this he handed them a piece of fat roast loin, which

had been set near him as being a prime part, and they laid their hands on the good things that were before them; as soon as they had had enough to eat and drink, Telemachus said to the son of Nestor, with his head so close that no one might hear, "Look, Peisistratus, man after my own heart, see the gleam of bronze and gold, of amber, ivory, and silver. Everything is so splendid that it is like seeing the palace of Olympian Zeus. I am lost in admiration."

Menelaus overheard him and said, "No one, my sons, can hold his own with Zeus, for his house and everything about him is immortal; but among mortal men—well there may be another who has as much wealth as I have, or there may not; but at all events I have travelled much and have undergone much hardship, for it was nearly eight years before I could get home with my fleet. I went to Cyprus, Phoenicia, and the Egyptians; I went also to the Ethiopians, the Sidonians, and the Erembi, and to Libya, where the lambs have horns as soon as they are born, and the sheep lamb down three times a year. Everyone in that country, whether master or man, has plenty of cheese, meat, and good milk, for the ewes yield all the year round. But while I was travelling and getting great riches among these people, my brother was secretly and shockingly murdered through the perfidy of his wicked wife, so that I have no pleasure in being lord of all this wealth. Whoever your parents may be, they must have told you about all this, and of my heavy loss in the ruin of a stately mansion fully and magnificently furnished. ° Would that I had only a third of what I now have so that I had stayed at home, and all those were living who perished on the plain of Troy, far from Argos. I often grieve, as I sit here in my house, for one and all of them. At times I cry aloud for sorrow, but presently I leave off again, for crying is cold comfort and one soon tires of it. Yet grieve for

°This no doubt refers to the story told in the lost poem of the Cypria about Paris and Helen robbing Menelaus of the greater part of his treasures, when they sailed together for Troy.

these as I may, I do so for one man more than for them all. I cannot even think of him without loathing both food and sleep, so miserable does he make me, for no one of all the Achaeans worked so hard or risked so much as he did. He gained nothing by it, and has left a legacy of sorrow to myself, for he has been gone a long time, and we know not whether he is alive or dead. His old father, his long-suffering wife, Penelope, and his son, Telemachus, whom he left behind him an infant in arms, are plunged in grief on his account."

Thus spoke Menelaus, and he aroused in Telemachus a desire to weep for his father. Tears fell from his eyes as he heard him thus mentioned, so that he held his cloak before his face with both hands. When Menelaus saw this he was uncertain whether to let him choose his own time for speaking, or to ask him at once and find what it was all about.

While he was thus in two minds, Helen came down from her high-vaulted and perfumed room, looking as lovely as Artemis herself. Adraste brought her a seat, Alcippe a soft woollen rug, while Phylo fetched her the silver workbox which Alcandra, wife of Polybus, had given her. Polybus lived in Egyptian Thebes, which is the richest city in the whole world; he gave Menelaus two baths, both of pure silver, two tripods, and ten talents of gold; besides all this, his wife gave Helen some beautiful presents—a golden distaff and a silver workbox that ran on wheels, with a gold band round the top of it. Phylo now placed this by her side, full of fine spun yarn, and a distaff charged with violet-coloured wool was laid upon the top of it. Then Helen took her seat, put her feet upon the footstool, and began to question her husband.

"Do we know, Menelaus," said she, "the names of these strangers who have come to visit us? Shall I guess right or wrong?—but I cannot help saying what I think. Never yet have I seen either man or woman so like somebody else (indeed, when I look at him I hardly know what to think) as this young man is like Telemachus, whom Odysseus left as a baby behind him, when you Achaeans went to Troy to make war, on account of my most shameless self."

"My dear wife," replied Menelaus, "I see the likeness just as you do. His hands and feet are just like Odysseus'; so is his hair, with the shape of his head and the expression of his eyes. Moreover, when I was talking about Odysseus, and saying how much he had suffered on my account, tears fell from his eyes, and he hid his face in his mantle."

Then Peisistratus said, "Menelaus, son of Atreus, you are right in thinking that this young man is Telemachus, but he is very modest, and is too respectful to come here and begin opening up discourse with one whose conversation is so divinely interesting as your own. My father, Nestor, sent me to escort him hither, for he wanted to know whether you could give him any counsel or suggestion. A son has always trouble at home when his father has gone away leaving him without supporters; and this is how Telemachus is now placed, for his father is absent, and there is no one among his own people to stand by him."

"Bless my heart," replied Menelaus, "then I am receiving a visit from the son of a very dear friend, who suffered much hardship for my sake. I had always hoped to entertain him with most marked distinction when heaven had granted us a safe return from beyond the seas. I should have founded a city for him in Argos, and built him a house. I should have made him leave Ithaca with his goods, his son, and all his people, and should have sacked for them some one of the neighbouring cities that are subject to me. We should thus have seen one another continually, and nothing but death could have interrupted so close and happy a friendship. I suppose, however, that heaven grudged us such great good fortune, for it has prevented the poor fellow from ever getting home at all."

Thus did he speak, and his words set them all a-weeping. Helen wept, Telemachus wept, and so did Menelaus, nor could Peisistratus keep his eyes from filling, when he remembered his dear brother Antilochus, whom Memnon, the son of bright Dawn, had killed. Thereon he said to Menelaus:

"Sir, my father, Nestor, when we used to talk about you at home, told me you were a person of rare and excellent understanding. If, then, it be possible, do as I would urge you. I am not fond of crying while I am getting my supper. Morning will come in due course, and in the forenoon I care not how much I cry for those that are dead and gone. This is all we can do for unhappy mortals. We can only shave our heads for them and let the tears fall from our cheeks. I had a brother who died at Troy; he was by no means the worst man there; you are sure to have known him—his name was Antilochus; I never set eyes upon him myself, but they say that he was very fleet of foot and in fight valiant."

"Your discretion, my friend," answered Menelaus, "is beyond your years. It is plain you take after your father. One can soon see when a man is son to one whom heaven has blessed both as regards wife and offspring—and it has blessed Nestor from first to last all his days, giving him a comfortable old age in his own house, with sons about him who are both well disposed and valiant. We will put an end therefore to all this weeping, and attend to our supper again. Let water be poured over our hands. Telemachus and I can talk with one another fully in the morning."

On this, Asphalion, one of the servants, poured water over their hands and they laid their hands on the good things that were before them.

Then Zeus's daughter Helen turned to other thoughts. She drugged the wine with an herb that banishes all care, sorrow, and ill humour. Whoever drinks wine thus drugged cannot shed a single tear all the rest of the day, not even though his father and mother both of them drop down dead, or he sees a brother or a son hewn in pieces before his very eyes. This drug, of such sovereign power and virtue, had been given to Helen by Polydamna, wife of Thon, a woman of Egypt, where there grow all sorts of herbs, some good to put into the mixing bowl and others poisonous. Moreover, everyone in the whole country is a skilled physician, for they are of the race of Paeëon. When Helen had put this drug in the bowl, and had told the servants to serve the wine round, she said:

"Menelaus, son of Atreus, and you, my good friends, sons of honourable men (which is as Zeus wills, for he is the giver both of good and evil, and can do what he chooses), feast here as you will, and listen while I tell you a tale in season. I cannot indeed name every single one of the exploits of Odysseus, but I can give an example of what he did in the land of Troy, where you Achaeans suffered hardship. He covered himself with wounds and bruises, dressed himself all in rags, and entered the enemy's city looking like a menial or a beggar, and quite different from when he was among his own people. In this disguise he entered the city of Troy, and no one said anything to him. I alone recognised him and began to question him, but he was too cunning for me. When, however, I had washed and anointed him and had given him clothes, and after I had sworn a solemn oath not to betray him to the Trojans till he had got safely back to his own camp and to the ships, he told me all that the Achaeans meant to do. He killed many Trojans and got much information before he reached the Argive camp, for all of which the Trojan women made lamentation, but for my own part I was glad, for my heart was beginning to yearn after my home, and I was unhappy about the wrong that Aphrodite had done me in taking me over there, away from my country, my little girl, and my lawful wedded husband, who is indeed by no means deficient either in person or in understanding."

Then Menelaus said, "All that you have been saying, my wife, is true. I have travelled much, and have had much to do with heroes, but I have never seen such another man as Odysseus. What endurance, too, and what courage he displayed within the wooden horse, wherein all the bravest of the Argives were lying in wait to bring death and destruction upon the Trojans. You came there then; some god who wished well to the Trojans must have set you on to it and you had Deiphobus with you. Three times did you go all round our hiding place and pat it; you called our chiefs each by his own name, and mimicked all our wives—Diomedes, Odysseus, and I from our seats inside heard what a noise you made. Diomedes and I could not make up our minds whether to spring out then and there, or to answer you from inside, but Odysseus held us all in check, so we sat quite still, all except Anticlus, who was beginning to answer you, when Odysseus clapped his two brawny hands over his mouth, and kept them there. It was this that saved us all, for he muzzled Anticlus till Athene took you away again."

"It makes it worse," exclaimed Telemachus, "that all this was of no avail to save him, nor yet his own iron courage. But now, sir, be pleased to send us all to bed, that we may lie down and enjoy the blessed boon of sleep."

On this, Helen told the maidservants to set beds in the room that was in the gatehouse, and to make them with good red rugs, and spread coverlets on the top of them with woollen cloaks for the guests to wear. So the maids went out, carrying a torch, and made the beds, to which a manservant presently conducted the strangers. Thus, then, did Telemachus and Peisistratus sleep there in the forecourt, while the son of Atreus lay in an inner room with lovely Helen by his side.

When the child of morning, rosy-fingered Dawn, appeared, Menelaus rose and dressed himself. He bound his sandals onto his feet, girded his sword about his shoulder, and left his room looking like an immortal god. Then, taking a seat near Telemachus, he said:

"And what, Telemachus, has led you to take this long sea voyage to Lacedaemon? Are you on public or private business? Tell me all about it."

"I have come, sir," replied Telemachus, "to see if you can tell me anything about my father. I am being eaten out of house and home; my fair estate is being wasted, and my house is full of miscreants who keep killing great numbers of my sheep and oxen, on the pretence of paying their addresses to my mother. Therefore, I have come to beseech you to tell me about my father's melancholy end, if you saw it with your own eyes, or heard it from some other traveller; for he was a man born to trouble. Do not soften things out of any pity for myself, but tell me in all plainness exactly what you saw. If my brave father, Odysseus, ever did you loyal service either by word or deed, when you Achaeans suffered hardship among the Trojans, bear it in mind now as in my favour and tell me truly all."

Menelaus, on hearing this, was very much shocked. "So," he exclaimed, "these cowards would usurp a brave man's bed? A hind might as well lay her newborn young in the lair of a lion, and then go off to feed in the forest or in some grassy dell; the lion when he comes back to his lair will make short work of them—and so will Odysseus with these suitors. By Father Zeus, Athene, and Apollo, if Odysseus is still the man that he was when he wrestled with Philomeleides in Lesbos, and threw him so heavily that all the Achaeans cheered him—if he is still such and were to come near these suitors, they would have a short shrift and a sorry wedding. As regards your questions, however, I will not prevaricate nor deceive you, but will tell you without concealment all that the old man of the sea told me.

"I was trying to come on here, but the gods detained me in Egypt, for my hecatombs had not given them full satisfaction, and the gods are very strict about having their dues. Now, off Egypt, about as far as a ship can sail in a day with a good stiff breeze behind her, there is an island called Pharos—it has a good harbour from which vessels can get out into open sea when they have taken in water—and here the gods becalmed me twenty days without so much as a breath of fair wind to help me forward. We should have run clean out of provisions and my men would have starved, if a goddess had not taken pity upon me and saved me in the person of Idothea, daughter of Proteus, the old man of the sea, for she had taken a great fancy to me.

"She came to me one day when I was by myself, as I often was, for the men used to go with their barbed hooks all over the island in the hope of catching a fish or two to save them from the pangs of hunger. 'Stranger,' said she, 'it seems to me that you like starving in this way—at any rate it does not greatly trouble you, for you stick here day after day, without even trying to get away, though your men are dying by inches.'

" 'Let me tell you,' said I, 'whichever of the goddesses you may happen to be, that I am not staying here of my own accord, but must have offended the gods that live in heaven. Tell me, therefore, for the gods know everything, which of the immortals it is that is hindering me in this way, and tell me also how I may sail the sea so as to reach my home.'

" 'Stranger,' replied she, 'I will make it all quite clear to you. There is an old immortal who lives under the sea hereabouts and whose name is Proteus. He is an Egyptian, and people say he is my father; he is Poseidon's head man and knows every inch of ground all over the bottom of the sea. If you can snare him and hold him tight, he will tell you about your voyage, what courses you are to take, and how you are to sail the sea so as to reach your home. He will also tell you, if you so will, all that has been going on at your house, both good and bad, while you have been away on your long and dangerous journey.'

" 'Can you show me,' said I, 'some stratagem by means of which I may catch this old god without his suspecting it and finding me out? For a god is not easily caught—not by a mortal man.'

" 'Stranger,' said she, 'I will make it all quite clear to you. About the time when the sun reaches mid-heaven, the old man of the sea comes up from under the waves, heralded by the west wind, which furs the water over his head. As soon as he has come up, he lies down and goes to sleep in a great sea cave, where the seals—Halosydne's chickens, as they call them—come up also from the grey sea, and go to sleep in shoals all round him; and a very strong and fishlike smell do they bring with them. Early tomorrow morning I will take you to this place and will lay you in ambush. Pick out, therefore, the three best men you have in your fleet, and I will tell you all the tricks that the old man will play you.

" 'First he will look over all his seals, and count them; then, when he has seen them and counted them on his five fingers, he will go to sleep among them, as a shepherd among his sheep. The moment you see that he is asleep, seize him; put forth all your strength and hold him fast, for he will do his very utmost to get away from you. He will turn himself into every kind of creature that goes upon the earth, and will become also both fire and water; but you must hold him fast and grip him tighter and tighter, till he begins to talk to you and comes back to what he was when you saw him go to sleep; then you may slacken your hold and let him go; and you can ask him which of the gods it is that is angry with you, and what you must do to reach your home over the seas.'

"Having so said, she dived under the waves, whereon I turned back to the place where my ships were ranged upon the shore; and my heart was clouded with care as I went along. When I reached my ship we got supper ready, for night was falling, and camped down upon the beach.

"When the child of morning, rosy-fingered Dawn, appeared, I took the three men on whose prowess of all kinds I could most rely, and went along by the seaside, praying heartily to heaven. Meanwhile the goddess fetched me up four sealskins from the bottom of the sea, all of them just skinned, for she meant to play a trick upon her father. Then she dug four pits for us to lie in, and sat down to wait till we should come. When we were close to her, she made us lie down in the

pits one after the other, and threw a sealskin over each of us.
Our ambuscade would have been intolerable, for the stench of
the fishy seals was most distressing—who would go to bed
with a sea monster if he could help it?—but here, too, the goddess helped us, and thought of something that gave us great
relief, for she put some ambrosia under each man's nostrils,
which was so fragrant that it killed the smell of the seals.

"We waited the whole morning and made the best of it,
watching the seals come up in hundreds to bask upon the
seashore, till at noon the old man of the sea came up, too,
and when he had found his fat seals he went over them and
counted them. We were among the first he counted, and he
never suspected any guile, but laid himself down to sleep as
soon as he had done counting. Then we rushed upon him
with a shout and seized him; on which he began at once with
his tricks, and changed himself first into a lion with a great
mane; then all of a sudden he became a dragon, a leopard, a
wild boar; the next moment he was running water, and then
again directly he was a tree, but we stuck to him and never
lost hold, till at last the cunning old creature became distressed, and said, 'Which of the gods was it, son of Atreus,
that hatched this plot with you for snaring me and seizing
me against my will? What do you want?'

" 'You know that yourself, old man,' I answered. 'You will
gain nothing by trying to put me off. It is because I have
been kept so long in this island, and see no sign of my being
able to get away. I am losing all heart; tell me, then, for you
gods know everything, which of the immortals it is that is
hindering me, and tell me also how I may sail the sea so as to
reach my home?'

" 'Well,' he said, 'you should have offered sacrifices to
Zeus and the rest of the gods before embarking, so that you
would finish your voyage and get home quickly; now it is decreed that you shall not get back to your friends, and to your
own house, till you have returned to the heaven-fed stream

of Egypt, and offered holy hecatombs to the immortal gods that reign in heaven. When you have done this they will let you finish your voyage.'

"I was brokenhearted when I heard that I must go back all that long and terrible voyage to Egypt; nevertheless I answered, 'I will do all, old man, that you have laid upon me; but now tell me, and tell me true, whether all the Achaeans whom Nestor and I left behind us when we set sail from Troy have got home safely, or whether any one of them came to a bad end either on board his own ship or among his friends when the days of his fighting were done.'

" 'Son of Atreus,' he answered, 'why ask me? You had better not know what I can tell you, for your eyes will surely fill when you have heard my story. Many of those about whom you ask are dead and gone, but many still remain, and only two of the chief men among the Achaeans perished during their return home. As for what happened on the field of battle—you were there yourself. A third Achaean leader is still at sea, alive, but hindered from returning. Ajax was wrecked, for Poseidon drove him onto the great rocks of Gyrae; nevertheless he let him get safe out of the water, and in spite of all Athene's hatred he would have escaped death, if he had not ruined himself by boasting. He said the gods could not drown him even though they had tried to do so, and when Poseidon heard this large talk, he seized his trident in his two brawny hands, and split the rock of Gyrae in two pieces. The base remained where it was, but the part on which Ajax was sitting fell headlong into the sea and carried Ajax with it; so he drank salt water and was drowned.

" 'Your brother and his ships escaped, for Hera protected him, but when he was just about to reach the high promontory of Malea, he was caught by a heavy gale, which carried him out to sea again sorely against his will, and drove him to the foreland where Thyestes used to dwell, but where Aegisthus, Thyestes' son, was then living. By and by, however, it seemed as though he was to return safely after all, for the gods backed the wind into its old quarter and they reached home; whereon Agamemnon kissed his native soil, and shed tears of joy at finding himself again in his own country.

" 'Now, there was a watchman whom Aegisthus kept always on the watch, and to whom he had promised two talents of gold. This man had been looking out for a whole year to make sure that Agamemnon did not give him the slip and prepare war; when, therefore, this man saw Agamemnon go by, he went and told Aegisthus, who at once began to lay a plot for him. He picked twenty of his bravest warriors and placed them in ambush, while on the opposite side of the hall he prepared a banquet. Then he sent his chariots and horsemen to Agamemnon, and invited him to the feast, but he meant foul play. He got him there, all unsuspicious of the doom that was awaiting him, and killed him when the banquet was over as though he were butchering an ox at the stall; not one of Agamemnon's followers was left alive, nor yet one of Aegisthus', but they were all killed there in the hall.'

"Thus spoke Proteus, and I was brokenhearted as I heard him. I sat down upon the sands and wept; I felt as though I could no longer bear to live nor look upon the light of the sun. Presently, when I had had my fill of weeping and writhing upon the ground, the old man of the sea said, 'Son of Atreus, do not waste any more time in crying so bitterly; it can do no manner of good; find your way home as fast as ever you can, for Aegisthus may be still alive, and even though Orestes has been beforehand with you in killing him, you may yet come in for his funeral.'

"On this I took comfort in spite of all my sorrow, and said, 'I know, then, about these two; tell me, therefore, about the third man of whom you spoke; is he still alive, but at sea, and unable to get home, or is he dead? Tell me, no matter how much it may grieve me.'

" 'The third man,' he answered, 'is Odysseus, who dwells

in Ithaca. I can see him on an island sorrowing bitterly in the house of the nymph Calypso, who is keeping him prisoner, and he cannot reach his home for he has no ships nor sailors to take him over the sea. As for your own end, Menelaus, you shall not die in Argos, but the gods will take you to the Elysian plain, which is at the ends of the world. There fair-haired Rhadamanthus reigns, and men lead an easier life than anywhere else in the world, for in Elysium there falls not rain, nor hail, nor snow, but Oceanus breathes ever with a west wind that sings softly from the sea, and gives fresh life to men. This will happen to you because you have married Helen, and are Zeus's son-in-law.'

"As he spoke he dived under the waves, whereon I turned back to the ships with my companions, and my heart was clouded with care as I went along. When we reached the ships we got supper ready, for night was falling, and camped down upon the beach. When the child of morning, rosy-fingered Dawn, appeared, we drew our ships into the water, and put our masts and sails within them; then we went on board ourselves, took our seats on the benches, and smote the grey sea with our oars. I again stationed my ships in the heaven-fed stream of Egypt, and offered hecatombs that were full and sufficient. When I had thus appeased heaven's anger, I raised a barrow to the memory of Agamemnon that his name might live forever, after which I had a quick passage home, for the gods sent me a fair wind.

"And now for yourself—stay here some ten or twelve days longer, and I will then speed you on your way. I will make you a noble present of a chariot and three horses. I will also give you a beautiful chalice that so long as you live you may think of me whenever you make a drink offering to the immortal gods."

"Son of Atreus," replied Telemachus, "do not press me to stay longer; I should be contented to remain with you for another twelve months; I find your conversation so delightful that I should never once wish myself at home with my parents; but my crew, whom I have left at Pylos, are already impatient, and you are detaining me from them. As for any present you may be disposed to make me, I had rather that it should be a piece of plate. I will take no horses back with me to Ithaca, but will leave them to adorn your own stables, for you have much flat ground in your kingdom, where lotus thrives, as also meadowsweet and wheat and barley, and oats with their white and spreading ears; whereas in Ithaca we have neither open fields nor racecourses, and the country is more fit for goats than horses, and I like it the better for that. None of our islands have much level ground, suitable for horses, and Ithaca least of all."

Menelaus smiled and patted Telemachus with his hand. "What you say," said he, "shows that you come of good stock. I both can, and will, make this exchange for you, by giving you the finest and most precious piece of plate in all my house. It is a mixing bowl by Hephaestus' own hand, of pure silver, except the rim, which is inlaid with gold. Phaedimus, king of the Sidonians, gave it to me in the course of a visit which I paid him when I returned thither on my homeward journey. I will make you a present of it."

Thus did they converse and guests kept coming to the king's house. They brought sheep and wine, while their wives had given bread for them to take with them; so they were busy preparing their meal in the courts.

Meanwhile the suitors were throwing the discus or aiming with spears at a mark on the levelled ground in front of Odysseus' house, and were behaving with all their old insolence. Antinous and Eurymachus, who were their ringleaders and much the foremost among them all, were sitting together when Noëmon, son of Phronius, came up and said to Antinous:

"Have we any idea, Antinous, on what day Telemachus returns from Pylos? He has a ship of mine, and I want it, to cross over to Elis. I have twelve brood mares there with yearling mule foals by their side not yet broken in, and I want to bring one of them over here and break him."

They were astounded when they heard this, for they had been sure that Telemachus had not gone to the city of Neleus. They thought he was only away somewhere on the farms, and was with the sheep, or with the swineherd; so Antinous said, "When did he go? Tell me truly, and what young men did he take with him? Were they freemen or his own bondsmen—for he might manage that, too. Tell me also, did you let him have the ship of your own free will because he asked you, or did he take it without your leave?"

"I lent it him," answered Noëmon. "What else could I do when a man of his position said he was in a difficulty, and asked me to oblige him? I could not possibly refuse. As for those who went with him, they were the best young men we have, and I saw Mentor go on board as captain—or some god who was exactly like him. I cannot understand it, for I saw Mentor here myself yesterday morning, and yet he was then setting out for Pylos."

Noëmon then went back to his father's house, but Antinous and Eurymachus were very angry. They told the others to leave off playing, and to come and sit down along with themselves. When they came, Antinous, son of Eupeithes, spoke in anger. His heart was black with rage, and his eyes flashed fire as he said:

"Good heavens, this voyage of Telemachus is a very serious matter; we had been sure that it would come to nothing, but the young fellow has got away in spite of us, and with a picked crew, too. He will be giving us trouble presently; may Zeus destroy him before he is full grown. Find me a ship, therefore, with a crew of twenty men, and I will lie in wait for him in the straits between Ithaca and Samos; he will then rue the day that he set out to try and get news of his father."

Thus did he speak, and the others applauded his words; they then all of them went inside the buildings.

It was not long before Penelope came to know what the suitors were plotting; for a manservant, Medon, overheard them from outside the outer court as they were laying their schemes within, and went to tell the queen. As he crossed the threshold of her room, Penelope said, "Medon, what have the suitors sent you here for? Is it to tell the maids to leave their work and cook dinner for them? I wish they may neither woo nor dine henceforward, neither here nor anywhere else, but let this be the very last time, for the waste you all make of my son's estate. Did not your fathers tell you, when you were children, how good Odysseus had been to them—never doing anything highhanded, nor speaking harshly to anybody? Kings may say things sometimes, and they may take a fancy to one man and dislike another, but Odysseus never did an unjust thing by anybody—which shows what bad hearts you have, and that there is no such thing as gratitude left in this world."

Then Medon said, "I wish, Madam, that this were all; but they are plotting something much more dreadful now—may heaven frustrate their design. They are going to try and murder Telemachus as he is coming home from Pylos and Lacedaemon, where he has been to get news of his father."

Then Penelope's heart sank within her, and for a long time she was speechless; her eyes filled with tears, and she could find no utterance. At last, however, she said, "Why did my son leave me? What business had he to go sailing off in ships that make long voyages over the ocean like sea horses? Does he want to die without leaving anyone behind him to keep up his name?"

"I do not know," answered Medon, "whether some god set him on to it, or whether he went on his own impulse to see if he could find out if his father was dead, or alive and on his way home."

Then he went downstairs again, leaving Penelope in an agony of grief. There were plenty of seats in the house, but she had no heart for sitting on any one of them; she could only fling herself on the floor of her own room and cry; whereon all the maids in the house, both old and young, gathered round her and began to cry, too, till at last in a transport of sorrow she exclaimed:

"My dears, heaven has been pleased to try me with more affliction than any other woman of my own age and country. First I lost my brave and lion-hearted husband, who had every good quality under heaven, and whose name was great throughout Hellas and Argos, and now my darling son is at the mercy of the winds and waves, without my having heard one word about his leaving home. Cruel creatures, there was not one of you would so much as think of giving me a call out of my bed, though you all of you very well knew when he was starting. If I had known he meant to take this voyage, he would have had to give it up, no matter how much he was bent upon it, or leave me a corpse behind him. Now, however, go some of you and call old Dolius, who was given me by my father on my marriage, and who is my gardener. Bid him go at once and tell everything to Laertes, who may be able to hit on some plan for enlisting public sympathy on our side, as against those who are trying to exterminate his own race and that of Odysseus."

Then the dear old nurse Eurycleia said, "You may kill me, Madam, or let me live on in your house, whichever you please, but I will tell you the real truth. I knew all about it, and gave him everything he wanted in the way of bread and wine, but he made me take my solemn oath that I would not tell you anything for twelve days, unless you asked or happened to hear of his having gone, for he did not want you to spoil your beauty by crying. And now, Madam, wash your face, change your dress, and go upstairs with your maids to offer prayers to Athene, daughter of aegis-bearing Zeus, for she can save him even though he be in the jaws of death. Do not trouble Laertes: he has trouble enough already. Besides, I cannot think that the gods hate the race of the son of Arceisius so much, but there will be a son left to come up after him, and inherit both the house and the fair fields that lie far all round it."

With these words she made her mistress leave off crying, and dried the tears from her eyes. Penelope washed her face, changed her dress, and went up upstairs with her maids. She then put some bruised barley into a basket and began praying to Athene.

"Hear me," she cried, "untiring daughter of aegis-bearing Zeus. If ever Odysseus while he was here burned you fat thigh bones of sheep or heifer, bear it in mind now as in my favour, and save my darling son from the villainy of the suitors."

She cried aloud as she spoke, and the goddess heard her prayer; meanwhile the suitors made a great uproar throughout the dark hall, and one of them said:

"The queen is preparing for her marriage with one or other of us. Little does she dream that her son has been now doomed to die."

This was what they said, but they did not know what was going to happen. Then Antinous said, "Comrades, let there be no loud talking, lest some of it get carried inside. Let us be up and do in silence what we have all decided."

He then chose twenty men, and they went down to their ship and to the seashore; they drew the vessel into the water and got her mast and sails inside her; they bound the oars to the thole pins with twisted thongs of leather, all as they should be, and spread the white sails aloft, while their fine servants brought them their armour. Then they made the ship fast a little way out, came on shore again, got their suppers, and waited till night should fall.

But Penelope lay in her own room upstairs, unable to eat or drink, and wondering whether her brave son would escape, or be overpowered by the wicked suitors. Like a lioness caught in the toils with huntsmen hemming her in on every side, she thought and thought till she sank into a slumber, and lay on her bed bereft of thought and motion.

Then Athene turned to other thoughts, and made a vision in the likeness of Penelope's sister Ipthime, daughter of Icarius, who had married Eumelus and lived in Pherae. She told the vision to go to the house of Odysseus, and to make Penelope leave off crying, so it came into her room by the hole through which the thong went for pulling the door to, and stood at her head, saying:

"You are asleep, Penelope: the gods who live at ease will not suffer you to weep and be so sad. Your son has done them no wrong, so he will yet come back to you."

Penelope, who was sleeping sweetly at the gates of dreamland, answered, "Sister, why have you come here? You do not come very often, because you live such a long way off. Am I, then, to leave off crying and refrain from all the sad thoughts that torture me? I, who have lost my brave and lion-hearted husband, who had every good quality under heaven, and whose name was great throughout Hellas and Argos; and now my darling son has gone off on board of a ship—a foolish boy who has never been used to roughing it, nor to going about among gatherings of men. I am even more anxious about him than about my husband; I am all in a tremble when I think of him, lest something should happen to him, either from the people among whom he has gone, or by sea, for he has many enemies who are plotting against him, and are bent on killing him before he can return home."

Then the vision said, "Take heart, and be not so much dismayed. There is one gone with him whom many a man would be glad enough to have stand by his side; I mean Athene; it is she who has compassion upon you, and who has sent me to bear you this message."

"Then," said Penelope, "if you are a god or have been sent here by divine commission, tell me also about that other unhappy one—is he still alive, or is he already dead and in the house of Hades?"

And the vision said, "I shall not tell you for certain whether he is alive or dead, and there is no use in idle conversation."

Then it vanished through the thong hole of the door and was dissipated into thin air; but Penelope rose from her sleep refreshed and comforted, so vivid had been her dream.

Meantime the suitors went on board and sailed over the sea, intent on murdering Telemachus. Now, there is a rocky islet called Asteris, of no great size, in mid-channel between Ithaca and Samos, and there is a harbour on either side of it where a ship can lie. Here then the Achaeans placed themselves in ambush.

BOOK V

❧

Calypso—Odysseus Reaches Scheria on a Raft

AND NOW, as Dawn rose from her couch beside Tithonus—to bring light alike to mortals and immortals—the gods met in council and with them Zeus, the lord of thunder, who is their king. Thereon Athene began to tell them of the many sufferings of Odysseus, for she pitied him away there in the house of the nymph Calypso.

"Father Zeus," said she, "and all you other gods that live in everlasting bliss, may there never be such a thing as a kind and well disposed ruler any more, nor one who will govern equitably. May they all henceforth be cruel and unjust, for there is not one of his subjects but has forgotten Odysseus, who ruled them as though he were their father. There he is, lying in great misery in an island where dwells the nymph Calypso, who will not let him go; and he cannot get back to his own country, for he can find neither ships nor sailors to take him over the sea. Furthermore, wicked people are now trying to murder his only son, Telemachus, who is coming home from Pylos and Lacedaemon, where he has been to see if he can get news of his father."

"What, my dear, are you talking about?" replied her father. "Did you not make this plan yourself, that Odysseus will come home and punish the suitors? Besides, you are perfectly able to protect Telemachus, and to see him safely home again, while the suitors have to come hurrying back without having killed him."

When he had thus spoken, he said to his son Hermes, "Hermes, you are our messenger; go therefore and tell Calypso we have decreed that poor Odysseus is to return home. He is to be convoyed neither by gods nor by men, but after a perilous voyage of twenty days upon a raft he is to reach fertile Scheria, the land of the Phaeacians, who are near of kin to the gods, and will honour him as though he were one of ourselves. They will send him in a ship to his own country, and will give him more bronze and gold and raiment than he would have brought back from Troy, if he had had all his prize money and had got home without disaster. This is how we have settled that he shall return to his country and his friends."

Thus he spoke, and Hermes, guide and guardian, slayer of Argus, did as he was told. Forthwith he bound on his glittering golden sandals, with which he could fly like the wind over land and sea. He took the wand with which he seals men's eyes in sleep or wakes them just as he pleases, and flew holding it in his hand over Pieria; then he swooped down through the sky till he reached the level of the sea, whose waves he skimmed like a cormorant that flies fishing close down on the vast swell of the ocean, and drenching its thick plumage in the spray. He flew and flew over many a wave, but when at last he got to the island which was his journey's end, he left the sea and went on by land till he came to the cave where the nymph Calypso lived.

He found her at home. There was a large fire burning on the hearth, and one could smell from far the fragrant reek of burning cedar and sandalwood. As for herself, she was busy at her loom, shooting her golden shuttle through the warp and singing beautifully. Round her cave there was a thick wood of alder, poplar, and sweet-smelling cypress trees, wherein all kinds of great birds had built their nests—owls, hawks, and chattering sea crows that occupy their business in the waters. A vine loaded with grapes was trained and grew luxuriantly about the mouth of the cave; there were also four running rills of water in channels cut close together, and turned hither and thither so as to irrigate the beds of violets and luscious herbage over which they flowed. Even a god could not help being charmed with such a lovely spot, so Hermes stood still and looked at it; but when he had admired it sufficiently he went inside the cave.

Calypso knew him at once—for the gods all know each other, no matter how far they live from one another—but Odysseus was not within; he was on the seashore as usual, looking out upon the barren ocean with tears in his eyes, groaning and breaking his heart for sorrow. Calypso gave Hermes a seat and said, "Why have you come to see me, Hermes—honoured, and ever welcome—for you do not visit me often. Say what you want; I will do it for you at once if I can, and if it can be done at all; but come inside, and let me set refreshment before you."

As she spoke she drew a table loaded with ambrosia beside him and mixed him some red nectar, so Hermes ate and drank till he had had enough, and then said:

"We are speaking god and goddess to one another, and you ask me why I have come here, and I will tell you truly as you would have me do. Zeus sent me; it was no doing of mine; who could possibly want to come all this way over the sea, where there are no cities full of people to offer me sacrifices or choice hecatombs? Nevertheless I had to come, for none of us other gods can cross Zeus, nor disobey his orders. He says that you have here the most ill-starred of all those who fought nine years before the city of King Priam and sailed home in the tenth year after having sacked it. On their way home they sinned against Athene, who raised both wind and waves against them, so that all his brave companions perished, and he alone was carried hither by wind and tide. Zeus says that you are to let this man go at once, for it is decreed that he shall not perish here, far from his own people, but shall return to his house and country and see his friends again."

Calypso trembled when she heard this. "You gods," she exclaimed, "ought to be ashamed of yourselves. You are always jealous, and hate seeing a goddess take a fancy to a mortal man, and live with him in open matrimony. So when rosy-fingered Dawn made love to Orion, you precious gods were all of you furious till Artemis went and killed him in Ortygia. So again when Demeter fell in love with Iasion, and lay with him in a thrice-ploughed fallow field, Zeus came to hear of it before so very long and killed Iasion with his thunderbolts. And now you are angry with me, too, because I have a man here. I found the poor creature sitting all alone astride of a keel, for Zeus had struck his ship with lightning and sunk it in mid-ocean, so that all his crew were drowned, while he himself was driven by wind and waves onto my island. I got fond of him and looked after him, and had set my heart on making him immortal, so that he should never grow old all his days; still I cannot cross Zeus, nor bring his counsels to nothing; therefore, if he insists upon it, let the man go beyond the seas again; but I cannot send him anywhere myself, for I have neither ships nor men who can take him. Nevertheless I will readily give him such advice, in all good faith, as will be likely to bring him safely to his own country."

"Then send him away," said Hermes, "or Zeus will be angry with you and punish you."

On this he took his leave, and Calypso went out to look for Odysseus, for she had heard Zeus's message. She found him sitting upon the beach with his eyes ever filled with tears, and dying of sheer homesickness; for he had got tired of Calypso, and though he was forced to sleep with her in the cave by night, it was she, not he, that would have it so. As for the daytime, he spent it on the rocks and on the seashore, weeping, crying aloud for his despair, and always looking out upon the sea. Calypso then went close up to him and said:

"My poor fellow, you shall not stay here grieving and fretting your life out any longer. I am going to send you away of my own free will; so go, cut some planks of wood, and make yourself a large raft with an upper deck that it may carry you safely over the sea. I will put bread, wine, and water on board to save you from starving. I will also give you clothes, and will send you a fair wind to take you home, if the gods in heaven so will it—for they know more about these things and can settle them better than I can."

Odysseus shuddered as he heard her. "Now, goddess," he answered, "there is something behind all this; you cannot be really meaning to help me home when you bid me do such a dreadful thing as put to sea on a raft. Not even a well-found ship with a fair wind could venture on such a distant voyage. Nothing that you can say or do shall make me go on board a raft unless you first solemnly swear that you mean me no mischief."

Calypso smiled at this and patted him with her hand. "You know a great deal," said she, "but you are quite wrong here. May heaven above and earth below be my witnesses, with the waters of the river Styx—and this is the most solemn oath which a blessed god can take—that I mean you no sort of harm, and am only advising you to do exactly what I should do myself in your place. I am dealing with you quite straightforwardly; my heart is not made of iron, and I am very sorry for you."

When she had thus spoken, she led the way rapidly before him, and Odysseus followed in her steps; so the pair, goddess and man, went on till they came to Calypso's cave, where Odysseus took the seat that Hermes had just left. Calypso set meat and drink before him of the food that mortals eat; but her maids brought ambrosia and nectar for herself, and they laid their hands on the good things that were before them. When they had satisfied themselves with meat and drink, Calypso spoke, saying:

"Odysseus, noble son of Laertes, so you would start home to your own land at once? Good luck go with you, but if you could only know how much suffering is in store for you before you get back to your own country, you would stay where you are, keep house along with me, and let me make you immortal, no matter how anxious you may be to see this wife of yours, of whom you are thinking all the time day after day; yet I flatter myself that I am no whit less tall or well-looking than she is, for it is not to be expected that a mortal woman should compare in beauty with an immortal."

"Goddess," replied Odysseus, "do not be angry with me about this. I am quite aware that my wife, Penelope, is nothing like so tall or so beautiful as yourself. She is only a woman, whereas you are an immortal. Nevertheless I want to get home, and can think of nothing else. If some god wrecks me when I am on the sea, I will bear it and make the best of it. I have had infinite trouble both by land and by sea already, so let this go with the rest."

Presently the sun set and it became dark, whereon the pair retired into the inner part of the cave and slept together.

When the child of morning, rosy-fingered Dawn, appeared, Odysseus put on his tunic and cloak, while the goddess wore a dress of a light gossamer fabric, very fine and graceful, with a beautiful golden belt about her waist and a veil to cover her head. She at once set herself to think how she could speed Odysseus on his way. So she gave him a great bronze axe that suited his hands; it was sharpened on both sides, and had a beautiful olivewood handle fitted firmly onto it. She also gave him a sharp adze, and then led the way to the far end of the island, where the largest trees grew—alder, poplar, and pine, that reached the sky—very dry and well seasoned, so as to sail light for him in the water. Then, when she had shown him where the best trees grew, Calypso went home, leaving him to cut them, which he soon finished doing. He cut down twenty trees in all and adzed them smooth, squaring them by rule in good workmanlike fashion. Meanwhile Calypso came back with some augers, so he bored holes with them and fitted the timbers together with bolts and rivets. He made the raft as broad as a skilled shipwright makes the beam of a large vessel, and he fixed a deck on top of the ribs, and ran a gunwale all round it. He also made a mast with a yardarm, and a rudder to steer with. He fenced the raft all round with wicker hurdles as a protection against the waves, and then he threw on a quantity of wood. By and by Calypso brought him some linen to make the sails, and he made these, too, excellently, making them fast with braces and sheets. Last of all, with the help of levers, he drew the raft down into the water.

In four days he had completed the whole work, and on the fifth Calypso sent him from the island after washing him and giving him some clean clothes. She gave him a goatskin full of deep-red wine, and another, larger one of water; she also gave him a wallet full of provisions, and put on board much good meat. Moreover, she made the wind fair and warm for him, and gladly did Odysseus spread his sail before it, while he sat and guided the raft skilfully by means of the rudder. He never closed his eyes, but kept them fixed on the Pleiads, on late-setting Boötes, and on the Bear—which men also call the wain, and which turns round and round where it is, facing Orion, and alone never dipping into the stream of Oceanus, for Calypso had told him to keep this to his left. Seventeen days did he sail over the sea, and on the eighteenth the dim outlines of the mountains on the nearest part of the Phaeacian coast appeared, rising like a shield on the horizon.

But King Poseidon, who was returning from the Ethiopians, caught sight of Odysseus a long way off, from the mountains of the Solymi. He could see him sailing upon the sea, and it made him very angry, so he shook his head and muttered to himself, "Good heavens, so the gods have been changing their minds about Odysseus while I was away in Ethiopia, and now he is close to the land of the Phaeacians, where it is decreed that he shall escape from the calamities that have befallen him. Still, he shall have plenty of hardship yet before he reaches it."

Thereon he gathered his clouds together, grasped his trident, stirred it round in the sea, and roused the rage of every wind that blows, till earth, sea, and sky were hidden in cloud, and night sprang forth out of the heavens. Winds from east, south, north, and west fell upon him all at the same time, and a tremendous sea got up, so that Odysseus' heart began to fail him. "Alas," he said to himself in his dismay, "whatever will become of me? I am afraid Calypso was right when she said I should have trouble by sea before I got back home. It is all coming true. How black is Zeus making heaven with his clouds, and what a sea the winds are raising from every quarter at once. I am now sure to perish. Blessed and thrice blessed were those Danaans who fell before Troy in the cause of the sons of Atreus. Would that I had been killed on the day when the Trojans were pressing me so sorely about the dead body of Achilles, for then I should have had due burial and the Achaeans would have honoured my name; but now it seems that I shall come to a most pitiable end."

As he spoke a sea broke over him with such terrific fury that the raft reeled, and he was carried overboard a long way off. He let go the helm, and the force of the hurricane was so great that it broke the mast halfway up, and both sail and yard went over into the sea. For a long time Odysseus was under water, and it was all he could do to rise to the surface again, for the clothes Calypso had given him weighed him down; but at last he got his head above water and spat out the bitter brine that was running down his face in streams. In spite of all this, however, he did not lose sight of his raft, but swam as fast as he could towards it, got hold of it, and climbed on board again so as to escape drowning. The sea took the raft and tossed it about as autumn winds whirl thistle down round and round upon a road. It was as though the south, north, east, and west winds were all tossing it backwards and forwards between them.

When he was in this plight, Ino, daughter of Cadmus, also called Leucothea, saw him. She had formerly been a mere mortal, but had been since raised to the rank of a marine goddess. Seeing in what great distress Odysseus now was, she had compassion upon him, and rising like a sea gull from the waves, took her seat upon the raft.

"My poor good man," said she, "why is Poseidon so furiously angry with you? He is giving you a great deal of trouble, but for all his bluster he will not kill you. You seem to be a sensible person; do then as I bid you. Strip, leave your raft to drive before the wind, and swim to the Phaeacian coast, where better luck awaits you. And here, take my veil and put it round your chest; it is enchanted, and you can come to no harm so long as you wear it. As soon as you touch land take it off, throw it back as far as you can into the sea, and then turn away." With these words she took off her veil and gave it to him. Then she dived down again like a sea gull and vanished beneath the dark-blue waters.

But Odysseus did not know what to think. "Alas," he said to himself in his dismay, "this is only some one or other of the gods who is luring me to ruin by advising me to quit my raft. At any rate I will not do so at present, for the land where she said I should be quit of all my troubles seems to be still a good way off. I know what I will do—I am sure it will be best. No matter what happens I will stick to the raft as long as her timbers hold together, but when the sea breaks her up I will swim for it; I do not see how I can do any better than this."

While he was thus in two minds, Poseidon sent a terrible great wave that seemed to rear itself above his head till it broke right over the raft, which then went to pieces as though it were a heap of dry chaff tossed about by a whirlwind. Odysseus got astride of one plank and rode upon it as if he were on horseback; he then took off the clothes Calypso had given him, bound Ino's veil under his arms, and plunged into the sea, meaning to swim to shore. King Poseidon watched him as he did so, and shook his head, muttering to himself, "There now, swim up and down as you best can till you come to those god-favoured people. I do not think you will be able to say that I have let you off too lightly." On this he lashed his horses and drove to Aegae, where his palace is.

But Athene resolved to help Odysseus, so she bound the paths of all the winds except one, and made them lie quite still; but she roused a good stiff breeze from the north that should calm the waters till Odysseus reached the land of the Phaeacians, where he would be safe.

Thereon he floated about for two nights and two days in the water, with a heavy swell on the sea and death staring him in the face; but when the third day broke, the wind fell and there was a dead calm without so much as a breath of air stirring. As he rose on the swell he looked eagerly ahead, and could see land quite near. Then, as children rejoice when their dear father begins to get better after having for a long time borne sore affliction sent him by some angry spirit, but the gods deliver him from evil, so was Odysseus thankful when he again saw land and trees, and swam on with all his strength that he might once more set foot upon dry ground. When, however, he got within earshot, he began to hear the surf thundering up against the rocks, for the swell still broke against them with a terrific roar. Everything was enveloped in spray; there were no harbours where a ship might ride, nor shelter of any kind, but only headlands, low-lying rocks, and cliffs.

Odysseus' heart now began to fail him, and he said despairingly to himself, "Alas, Zeus has let me see land after swimming so far that I had given up all hope, but I can find no landing place, for the coast is rocky and surf-beaten, the rocks are smooth and rise sheer from the sea, with deep water close under them so that I cannot climb out for want of foothold. I am afraid some great wave will lift me off my legs and dash me against the rocks as I leave the water—which would give me a sorry landing. If, on the other hand, I swim further in search of some shelving beach or harbour, a hurricane may carry me out to sea again sorely against my will, or heaven may send some great monster of the deep to attack me; for Amphitrite breeds many such, and I know that Poseidon is very angry with me."

While he was thus in two minds, a wave caught him and took him with such force against the rocks that he would have been smashed and torn to pieces if Athene had not shown him what to do. He caught hold of the rock with both hands and clung to it, groaning with pain, till the wave ran past him, so he was saved that time; but presently the wave came back again and carried him with it far into the sea—tearing his hands as the suckers of a polypus are torn when someone plucks it from its bed, and the stones come up along with it— even so did the rocks tear the skin from his strong hands, and then the wave drew him deep down under the water.

Here poor Odysseus would have certainly perished even in spite of his own destiny, if Athene had not helped him to keep his wits about him. He swam seaward again, beyond reach of the surf that was beating against the land, and at the same time he kept looking towards the shore to see if he could find some haven, or a spit that should take the waves aslant. By and by, as he swam on, he came to the mouth of a river, and here he thought would be the best place, for there were no rocks, and it afforded shelter from the wind. He felt that there was a current, so he prayed inwardly and said:

"Hear me, O king, whoever you may be, and save me from the anger of the sea god, Poseidon, for I approach you prayerfully. Any stranger who comes has at all times a claim even upon the gods, wherefore in my distress I draw near to your stream, and beg your help. Have mercy upon me, O king, for I declare myself your suppliant."

Then the god stopped his stream and stilled the waves,

making all calm before him, and bringing him safely into the mouth of the river. Here at last Odysseus' knees and strong hands failed him, for the sea had completely broken him. His body was all swollen, and sea water ran out through his mouth and nostrils, so that he could neither breathe nor speak, and lay swooning from sheer exhaustion; presently, when he had got his breath and came to himself again, he took off the scarf that Ino had given him and threw it back into the salt stream of the river, whereon Ino received it into her hands from the wave that bore it towards her. Then he left the river, laid himself down among the rushes, and kissed the bounteous earth.

"Alas," he cried to himself in his dismay, "whatever will become of me, and how is it all to end? If I stay here upon the riverbed through the long watches of the night, I am so exhausted that the bitter cold and damp may make an end of me—for towards sunrise there will be a keen wind blowing from off the river. If, on the other hand, I climb the hillside, find shelter in the woods, and sleep in some thicket, I may escape the cold and have a good night's rest, but some savage beast may take advantage of me and devour me."

In the end he deemed it best to take to the woods, and he found one upon some high ground not far from the water. There he crept beneath two shoots of olive that grew from a single stock—the one an ungrafted sucker, while the other had been grafted. No wind, however squally, could break through the cover they afforded, nor could the sun's rays pierce them, nor the rain get through them, so closely did they grow into one another. Odysseus crept under these and began to make himself a bed to lie on, for there was a great litter of dead leaves lying about, enough to make a covering for two or three men even in hard winter weather. He was glad enough to see this, so he laid himself down and heaped the leaves all round him. Then, as one who lives alone in the country, far from any neighbour, hides a brand in the ashes, keeping the flame alight, to save himself from having to get a light elsewhere, even so did Odysseus cover himself up with leaves; and Athene shed a sweet sleep upon his eyes, closed his eyelids, and made him lose all memory of his sorrows.

BOOK VI

The Meeting between Nausicaa and Odysseus

SO HERE Odysseus slept, overcome by sleep and toil; but Athene went off to the country and city of the Phaeacians—a people who used to live in the fair town of Hypereia, near the lawless Cyclopes. The Cyclopes were stronger than they and plundered them, so their king, Nausithous, moved them from there and settled them in Scheria, far from all other people. He surrounded the city with a wall, built houses and temples, and divided the land among his people; but he was dead and gone to the house of Hades, and King Alcinous, whose counsels were inspired of heaven, was now reigning. To his house, then, did Athene go in furtherance of the return of Odysseus.

She went straight to the beautifully decorated bedroom in which there slept a girl who was as lovely as a goddess, Nausicaa, daughter of King Alcinous. Two maidservants were sleeping near her, both very pretty, one on either side of the doorway, which was closed with well-made folding doors. Athene took the form of the famous sea captain Dymas' daughter, who was a bosom friend of Nausicaa and just her own age; then, coming up to the girl's bedside like a breath of wind, she stood at her head and said:

"Nausicaa, what can your mother have been about, to have such a lazy daughter? Here are your clothes all lying in disorder, yet you are going to be married almost immediately, and should not only be well dressed yourself, but should find good clothes for those who attend you. This is the way to get yourself a good name, and to make your father and mother proud of you. Suppose, then, that we make tomorrow a washing day, and start at daybreak. I will come and help you so that you may have everything ready as soon as possible, for all the best young men among your own people are courting you, and you are not going to remain a maid much longer. Ask your father, therefore, to have a wagon and mules ready for us at daybreak, to take the rugs, robes, and other clothes, and you can ride, too, which will be much pleasanter for you than walking, for the washing cisterns are some way from the town."

When she had said this, Athene went away to Olympus, which they say is the everlasting home of the gods. There no wind beats roughly, and neither rain nor snow can fall; but there is clear, cloudless sky and bright light is shed over the land; there the blessed gods live happily forever. There the goddess went when she had given instructions to the girl.

By and by morning came and woke Nausicaa, who began wondering about her dream; she therefore went to the other end of the house to tell her father and mother all about it, and found them in their own room. Her mother was sitting by the fireside spinning her purple yarn with her maids around her, and she happened to catch her father just as he was going out to attend a meeting of the town council, which the Phaeacian aldermen had convened. She stopped him and said:

"Father dear, could you manage to let me have a good big wagon? I want to take all our dirty clothes to the river and wash them. You are the chief man here, so it is only right that you should have a clean shirt when you attend meetings of the council. Moreover, you have five sons at home, two of them married, while the other three are good-looking bachelors; you know they always like to have clean linen when they go to a dance, and I have been thinking about all this."

She did not say a word about her own wedding, for she did not like to, but her father knew and said, "You shall have the mules, my love, and whatever else you have a mind for.

Be off with you, and the men shall get you a good strong wagon with a body to it that will hold all your clothes."

On this he gave his orders to the servants, who got the wagon out, harnessed the mules, and yoked them, while the girl brought the clothes down from the linen room and placed them on the wagon. Her mother prepared her a basket of provisions with all sorts of good things, and a goatskin full of wine; the girl now got into the wagon, and her mother gave her also a golden cruse of oil, that she and her women might anoint themselves. Then she took the whip and reins and lashed the mules on, whereon they set off, and their hoofs clattered on the road. They pulled without flagging, and carried not only Nausicaa and her wash of clothes, but the maids also who were with her.

When they reached the waterside they went to the washing cisterns, through which there ran at all times enough pure water to wash any quantity of linen, no matter how dirty. Here they unharnessed the mules and turned them out to feed on the sweet juicy herbage that grew by the waterside. They took the clothes out of the wagon, put them in the water, and vied with one another in treading them in the pits to get the dirt out. After they had washed them and got them quite clean, they laid them out by the seaside, where the waves had raised a high beach of shingle, and set about washing themselves and anointing themselves with olive oil. Then they got their dinner by the side of the stream, and waited for the sun to finish drying the clothes. When they had done dinner they threw off the veils that covered their heads and began to play ball, and Nausicaa began the game. As the huntress Artemis goes forth upon the mountains of Taÿgetus or Erymanthus to hunt wild boars or deer, and the wood nymphs, daughters of aegis-bearing Zeus, take their sport along with her, then is Leto proud at seeing her daughter stand a full head taller than the others, and eclipse the loveliest amid a whole bevy of beauties—even so did the girl outshine her handmaids.

When it was time for them to start home, and they were folding the clothes and putting them into the wagon, Athene began to consider how Odysseus should wake up and see the handsome girl who was to conduct him to the city of the Phaeacians. The girl, therefore, threw a ball at one of the maids, which missed her and fell into deep water. On this they all shouted, and the noise they made woke Odysseus, who sat up in his bed of leaves and began to wonder what it might all be.

"Alas," said he to himself, "what kind of people have I come amongst? Are they cruel, savage, and uncivilized, or hospitable and humane? I seem to hear the voices of young women, and they sound like those of the nymphs that haunt mountaintops, or springs of rivers and meadows of green grass. At any rate I am among a race of men and women. Let me try if I cannot manage to get a look at them."

As he said this he crept from under his bush, and broke off a bough covered with thick leaves to hide his nakedness. He looked like some lion of the wilderness that stalks about exulting in his strength and defying both wind and rain; his eyes glare as he prowls in quest of oxen, sheep, or deer, for he is famished, and will dare break even into a well-fenced homestead, trying to get at the sheep—even such did Odysseus seem to the young women, as he drew near to them all naked as he was, for he was in great need. On seeing one so unkempt and so begrimed with salt water, the others scampered off along the spits that jutted out into the sea, but the daughter of Alcinous stood firm, for Athene put courage into her heart and took away all fear from her. She stood right in front of Odysseus, and he hesitated whether he should go up to her, throw himself at her feet, and embrace her knees as a suppliant, or stay where he was and entreat her to give him some clothes and show him the way to the town. In the end he deemed it best to entreat her from a distance in case the girl should take offence at his coming near enough to clasp her knees, so he addressed her in honeyed and persuasive language.

"O queen," he said, "I implore your aid—but tell me, are you a goddess or are you a mortal woman? If you are a goddess and dwell in heaven, I can only conjecture that you are Zeus's daughter Artemis, for your face and figure resemble none but hers; if on the other hand you are a mortal and live on earth, thrice happy are your father and mother—thrice happy, too, are your brothers and sisters; how proud and delighted they must feel when they see so fair a creature as yourself going out to a dance; most happy, however, of all will he be whose wedding gifts have been the richest, and who takes you to his own home. I never yet saw anyone so beautiful, neither man nor woman, and am lost in admiration as I behold you. I can only compare you to a young palm tree which I saw when I was at Delos growing near the altar of Apollo—for I was there, too, and a large company with me, when I was on that journey which has been the source of all my troubles. Never yet did such a young plant shoot out of the ground as that was, and I admired and wondered at it exactly as I now admire and wonder at yourself. I dare not clasp your knees, but I am in great distress; yesterday made the twentieth day that I have been tossing about upon the sea. The winds and waves have taken me all the way from the Ogygian island, and now fate has flung me upon this coast that I may endure still further suffering; for I do not think that I have yet come to the end of it, but rather that heaven has still much evil in store for me.

"And now, O queen, have pity upon me, for you are the first person I have met, and I know no one else in this country. Show me the way to your town, and let me have anything that you may have brought hither to wrap your clothes in. May heaven grant you in all things your heart's desire—husband, house, and a happy, peaceful home; for there is nothing better in this world than that man and wife should be of one mind in a house. It discomfits their enemies, makes the hearts of their friends glad, and they themselves know more about it than anyone."

To this Nausicaa answered, "Stranger, you appear to be a sensible, well-disposed person. There is no accounting for luck; Zeus gives prosperity to rich and poor just as he chooses, so you must take what he has seen fit to send you, and make the best of it. Now, however, that you have come to this our country, you shall not want for clothes nor for anything else that a foreigner in distress may reasonably look for. I will show you the way to the town, and will tell you the name of our people; we are called Phaeacians, and I am the daughter of Alcinous, in whom the whole power of the state is vested."

Then she called her maids and said, "Stay where you are, you girls. Can you not see a man without running away from him? Do you take him for a robber or a murderer? Neither he nor anyone else can come here to do us Phaeacians any harm, for we are dear to the gods, and live apart on an island, far away, and have nothing to do with any other people. This is only some poor man who has lost his way, and we must be kind to him, for strangers and foreigners in distress are under Zeus's protection, and will take what they can get and be thankful; so, girls, give the stranger something to eat and drink, and wash him in the stream at some place that is sheltered from the wind."

On this the maids left off running away and began calling one another back. They made Odysseus sit down in the shelter as Nausicaa had told them, and brought him a tunic and cloak. They also brought him the little golden cruse of oil, and told him to go and wash in the stream. But Odysseus said, "Young women, please to stand a little on one side that I may wash the brine from my shoulders and anoint myself with oil, for it is long enough since my skin has had a drop of oil upon it. I cannot wash as long as you all keep standing there. I am ashamed to strip before a number of good-looking young women."

Then they stood on one side and went to tell the girl,

while Odysseus washed himself in the stream and scrubbed the brine from his back and from his broad shoulders. When he had thoroughly washed himself, and had got the brine out of his hair, he anointed himself with oil, and put on the clothes which the girl had given him; Athene then made him look taller and stronger than before, she also made the hair grow thick on the top of his head, and flow down in curls like hyacinth blossoms; she glorified him about the head and shoulders as a skilful workman who has studied art of all kinds under Hephaestus and Athene enriches a piece of silver by gilding it—and his work is full of beauty. Then he went and sat down a little way off upon the beach, looking young and handsome, and the girl gazed on him with admiration; then she said to her maids:

"Hush, my dears, for I want to say something. I believe the gods who live in heaven have sent this man to the Phaeacians. When I first saw him I thought him unattractive, but now his appearance is like that of the gods who dwell in heaven. I should like my future husband to be just such a one as he is, if he would only stay here and not want to go away. However, give him something to eat and drink."

They did as they were told, and set food before Odysseus, who ate and drank ravenously, for it was long since he had had food of any kind. Meanwhile Nausicaa turned to other thoughts. She got the linen folded and placed in the wagon, she then yoked the mules, and as she took her seat, she called Odysseus:

"Stranger," said she, "rise and let us be going back to the town; I will bring you to the house of my excellent father, where I can tell you that you will meet all the best people among the Phaeacians. But be sure and do as I bid you, for you seem to be a sensible person. As long as we are going past the fields and farmlands, follow briskly behind the wagon along with the maids and I will lead the way myself. Presently, however, we shall come to the town, where you will find a high wall running all round it, and a good harbour on either side with a narrow entrance into the city, and the ships are drawn up by the roadside, for everyone has a place where his own ship can lie. You will see the market place with a temple of Poseidon in the middle of it, and paved with large stones bedded in the earth. Here people work at ship's gear of all kinds, such as cables and sails, and here, too, are the places where oars are made, for the Phaeacians are not a nation of archers; they know nothing about bows and arrows, but are a seafaring folk, and pride themselves on their masts, oars, and ships, with which they travel far over the sea.

"I am afraid of the gossip and scandal that may be set on foot against me later on; for the people here are very ill-natured, and some low fellow, if he met us, might say, 'Who is this fine-looking stranger that is going about with Nausicaa? Where did she find him? I suppose she is going to marry him. Perhaps he is a vagabond sailor whom she has taken from some foreign vessel, for we have no neighbours; or some god has at last come down from heaven in answer to her prayers, and she is going to live with him all the rest of her life. It would be a good thing if she would take herself off and find a husband somewhere else, for she will not look at one of the many excellent young Phaeacians who are in love with her.' This is the kind of disparaging remark that would be made about me, and I could not complain, for I should myself be scandalised at seeing any other girl do the like, and go about with men in spite of everybody, while her father and mother were still alive, and without having been married in the face of all the world.

"If, therefore, you want my father to give you an escort and to help you home, do as I bid you; you will see a beautiful grove of poplars by the roadside dedicated to Athene; it has a well in it and a meadow all round it. Here my father has a field of rich garden ground, about as far from the town as a man's voice will carry. Sit down there and wait for a while till the rest of us can get into the town and reach my father's house. Then, when you think we must have done this, come into the town and ask the way to the house of my father, Alcinous. You will have no difficulty in finding it; any child will point it out to you, for no one else in the whole town has anything like such a fine house as he has. When you have got past the gates and through the outer court, go right across the hall till you come to my mother. You will find her sitting by the fire and spinning her purple wool by fire-light. It is a fine sight to see her as she leans back against one of the pillars with her maids all ranged behind her. Close to her seat stands that of my father, on which he sits and drinks his wine like an immortal god. Never mind him, but go up to my mother, and lay your hands upon her knees if you would get home quickly. If you can gain her over, you may hope to see your own country again, no matter how distant it may be."

So saying, she lashed the mules with her whip and they left the river. The mules drew well, and their hoofs went up and down upon the road. She was careful not to go too fast for Odysseus and the maids, who were following on foot along with the wagon, so she plied her whip with judgement. As the sun was going down they came to the sacred grove of Athene, and there Odysseus sat down and prayed to the mighty daughter of Zeus.

"Hear me," he cried, "untiring daughter of aegis-bearing Zeus, hear me now, for you gave no heed to my prayers when Poseidon was wrecking me. Now, therefore, have pity upon me and grant that I may find friends and be hospitably received by the Phaeacians."

Thus did he pray, and Athene heard his prayer, but she would not show herself to him openly, for she was afraid of her uncle Poseidon, who was still furious with Odysseus, until he reached his own land.

BOOK VII

❦

*Reception of Odysseus at the Palace of King
Alcinous*

THUS, THEN, did Odysseus wait and pray; but the girl drove
on to the town. When she reached her father's house she
drew up at the gateway, and her brothers—handsome as the
gods—gathered round her, took the mules out of the wagon,
and carried the clothes into the house, while she went to her
own room, where an old servant, Eurymedusa of Apeira, lit
the fire for her. This old woman had been brought by sea
from Apeira, and had been chosen as a prize for Alcinous
because he was king over the Phaeacians, and the people
obeyed him as though he were a god. She had been nurse to
Nausicaa, and had now lit the fire for her, and brought her
supper for her into her own room.

Presently Odysseus got up to go towards the town; and
Athene shed a thick mist all round him to hide him in case
any of the proud Phaeacians who met him should be rude to
him, or ask him who he was. Then, as he was just entering the
town, she came towards him in the likeness of a girl carrying
a pitcher. She stood right in front of him, and Odysseus said:

"My dear, will you be so kind as to show me the house of
King Alcinous? I am an unfortunate foreigner in distress,
and do not know anyone in your town and country."

Then Athene said, "Yes, father stranger, I will show you
the house you want, for Alcinous lives quite close to my own
father. I will go before you and show the way, but say not a

word as you go, and do not look at any man, nor ask him questions; for the people here cannot abide strangers, and do not like men who come from some other place. They are a seafaring folk, and sail the seas by the grace of Poseidon in ships that glide along like thought, or as a bird in the air."

On this she led the way, and Odysseus followed in her steps; but not one of the Phaeacians could see him as he passed through the city in the midst of them; for the great goddess Athene in her good will towards him had hidden him in a thick cloud of darkness. He admired their harbours, ships, places of assembly, and the lofty walls of the city, which, with the palisade on top of them, were very striking, and when they reached the king's house Athene said:

"This is the house, father stranger, which you would have me show you. You will find a number of great people sitting at table, but do not be afraid; go straight in, for the bolder a man is the more likely he is to carry his point, even though he is a stranger. First find the queen. Her name is Arete, and she comes of the same family as her husband, Alcinous. They both descend originally from Poseidon, who was father to Nausithous by Periboea, a woman of great beauty. Periboea was the youngest daughter of Eurymedon, who at one time reigned over the giants, but he ruined his ill-fated people, and lost his own life to boot.

"Poseidon, however, lay with his daughter, and she had a son by him, the great Nausithous, who reigned over the Phaeacians. Nausithous had two sons, Rhexenor and Alcinous; Apollo killed the first of them while he was still a bridegroom and without male issue; but he left a daughter, Arete, whom Alcinous married, and honours as no other woman is honoured of all those that keep house along with their husbands.

"Thus she both was, and still is, respected beyond measure by her children, by Alcinous himself, and by the whole people, who look upon her as a goddess, and greet her whenever she goes about the city, for she is a thoroughly good woman both in head and heart, and when any are friends of hers, she will help even men to settle their disputes. If you can gain her good will, you may have every hope of seeing your friends again, and getting safely back to your home and country."

Then Athene left Scheria and went away over the sea. She went to Marathon and to the spacious streets of Athens, where she entered the house of Erechtheus; but Odysseus went on to the house of Alcinous, and he pondered much as he paused before reaching the threshold of bronze, for the splendour of the palace was like that of the sun or moon. The walls on either side were of bronze from end to end, and the cornice was of blue enamel. The doors were gold, and hung on pillars of silver that rose from a floor of bronze, while the lintel was silver and the hook of the door was of gold.

On either side there stood gold and silver mastiffs which Hephaestus, with his consummate skill, had fashioned expressly to keep watch over the palace of King Alcinous; so they were immortal and could never grow old. Seats were ranged all along the wall, here and there from one end to the other, with coverings of fine woven work which the women of the house had made. Here the chief persons of the Phaeacians used to sit and eat and drink, for there was abundance at all seasons; and there were golden figures of young men with lighted torches in their hands, raised on pedestals, to give light by night to those who were at table. There are fifty maidservants in the house, some of whom are always grinding rich yellow grain at the mill, while others work at the loom, or sit and spin, and their shuttles go backwards and forwards like the fluttering of poplar leaves, while the linen is so closely woven that oil runs off it. As the Phaeacians are the best sailors in the world, so their women excel all others in weaving, for Athene has taught them all manner of useful arts, and they are very intelligent.

Outside the gate of the outer court there is a large garden of about four acres with a wall all round it. It is full of beautiful trees—pears, pomegranates, and the most delicious apples. There are luscious figs also, and olives in full growth. The fruits never rot nor fail all the year round, neither winter nor summer, for the air is so soft that a new crop ripens before the old has dropped. Pear grows on pear, apple on apple, and fig on fig, and so also with the grapes, for there is an excellent vineyard. On the level ground of a part of this, the grapes are being made into raisins; in another part they are being gathered; some are being trodden in the wine tubs, others further on have shed their blossom and are beginning to show fruit, others again are just changing colour. In the furthest part of the ground there are beautifully arranged beds of flowers that are in bloom all the year round. Two streams go through it, the one turned in ducts throughout the whole garden, while the other is carried under the ground of the outer court to the house itself, and the town's people draw water from it. Such, then, were the splendours with which the gods had endowed the house of King Alcinous.

So here Odysseus stood for a while and looked about him, but when he had looked long enough he crossed the threshold and went within the precincts of the house. There he found all the chief people among the Phaeacians making their drink offerings to Hermes, which they always did the last thing before going away for the night. He went straight through the court, still hidden by the cloak of darkness in which Athene had enveloped him, till he reached Arete and King Alcinous; then he laid his hands upon the knees of the queen, and at that moment the miraculous darkness fell away from him and he became visible. Everyone was speechless with surprise at seeing a man there, but Odysseus began at once with his petition.

"Queen Arete," he exclaimed, "daughter of great Rhexenor, in my distress I humbly pray you, as also your husband and these your guests (whom may heaven prosper with long life and happiness, and may they leave their possessions to their children, and all the honours conferred upon them by the state), to help me home to my own country as soon as possible; for I have been long in trouble and away from my friends."

Then he sat down on the hearth among the ashes and they all held their peace, till presently the old hero Echeneüs, who was an excellent speaker and an elder among the Phaeacians, plainly and in all honesty addressed them thus:

"Alcinous," said he, "it is not creditable to you that a stranger should be sitting among the ashes of your hearth; everyone is waiting to hear what you are about to say; tell him, then, to rise and take a seat on a stool inlaid with silver, and bid your servants mix some wine and water that we may make a drink offering to Zeus, the lord of thunder, who takes all suppliants under his protection; and let the housekeeper give him some supper, of whatever there may be in the house."

When Alcinous heard this he took Odysseus by the hand, raised him from the hearth, and bade him take the seat of Laodamas, who had been sitting beside him, and was his favourite son. A maidservant then brought him water in a beautiful golden ewer and poured it over a silver basin for him to wash his hands, and she drew a clean table beside him; a housekeeper brought him bread and offered him many good things, of what there was in the house, and Odysseus ate and drank. Then Alcinous said to one of the servants, "Pontonous, mix a cup of wine and hand it round that we may make drink offerings to Zeus, the lord of thunder, who is the protector of all suppliants."

Pontonous then mixed wine and water, and handed it round after giving every man his drink offering. When they had made their offerings, and had drunk each as much as he wished, Alcinous said:

"Leaders and councillors of the Phaeacians, hear my words. You have had your supper, so now go home to bed. Tomorrow morning I shall invite a still larger number of leading citizens, and will give a sacrificial banquet in honour of our guest; we can then discuss the question of his escort, and consider how we may at once send him back rejoicing to his own country without trouble or inconvenience to himself, no matter how distant it may be. We must see that he comes to no harm while on his homeward journey, but when he is once at home he will have to take the luck he was born with for better or worse like other people. It is possible, however, that the stranger is one of the immortals, who has come down from heaven to visit us; but in this case the gods are departing from their usual practice, for hitherto they have made themselves, perfectly clear to us when we have been offering them hecatombs. They come and sit at our feasts just like one of ourselves, and if any solitary wayfarer happens to stumble upon some one or other of them, they affect no concealment, for we are as near of kin to the gods as the Cyclopes and the savage giants are."

Then Odysseus said, "Pray, Alcinous, do not take any such notion into your head. I have nothing of the immortal about me, neither in body nor mind, and most resemble those whom you know who are the most afflicted. Indeed were I to tell you all that heaven has seen fit to lay upon me, you would say that I was still worse off than they are. Nevertheless, let me sup in spite of sorrow, for an empty stomach is a very importunate thing, and thrusts itself on a man's notice no matter how dire is his distress. I am in great trouble, yet it insists that I shall eat and drink, bids me lay aside all memory of my sorrows and dwell only on the due replenishing of itself. As for yourselves, do as you propose, and at break of day set about helping me to get home. I shall be content to die if I may first behold my property, my bondsmen, and all the greatness of my house."

Thus did he speak. Everyone approved his words, and agreed that he should have his escort because he had spoken properly. Then when they had made their drink offerings, and had drunk each as much as he wished, they went home to bed, every man in his own house, leaving Odysseus in the hall with Arete and Alcinous while the servants were taking the things away after supper. Arete was the first to speak, for she recognised the tunic and cloak, the good clothes that Odysseus was wearing, as the work of herself and of her maids; so she said, "Stranger, before we go any further, there is a question I should like to ask you. Who and whence are you, and who gave you those clothes? Did you not say you had come here from beyond the sea?"

And Odysseus answered, "It would be a long story, Madam, were I to relate in full the tale of my misfortunes, for the hand of heaven has been laid heavy upon me; but as regards your question, there is an island far away in the sea which is called the Ogygian. Here dwells the cunning and powerful goddess Calypso, daughter of Atlas. She lives by herself far from all neighbours, human or divine. Fortune, however, brought me to her hearth all desolate and alone, for Zeus struck my ship with his thunderbolts, and broke it up in mid-ocean. My brave comrades were drowned, every man of them, but I stuck to the keel and was carried hither and thither for the space of nine days, till at last during the darkness of the tenth night the gods brought me to the Ogygian island, where the great goddess Calypso lives. She took me in and treated me with the utmost kindness; indeed she wanted to make me immortal that I might never grow old, but she could not persuade me to let her do so.

"I stayed with Calypso seven years straight on end, and watered the good clothes she gave me with my tears during the whole time; but at last when the eighth year came round she bade me depart of her own free will, either because Zeus had told her she must, or because she had changed her mind. She sent me from her island on a raft, which she provisioned with abundance of bread and wine. Moreover, she gave me good stout clothing, and sent me a wind that blew both warm and fair. Seventeen days did I sail over the sea, and on the eighteenth I caught sight of the faint outlines of the mountains upon your coast—and glad indeed was I to set eyes upon them. Nevertheless there was still much trouble in store for me, for at this point Poseidon would let me go no further, and raised a great storm against me; the sea was so terribly high that I could no longer keep to my raft, which went to pieces under the fury of the gale, and I had to swim for it, till wind and current brought me to your shores.

"There I tried to land, but could not, for it was a bad place and the waves dashed me against the rocks, so I again took to the sea and swam on till I came to a river that seemed the most likely landing place, for there were no rocks and it was sheltered from the wind. Here, then, I got out of the water and gathered my senses together again. Night was coming on, so I left the river, and went into a thicket, where I covered myself all over with leaves, and presently heaven sent me off into a very deep sleep. Sick and sorry as I was, I slept among the leaves all night, and through the next day till afternoon, when I woke as the sun was westering, and saw your daughter's maidservants playing upon the beach, and your daughter among them looking like a goddess. I besought her aid, and she proved to be of an excellent disposition, much more so than could be expected from so young a person—for young people are apt to be thoughtless. She gave me plenty of bread and wine, and when she had had me washed in the river she also gave me the clothes in which you see me. Now, therefore, though it has pained me to do so, I have told you the whole truth."

Then Alcinous said, "Stranger, it was very wrong of my daughter not to bring you on at once to my house along with the maids, seeing that she was the first person whose aid you asked."

"Pray do not scold her," replied Odysseus, "she is not to blame. She did tell me to follow along with the maids, but I was ashamed and afraid, for I thought you might perhaps be displeased if you saw me. Every human being is sometimes a little suspicious and irritable."

"Stranger," replied Alcinous, "I am not the kind of man to

get angry about nothing; it is always better to be reasonable; but by Father Zeus, Athene, and Apollo, now that I see what kind of person you are, and how much you think as I do, I wish you would stay here, marry my daughter, and become my son-in-law. If you will stay I will give you a house and an estate, but no one (heaven forbid) shall keep you here against your own wish, and that you may be sure of this, I will attend tomorrow to the matter of your escort. You can sleep during the whole voyage if you like, and the men shall sail you over smooth waters either to your own home, or wherever you please, even though it be a long way further off than Euboea, which those of my people who saw it when they took fair-haired Rhadamanthus to see Tityus, the son of Gaia, tell me is the furthest of any place—and yet they did the whole voyage in a single day without distressing themselves, and came back again afterwards. You will thus see how much my ships excel all others, and what magnificent oarsmen my sailors are."

Then Odysseus was glad and prayed aloud, saying, "Father Zeus, grant that Alcinous may do all as he has said, for so he will win an imperishable name among mankind, and at the same time I shall return to my own country."

Thus did they converse. Then Arete told her maids to set a bed in the room that was in the gatehouse, and make it with good red rugs, and to spread coverlets on the top of them with woollen cloaks for Odysseus to wrap round himself. The maids went out with torches in their hands, and when they had made the bed they came up to Odysseus and said, "Rise, sir stranger, and come with us, for your bed is ready," and glad indeed was he to go to his rest.

So Odysseus slept in a bed placed in a room under the echoing porch; but Alcinous lay in the inner part of the house, with the queen his wife by his side.

BOOK VIII

Banquet in the House of Alcinous—The Games

NOW, WHEN the child of morning, rosy-fingered Dawn, appeared, Alcinous and Odysseus both rose, and Alcinous led the way to the Phaeacian place of assembly, which was near the ships. When they got there they sat down side by side on a seat of polished stone, while Athene took the form of one of Alcinous' servants, and went round the town in order to help Odysseus to get home. She went up to the citizens, man by man, and said, "Leaders and councillors of the Phaeacians, come to the assembly all of you and listen to the stranger who has just come off a long voyage to the house of King Alcinous; he looks like an immortal god."

With these words she made them all want to come, and they flocked to the assembly till seats and standing room were alike crowded. Everyone was struck with the appearance of Odysseus, for Athene had beautified him about the head and shoulders, making him look taller and bigger than he really was, that he might impress the Phaeacians favourably as being a very remarkable man, and might come off well in the many trials of skill to which they would challenge him. Then, when they were got together, Alcinous spoke:

"Hear me," said he, "leaders and councillors of the Phaeacians, that I may speak as I am minded. This stranger, whoever he may be, has found his way to my house from somewhere or other either east or west. He wants an escort and wishes to have the matter settled. Let us then get one ready for him, as we have done for others before him; indeed no one who ever yet came to my house has been able to complain of me for not speeding him on his way soon enough. Let us draw a ship into the sea—one that has never yet made a voyage—and man her with two and fifty of our smartest young sailors. Then when you have made fast your oars, each by his own seat, leave the ship and come to my house to prepare a feast. I will provide everything. I am giving these instructions to the young men who will form the crew, for as regards you leading citizens, you will join me in entertaining our guest in the palace. I will take no excuses, and we will have Demodocus to sing to us; for there is no bard like him, whatever he may choose to sing about."

Alcinous then led the way, and the others followed after, while a servant went to fetch Demodocus. The fifty-two picked oarsmen went to the seashore as they had been told, and when they got there they drew the ship into the water, got her mast and sails inside her, and bound the oars to the thole pins with twisted thongs of leather, all as they should be, and spread the white sails aloft. They moored the vessel a little way out from land, and then came on shore and went to the house of King Alcinous. The outhouses, yards, and all the precincts were filled with crowds of men in great multitudes, both old and young; and Alcinous killed them a dozen sheep, eight full-grown pigs, and two oxen. These they skinned and dressed so as to provide a magnificent banquet.

A servant presently led in the famous bard Demodocus, whom the muse had dearly loved, but to whom she had given both good and evil, for though she had endowed him with a divine gift of song, she had robbed him of his eyesight. Pontonous set a seat for him among the guests, leaning it up against a pillar. He hung the lyre for him on a peg over his head, and showed him where he was to feel for it with his hands. He also set a fair table with a basket of food by his side, and a cup of wine from which he might drink whenever he was so disposed.

The company then laid their hands upon the good things that were before them, but as soon as they had had enough to eat and drink, the muse inspired Demodocus to sing the feats of heroes, and more especially a matter that was then in the mouths of all men, the quarrel between Odysseus and Achilles, and the fierce words that they heaped on one another as they sat together at a banquet. But Agamemnon was glad when he heard his chieftains quarrelling with one another, for Apollo had foretold him this at Pytho when he crossed the stone floor to consult the oracle. Then was the beginning of the evil that by the will of Zeus fell both upon Danaans and Trojans.

Thus sang the bard, but Odysseus drew his purple mantle over his head and covered his face, for he was ashamed to let the Phaeacians see that he was weeping. When the bard left off singing, he wiped the tears from his eyes, uncovered his face, and, taking his cup, made a drink offering to the gods; but when the Phaeacians pressed Demodocus to sing further, for they delighted in his lays, then Odysseus again drew his mantle over his head and wept bitterly. No one noticed his distress except Alcinous, who was sitting near him, and heard the heavy sighs that he was heaving. So he at once said, "Leaders and councillors of the Phaeacians, we have had enough now, both of the feast and of the minstrelsy that is its due accompaniment; let us proceed therefore to the athletic sports, so that our guest on his return home may be able to tell his friends how much we surpass all other nations as boxers, wrestlers, jumpers, and runners."

With these words he led the way, and the others followed after. A servant hung Demodocus' lyre on its peg for him, led him out of the hall, and set him on the same way as that along which all the chief men of the Phaeacians were going to see the sports; a crowd of several thousands of people followed them, and there were many excellent competitors for all the prizes. Acroneos, Ocyalus, Elatreus, Nauteus, Prymneus, Anchialus, Eretmeus, Ponteus, Proreus, Thoön, Anabesineos, and Amphialus, son of Polyneüs, son of Tecton. There was also Euryalus, son of Naubolus, who was like Ares himself, and was the best-looking man among the Phaeacians except Laodamas. Three sons of Alcinous—Laodamas, Halius, and Clytoneüs—competed also.

The foot races came first. The course was set out for them from the starting post, and they raised a dust upon the plain as they all flew forward at the same moment. Clytoneüs came in first by a long way; he left everyone else behind him by the width of a field that a yoke of mules can plough in a day. They then turned to the painful art of wrestling, and here Euryalus proved to be the best man. Amphialus excelled all the others in jumping, while at throwing the discus there was no one who could approach Elatreus. Alcinous' son Laodamas was the best boxer, and he it was who presently said, when they had all enjoyed the games, "Let us ask the stranger whether he excels in any of these sports; he seems powerfully built; his thighs, calves, hands, and neck are of great strength, nor is he at all old, but he has suffered much lately, and there is nothing like the sea for making havoc with a man, no matter how strong he is."

"You are quite right, Laodamas," replied Euryalus. "Go up to your guest and speak to him about it yourself."

When Laodamas heard this, he made his way into the middle of the crowd and said to Odysseus, "I hope, Sir, that you will enter yourself for some one or other of our competitions if you are skilled in any of them—and you must have gone in for many a one before now. There is nothing that does anyone so much credit all his life long as the showing himself a proper man with his hands and feet. Have a try, therefore, at something, and banish all care from your mind.

Your return home will not be long delayed, for the ship is already drawn into the water, and the crew is found."

Odysseus answered, "Laodamas, why do you taunt me in this way? My mind is set rather on cares than on contests; I have been through infinite trouble, and am come among you now as a suppliant, praying your king and people to further me on my return home."

Then Euryalus reviled him outright and said, "I gather, then, that you are unskilled in any of the many sports that men generally delight in. I suppose you are one of those grasping traders that go about in ships as captains or merchants, and who think of nothing but of their outward freights and homeward cargoes. There does not seem to be much of the athlete about you."

"For shame, Sir," answered Odysseus fiercely, "you are an insolent fellow—so true is it that the gods do not grace all men alike in speech, person, and understanding. One man may be of weak presence, but heaven has adorned this with such a good conversation that he charms everyone who sees him; his honeyed moderation carries his hearers with him so that he is leader in all assemblies of his fellows, and wherever he goes he is looked up to. Another may be as handsome as a god, but his good looks are not crowned with discretion. This is your case. No god could make a finer-looking fellow than you are, but you are a fool. Your ill-judged remarks have made me exceedingly angry, and you are quite mistaken, for I excel in a great many athletic exercises; indeed, so long as I had youth and strength, I was among the first athletes of the age. Now, however, I am worn out by labour and sorrow, for I have gone through much both on the field of battle and by the waves of the weary sea; still, in spite of all this I will compete, for your taunts have stung me to the quick."

So he hurried up without even taking his cloak off, and seized a discus, larger, more massive, and much heavier than those used by the Phaeacians when throwing the discus among themselves. Then, swinging it back, he threw it from his brawny hand, and it made a humming sound in the air. The Phaeacians quailed beneath the rushing of its flight as it sped from his hand, and flew beyond any mark that had been made yet. Athene, in the form of a man, came and marked the place where it had fallen. "A blind man, Sir," said she, "could easily tell your mark by groping for it—it is so far ahead of any other. You may make your mind easy about this contest, for no Phaeacian can come near to such a throw as yours."

Odysseus was glad when he found he had a friend among the lookers on, so he began to speak more pleasantly. "Young men," said he, "come up to that throw if you can, and I will throw another discus as heavy or even heavier. If anyone wants to have a bout with me, let him come on, for I am exceedingly angry; I will box, wrestle, or run, I do not care what it is, with any man of you all except Laodamas, but not with him because I am his guest, and one cannot compete with one's own personal friend. At least I do not think it a prudent or a sensible thing for a guest to challenge his host's family at any game, especially when he is in a foreign country. He will cut the ground from under his own feet if he does; but I make no exception as regards anyone else, for I want to have the matter out and know which is the best man. I am a good hand at every kind of athletic sport known among mankind. I am an excellent archer. In battle I am always the first to bring a man down with my arrow, no matter how many more are taking aim alongside of me. Philoctetes was the only man who could shoot better than I could when we Achaeans were before Troy and in practice. I far excel everyone else in the whole world, of those who still eat bread upon the face of the earth, but I should not like to shoot against the mighty dead, such as Heracles, or Eurytus the Oechalian—men who could shoot against the gods themselves. This in fact was how Eurytus came prematurely by his end, for Apollo was angry with him and killed him because he challenged him as an archer. I can throw a dart farther than anyone else can shoot an arrow. Running is the only point in respect of which I am afraid some of the Phaeacians might beat me, for I have been brought down very low at sea; my provisions ran short, and therefore I am still weak."

They all held their peace except King Alcinous, who began, "Sir, we have had much pleasure in hearing all that you have told us, from which I understand that you are willing to show your prowess, as having been displeased with some insolent remarks that have been made to you by one of our athletes, and which could never have been uttered by anyone who knows how to talk with propriety. But now, pay attention to my words, so that you can explain to any one of your chief men who may be dining with yourself and your family when you get home that we have hereditary aptitude for accomplishments of all kinds. We are not particularly remarkable for our boxing, nor yet as wrestlers, but we are singularly fleet of foot and are excellent sailors. We are extremely fond of good dinners, music, and dancing; we also like frequent changes of linen, warm baths, and good beds. So now, please, some of you who are the best dancers set about dancing, that our guest on his return home may be able to tell his friends how much we surpass all other nations as sailors, runners, dancers, and minstrels. Demodocus has left his lyre at my house, so run, some one or other of you, and fetch it for him."

On this a servant hurried off to bring the lyre from the king's house, and the nine men who had been chosen as stewards stood forward. It was their business to manage everything connected with the sports, so they made the ground smooth and marked a wide space for the dancers. Presently the servant came back with Demodocus' lyre, and he took his place in the midst of them, whereon the best young dancers in the town began to foot and trip it so nimbly that Odysseus was delighted with the merry twinkling of their feet.

Meanwhile the bard began to sing the loves of Ares and

Aphrodite, and how they first began their intrigue in the
house of Hephaestus. Ares made Aphrodite many presents,
and dishonoured King Hephaestus' marriage bed, so the sun,
who saw what they were about, told Hephaestus. Hephaestus
was very angry when he heard such dreadful news, so he went
to his smithy, brooding mischief, got his great anvil into its
place, and began to forge some chains which none could either unloose or break, so that they might stay in their place.
When he had finished his snare, he went into his bedroom and
festooned the bedposts all over with chains like cobwebs; he
also let many hang down from the great beam of the ceiling.
Not even a god could see them, so fine and subtle were they.
As soon as he had spread the chains all over the bed, he made
as though he were setting out for the fair state of Lemnos,
which of all places in the world was the one he was most fond
of. But Ares kept no blind lookout, and as soon as he saw him
start, hurried off to his house, burning with love for Aphrodite.

Now, Aphrodite was just come in from a visit to her father, Zeus, and was sitting down when Ares came inside the
house, and said as he took her hand in his own, "Let us go to
the couch of Hephaestus: he is not at home, but is gone off to
Lemnos among the Sintians, whose speech is barbarous."

She was nothing loth, so they went to the couch to sleep
together, whereon they were caught in the toils which cunning Hephaestus had spread for them, and could neither get
up nor stir hand or foot, but found too late that they were in
a trap. Then Hephaestus came up to them, for he had
turned back before reaching Lemnos, since the sun had
kept watch and told him what was going on. He was in a furious passion, and stood in the vestibule making a dreadful
noise as he shouted to all the gods.

"Father Zeus," he cried, "and all you other blessed gods
who live forever, come here and see the ridiculous and disgraceful sight that I will show you. Zeus's daughter
Aphrodite is always dishonouring me because I am lame.

She is in love with Ares, who is handsome and clean-built, whereas I am a cripple—but my parents are to blame for that, not I; they ought never to have begotten me. Come and see the pair together asleep on my bed. It makes me furious to look at them. They are very fond of one another, but I do not think they will lie there longer than they can help, nor do I think that they will sleep much; there, however, they shall stay till her father has repaid me the sum I gave him for his baggage of a daughter, who is fair but not honest."

On this the gods gathered to the house of Hephaestus. Earth-encircling Poseidon came, and Hermes, the bringer of luck, and King Apollo, but the goddesses stayed at home, all of them, for shame. Then the gods, the givers of all good things, stood in the doorway, and the blessed gods roared with inextinguishable laughter as they saw how cunning Hephaestus had been, and one would turn towards his neighbour, saying:

"Ill deeds do not prosper, and the weak confound the strong. See how limping Hephaestus, lame as he is, has caught Ares, who is the fastest god in heaven; and now Ares will have to pay heavy damages."

Thus did they converse, but King Apollo said to Hermes, "Messenger Hermes, giver of good things, would you care how strong the chains were if you could sleep with Aphrodite?"

"King Apollo," answered Hermes, "I only wish I might get the chance, though there were three times as many chains—and you might look on, all of you, gods and goddesses, but I would sleep with her if I could."

The immortal gods burst out laughing as they heard him, but Poseidon took it all seriously, and kept on imploring Hephaestus to set Ares free again. "Let him go," he cried, "and I will undertake, as you require, that he shall pay you all the damages that are held reasonable among the immortal gods."

"Do not," replied Hephaestus, "ask me to do this; a bad man's bond is bad security; what remedy could I enforce against you if Ares should go away and leave his debts behind him along with his chains?"

"Hephaestus," said Poseidon, "if Ares goes away without paying his damages, I will pay you myself." So Hephaestus answered, "In this case I cannot and must not refuse you."

Thereon he loosed the bonds that bound them, and as soon as they were free they scampered off, Ares to Thrace and laughter-loving Aphrodite to Cyprus and to Paphos, where is her grove and her altar fragrant with burnt offerings. Here the Graces bathed her, and anointed her with oil of ambrosia such as the immortal gods make use of, and they clothed her in raiment of the most enchanting beauty.

Thus sang the bard, and both Odysseus and the seafaring Phaeacians were charmed as they heard him.

Then Alcinous told Laodamas and Halius to dance alone, for there was no one to compete with them. So they took a red ball which Polybus had made for them, and one of them bent himself backwards and threw it up towards the clouds, while the other jumped from off the ground and caught it with ease before it came down again. When they had done throwing the ball straight up into the air, they began to dance, and at the same time kept on throwing it backwards and forwards to one another, while all the young men in the ring applauded and made a great stamping with their feet. Then Odysseus said:

"King Alcinous, you said your people were the nimblest dancers in the world, and indeed they have proved themselves to be so. I was astonished as I saw them."

The king was delighted at this, and exclaimed to the Phaeacians, "Leaders and councillors of the Phaeacians, our guest seems to be a person of singular judgement; let us give him such proof of our hospitality as he may reasonably expect. There are twelve chief men among you, and counting myself there are thirteen; contribute, each of you, a clean cloak, a tunic, and a talent of fine gold; let us give him all this in a lump down at once, so that when he gets his supper he may do so with a light heart. As for Euryalus, he will have to make a formal apology and a present, too, for he has been rude."

Thus did he speak. The others all of them applauded his words, and sent their servants to fetch the presents. Then Euryalus said, "King Alcinous, I will give the stranger all the satisfaction you require. He shall have my sword, which is of bronze, all but the hilt, which is of silver. I will also give him the scabbard of newly sawn ivory into which it fits. It will be worth a great deal to him."

As he spoke he placed the sword in the hands of Odysseus and said, "Good luck to you, father stranger; if anything has been said amiss, may the winds blow it away with them, and may heaven grant you a safe return, for I understand you have been long away from home, and have gone through much hardship."

To which Odysseus answered, "Good luck to you, too, my friend, and may the gods grant you every happiness. I hope you will not miss the sword you have given me along with your apology."

With these words he girded the sword about his shoulders, and towards sundown the presents began to make their appearance, as the servants of the donors kept bringing them to the house of King Alcinous; here his sons received them, and placed them under their mother's charge. Then Alcinous led the way to the house and bade his guests take their seats.

"Wife," said he, turning to Queen Arete, "go, fetch the best chest we have, and put a clean cloak and shirt in it. Also, set a cauldron on the fire and heat some water; our guest will take a warm bath; see also to the careful packing of the presents that the noble Phaeacians have given him; he will thus better enjoy both his supper and the singing that will follow. I shall myself give him this golden goblet—which is of exquisite workmanship—that he may be reminded of me for the rest of his life whenever he makes a drink offering to Zeus, or to any of the gods."

Then Arete told her maids to set a large tripod upon the fire as fast as they could, whereon they set a tripod full of bath water onto a clear fire; they threw on sticks to make it blaze, and the water became hot as the flame played about the belly of the tripod. Meanwhile Arete brought a magnificent chest from her own room, and inside it she packed all the beautiful presents of gold and clothing which the Phaeacians had brought. Lastly she added a cloak and a good tunic from Alcinous, and said to Odysseus:

"See to the lid yourself, and tie it with a knot at once, for fear anyone should rob you by the way when you are asleep in the ship."

When Odysseus heard this, he put the lid on the chest and made it fast with a knot that Circe had taught him. He had hardly done so before a housekeeper told him to come to the bath and wash himself. He was very glad of a warm bath, for he had had no one to wait upon him ever since he left the house of Calypso, who as long as he remained with her had taken as good care of him as though he had been a god. When the servants had done washing and anointing him with oil, and had given him a clean cloak and tunic, he left the bath room and joined the guests, who were sitting over their wine. Lovely Nausicaa stood by one of the pillars supporting the roof of the hall, and admired him as she saw him pass. "Farewell, stranger," said she. "Do not forget me when you are safe at home again, for it is to me first that you owe a ransom for having saved your life."

And Odysseus said, "Nausicaa, daughter of great Alcinous, may Zeus, the mighty husband of Hera, grant that I may reach my home; so shall I bless you as my guardian angel all my days, for it was you who saved me."

When he had said this, he seated himself beside Alcinous. Supper was then served, and the wine was mixed for drinking. A servant led in the favourite bard, Demodocus, and set him in the midst of the company, near one of the pillars supporting the hall, that he might lean against it. Then Odysseus cut off a piece of roast pork with plenty of fat (for there was abundance left on the joint) and said to a servant, "Take this piece of pork over to Demodocus and tell him to eat it; for all the pain his lays may cause me, I will salute him none the less; bards are honoured and respected throughout the world, for the Muse teaches them their songs and loves them."

The servant carried the pork over to Demodocus, who took it and was very much pleased. They then laid their hands on the good things that were before them, and as soon as they had had enough to eat and drink, Odysseus said to Demodocus, "Demodocus, there is no one in the world whom I admire more than I do you. You must have been taught by the Muse, Zeus's daughter, or by Apollo, so accurately do you sing the return of the Achaeans with all their sufferings and adventures. If you were not there yourself, you must have heard it all from someone who was. Now, however, change your song and tell us of the wooden horse which Epeüs made with the assistance of Athene, and which Odysseus got by stratagem into the fort of Troy after filling it with the men who afterwards sacked the city. If you will sing this tale aright, I will tell all the world how magnificently heaven has endowed you."

The bard inspired of heaven took up the story at the point where some of the Argives set fire to their tents and sailed away, while others, hidden within the horse, were waiting with Odysseus in the Trojan place of assembly. For the Trojans themselves had drawn the horse into their fortress, and it stood there while they sat in council round it, and were in three minds as to what they should do. Some were for breaking it up then and there; others would have it dragged to the top of the rock on which the fortress stood, and then thrown down the precipice; while yet others were for letting it remain as an offering and propitiation for the gods. And this was how they settled it in the end, for the city was doomed when it took in that horse, within which were all the bravest of the Argives waiting to bring death and destruction on the Trojans. Anon he sang how the sons of the Achaeans issued from the horse, and sacked the town, breaking out from their ambuscade. He sang how they overran the city and ravaged it, and how Odysseus went raging like Ares along with Menelaus to the house of Deiphobus. It was there that the fight raged most furiously; nevertheless, by Athene's help, he was victorious.

All this he told, but Odysseus was overcome as he heard him, and his cheeks were wet with tears. He wept as a woman weeps when she throws herself on the body of her husband who has fallen before his own city and people, fighting bravely in defence of his home and children. She screams aloud and flings her arms about him as he lies gasping for breath and dying, but her enemies beat her from behind about the back and shoulders, and carry her off into slavery, to a life of labour and sorrow, and the beauty fades from her cheeks—even so piteously did Odysseus weep, but none of those present perceived his tears except Alcinous, who was sitting near him, and could hear his sobs and sighs. The king, therefore, at once rose and said:

"Leaders and councillors of the Phaeacians, let Demodocus cease his song, for there are those present who do not seem to like it. From the moment that we had done supper and Demodocus began to sing, our guest has been all the time groaning and lamenting. He is evidently in great distress, so let the bard leave off, that we may all enjoy ourselves, hosts and guest alike. This will be much more as it should be, for all these festivities with the escort and the presents that we are making with so much good will are wholly in his honour, and anyone with even a moderate amount of right feeling knows that he ought to treat a guest and a suppliant as though he were his own brother.

"Therefore, Sir, do you on your part affect no more concealment nor reserve in the matter about which I shall ask you; it will be more polite in you to give me a plain answer;

tell me the name by which your father and mother over yonder used to call you, and by which you were known among your neighbours and fellow-citizens. There is no one, neither rich nor poor, who is absolutely without any name whatever, for people's fathers and mothers give them names as soon as they are born. Tell me also your country, nation, and city, that our ships may shape their purpose accordingly and take you there. For the Phaeacians have no pilots; their vessels have no rudders as those of other nations have, but the ships themselves understand what it is that we are thinking about and want; they know all the cities and countries in the whole world, and can traverse the sea just as well even when it is covered with mist and cloud, so that there is no danger of being wrecked or coming to any harm. Still I do remember hearing my father say that Poseidon was angry with us for being too easygoing in the matter of giving people escorts. He said that one of these days he should wreck a ship of ours as it was returning from having escorted someone, and hide our city under a high mountain. This is what my father used to say, but whether the god will carry out his threat or no is a matter which he will decide for himself.

"And now, tell me and tell me true. Where have you been wandering, and in what countries have you travelled? Tell us of the peoples themselves, and of their cities—who were hostile, savage, and uncivilised, and who, on the other hand, hospitable and humane. Tell us also why you are made so unhappy on hearing about the fate of the Greeks and of Troy. The gods arranged all this, and sent them their misfortunes in order that future generations might sing about them. Did you lose some brave kinsman of your wife's before Troy? A son-in-law or father-in-law—which are the nearest relations a man has outside his own flesh and blood—or was it some brave and kindly natured comrade—for a good friend is as dear to a man as his own brother."

BOOK IX

❦

Odysseus Declares Himself and Begins His Story—
The Cicones, Lotophagi, and Cyclopes

AND ODYSSEUS answered, "King Alcinous, it is a good thing to
hear a bard with such a divine voice as this man has. There is
nothing better or more delightful than when a whole people
make merry together, with the guests sitting in their places to
listen, while the table is loaded with bread and meats, and the
cupbearer draws wine and fills his cup for every man. This is
indeed as fair a sight as a man can see. Now, however, since
you are inclined to ask the story of my sorrows, and rekindle
my own sad memories in respect of them, I do not know how
to begin, nor yet how to continue and conclude my tale, for
the hand of heaven has been laid heavily upon me.

"Firstly, then, I will tell you my name that you too may
know it, and one day, if I outlive this time of sorrow, may become my guests though I live so far away from all of you. I am
Odysseus, son of Laertes, renowned among mankind for all
manner of subtlety, so that my fame ascends to heaven. I live
in Ithaca, where there is a high mountain called Neritum, covered with forests; and not far from it there is a group of islands
very near to one another—Dulichium, Same, and the wooded
island of Zacynthus. It lies squat on the horizon, furthest off in
the sea towards the sunset, while the others lie away from it towards dawn. It is a rugged island, but it breeds brave men, and
my eyes know none that they better love to look upon. The
goddess Calypso kept me with her in her cave, and wanted me

to marry her, as did also cunning Aeaean Circe; but they could neither of them persuade me, for there is nothing dearer to a man than his own country and his parents, and however splendid a home he may have in a foreign country, if it be far from his father or mother, he does not care about it. Now, however, I will tell you of the many hazardous adventures which by Zeus's will I met with on my return from Troy.

"When I had set sail from there, the wind took me first to Ismarus, which is the city of the Cicones. There I sacked the town and put the people to the sword. We took their wives and also much booty, which we divided fairly amongst us, so that none might have reason to complain. I then said that we had better make off at once, but my men very foolishly would not obey me, so they stayed there drinking much wine and killing great numbers of sheep and oxen on the seashore. Meanwhile the Cicones cried out for help to other Cicones who lived inland. These were more in number, and stronger, and they were more skilled in the art of war, for they could fight either from chariots or on foot, as the occasion served; in the morning, therefore, they came as thick as leaves and blossom in summer, and the hand of heaven was against us, so that we were hard pressed. They set the battle in array near the ships, and the hosts aimed their bronze-shod spears at one another. So long as the day waxed and it was still morning, we held our own against them, though they were more in number than we; but as the sun went down, towards the time when men loose their oxen, the Cicones got the better of us, and we lost six men from every ship we had; so we got away with those that were left.

"Thence we sailed onward with sorrow in our hearts, but glad to have escaped death though we had lost our comrades, nor did we leave till we had thrice called out the name of each one of the poor fellows who had perished by the hands of the Cicones. Then Zeus raised the north wind against us till it blew a hurricane, so that land and sky were hidden in thick clouds, and night sprang forth out of the heavens. We let the ships run before the gale, but the force of the wind tore our sails to tatters, so we took them down for fear of shipwreck, and rowed our hardest towards the land. There we lay two days and two nights, suffering much alike from toil and distress of mind, but on the morning of the third day we again raised our masts, set sail, and took our places, letting the wind and steersmen direct our ships. I should have got home at that time unharmed had not the north wind and the currents been against me as I was doubling Cape Malea, and set me off my course hard by the island of Cythera.

"I was driven thence by adverse winds for a space of nine days upon the sea, but on the tenth day we reached the land of the lotus-eaters, who live on a food that comes from a kind of flower. Here we landed to take in fresh water, and our crews got their midday meal on the shore near the ships. When they had eaten and drunk, I sent two of my company to see what manner of men the people of the place might be, and they had a third man under them. They started at once, and went about among the lotus-eaters, who did them no hurt, but gave them to eat of the lotus, which was so delicious that those who ate it left off caring about home, and did not even want to go back and say what had happened to them, but were for staying and munching lotus with the lotus-eaters without thinking further of their return; nevertheless, though they wept bitterly, I forced them back to the ships and made them fast under the benches. Then I told the rest to go on board at once, lest any of them should taste of the lotus, and leave off wanting to get home, so they took their places and smote the grey sea with their oars.

"We sailed hence, always in much distress, till we came to the land of the lawless and inhuman Cyclopes. Now, the Cyclopes neither plant nor plough, but trust in providence, and live on the wheat, barley, and grapes which grow wild without any kind of tillage, and their wild grapes yield them wine as the sun and the rain make them grow. They have no laws nor assemblies of the people, but live in caves on the tops of high mountains; each is lord and master in his family, and they take no account of their neighbours.

"Now, off their harbour there lies a wooded and fertile island not quite close to the land of the Cyclopes, but still not far. It is overrun with wild goats, that breed there in great numbers and are never disturbed by foot of man; for hunters—who as a rule will suffer so much hardship in forest or among mountain precipices—do not go there, nor yet again is it ever ploughed or fed down, but it lies a wilderness untilled and unsown from year to year, and has no living thing upon it but only goats. For the Cyclopes have no ships, nor yet shipwrights who could make ships for them; they cannot therefore go from city to city, or sail over the sea to one another's country as people who have ships can do; if they had had these they would have colonised the island, for it is a very good one, and would yield everything in due season. There are meadows that in some places come right down to the seashore, well watered and full of luscious grass; grapes would do there excellently; there is level land for ploughing, and it would always yield heavily at harvest time, for the soil is deep. There is a good harbour where no cables are wanted, nor yet anchors, nor need a ship be moored, but all one has to do is to beach one's vessel and stay there till the wind becomes fair for putting out to sea again. At the head of the harbour there is a spring of clear water coming out of a cave, and there are poplars growing all round it.

"Here we entered, but so dark was the night that some god must have brought us in, for there was nothing whatever to be seen. A thick mist hung all round our ships; the moon was hidden behind a mass of clouds so that no one could have seen the island if he had looked for it, nor were there any breakers to tell us we were close inshore before we found ourselves upon the land itself; when, however, we had beached the ships, we took down the sails, went ashore, and camped upon the beach till daybreak.

"When the child of morning, rosy-fingered Dawn, appeared, we admired the island and wandered all over it, while the nymphs, Zeus's daughters, roused the wild goats that we might get some meat for our dinner. On this we fetched our spears and bows and arrows from the ships, and dividing ourselves into three bands, began to shoot the goats. Heaven sent us excellent hunting; I had twelve ships with me, and each ship got nine goats, while my own ship had ten; thus through the livelong day to the going down of the sun we ate and drank our fill, and we had plenty of wine left, for each one of us had taken many jars full when we sacked the city of the Cicones, and this had not yet run out. While we were feasting we kept turning our eyes towards the land of the Cyclopes, which was hard by, and saw the smoke of their fires, and heard their voices and the bleating of their sheep and goats, but when the sun went down and it became dark, we camped down upon the beach, and next morning I called a council.

" 'Stay here, my brave fellows,' said I, 'all the rest of you, while I go with my ship and reconnoitre these people myself: I want to see if they are uncivilised savages, or a hospitable and humane race.'

"I went on board, bidding my men to do so also and loose the hawsers; so they took their places and smote the grey sea with their oars. When we got to the land, which was not far, there, on the face of a cliff near the sea, we saw a great cave overhung with laurels. It was a station for a great many sheep and goats, and outside there was a large yard, with a high wall round it made of stones sunk into the ground and of trees both pine and oak. This was the abode of a huge monster who used to pasture his flocks alone, away from the others. He would have nothing to do with other people, but led the life of an outlaw. He was a horrid creature, not like a human

being at all, but resembling rather some crag that stands out
boldly against the sky on the top of a high mountain.

"I told my men to draw the ship ashore, and stay where
they were, all but the twelve best among them, who were to
go along with myself. I also took a goatskin of sweet red wine
which had been given me by Maron, son of Euanthes, who
was priest of Apollo, the patron god of Ismarus, and lived
within the wooded precincts of the temple. When we were
sacking the city we respected him, and spared his life, as also
his wife and child; so he made me some presents of great
value—seven talents of fine gold, and a bowl of silver, with
twelve jars of sweet wine, unblended, and of the most exquisite flavour. Not a man nor maid in the house knew about
it, but only himself, his wife, and one housekeeper; when he
drank it he mixed twenty parts of water to one of wine, and
yet the fragrance from the mixing bowl was so exquisite that
it was impossible to refrain from drinking. I filled a large
skin with this wine, and took a wallet full of provisions with
me, for my mind misgave me that I might have to deal with
some savage who would be of great strength, and would respect neither right nor law.

"We soon reached his cave, but he was out with his flocks,
so we went inside and took stock of all that we could see. His
cheese racks were loaded with cheeses, and he had more
lambs and kids than his pens could hold. They were kept in
separate flocks; first there were the yearlings, then the oldest of the younger lambs, and lastly the very young ones, all
kept apart from one another; as for his dairy, all the vessels,
bowls, and milk pails into which he milked were swimming
with whey. When they saw all this, my men begged me to let
them first steal some cheeses, and make off with them to the
ship; they would then return, drive down the lambs and
kids, put them on board, and sail away with them. It would
have been indeed better if we had done so but I would not
listen to them, for I wanted to see the owner himself, in the

hope that he might give me hospitality. When, however, we saw him, my poor men found him ill to deal with.

"We lit a fire, and ate some of the cheese, having first made an offering of it to the gods, and then sat waiting till the Cyclops should come in with his sheep. When he came, he brought in with him a huge load of dry firewood to light the fire for his supper, and this he flung with such a noise onto the floor of his cave that we hid ourselves for fear at the far end of the cavern. Meanwhile he drove all the ewes inside, as well as the she-goats that he was going to milk, leaving the males, both rams and he-goats, outside in the yards. Then he rolled a huge stone to the mouth of the cave—so huge that two and twenty strong four-wheeled wagons would not be enough to draw it from its place against the doorway. When he had so done, he sat down and milked his ewes and goats, one after another, and then let each of them have her own young. He curdled half the milk and set it aside in wicker strainers, but the other half he poured into bowls that he might drink it for his supper. When he had got through with all his work, he lit the fire, and then caught sight of us, whereon he said:

" 'Strangers, who are you? Where do you sail from? Are you traders, or do you sail the sea as pirates, with your hands against every man, and every man's hand against you?'

"We were frightened out of our senses by his loud voice and monstrous form, but I managed to say, 'We are Achaeans on our way home from Troy, but by the will of Zeus, and stress of weather, we have been driven far out of our course. We are the people of Agamemnon, son of Atreus, who has won infinite renown throughout the whole world, by sacking so great a city and killing so many people. We therefore humbly pray you to show us some hospitality, and otherwise make us such presents as visitors may reasonably expect. May your excellency fear the wrath of heaven, for we are your suppliants, and Zeus takes all travellers under his protection, for he is the avenger of all suppliants and foreigners in distress.'

"To this he gave me a pitiless answer. 'Stranger,' said he, 'you are a fool, or else you know nothing of this country. You talk to me indeed about fearing the gods or shunning their anger. We Cyclopes do not care about Zeus or any of your blessed gods, for we are ever so much stronger than they. I shall not spare either yourself or your companions out of any regard for Zeus, unless I am in the humour for doing so. And now tell me where you made your ship fast when you came on shore. Was it round the point, or is she lying straight off the land?'

"He said this to draw me out, but I was too cunning to be caught in that way, so I answered with a lie. 'Poseidon,' said I, 'sent my ship onto the rocks at the far end of your country, and wrecked it. We were driven onto them from the open sea, but I and those who are with me escaped the jaws of death.'

"The cruel wretch vouchsafed me not one word of answer, but with a sudden clutch he gripped up two of my men at once and dashed them down upon the ground as though they had been puppies. Their brains were shed upon the ground, and the earth was wet with their blood. Then he tore them limb from limb and supped upon them. He gobbled them up like a lion in the wilderness, flesh, bones, marrow, and entrails, without leaving anything uneaten. As for us, we wept and lifted up our hands to heaven on seeing such a horrid sight, for we did not know what to do; but when the Cyclops had filled his huge paunch, and had washed down his meal of human flesh with a drink of neat milk, he stretched himself full length upon the ground among his sheep, and went to sleep. I was at first inclined to seize my sword, draw it, and drive it into his breast, but I reflected that if I did we should all certainly be lost, for we should never be able to shift the stone which the monster had put in front of the door. So we stayed sobbing and sighing where we were till morning came.

"When the child of morning, rosy-fingered Dawn, appeared, he again lit his fire, milked his goats and ewes, one after another, and then let each have her own young one; as soon as he had got through with all his work, he snatched up two more of my men, and began eating them for his morning meal. Presently, with the utmost ease, he rolled the stone away from the door and drove out his sheep, but he at once put it back again—as easily as though he were merely clapping the lid onto a quiver full of arrows. As soon as he had done so he shouted after his sheep to drive them onto the mountain; so I was left to scheme some way of taking my revenge and covering myself with glory.

"In the end I deemed it would be the best plan to do as follows: The Cyclops had a great club which was lying near one of the sheep pens; it was of green olive wood, and he had cut it intending to use it for a staff as soon as it should be dry. It was so huge that we could only compare it with the mast of a twenty-oared merchant vessel of large burden, and able to venture out into open sea. I went up to this club and cut off about six feet of it; I then gave this piece to the men and told them to make it smooth at one end, which they proceeded to do, and lastly I brought it to a point myself, charring the end in the fire to make it harder. When I had done this, I hid it under the dung which was lying about all over the cave, and told the men to cast lots which of them should venture along with myself to lift it and bore it into the monster's eye while he was asleep. The lot fell upon the very four whom I should have chosen, and I myself made five. In the evening the wretch came back from shepherding, and drove his flocks into the cave—this time driving them all inside, and not leaving any in the yards; I suppose some fancy must have taken him, or a god must have prompted him to do so. As soon as he had put the stone back to its place against the door, he sat down, milked his ewes and his goats, one after another, and then let each have her own young one; when he had got through with all this work, he snatched up two more of my men, and made his supper off them. So I went up to him with an ivy-wood bowl of deep red wine in my hands.

" 'Look here, Cyclops,' said I, 'you have been eating a great deal of man's flesh, so take this and drink some wine, that you may see what kind of liquor we had on board my ship. I was bringing it to you as a drink offering, in the hope that you would take compassion upon me and further me on my way home, whereas all you do is to go on ramping and raving most intolerably. You ought to be ashamed of yourself; how can you expect people to come and see you any more if you treat them in this way?'

"He then took the cup and drank. He was so delighted with the taste of the wine that he asked me for another bowlful. 'Be so kind,' he said, 'as to give me some more, and tell me your name at once. I want to make you a present that you will be glad to have. We have wine also in this country, for our soil bears grapes and the rain fills them out, but this drinks like nectar and ambrosia all in one.'

"I then gave him some more; three times did I fill the bowl for him, and three times did he drain it without thought or heed; then, when I saw that the wine had got into his head, I said to him as plausibly as I could: 'Cyclops, you ask my name and I will tell it to you; give me, therefore, the present you promised me; my name is Noman; this is what my father and mother and my friends have always called me.'

"But the cruel wretch said, 'Then I will eat all Noman's comrades before Noman himself, and will keep Noman for the last. This is the present that I will make him.'

"As he spoke he reeled, and fell back face upwards on the ground. His great neck hung sideways and a deep sleep took hold upon him. Presently he turned sick, and threw up both wine and the gobbets of human flesh on which he had been gorging, for he was very drunk. Then I thrust the beam of wood far into the embers to heat it, and encouraged my men lest any of them should turn fainthearted. When the wood, green though it was, was about to blaze, I drew it out of the fire glowing with heat, and my men gathered round me, for heaven had filled their hearts with courage. We drove the sharp end of the beam into the monster's eye, and bearing upon it with all my weight, I kept turning it round and round as though I were boring a hole in a ship's plank with an auger, which two men with a wheel and strap can keep on turning as long as they choose. Even thus did we bore the red-hot beam into his eye, till the boiling blood bubbled all over it as we worked it round and round, so that the steam from the burning eyeball scalded his eyelids and eyebrows, and the roots of the eye sputtered in the fire. As a blacksmith plunges an axe or hatchet into cold water to temper it—for it is this that gives strength to the iron—and it makes a great hiss as he does so, even thus did the Cyclops' eye hiss round the beam of olive wood, and his hideous yells made the cave ring again. We ran away in a fright, but he plucked the beam, all spattered with gore, from his eye, and hurled it from him in a frenzy of rage and pain, shouting as he did so to the other Cyclopes who lived on the bleak headlands near him; so they gathered from all quarters round his cave when they heard him shouting, and asked what was the matter with him.

" 'What ails you, Polyphemus,' said they, 'that you make such a noise, breaking the stillness of the night, and preventing us from being able to sleep? Surely no man is carrying off your sheep? Surely no man is trying to kill you either by fraud or by force?'

"But Polyphemus shouted to them from inside the cave, 'Noman is killing me by fraud; Noman is killing me by force.'

" 'Then,' said they, 'if no man is attacking, you must be ill; when Zeus makes people ill, there is no help for it, and you had better pray to your father, Poseidon.'

"Then they went away, and I laughed inwardly at the success of my clever stratagem, but the Cyclops, groaning and in an agony of pain, felt about with his hands till he found the stone and took it from the door; then he sat in the doorway and stretched his hands in front of it to catch anyone going out with the sheep, for he thought I might be foolish enough to attempt this.

"As for myself, I kept on puzzling to think how I could best save my own life and those of my companions; I schemed and schemed, as one who knows that his life depends upon it, for the danger was very great. In the end I decided that this plan would be the best: the male sheep were well grown, and carried a heavy black fleece, so I quietly bound them in threes together, with some of the withes on which the wicked monster used to sleep. There was a man under the middle sheep, and the two on either side were to cover him, so that there were three sheep to each man. As for myself, there was a ram finer than any of the others, so I caught hold of him by the back, slid down in the thick wool under his belly, and hung on patiently to his fleece, face upwards, keeping a firm hold on it all the time.

"Thus, then, did we wait in great fear of mind till morning came, but when the child of morning, rosy-fingered Dawn, appeared, the male sheep hurried out to feed, while the ewes remained bleating about the pens waiting to be milked, for their udders were full to bursting; but their master, in spite of all his pain, felt the backs of all the sheep as they stood upright, without being sharp enough to find out that the men were underneath their bellies. As the ram was going out, last of all, heavy with its fleece and with the weight of my crafty self, Polyphemus laid hold of it and said:

" 'My good ram, what is it that makes you the last to leave my cave this morning? You are not wont to let the ewes go before you, but lead the mob with a run whether to flowery mead or bubbling fountain, and are the first to come home again at night; but now you lag last of all. Is it because you know your master has lost his eye, and are sorry because that wicked Noman and his horrid crew have overcome him with drink and blinded him? But I will have his life yet. If you could understand and talk, you would tell me where the wretch is hiding, and I would dash his brains upon the ground till they flew all over the cave. I should thus have some satisfaction for the harm this no-good Noman has done me.'

"As he spoke he drove the ram outside, but when we were a little way out from the cave and yards, I first got from under the ram's belly, and then freed my comrades; as for the sheep, which were very fat, by constantly heading them in the right direction we managed to drive them down to the ship. The crew rejoiced greatly at seeing those of us who had escaped death, but wept for the others whom the Cyclops had killed. However, I made signs to them by nodding and frowning that they were to hush their crying, and told them to get all the sheep on board at once and put out to sea; so they went aboard, took their places, and smote the grey sea with their oars. Then, when I had got as far out as my voice would reach, I began to jeer at the Cyclops.

" 'Cyclops,' said I, 'you should have taken better measure of your man before eating up his comrades in your cave. You wretch, to eat up your visitors in your own house! You might have known that your sin would find you out, and now Zeus and the other gods have punished you.'

"He got more and more furious as he heard me, so he tore the top from off a high mountain, and flung it just in front of my ship. The sea heaved as the rock fell into it, and the wash of the wave it raised carried us back towards the mainland, and forced us towards the shore. But I snatched up a long pole and kept the ship off, making signs to my men, by nodding my head, that they must row for their lives, whereon they laid out with a will. When we had got twice as far as we were before, I was for jeering at the Cyclops again, but the men begged and prayed me to hold my tongue.

" 'Do not,' they exclaimed, 'be mad enough to provoke this savage creature further; he has thrown one rock at us already, which drove us back again to the mainland, and we thought it had been the death of us; if he had then heard any further sound of voices he would have pounded our heads and our ship's timbers into a jelly with the jagged rocks he would have hurled at us, for he can throw them a long way.'

"But I would not listen to them, and shouted out to him in my rage, 'Cyclops, if anyone asks you who it was that put your eye out and spoiled your beauty, say it was the valiant warrior Odysseus, son of Laertes, who lives in Ithaca.'

"On this he groaned, and cried out, 'Alas, alas, then the old prophecy about me is coming true. There was a prophet here, at one time, a man both brave and of great stature, Telemus, son of Eurymus, who was an excellent seer, and did all the prophesying for the Cyclopes till he grew old; he told me that all this would happen to me someday, and said I should lose my sight by the hand of Odysseus. I have been all along expecting someone of imposing presence and super-human strength, whereas he turns out to be a little insignificant weakling, who has managed to blind my eye by taking advantage of me in my drink; come here, then, Odysseus, that I may make you presents to show my hospitality, and urge Poseidon to help you forward on your journey—for Poseidon and I are father and son. He, if he so will, shall heal me, which no one else, neither god nor man, can do.'

"Then I said, 'I wish I could be as sure of killing you outright and sending you down to the house of Hades, as I am that it will take more than Poseidon to cure that eye of yours.'

"On this he lifted up his hands to the firmament of heaven and prayed, saying, 'Hear me, great Poseidon; if I am indeed your own son, grant that Odysseus may never reach his home alive; or if he must get back to his friends at last, let him do so late and in sore plight after losing all his men. Let him reach his home in another man's ship and find trouble in his house.'

"Thus did he pray, and Poseidon heard his prayer. Then he picked up a rock much larger than the first, swung it aloft, and hurled it with prodigious force. It fell just short of the ship, and was within a little of hitting the end of the rudder. The sea heaved as the rock fell into it, and the wash of the wave it raised drove us onwards on our way towards the shore of the island.

"When at last we got to the island where we had left the rest of our ships, we found our comrades lamenting us, and anxiously awaiting our return. We ran our vessel upon the sands and got out of her onto the seashore; we also landed the Cyclops' sheep, and divided them fairly amongst us so that none might have reason to complain. As for the ram, my companions agreed that I should have it as an extra share; so I sacrificed it on the seashore, and burned its thighbones to Zeus, who is the lord of all. But he heeded not my sacrifice, and only thought how he might destroy both my ships and my comrades.

"Thus through the livelong day to the going down of the sun we feasted our fill on meat and drink, but when the sun went down and it became dark, we camped upon the beach. When the child of morning, rosy-fingered Dawn, appeared, I bade my men go on board and loose the hawsers. Then they took their places and smote the grey sea with their oars; so we sailed on with sorrow in our hearts, but glad to have escaped death though we had lost our comrades.

BOOK X

Aeolus, the Laestrygonians, Circe

"THENCE WE went on to the Aeolian island, where lives Aeolus, son of Hippotas, dear to the immortal gods. It is an island that floats upon the sea; all around it is an unbroken wall of bronze, and the cliffs drop sheer to the sea. Now, Aeolus has six daughters and six young sons, so he made the sons marry the daughters, and they all live with their dear father and mother, feasting and enjoying every conceivable kind of luxury. All day long the house and the courtyard are full of the savour of roasting meats and ring with the sounds of feasting; but by night they sleep on their well-made bedsteads, each with his own wife between the blankets. These were the people among whom we had now come.

"Aeolus entertained me for a whole month, asking me questions all the time about Troy, the Argive fleet, and the return of the Achaeans. I told him exactly how everything had happened, and when I said I must go, and asked him to further me on my way, he made no sort of difficulty, but set about doing so at once. Moreover, he flayed me a prime oxhide to hold the ways of the roaring winds, which he shut up in the hide as in a sack—for Zeus had made him captain over the winds, and he could stir or still each one of them according to his own pleasure. He put the sack in the ship, and bound the mouth so tightly with a silver thread that not even a breath of a side wind could blow from any quarter. The west wind, which was fair for us, did he alone let blow as it chose; but it all came to nothing, for we were lost through our own folly.

"Nine days and nine nights did we sail, and on the tenth day our native land showed on the horizon. We got so close in that we could see the fires burning, and I, being then dead beat, fell into a light sleep, for I had never let the rudder out of my own hands, that we might get home the faster. On this the men fell to talking among themselves, and said I was bringing back gold and silver in the sack that Aeolus had given me. 'Bless my heart,' one would turn to his neighbour and say, 'how this man gets honoured and makes friends whatever city or country he visits. See what fine prizes he is taking home from Troy, while we, who have travelled just as far as he has, come back with hands as empty as we set out with—and now Aeolus has given him ever so much more. Quick—let us see what it all is, and how much gold and silver there is in the sack he gave him.'

"Thus they talked and evil counsels prevailed. They loosed the sack, whereupon the winds flew howling forth and raised a storm that carried us weeping out to sea and away from our own country. Then I awoke, and knew not whether to throw myself into the sea or to live on and make the best of it; but I bore it, covered myself up, and lay down in the ship, while the men lamented bitterly as the fierce winds bore our fleet back to the Aeolian island.

"When we reached it we went ashore to take in water, and dined hard by the ships. Immediately after dinner I took a herald and one of my men and went straight to the house of Aeolus, where I found him feasting with his wife and family; so we sat down as suppliants on the threshold. They were astounded when they saw us and said, 'Odysseus, what brings you here? What god has been ill-treating you? We took great pains to further you on your way home to Ithaca, or wherever it was that you wanted to go to.'

"Thus did they speak, but I answered sorrowfully, 'My men have undone me; they, and cruel sleep, have ruined me. My friends, mend me this mischief, for you can if you will.'

"I spoke as movingly as I could, but they said nothing, till their father answered, 'Vilest of mankind, get you gone at once out of the island; him whom heaven hates will I in no wise help. Be off, for you come here as one abhorred of heaven.' And with these words he sent me sorrowing from his door.

"Thence we sailed sadly on till the men were worn out with long and fruitless rowing, for there was no longer any wind to help them. Six days, night and day, did we toil, and on the seventh day we reached the rocky stronghold of Lamus—Telepylus, the city of the Laestrygonians, where the shepherd who is driving in his sheep and goats salutes him who is driving out his flock, and this last answers the salute. In that country a man who could do without sleep might earn double wages, one as a herdsmen of cattle, and another as a shepherd, for the paths of night and day are close together.

"When we reached the harbour we found it landlocked under steep cliffs, with a narrow entrance between two headlands. My captains took all their ships inside, and made them fast close to one another, for there was never so much as a breath of wind inside, but it was always dead calm. I kept my own ship outside, and moored it to a rock at the very end of the point; then I climbed a high rock to reconnoitre, but could see no sign neither of man nor of cattle, only some smoke rising from the ground. So I sent two of my company with an attendant to find out what sort of people the inhabitants were.

"The men when they got on shore followed a level road by which the people draw their firewood from the mountains into the town, till presently they met a young woman who had come outside to fetch water, and who was daughter to a Laestrygonian named Antiphates. She was going to the fountain Artacia, from which the people bring in their water, and when my men had come close up to her, they asked her who the king of that country might be, and over what kind of people he ruled; so she directed them to her father's house, but when they got there they found his wife to be a giantess as huge as a mountain, and they were horrified at the sight of her.

"She at once called her husband, Antiphates, from the place of assembly, and forthwith he set about killing my men. He snatched up one of them, and began to make his dinner off him then and there, whereon the other two ran back to the ships as fast as ever they could. But Antiphates raised a hue and cry after them, and thousands of sturdy Laestrygonians sprang up from every quarter—ogres, not men. They threw vast rocks at us from the cliffs as though they had been mere stones, and I heard the horrid sound of the ships crunching up against one another, and the death cries of my men, as the Laestrygonians speared them like fishes and took them home to eat them. While they were thus killing my men within the harbour, I drew my sword, cut the cable of my own ship, and told my men to row with all their might if they too would not fare like the rest; so they laid out for their lives, and we were thankful enough when we got into open water out of reach of the rocks they hurled at us. As for the others, there was not one of them left.

"Thence we sailed sadly on, glad to have escaped death, though we had lost our comrades, and came to the Aeaean island, where Circe lives—a great and cunning goddess who is own sister to the magician Aeëtes—for they are both children of the sun by Perse, who is daughter to Oceanus. We brought our ship into a safe harbour silently, for some god guided us thither, and having landed, we lay there for two days and two nights, worn out in body and mind. When the morning of the third day came, I took my spear and my sword, and went away from the ship to reconnoitre, and see if I could discover signs of human handiwork, or hear the sound of voices. Climbing to the top of a high lookout, I espied the smoke of Circe's house rising upwards amid a dense forest of trees, and when I saw this I wondered whether, having seen the smoke, I would not go on at once and find out more, but in the end I thought it best to go back to the ship, give the men their dinners, and send some of them instead of going myself.

"When I had nearly got back to the ship, some god took pity upon my solitude, and sent a fine-antlered stag right into the very middle of my path. He was coming down from his pasture in the forest to drink of the river, for the heat of the sun drove him, and as he passed I struck him in the middle of the back; the bronze point of the spear went clean through him, and he lay groaning in the dust until the life went out of him. Then I set my foot upon him, drew my spear from the wound, and laid it down; I also gathered rough grass and rushes and twisted them into a fathom or so of good stout rope, with which I bound the four feet of the noble creature together; having so done, I hung him round my neck and walked back to the ship leaning upon my spear, for the stag was much too big for me to be able to carry him on my shoulder, steadying him with one hand. As I threw him down in front of the ship, I called the men and spoke cheeringly man by man to each of them. 'Look here, my friends,' said I, 'we are not going to die so much before our time after all, and at any rate let us not starve so long as we have got something to eat and drink on board.' On this they uncovered their heads upon the seashore and admired the stag, for he was indeed a splendid fellow. Then, when they had feasted their eyes upon him sufficiently, they washed their hands and began to cook him for dinner.

"Thus through the livelong day to the going down of the sun we stayed there, eating and drinking our fill, but when the sun went down and it became dark, we camped upon the seashore. When the child of morning, rosy-fingered Dawn, appeared, I called a council and said, 'My friends, we are in very great difficulties; listen therefore to me. We have no idea where the sun either sets or rises, so that we do not even know east from west. I see no way out of it; nevertheless we must try and find one. We are certainly on an island, for I went as high as I could this morning, and saw the sea reaching all round it to the horizon; it lies low, but towards the middle I saw smoke rising from out of a thick forest of trees.'

"Their hearts sank as they heard me, for they remembered how they had been treated by the Laestrygonian Antiphates, and by the savage ogre Polyphemus. They wept bitterly in their dismay, but there was nothing to be got by crying, so I divided them into two companies and set a captain over each; I gave one company to Eurylochus, while I took command of the other myself. Then we cast lots in a helmet, and the lot fell upon Eurylochus; so he set out with his twenty-two men, and they wept, as also did we who were left behind.

"When they reached Circe's house they found it built of cut stones, on a site that could be seen from far, in the middle of the forest. There were wild mountain wolves and lions prowling all round it—poor bewitched creatures whom she had tamed by her enchantments and drugged into subjection. They did not attack my men, but wagged their great tails, fawned upon them, and rubbed their noses lovingly against them. As hounds crowd round their master when they see him coming from dinner—for they know he will bring them something—even so did these wolves and lions with their great claws fawn upon my men, but the men were terribly frightened at seeing such strange creatures. Presently they reached the gates of the goddess' house, and as they stood there they could hear Circe within, singing most beautifully as she worked at her loom, making a web so fine, so soft, and of such dazzling colours as no one but a goddess could weave. On this Polites, whom I valued and trusted more than any others of my men, said, 'There is someone inside working at a loom and singing most beautifully; the whole place resounds with it; let us call her and see whether she is woman or goddess.'

"They called her and she came down, unfastened the door, and bade them enter. They, thinking no evil, followed her, all except Eurylochus, who suspected mischief and

stayed outside. When she had got them into her house, she
set them upon benches and seats and mixed them a mess
with cheese, honey, meal, and Pramnian wine, but she
drugged it with wicked poisons to make them forget their
homes, and when they had drunk she turned them into pigs
by a stroke of her wand, and shut them up in her pigstys.
They were like pigs—head, hair, and all, and they grunted
just as pigs do; but their senses were the same as before, and
they remembered everything.

"Thus then were they shut up squealing, and Circe threw
them some acorns and beech mast such as pigs eat, but Eurylochus hurried back to tell me about the sad fate of our
comrades. He was so overcome with dismay that though he
tried to speak he could find no words to do so; his eyes filled
with tears and he could only sob and sigh, till at last we
forced his story out of him, and he told us what had happened to the others.

" 'We went,' said he, 'as you told us, through the forest,
and in the middle of it there was a fine house built with cut
stones in a place that could be seen from far. There we
found a woman, or else she was a goddess, working at her
loom and singing sweetly; so the men shouted to her and
called her, whereon she at once came down, opened the
door, and invited us in. The others did not suspect any mischief, so they followed her into the house, but I stayed
where I was, for I thought there might be some treachery.
From that moment I saw them no more, for not one of them
ever came out, though I sat a long time watching for them.'

"Then I took my sword of bronze and slung it over my
shoulders; I also took my bow, and told Eurylochus to come
back with me and show me the way. But he laid hold of me
with both his hands and spoke piteously, saying, 'Sir, do not
force me to go with you, but let me stay here, for I know you
will not bring one of them back with you, nor even return
alive yourself; let us rather see if we cannot escape at any

rate with the few that are left us, for we may still save our lives.'

" 'Stay where you are, then,' answered I, 'eating and drinking at the ship, but I must go, for I am most urgently bound to do so.'

"With this I left the ship and went up inland. When I got through the charmed grove, and was near the great house of the enchantress Circe, I met Hermes, god of the golden wand, disguised as a young man in the heyday of his youth and beauty, with the down just coming upon his face. He came up to me and took my hand within his own, saying, 'My poor unhappy man, where are you going over these hills, alone and without knowing the way? Your men are shut up in Circe's pigstys, like so many wild boars in their lairs. Are you coming to set them free? I fear that you yourself will not return either and will have to stay there with the rest of them. But never mind, I will protect you and get you out of your difficulty. Take this herb, which is one of great virtue, and keep it about you when you go to Circe's house; it will be a talisman to you against every kind of mischief.

" 'And I will tell you of all the witchcraft that Circe will try to practice upon you. She will mix a drink for you, and she will drug the meal with which she makes it, but she will not be able to charm you, for the virtue of the herb that I shall give you will prevent her spells from working. I will tell you all about it. When Circe strikes you with her wand, draw your sword and spring upon her as though you were going to kill her. She will then be frightened, and will desire you to go to bed with her; on this you must not point-blank refuse her, for you want her to set your companions free, and to take good care also of yourself, but you must make her swear solemnly by all the blessed gods that she will plot no further mischief against you, or else when she has got you naked she will unman you and make you fit for nothing.'

"As he spoke, he pulled the herb out of the ground and

showed me what it was like. The root was black, while the flower was as white as milk; the gods call it moly, and mortal men cannot uproot it, but the gods can do whatever they like.

"Then Hermes went back to high Olympus, passing over the wooded island; but I fared onward to the house of Circe, and my heart was clouded with care as I walked along. When I got to the gates I stood there and called the goddess, and as soon as she heard me she came down, opened the door, and asked me to come in; so I followed her, much troubled in my mind. She set me on a richly decorated seat inlaid with silver, there was a footstool also under my feet, and she mixed a drink for me in a golden goblet; but she drugged it, for she meant me mischief. When she had given it to me, and I had drunk it without its charming me, she struck me with her wand. 'There now,' she cried, 'be off to the pigsty, and make your lair with the rest of them.'

"But I rushed at her with my sword drawn as though I would kill her, whereon she fell with a loud scream, clasped my knees, and spoke piteously, saying, 'Who and whence are you? From what place and people have you come? How can it be that my drugs have no power to charm you? Never yet was any man able to stand so much as a taste of the herb I gave you; you must be spellproof; surely you can be none other than the bold hero Odysseus, who Hermes always said would come here someday with his ship while on his way home from Troy; so be it then; sheathe your sword and let us go to bed, that we may make friends and learn to trust each other.'

"And I answered, 'Circe, how can you expect me to be friendly with you when you have just been turning all my men into pigs? And now that you have got me here myself, you mean me mischief when you ask me to go to bed with you, and will unman me and make me fit for nothing. I shall certainly not consent to go to bed with you unless you will first take your solemn oath to plot no further harm against me.'

"So she swore at once as I had told her, and when she had completed her oath then I went to bed with her.

"Meanwhile her four servants, who are her housemaids, set about their work. They are the children of the groves and fountains, and of the holy waters that run down into the sea. One of them spread a fair purple cloth over a seat, and laid a carpet underneath it. Another brought tables of silver up to the seats, and set them with baskets of gold. A third mixed some sweet wine with water in a silver bowl and put golden cups upon the tables, while the fourth brought in water and set it to boil in a large cauldron over a good fire which she had lighted. When the water in the cauldron was boiling, she poured cold into it till it was just as I liked it, and then she set me in a bath and began washing me from the cauldron about the head and shoulders, to take the tiredness and stiffness out of my limbs. As soon as she had done washing me and anointing me with oil, she arrayed me in a good cloak and tunic and led me to a richly decorated seat inlaid with silver; there was a footstool also under my feet. A maidservant then brought me water in a beautiful golden ewer and poured it over a silver basin for me to wash my hands, and she drew a clean table beside me; a housekeeper brought me bread and offered me many good things of what there was in the house, and then Circe bade me eat, but I would not, and sat without heeding what was before me, still moody and suspicious.

"When Circe saw me sitting there without eating, and in great grief, she came to me and said, 'Odysseus, why do you sit like that as though you were dumb, gnawing at your own heart, and refusing both meat and drink? Is it that you are still suspicious? You ought not to be, for I have already sworn solemnly that I will not hurt you.'

"And I said, 'Circe, no man with any sense of what is right can think of either eating and drinking in your house until you have set his friends free and let him see them. If you want me to eat and drink, you must free my men and bring them to me that I may see them with my own eyes.'

"When I had said this, she went straight through the court with her wand in her hand and opened the pigsty doors. My men came out like so many prime hogs and stood looking at her, but she went about among them and anointed each with a second drug, whereon the bristles that the bad drug had given them fell off, and they became men again, younger than they were before, and much taller and better-looking. They knew me at once, seized me each of them by the hand, and wept for joy till the whole house was filled with the sound, and Circe herself was so sorry for them that she came up to me and said, 'Odysseus, noble son of Laertes, go back at once to the sea where you have left your ship, and first draw it onto the land. Then hide all your ship's gear and property in some cave, and come back here with your men.'

"I agreed to this, so I went back to the seashore, and found the men at the ship weeping and wailing most piteously. When they saw me, the silly blubbering fellows began frisking round me as calves break out and gambol round their mothers, when they see them coming home to be milked after they have been feeding all day, and the homestead resounds with their lowing. They seemed as glad to see me as though they had got back to their own rugged Ithaca, where they had been born and bred. 'Sir,' said the affectionate creatures, 'we are as glad to see you back as though we had got safe home to Ithaca; but tell us all about the fate of our comrades.'

"I spoke comfortingly to them and said, 'We must draw our ship onto the land, and hide the ship's gear with all our property in some cave; then come with me all of you as fast as you can to Circe's house, where you will find your comrades eating and drinking in the midst of great abundance.'

"On this the men would have come with me at once, but Eurylochus tried to hold them back and said, 'Alas, poor wretches that we are, what will become of us? Rush not on your ruin by going to the house of Circe, who will turn us all into pigs or wolves or lions, and we shall have to keep guard over her house. Remember how the Cyclops treated us when our comrades went inside his cave, and Odysseus with them. It was all through his sheer folly that those men lost their lives.'

"When I heard him, I was in two minds whether or no to draw the keen blade that hung by my sturdy thigh and cut his head off in spite of his being a near relation of my own; but the men interceded for him and said, 'Sir, if it may so be, let this fellow stay here and mind the ship, but take the rest of us with you to Circe's house.'

"On this we all went inland, and Eurylochus was not left behind after all, but came on too, for he was frightened by the severe reprimand that I had given him.

"Meanwhile Circe had been seeing that the men who had been left behind were washed and anointed with olive oil; she had also given them woollen cloaks and tunics, and when we came we found them all comfortably at dinner in her house. As soon as the men saw each other face to face and knew one another, they wept for joy and cried aloud till the whole palace rang again. Thereon Circe came up to me and said, 'Odysseus, noble son of Laertes, tell your men to leave off crying; I know how much you have all of you suffered at sea, and how ill you have fared among cruel savages on the mainland, but that is over now, so stay here, and eat and drink till you are once more as strong and hearty as you were when you left Ithaca; for at present you are weakened both in body and mind; you keep all the time thinking of the hardships you have suffered during your travels, so that you have no more cheerfulness left in you.'

"Thus did she speak and we assented. We stayed with Circe for a whole twelvemonth, feasting upon an untold quantity both of meat and wine. But when the year had passed in the waning of moons and the long days had come round, my men called me apart and said, 'Sir, it is time you began to think about going home, if so be you are to be spared to see your house and native country at all.'

"Thus did they speak and I assented. Thereon through the livelong day to the going down of the sun we feasted our fill on meat and wine, but when the sun went down and it became dark the men laid themselves down to sleep in the dark hall. I, however, after I had got into bed with Circe, besought her by her knees, and the goddess listened to what I had to say. 'Circe,' said I, 'please to keep the promise you made me about furthering me on my homeward voyage. I want to get back and so do my men; they are always pestering me with their complaints as soon as ever your back is turned.'

"And the goddess answered, 'Odysseus, noble son of Laertes, you shall none of you stay here any longer if you do not want to, but there is another journey which you have got to take before you can sail homewards. You must go to the house of Hades and of dread Persephone to consult the ghost of the blind Theban prophet Teiresias, whose reason is still unshaken. To him alone has Persephone left his understanding even in death, but the other ghosts flit about aimlessly.'

"I was dismayed when I heard this. I sat up in bed and wept, and would gladly have lived no longer to see the light of the sun, but presently, when I was tired of weeping and tossing myself about, I said, 'And who shall guide me upon this voyage, for the house of Hades is a port that no ship can reach.'

" 'You will want no guide,' she answered. 'Raise your mast, set your white sails, sit quite still, and the north wind will blow you there of itself. When your ship has traversed the waters of Oceanus, you will reach the fertile shore of Persephone's country, with its groves of tall poplars and willows that shed their fruit untimely; here beach your ship upon the shore of Oceanus, and go straight on to the dark abode of Hades. You will find it near the place where the rivers Pyriphlegethon and Cocytus (which is a branch of the river Styx) flow into Acheron, and you will see a rock near it, just where the two roaring rivers run into one another.

" 'When you have reached this spot, as I now tell you, dig a trench a cubit or so in length and breadth, and pour into it as a drink offering to all the dead, first, honey mixed with milk, then wine, and in the third place water—sprinkling white barley meal over the whole. Moreover, you must offer many prayers to the poor feeble ghosts, and promise them that when you get back to Ithaca you will sacrifice a barren heifer to them, the best you have, and will load the pyre with good things. More particularly you must promise that Teiresias shall have a black sheep all to himself, the finest in all your flocks.'

" 'When you shall have thus besought the ghosts with your prayers, offer them a ram and a black ewe, bending their heads towards Erebus; but yourself turn away from them as though you would make towards the river. On this, many dead men's ghosts will come to you, and you must tell your men to skin the two sheep that you have just killed, and offer them as a burnt sacrifice with prayers to Hades and to Persephone. Then draw your sword and sit there, so as to prevent any other poor ghost from coming near the spilled blood before Teiresias shall have answered your questions. The seer will presently come to you, and will tell you about your voyage—what stages you are to make, and how you are to sail the sea so as to reach your home.'

"It was daybreak by the time she had done speaking, so she dressed me in my tunic and cloak. As for herself, she threw a beautiful light gossamer fabric over her shoulders, fastening it with a golden belt round her waist, and she covered her head with a mantle. Then I went about among the men everywhere all over the house, and spoke kindly to each of them man by man. 'You must not lie sleeping here any longer,' said I to them. 'We must be going, for Circe has told me all about it.' And on this they did as I bade them.

"Even so, however, I did not get them away without misadventure. We had with us a certain youth named Elpenor, not very remarkable for sense or courage, who had got drunk and was lying on the housetop away from the rest of the men, to sleep off his liquor in the cool. When he heard the noise of the men bustling about, he jumped up on a sudden and forgot all about coming down by the main staircase, so he tumbled right off the roof and broke his neck, and his soul went down to the house of Hades.

"When I had got the men together I said to them, 'You think you are about to start home again, but Circe has explained to me that instead of this, we have got to go to the house of Hades and Persephone to consult the ghost of the Theban prophet Teiresias.'

"The men were brokenhearted as they heard me, and threw themselves on the ground, groaning and tearing their hair, but they did not mend matters by crying. When we reached the seashore, weeping and lamenting our fate, Circe had brought the ram and the ewe, and made them fast hard by the ship. She passed through the midst of us without our knowing it, for who can see the comings and goings of a god, if the god does not wish to be seen?"

BOOK XI

The Visit to the Dead

"WHEN WE had got down to the seashore we drew our ship into the water and got her mast and sails into her; we also put the sheep on board and took our places, weeping and in great distress of mind. Circe, that great and cunning goddess, sent us a fair wind that blew dead aft and stayed steadily with us, keeping our sails all the time well-filled; so we set in order the ship's gear and let her go as the wind and helmsman headed her. All day long her sails were full as she held her course over the sea, but when the sun went down and darkness was over all the earth, we got into the deep waters of the river Oceanus, where lie the land and city of the Cimmerians, who live enshrouded in mist and darkness which the rays of the sun never pierce neither at his rising nor as he goes down again out of the heavens, but the poor wretches live in one long melancholy night. When we got there we beached the ship, took the sheep out of her, and went along by the waters of Oceanus till we came to the place of which Circe had told us.

"Here Perimedes and Eurylochus held the victims, while I drew my sword and dug the trench a cubit each way. I made a drink offering to all the dead, first with honey and milk, then with wine, and thirdly with water, and I sprinkled white barley meal over the whole, praying earnestly to the poor feeble ghosts, and promising them that when I got back to Ithaca I would sacrifice a barren heifer for them, the best I had, and would load the pyre with good things. I also particularly promised that Teiresias should have a black sheep to himself, the best in all my flocks. When I had prayed sufficiently to the dead, I cut the throats of the two sheep and let the blood run into the trench, whereon the ghosts came trooping up from Erebus—brides, young bachelors, old men worn out with toil, maids with fresh sorrow in their hearts, and brave men who had been killed in battle, with their armour still stained with blood; they came from every quarter and flitted round the trench with a strange kind of screaming sound that made me turn pale with fear. When I saw them coming, I told the men to be quick and flay the carcasses of the two dead sheep and make burnt offerings of them, and at the same time to repeat prayers to Hades and to Persephone; but I sat where I was with my sword drawn and would not let the poor feeble ghosts come near the blood till Teiresias should have answered my questions.

"The first ghost that came was that of my comrade Elpenor, for he had not yet been laid beneath the earth. We had left his body unwept and unburied in Circe's house, for we had had too much else to do. I was very sorry for him, and cried when I saw him; 'Elpenor,' said I, 'how did you come down here into this gloom and darkness? You have got here on foot quicker than I have with my ship.'

" 'Sir,' he answered with a groan, 'it was all bad luck, and my own unspeakable drunkenness. I was lying asleep on the top of Circe's house, and never thought of coming down again by the great staircase but fell right off the roof and broke my neck, so my soul came down to the house of Hades. And now I beseech you by all those whom you have left behind you, though they are not here, by your wife, by the father who brought you up when you were a child, and by Telemachus, who is the one hope of your house, do what I shall now ask you. I know that when you leave this house of Hades you will again sail your ship to the Aeaea island. Do not go thence leaving me unwept and unburied behind you, or I may bring heaven's anger upon you; but burn me with my armour, build a barrow for me on the seashore, that may tell people in days to come what a poor unlucky fellow I was, and plant over my grave the oar I used to row with when I was yet alive and with my messmates.' And I said, 'My poor fellow, I will do all that you have asked of me.'

"Thus, then, did we sit and hold sad talk with one another, I on the one side of the trench with my sword held over the blood, and the ghost of my comrade saying all this to me from the other side. Then came the ghost of my dead mother, Anticleia, daughter to Autolycus. I had left her alive when I set out for Troy and was moved to tears when I saw her, but even so, for all my sorrow, I would not let her come near the blood till I had asked my questions of Teiresias.

"Then came also the ghost of Theban Teiresias, with his golden sceptre in his hand. He knew me and said, 'Odysseus, noble son of Laertes, why, poor man, have you left the light of day and come down to visit the dead in this sad place? Stand back from the trench and withdraw your sword that I may drink of the blood and answer your questions truly.'

"So I drew back, and sheathed my sword, whereon when he had drank of the blood he began with his prophecy.

" 'You want to know,' said he, 'about your return home, but heaven will make this hard for you. I do not think that you will escape the eye of Poseidon, who still nurses his bitter grudge against you for having blinded his son. Still, after much suffering you may get home if you can restrain yourself and your companions when your ship reaches the Thrinacian island, where you will find the sheep and cattle belonging to the sun, who sees and hears everything. If you leave these flocks unharmed and think of nothing but getting home, you may yet after much hardship reach Ithaca; but if you harm them, then I forewarn you of the destruction of your ship and your men. Even though you may yourself escape, you will return in bad plight after losing all your men, in another man's ship, and you will find trouble in your house, which will be overrun by highhanded people, who are devouring your substance under the pretext of paying court and making presents to your wife.

" 'When you get home you will take your revenge on these suitors; and after you have killed them by force or fraud in your own house, you must take a well-made oar and carry it on and on, till you come to a country where the people have never heard of the sea and do not even mix salt with their food, nor do they know anything about ships, and oars that are as the wings of a ship. I will give you this certain token which cannot escape your notice. A wayfarer will meet you and will say it is a winnowing shovel that you have got upon your shoulder; on this, you must fix the oar in the ground and sacrifice a ram, a bull, and a boar to Poseidon. Then go home and offer hecatombs to all the gods in heaven one after the other. As for yourself, death shall come to you from the sea, a very gentle death when you are full of years and peace of mind, and your people will be happy around you. All that I have said will come true.'

" 'This,' I answered, 'must be as it may please heaven, but tell me and tell me true: I see my poor mother's ghost close by us; she is sitting by the blood without saying a word, and though I am her own son she does not remember me and speak to me; tell me, Sir, how I can make her know me.'

" 'That,' said he, 'I can soon do. Any ghost that you let taste of the blood will talk with you like a reasonable being, but if you do not let them have any blood they will go away again.'

"On this, the ghost of Teiresias went back to the house of Hades, for his prophecies had now been spoken, but I sat still where I was until my mother came up and tasted the blood. Then she knew me at once and spoke fondly to me, saying, 'My son, how did you come down to this abode of darkness while you are still alive? It is a hard thing for the living to see these places, for between us and them there are great and terrible waters, and there is Oceanus, which no man can cross on foot, but he must have a good ship to take him. Are you all this time trying to find your way home from Troy, and have you never yet got back to Ithaca nor seen your wife in your own house?'

" 'Mother,' said I, 'I was forced to come here to consult the ghost of the Theban prophet Teiresias. I have never yet been near the Achaean land nor set foot on my native country, and I have had nothing but one long series of misfortunes from the very first day that I set out with Agamemnon for Ilium, the land of noble steeds, to fight the Trojans. But tell me, and tell me true, in what way did you die? Did you have a long illness, or did heaven vouchsafe you a swift and gentle death? Tell me also about my father, and the son whom I left behind me; is my property still in their hands, or has someone else got hold of it, who thinks that I shall not return to claim it? Tell me again what my wife intends doing, and in what mind she is; does she live with my son and guard my estate securely, or has she made the best match she could and married again?'

"My mother answered, 'Your wife still remains in your house, but she is in great distress of mind and spends her whole time in tears both night and day. No one as yet has got possession of your fine property, and Telemachus still holds your lands undisturbed. He has to entertain largely, as of course he must, considering his position as a magistrate, and how everyone invites him. Your father remains at his old place in the country and never goes near the town. He has no comfortable bed nor bedding; in the winter he sleeps on the floor in front of the fire with the men and goes about all in rags, but in summer, when the warm weather comes on again, he lies out in the vineyard on a bed of vine leaves thrown anyhow upon the ground. He grieves continually about your never having come home, and suffers more and more as he grows older. As for my own end, it was in this wise: heaven did not take me swiftly and painlessly in my own house, nor was I attacked by any illness such as those that generally wear people out and kill them, but my longing to know what you were doing and the force of my affection for you—this it was that was the death of me.'

"Then I tried to find some way of embracing my poor mother's ghost. Thrice I sprang towards her and tried to clasp her in my arms, but each time she slipped from my embrace as though it were a dream or phantom, and in great distress I said to her, 'Mother, why do you not stay still when I would embrace you? If we could throw our arms around one another we might find sad comfort in the sharing of our sorrow even in the house of Hades; does Persephone want to lay a still further load of grief upon me by mocking me with a phantom only?'

" 'My son,' she answered, 'most ill-fated of all mankind, it is not Persephone that is beguiling you, but all people are like this when they are dead. The sinews no longer hold the flesh and bones together; these perish in the fierceness of consuming fire as soon as life has left the body, and the soul flies away as though it were a dream. Now, however, go back to the light of day as soon as you can, and note all these things that you may tell them to your wife hereafter.'

"Thus did we converse, and anon Persephone sent up the ghosts of the wives and daughters of famous men. They gathered in crowds about the blood, and I considered how I might question them severally. In the end I decided that it would be best to draw the keen blade that hung by my sturdy thigh, and keep them from all drinking the blood at once. So they came up one after the other, and each one as I questioned her told me her race and lineage.

"The first I saw was Tyro. She was daughter of Salmoneus and wife of Cretheus, the son of Aeolus. She fell in love with the river Enipeus, who is much the most beautiful river in the whole world. Once when she was taking a walk by his side as usual, Poseidon, disguised as her lover, lay with her at the mouth of the river, and a huge blue wave arched itself like a mountain over them to hide both woman and god, whereon he loosed her girdle and laid her in a deep slumber.

When the god had accomplished the deed of love, he took her hand in his own and said, 'Tyro, rejoice in our lovemaking; the embraces of the gods are not fruitless, and you will have fine twins about this time twelvemonth. Take great care of them. I am Poseidon, so now go home, but keep silence and do not tell anyone.'

"Then he dived under the sea, and she in due course bore Pelias and Neleus, who both of them served Zeus with all their might. Pelias was a great breeder of sheep and lived in Iolcus, but the other lived in Pylos. The rest of her children were by Cretheus, namely, Aeson, Pheres, and Amythaon, who was a mighty warrior and charioteer.

"Next to her I saw Antiope, daughter of Asopus, who could boast of having slept in the arms of Zeus himself, and who bore him two sons, Amphion and Zethus. These founded Thebes with its seven gates, and built a wall all round it; for strong though they were, they could not hold Thebes till they had walled it.

"Then I saw Alcmene, the wife of Amphitryon, who bore to Zeus indomitable Heracles; and Megara, who was daughter of great King Creon, and married the redoubtable son of Amphitryon.

"I also saw fair Epicaste, mother of King Oedipodes, whose awful lot it was to marry her own son without suspecting it. He married her after having killed his father, but the gods exposed the whole story to the world; whereon he remained king of Thebes, in great grief for the spite the gods had borne him; but Epicaste went to the house of the mighty jailor Hades, having hanged herself for grief, and she left behind for him the many sorrows that are caused by the spirits that avenge a mother.

"Then I saw Chloris, whom Neleus married for her beauty, having given priceless presents for her. She was youngest daughter of Amphion, son of Iasus and king of Minyan Orchomenus, and was queen in Pylos. She bore Nestor, Chromius, and Periclymenus, and she also bore that marvellously lovely woman Pero, who was wooed by all the country round; but Neleus would only give her to him who should drive the cattle of Iphicles from the grazing grounds of Phylace, and this was a hard task. The only man who would undertake to aid them was a certain excellent seer,* but the will of heaven was against him, for the herdsmen of the cattle caught him and bound him; nevertheless, when a full year had passed and the same season came round again, Iphicles set him at liberty, after he had expounded all the oracles of heaven. Thus, then, was the will of Zeus accomplished.

"And I saw Leda, the wife of Tyndareus, who bore him two famous sons, Castor, tamer of horses, and Pollux, the mighty boxer. Both these heroes are lying under the earth, though they are still alive, for by a special dispensation of Zeus, they die and come to life again, each one of them every other day, and they have the rank of gods.

"After her I saw Iphimedeia, wife of Aloeus, who boasted the embrace of Poseidon. She bore two sons, Otus and Ephialtes, but both were short-lived. They were the finest children that were ever born in this world, and the best-looking, Orion only excepted; for at nine years old they were nine fathoms high, and measured nine cubits round the chest. They threatened to make war with the gods in Olympus, and tried to set Mount Ossa on the top of Mount Olympus, and Mount Pelion on the top of Ossa, that they might scale heaven itself, and they would have done it too if they had been grown up, but Apollo, son of Leto, killed both of them before they had got so much as a sign of hair upon their cheeks or chin.

"Then I saw Phaedra, and Procris, and fair Ariadne, daughter of the magician Minos, whom Theseus was carrying off from Crete to Athens, but he did not enjoy her, for

*Melampus; see Book XV, p. 195.

before he could do so Artemis killed her in the island of Dia on account of what Dionysus had said against her.

"I also saw Maera and Clymene and hateful Eriphyle, who sold her own husband for gold. But it would take me all night if I were to name every single one of the wives and daughters of heroes whom I saw, and it is time for me to go to bed, either on board ship with my crew, or here. As for my journey, heaven and yourselves will see to it."

Here he ended, and the guests sat all of them enthralled and speechless throughout the dark hall. Then Arete said to them:

"What do you think of this man, Phaeacians? Is he not tall and good-looking, and is he not clever? True, he is my own guest, but you all of you share in the distinction. Do not be in a hurry to send him away, nor niggardly in the presents you make to one who is in such great need, for heaven has blessed all of you with great abundance."

Then spoke the aged hero Echeneüs who was one of the oldest men among them. "My friends," said he, "what our august queen has just said to us is both reasonable and to the purpose, therefore be persuaded by it; but the decision, whether in word or deed, rests ultimately with King Alcinous."

"The thing shall be done," exclaimed Alcinous, "as surely as I still live and reign over the Phaeacians. Our guest is indeed very anxious to get home; still we must persuade him to remain with us until tomorrow, by which time I shall be able to get together the whole sum that I mean to give him. As regards his escort, it will be a matter for you all, and mine above all others as the chief person among you."

And Odysseus answered, "King Alcinous, if you were to bid me to stay here for a whole twelve months, and then speed me on my way, loaded with your noble gifts, I should obey you gladly and it would redound greatly to my advantage, for I should return fuller handed to my own people, and should thus be more respected and beloved by all who see me when I get back to Ithaca."

"Odysseus," replied Alcinous, "not one of us who sees you has any idea that you are a charlatan or a liar. I know there are many people going about who tell such plausible stories that it is very hard to see through them, but there is a style about your language which assures me of your good disposition. Moreover, you have told the story of your own misfortunes, and those of the Argives, as though you were a practised bard; but tell me, and tell me true, whether you saw any of the mighty heroes who went to Troy at the same time with yourself, and perished there. The evenings are still at their longest, and it is not yet bedtime; go on, therefore, with your divine story, for I could stay here listening till tomorrow morning, so long as you will continue to tell us of your adventures."

"Alcinous," answered Odysseus, "there is a time for making speeches, and a time for going to bed; nevertheless, since you so desire, I will not refrain from telling you the still sadder tale of those of my comrades who did not fall fighting with the Trojans, but perished on their return, through the treachery of a wicked woman.

"When Persephone had dismissed the female ghosts in all directions, the ghost of Agamemnon, son of Atreus, came sadly up to me, surrounded by those who had perished with him in the house of Aegisthus. As soon as he had tasted the blood, he knew me, and weeping bitterly, stretched out his arms towards me to embrace me; but he had no strength nor substance any more, and I too wept and pitied him as I beheld him. 'How did you come by your death,' said I, 'King Agamemnon? Did Poseidon raise his winds and waves against you when you were at sea, or did your enemies make an end of you on the mainland when you were cattle-lifting or sheep-stealing, or while they were fighting in defence of their wives and city?'

" 'Odysseus,' he answered, 'noble son of Laertes, I was not

lost at sea in any storm of Poseidon's raising, nor did my foes despatch me upon the mainland, but Aegisthus and my wicked wife were the death of me between them. He asked me to his house, feasted me, and then butchered me most miserably as though I were an ox at the stall, while all around me my comrades were slaughtered like sheep or pigs for the wedding breakfast, or picnic, or gorgeous banquet of some great nobleman. You must have seen numbers of men killed either in a general engagement or in single combat, but you never saw anything so truly pitiable as the way in which we fell in that hall, with the mixing bowl and the loaded tables lying all about, and the ground reeking with our blood. I heard Priam's daughter Cassandra scream as Clytemnestra killed her close beside me. I lay dying upon the earth with the sword in my body, and tried to raise my hands, but failed. My shameless wife turned away from me; she would not even close my lips or my eyes when I was dying, for there is nothing in this world so cruel and so shameless as a woman when she has fallen into such guilt as hers was. She committed the crime of murdering her own husband. I thought I was going to be welcomed home by my children and my servants, but her abominable crime has brought disgrace on herself and all women who shall come after—even on the good ones.'

"And I said, 'In truth, Zeus has hated the house of Atreus from first to last in the matter of their women's counsels. Many of us fell for Helen's sake; and Clytemnestra hatched mischief against you during your absence.'

" 'Be sure, therefore,' continued Agamemnon, 'and not be too friendly even with your own wife. Do not tell her all that you know perfectly well yourself. Tell her a part only, and keep your own counsel about the rest. Not that your wife, Odysseus, is likely to murder you, for Penelope is a very admirable woman, and has an excellent nature. We left her a young bride with an infant at her breast when we set out for Troy. This child no doubt is now grown up happily to man's estate, and he and his father will have a joyful meeting and embrace one another as it is right they should do, whereas my wicked wife did not even allow me the happiness of looking upon my son, but killed me ere I could do so. Furthermore I say—and lay my saying to your heart—do not tell people when you are bringing your ship to Ithaca, but steal a march upon them, for after all this there is no trusting women. But now tell me, and tell me true, can you give me any news of my son, Orestes? Is he in Orchomenus, or at Pylos, or is he at Sparta with Menelaus—for I presume that he is still living.'

"And I said, 'Agamemnon, why do you ask me? I do not know whether your son is alive or dead, and it is not right to talk when one does not know.'

"As we two sat weeping and talking thus sadly with one another, the ghost of Achilles came up to us with Patroclus, Antilochus, and Ajax, who was the finest and goodliest man of all the Danaans after the son of Peleus. The fleet descendant of Aeacus knew me and spoke piteously, saying, 'Odysseus, noble son of Laertes, what deed of daring will you undertake next, that you venture down to the house of Hades among us senseless dead, who are but the ghosts of them that can labour no more?'

"And I said, 'Achilles, son of Peleus, foremost champion of the Achaeans, I came to consult Teiresias, and see if he could advise me about my return home to Ithaca, for I have never yet been able to get near the Achaean land, nor to set foot in my own country, but have been in trouble all the time. As for you, Achilles, no one was ever yet so fortunate as you have been, nor ever will be, for you were adored by all us Argives as long as you were alive, and now that you are here you are a great prince among the dead. Do not, therefore, take it so much to heart even if you are dead.'

" 'Say not a word,' he answered, 'in death's favour; I would rather be a paid servant in a poor man's house and be above ground than king of kings among the dead. But give me news

about my son; is he gone to the wars and will he be a great
soldier, or is this not so? Tell me also if you have heard anything about my father, Peleus—does he still rule among the
Myrmidons, or do they show him no respect throughout
Hellas and Phthia now that he is old and his limbs fail him?
Could I but stand by his side, in the light of day, with the
same strength that I had when I killed the bravest of our foes
upon the plain of Troy—could I but be as I then was and go
even for a short time to my father's house, anyone who tried
to do him violence or supersede him would soon regret it.'

" 'I have heard nothing,' I answered, 'of Peleus, but I can
tell you all about your son, Neoptolemus, for I took him in
my own ship from Scyros to the Achaeans. In our councils of
war before Troy he was always first to speak, and his judgement was unerring. Nestor and I were the only two who
could surpass him; and when it came to fighting on the plain
of Troy, he would never remain with the body of his men,
but would dash on far in front, foremost of them all in valour. Many a man did he kill in battle—I cannot name every
single one of those whom he slew while fighting on the side
of the Argives, but will only say how he killed that valiant
hero Eurypylus, son of Telephus, who was the handsomest
man I ever saw except Memnon; many others also of the
Ceteians fell around him by reason of a woman's bribes.
Moreover, when all the bravest of the Argives went inside
the horse that Epeus had made, and it was left to me to settle when we should either open the door of our ambuscade,
or close it, though all the other leaders and chief men among
the Danaans were drying their eyes and quaking in every
limb, I never once saw him turn pale nor wipe a tear from
his cheek; he was all the time urging me to break out from
the horse—grasping the handle of his sword and his bronze-
shod spear, and breathing fury against the foe. Yet when we
had sacked the city of Priam, he got his handsome share of
the prize money and went on board (such is the fortune of

war) without a wound upon him, neither from a thrown spear nor in close combat, for the rage of Ares is a matter of great chance.'

"When I had told him this, the ghost of Achilles strode off across the meadow of asphodel, exulting over what I had said concerning the prowess of his son.

"The ghosts of other dead men stood near me and told me each his own melancholy tale; but that of Ajax, son of Telamon, alone held aloof—still angry with me for having won in our dispute about the armour of Achilles. Thetis had offered it as a prize, but the Trojan prisoners and Athene were the judges. Would that I had never won in such a contest, for it cost the life of Ajax, who was foremost of all the Danaans after the son of Peleus, alike in stature and prowess.

"When I saw him I tried to pacify him and said, 'Ajax, will you not forget and forgive even in death, but must the judgement about that hateful armour still rankle with you? It cost us Argives dear enough to lose such a tower of strength as you were to us. We mourned you as much as we mourned Achilles, son of Peleus, himself, nor can the blame be laid on anything but on the spite which Zeus bore against the Danaans, for it was this that made him counsel your destruction. Come hither, therefore, bring your proud spirit into subjection, and hear what I can tell you.'

"He would not answer, but turned away to Erebus and to the other ghosts; nevertheless I should have made him talk to me in spite of his being so angry, or I should have gone on talking to him, only that there were still others among the dead whom I desired to see.

"Then I saw Minos, son of Zeus, with his golden sceptre in his hand sitting in judgement on the dead, and the ghosts were gathered sitting and standing round him in the spacious house of Hades, to learn his sentences upon them.

"After him I saw huge Orion in a meadow full of asphodel, driving the ghosts of the wild beasts that he had killed upon the mountains, and he had a great bronze club in his hand, unbreakable for ever and ever.

"And I saw Tityus, son of Gaia, stretched upon the plain and covering some nine acres of ground. Two vultures, one on either side of him, were digging their beaks into his liver, and he kept on trying to beat them off with his hands, but could not; for he had violated Zeus's mistress Leto as she was going through Panopeus on her way to Pytho.

"I saw also the cruel fate of Tantalus, who stood in a lake that reached his chin; he longed to quench his thirst, but could never reach the water, for whenever the old man stooped to drink, it dried up and vanished, so that there was nothing but dry ground—parched by the spite of heaven. There were tall trees, moreover, that shed their fruit over his head—pears, pomegranates, apples, sweet figs, and juicy olives—but whenever the old man stretched out his hand to take some, the wind tossed the branches back again to the clouds.

"And I saw Sisyphus at his endless task, raising his prodigious stone with both his hands. Straining with hands and feet, he tried to roll it up to the top of the hill, but always, just before he could roll it over onto the other side, its weight would be too much for him, and the pitiless stone would come thundering down again onto the plain. Then he would begin trying to push it uphill again, and the sweat ran off him and the dust rose about his head.

"After him I saw mighty Heracles, but it was his phantom only, for he is feasting ever with the immortal gods, and has lovely Hebe to wife, who is daughter of Zeus and Hera. The ghosts were screaming round him like scared birds, flying in all directions. He looked black as night with his bow in his hands and his arrow on the string, glaring around as though ever on the point of taking aim. About his breast there was a wondrous golden belt adorned in the most marvellous fashion with bears, wild boars, and lions with gleaming eyes; there was also war, battle, and death. The man who made that belt, do what he might, would never be able to make another like it. Heracles knew me at once when he saw me, and spoke piteously, saying, 'My poor Odysseus, noble son of Laertes, are you too leading the same sorry kind of life that I did when I was above ground? I was son of Zeus, but I went through an infinity of suffering, for I became bondsman to one who was far beneath me—a low fellow who set me all manner of labours. He once sent me here to fetch the hell hound—for he did not think he could find anything harder for me than this, but I got the hound out of Hades and brought him to him, for Hermes and Athene helped me.'

"On this Heracles went down again into the house of Hades, but I stayed where I was in case some other of the mighty dead should come to me. And I should have seen still others of them that are gone before, whom I would fain have seen—Theseus and Pirithous—glorious children of the gods, but so many thousands of ghosts came round me and uttered such appalling cries, that I was panic-stricken lest Persephone should send up from the house of Hades the head of that awful monster Gorgon. On this, I hastened back to my ship and ordered my men to go on board at once and loose the hawsers; so they embarked and took their places, whereon the ship went down the stream of the river Oceanus. We had to row at first, but presently a fair wind sprang up."

BOOK XII

❧

*The Sirens, Scylla and Charybdis, the Cattle
of the Sun*

"AFTER WE were clear of the river Oceanus, and had got out
into the open sea, we went on till we reached the Aeaean island, where there is the house and dancing place of the
dawn, and the rising of the sun. We then drew our ship onto
the sands and got out of her onto the shore, where we went
to sleep and waited till day should break.

"Then, when the child of morning, rosy-fingered Dawn,
appeared, I sent some men to Circe's house to fetch the
body of Elpenor. We cut firewood from a wood where the
headland jutted out into the sea, and after we had wept over
him and lamented him, we performed his funeral rites.
When his body and armour had been burned to ashes, we
raised a cairn, set a stone over it, and at the top of the cairn
we fixed the oar that he used to row with.

"While we were doing all this, Circe, who knew that we
had got back from the house of Hades, dressed herself and
came to us as fast as she could; and her maidservants came
with her, bringing us bread, meat, and wine. Then she stood
in the midst of us and said, 'You have done a bold thing in
going down alive to the house of Hades, and you will have
died twice, to other people's once; now, then, stay here for
the rest of the day, feast your fill, and go on with your voyage
at daybreak tomorrow morning. In the meantime I will tell
Odysseus about your course, and will explain everything to

him so as to prevent your suffering from misadventure either by land or by sea.'

"We agreed to do as she had said, and feasted through the livelong day to the going down of the sun, but when the sun had set and it became dark, the men laid themselves down to sleep by the stern cables of the ship. Then Circe took me by the hand and bade me be seated away from the others, while she reclined by my side and asked me all about our adventures.

" 'So far so good,' said she, when I had ended my story, 'and now pay attention to what I am about to tell you—heaven itself, indeed, will recall it to your recollection. First you will come to the Sirens, who enchant all who come near them. If anyone unwarily draws in too close and hears the singing of the Sirens, his wife and children will never welcome him home again, for they sit in a green field and bewitch him with the sweetness of their song. There is a great heap of dead men's bones lying all around, with the flesh still rotting off them. Therefore pass these Sirens by, and stop your men's ears with wax that none of them may hear; but if you like, you can listen yourself, for you may get the men to bind you as you stand upright at the base of the mast, and they must lash the rope's ends to the mast itself, that you may have the pleasure of listening. If you beg and pray the men to unloose you, then they must bind you faster.

" 'When your crew have taken you past these Sirens, I will not give you definite directions as to which of two courses you are to take; I will lay the two alternatives before you, and you must consider them for yourself. On the one hand there are some overhanging rocks against which the deep blue waves of Amphitrite beat with terrific fury; the blessed gods call these rocks the Wanderers. Here not even a bird may pass, no, not even the timid doves that bring ambrosia to Father Zeus, but the sheer rock always carries off one of them, and Father Zeus has to send another to make up their number; no ship that ever yet came to these rocks has got away again, but the waves and whirlwinds of fire carry the wreckage and the bodies of dead men. The only vessel that ever sailed and got through was the famous Argo on her way from the house of Aeëtes, and she too would have gone against these great rocks, only that Hera piloted her past them for the love she bore to Jason.

" 'In the other direction are two rocks, of which the one reaches heaven and its peak is lost in a dark cloud. This never leaves it, so that the top is never clear, not even in summer and early autumn. No man, though he had twenty hands and twenty feet, could get a foothold on it and climb it, for it runs sheer up, as smooth as though it had been polished. In the middle of it there is a large cavern, looking west and turned towards Erebus; you must take your ship this way, but the cave is so high up that not even the stoutest archer could send an arrow into it. Inside it Scylla sits and yelps with a voice that you might take to be that of a young hound, but in truth she is a dreadful monster and no one— not even a god—could face her without being terror-struck. She has twelve misshapen feet, and six necks of the most prodigious length; and at the end of each neck she has a frightful head with three rows of teeth in each, all set very close together, so that they would crunch anyone to death in a moment, and she sits deep within her shady cell thrusting out her heads and peering all round the rock, fishing for dolphins or dog-fish or any larger monster that she can catch, of the thousands with which Amphitrite teems. No ship ever yet got past her without losing some men, for she shoots out all her heads at once, and carries off a man in each mouth.

" 'You will find the other rock lies lower, but they are so close together that there is not more than a bowshot between them. A large fig tree in full leaf grows upon it, and under it lies the sucking whirlpool of Charybdis. Three times in the day does she vomit forth her waters, and three times she sucks them down again; see that you be not there when she is sucking, for if you are, Poseidon himself could not save you; you must hug the Scylla side and drive your ship by as fast as you can, for you had better lose six men than your whole crew.'

" 'Is there no way,' said I, 'of escaping Charybdis, and at the same time keeping Scylla off when she is trying to harm my men?'

" 'You daredevil,' replied the goddess, 'you are always wanting to fight somebody or something; you will not let yourself be beaten even by the immortals. For Scylla is not mortal; moreover, she is terrible, savage, cruel, and invincible. There is no help for it; your best chance will be to get by her as fast as ever you can, for if you dawdle about her rock while you are putting on your armour, she may catch you with a second cast of her six heads, and snap up another half dozen of your men; so drive your ship past her at full speed, and roar out lustily to Crataiis, who is Scylla's dam, bad luck to her; she will then stop her from making a second raid upon you.'

" 'You will now come to the Thrinacian island, and here you will see many cattle and sheep belonging to the sun god—seven herds of cattle and seven flocks of sheep, with fifty head in each flock. They do not breed, nor do they become fewer in number, and they are tended by the goddesses Phaëthusa and Lampetie, who are children of the sun god Hyperion by Neaera. Their mother, when she had borne them and reared them, sent them to the Thrinacian island, which was a long way off, to live there and look after their father's flocks and herds. If you leave these flocks unharmed, and think of nothing but getting home, you may yet after much hardship reach Ithaca; but if you harm them, then I forewarn you of the destruction both of your ship and of your comrades; and even though you may yourself escape, you will return late, in bad plight, after losing all your men.'

"Here she ended, and dawn, enthroned in gold, began to show in heaven, whereon she returned inland. I then went on board and told my men to loose the ship from her moorings; so they at once got into her, took their places, and began to smite the grey sea with their oars. Presently the great and cunning goddess Circe befriended us with a fair wind that blew dead aft, and stayed steadily with us, keeping our sails well filled, so we set in order the ship's gear, and let her go as wind and helmsman headed her.

"Then, being much troubled in mind, I said to my men, 'My friends, it is not right that one or two of us alone should know the prophecies that Circe has made me; I will therefore tell you about them, so that whether we live or die, we may do so with our eyes open. First she said we were to keep clear of the Sirens, who sit and sing most beautifully in a field of flowers; but she said I might hear them myself so long as no one else did. Therefore take me and bind me to the base of the mast; bind me as I stand upright, with a bond so fast that I cannot possibly break away, and lash the rope's ends to the mast itself. If I beg and pray you to set me free, then bind me more tightly still.'

"I had hardly finished telling everything to the men before we reached the island of the two Sirens, for the wind had been very favourable. Then all of a sudden it fell dead calm; there was not a breath of wind nor a ripple upon the water, so the men furled the sails and stowed them; then taking to their oars, they whitened the water with the foam they raised in rowing. Meanwhile I took a large wheel of wax and cut it up small with my sword. Then I kneaded the wax in my strong hands till it became soft, which it soon did between the kneading and the rays of the sun god, son of Hyperion. Then I stopped the ears of all my men, and they bound me hands and feet to the mast as I stood upright at its base; but they went on rowing themselves. When we had got within earshot of the land, and the ship was going at a good rate, the Sirens saw that we were getting close inshore and began with their singing.

" 'Come here,' they sang, 'renowned Odysseus, honour to the Achaean name, and listen to our voices. No one ever sailed past us without staying to hear the enchanting sweetness of our song—and he who listens will go on his way not only charmed, but wiser, for we know all the ills that the gods laid upon the Argives and Trojans before Troy, and can tell you everything that happens over the whole world.'

"They sang these words most musically, and as I longed to hear them further, I made signs by frowning to my men that they should set me free; but they quickened their stroke, and Eurylochus and Perimedes bound me with still stronger bonds till we had got out of hearing of the Sirens' voices. Then my men took the wax from their ears and unbound me.

"Immediately after we had got past the island, I saw a great wave from which spray was rising, and I heard a loud roaring sound. The men were so frightened that they loosed hold of their oars, for the whole sea resounded with the rushing of the waters, but the ship stayed where it was, for the men had left off rowing. I went round, therefore, and exhorted them man by man not to lose heart.

" 'My friends,' said I, 'this is not the first time that we have been in danger, and we are in nothing like so bad a case as when the Cyclops shut us up in his cave; nevertheless my courage and wise counsel saved us then, and we shall live to look back on all this as well. Now, therefore, let us all do as I say, trust in Zeus and row on with might and main. As for you, steersman, these are your orders; attend to them, for the ship is in your hands; turn her head away from these steaming rapids and hug the rock, or she will give you the slip and be over yonder before you know where you are, and you will be the death of us.'

"So they did as I told them; but I said nothing about the awful monster Scylla, for I knew the men would not go on rowing if I did, but would huddle together in the hold. In one thing only did I disobey Circe's strict instructions—I put on my armour. Then seizing two strong spears, I took my stand on the ship's bows, for it was there that I expected first to see the monster of the rock, who was to do my men so much harm; but I could not make her out anywhere, though I strained my eyes with looking the gloomy rock all over and over.

"Then we entered the straits in great fear of mind, for on the one hand was Scylla, and on the other dread Charybdis kept sucking up the salt water. When she vomited it up, it was like the water in a cauldron when it is boiling over upon a great fire, and the spray reached the top of the rocks on either side. When she began to suck again, we could see the water all inside whirling round and round, and a frightening roar sounded all round the rock. We could see the bottom of the whirlpool all black with sand and mud, and the men were at their wits' ends for fear. While we were looking at this, and were expecting each moment to be our last, Scylla pounced down suddenly upon us and snatched up my six best men. I was looking at the ship and my men, and then I saw their hands and feet ever so high above me, struggling in the air as Scylla was carrying them off, and I heard them call out my name in one last despairing cry. As a fisherman, seated with his long fishing rod upon some jutting rock, throws bait into the water to deceive the poor little fishes, and casts his line, protected by ox horn, into the sea, and throws them gasping onto the land as he catches them one by one—even so did Scylla land these panting creatures on her rock and munch them up at the mouth of her den, while they screamed and stretched out their hands to me in their mortal agony. This was the most sickening sight that I saw throughout all my voyages.

"When we had passed the Wandering rocks, with Scylla and terrible Charybdis, we reached the noble island of the sun god, where were the goodly cattle and sheep belonging to the sun, Hyperion. While still at sea in my ship, I could hear the cattle lowing as they came home to the stalls, and the sheep bleating. Then I remembered what the blind Theban prophet Teiresias had told me, and how carefully Aeaean Circe had warned me to shun the island of the blessed sun god. So being much troubled, I said to the men, 'My men, I know you are hard pressed, but listen while I tell you the prophecy that Teiresias made me, and how carefully Aeaean Circe warned me to shun the island of the blessed sun god, for it was here, she said, that our worst danger would lie. Head the ship, therefore, away from the island.'

"The men were in despair at this, and Eurylochus at once gave me an insolent answer. 'Odysseus,' said he, 'you are hard; you are very strong yourself and never get worn out; you seem to be made of iron, and now, though your men are exhausted with toil and want of sleep, you will not let them land and cook themselves a good supper upon this island, but bid them put out to sea and go faring fruitlessly on through the watches of the night. It is by night that the winds blow hardest and do so much damage; how can we escape should one of those sudden squalls spring up from southwest or west, which so often wreck a vessel when our lords the gods are unpropitious? Now, therefore, let us obey the night and prepare our supper here hard by the ship; tomorrow morning we will go on board again and put out to sea.'

"Thus spoke Eurylochus, and the men approved his words. I saw that heaven meant us a mischief, and said, 'You force me to yield, for you are many against one, but at any rate each one of you must take his solemn oath that if he meet with a herd of cattle or a large flock of sheep, he will not be so mad as to kill a single head of either, but will be satisfied with the food that Circe has given us.'

"They all swore as I bade them, and when they had completed their oath we made the ship fast in a harbour that was near a stream of fresh water, and the men went ashore and cooked their suppers. As soon as they had had enough to eat and drink, they began talking about their poor comrades whom Scylla had snatched up and eaten; this set them weeping, and they went on crying till they fell off into a sound sleep.

"In the third watch of the night, when the stars had

shifted their places, Zeus raised a great gale of wind that
blew a hurricane, so that land and sea were covered with
thick clouds, and night sprang forth out of the heavens.
When the child of morning, rosy-fingered Dawn, appeared,
we brought the ship to land and drew her into a cave
wherein the sea nymphs hold their assemblies and dances,
and I called the men together in council.

" 'My friends,' said I, 'we have meat and drink in the ship;
let us mind, therefore, and not touch the cattle, or we shall
suffer for it; for these cattle and sheep belong to the mighty
sun, who sees and hears everything. And again they
promised that they would obey.'

"For a whole month the wind blew steadily from the
south, and there was no other wind, but only south and east.
As long as corn and wine held out, the men did not touch
the cattle when they were hungry; when, however, they had
eaten all there was in the ship, they were forced to go further afield, fishing with hook and line, catching birds, and
taking whatever they could lay their hands on; for they were
starving. One day, therefore, I went up inland that I might
pray heaven to show me some means of getting away. When
I had gone far enough to be clear of all my men, and had
found a place that was well sheltered from the wind, I
washed my hands and prayed to all the gods in Olympus till
by and by they sent me off into a sweet sleep.

"Meanwhile Eurylochus had been giving evil counsel to
the men. 'Listen to me,' said he, 'my poor comrades. All
deaths are bad enough, but there is none so bad as famine.
Why should not we drive in the best of these cows and offer
them in sacrifice to the immortal gods? If we ever get back
to Ithaca, we can build a fine temple to the sun god and en-
rich it with every kind of ornament; if, however, he is determined to sink our ship out of revenge for these horned
cattle, and the other gods are of the same mind, I for one
would rather drink salt water once for all and have done

with it, than be starved to death by inches in such a desert island as this is.'

"Thus spoke Eurylochus, and the men approved his words. Now, the cattle, so fair and goodly, were feeding not far from the ship; the men, therefore, drove in the best of them, and they all stood round them saying their prayers, and using young oak shoots instead of barley meal, for there was no barley left. When they had done praying, they killed the cows and skinned them; they cut out the thighbones, wrapped them round in two layers of fat, and set some pieces of raw meat on the top of them. They had no wine with which to make drink offerings over the sacrifice while it was burning, so they kept pouring on a little water from time to time while the inner parts were being grilled; then, when the thighbones were burned and they had tasted the inner parts, they cut the rest up small and put the pieces upon the spits.

"By this time my deep sleep had left me, and I turned back to the ship and to the seashore. As I drew near I began to smell hot roast meat, so I groaned out a prayer to the immortal gods. 'Father Zeus,' I exclaimed, 'and all you other gods who live in everlasting bliss, you have done me a cruel mischief by the sleep into which you have sent me; see what fine work these men of mine have been making in my absence.'

"Meanwhile Lampetie went straight off to the sun and told him we had been killing his cows, whereon he flew into a great rage, and said to the immortals, 'Father Zeus, and all you other gods who live in everlasting bliss, I must have vengeance on the crew of Odysseus' ship: they have had the insolence to kill my cows, which were the one thing I loved to look upon, whether I was going up heaven or down again. If they do not square accounts with me about my cows, I will go down to Hades and shine there among the dead.'

" 'Sun,' said Zeus, 'go on shining upon us gods and upon mankind over the fruitful earth. I will shiver their ship into

little pieces with a bolt of white lightning as soon as they get
out to sea.'

"I was told all this by Calypso, who said she had heard it
from the mouth of Hermes.

"As soon as I got down to my ship and to the seashore, I
rebuked each one of the men separately, but we could see no
way out of it, for the cows were dead already. And indeed the
gods began at once to show signs and wonders among us, for
the hides of the cattle crawled about, and the joints upon the
spits began to low like cows, and the meat, whether cooked
or raw, kept on making a noise like the lowing of cattle.

"For six days my men kept driving in the best cows and
feasting upon them, but when Zeus, the son of Cronus, had
added a seventh day, the fury of the gale abated; we therefore went on board, raised our masts, spread sail, and put out
to sea. As soon as we were well away from the island, and
could see nothing but sky and sea, the son of Cronus set a
black cloud over our ship, and the sea grew dark beneath it.
We did not get on much further, for in another moment we
were caught by a terrific squall from the west that snapped
the forestays of the mast so that it fell aft, while all the ship's
gear tumbled about at the bottom of the vessel. The mast fell
upon the head of the helmsman in the ship's stern, so that the
bones of his head were crushed to pieces, and he fell overboard as though he were diving, with no more life left in him.

"Then Zeus let fly with his thunderbolts, and the ship
went round and round, and was filled with fire and brimstone as the lightning struck it. The men all fell into the sea;
they were carried about in the water round the ship, looking
like so many sea gulls, but the god presently deprived them
of all chance of getting home again.

"I stuck to the ship till the sea knocked her sides from her
keel (which drifted about by itself) and struck the mast out
of her in the direction of the keel; but there was a backstay
of stout ox thong still hanging about it, and with this I lashed

the mast and keel together, and getting astride of them, was carried wherever the winds chose to take me.

"The gale from the west had now spent its force, and the wind got into the south again, which frightened me lest I should be taken back to the terrible whirlpool of Charybdis. This indeed was what actually happened, for I was borne along by the waves all night, and by sunrise had reached the rock of Scylla, and the whirlpool. She was then sucking down the salt sea water, but I jumped up to the fig tree, which I caught hold of and clung onto like a bat. I could not plant my feet anywhere so as to stand securely, for the roots were a long way off and the boughs that overshadowed the whole pool were too high, too vast, and too far apart for me to reach them; so I hung patiently on, waiting till the pool should discharge my mast and raft again—and a very long while it seemed. At the time when a man goes home from the market place to supper, after judging many quarrels of young men at law, then I saw my raft beginning to work its way out of the whirlpool again. At last I let go with my hands and feet, and fell heavily into the sea, hard by my raft, onto which I then got, and began to row with my hands. As for Scylla, the father of gods and men would not let her get further sight of me—otherwise I should have certainly been lost.

"Hence I was carried along for nine days, till on the tenth night the gods brought me to the Ogygian island, where dwells the great and powerful goddess Calypso. She took me in and was kind to me, but I need say no more about this, for I told you and your noble wife all about it yesterday, and I hate telling again what has already been clearly told."

BOOK XIII

❧

Odysseus Leaves Scheria and Returns to Ithaca

THUS DID he speak, and they all held their peace throughout the dark hall, enthralled by the charm of his story, till presently Alcinous began to speak.

"Odysseus," said he, "now that you have reached my house, I doubt not you will get home without further misadventure, no matter how much you have suffered in the past. To you others, however, who come here night after night to drink my choicest wine and listen to my bard, I would insist as follows. Our guest has already packed up the clothes, wrought gold, and other valuables which you have brought; let us now, therefore, present him further, each one of us, with a large tripod and a cauldron. We will recoup ourselves by the levy of a general rate; for private individuals cannot be expected to bear the burden of such a handsome present."

Everyone approved of this, and then they went home to bed, each in his own abode. When the child of morning, rosy-fingered Dawn, appeared, they hurried down to the ship and brought their cauldrons with them. Alcinous went on board and saw everything so securely stowed under the ship's benches that nothing could break adrift and injure the rowers. Then they went to the house of Alcinous to get dinner, and he sacrificed a bull for them in honour of Zeus, who is the lord of all. When they had made a burnt offering of the thighs, they enjoyed an excellent dinner, after which the inspired bard Demodocus, who was a favourite with everyone, sang to them;

but Odysseus kept on turning his eyes towards the sun, as though to hasten his setting, for he was longing to be on his way. As one who has been all day ploughing a fallow field with a couple of oxen keeps thinking about his supper and is glad when night comes that he may go and get it, for it is all his legs can do to carry him, even so did Odysseus rejoice when the sun went down, and he at once said to the Phaeacians, addressing himself more particularly to King Alcinous:

"Sir, and all of you, farewell. Make your drink offerings and send me on my way rejoicing, for you have fulfilled my heart's desire by giving me an escort, and making me presents, which heaven grant that I may turn to good account; may I find my admirable wife living in peace among friends, and may you whom I leave behind me give happiness to your wives and children; may heaven vouchsafe you every good grace, and may no evil thing come among your people."

Thus did he speak. His hearers all of them approved his words and agreed that he should have his escort inasmuch as he had spoken properly. Alcinous therefore said to his servant, "Pontonous, mix some wine and hand it round to everybody, that we may offer a prayer to Father Zeus, and speed our guest upon his way."

Pontonous mixed the wine and handed it to everyone in turn; the others, each from his own seat, made a drink offering to the blessed gods that live in heaven, but Odysseus rose and placed the double cup in the hands of Queen Arete.

"Farewell, queen," said he, "henceforward and forever, till age and death, the common lot of mankind, lay their hands upon you. I now take my leave; be happy in this house with your children, your people, and with King Alcinous."

As he spoke, he crossed the threshold, and Alcinous sent a man to conduct him to his ship and to the seashore. Arete also sent some maidservants with him—one with a clean tunic and cloak, another to carry his strongbox, and a third with corn and wine. When they got to the waterside the crew took these things and put them on board, with all the meat and drink; but for Odysseus they spread a rug and a linen sheet on deck that he might sleep soundly in the stern of the ship. Then he too went on board and lay down without a word, but the crew took every man his place and loosed the hawser from the pierced stone to which it had been bound. Thereon, when they began rowing out to sea, Odysseus fell into a deep, sweet, and almost deathlike slumber.

The ship bounded forward on her way as a four-in-hand chariot flies over the course when the horses feel the whip. Her prow curvetted as though it were the neck of a stallion, and a great wave of dark-blue water seethed in her wake. She held steadily on her course, and even a falcon, swiftest of all birds, could not have kept pace with her. Thus, then, she cut her way through the water, carrying one who was as cunning as the gods, but who was now sleeping peacefully, forgetful of all that he had suffered both on the field of battle and by the waves of the weary sea.

When the bright star that heralds the approach of dawn began to show, the ship drew near to land. Now, there is in Ithaca a haven of the old merman Phorcys, which lies between two points that break the line of the sea and shut the harbour in. These shelter it from the storms of wind and sea that rage outside, so that, when once within it, a ship may lie without even being moored. At the head of this harbour there is a large olive tree, and at no great distance a fine overarching cavern sacred to the nymphs who are called Naiads. There are mixing bowls and wine jars of stone within it, and the bees hive there. Moreover, there are great looms of stone on which the nymphs weave their robes of sea purple—very wonderful to see—and at all times there is flowing water within it. It has two entrances, one facing north, by which mortals can go down into the cave, while the other comes from the south and is more mysterious; mortals cannot possibly get in by it; it is the way taken by the gods.

Into this harbour, then, they took their ship, for they knew the place. She had so much way upon her that she ran half her own length onto the shore; when, however, they had landed, the first thing they did was to lift Odysseus with his rug and linen sheet out of the ship, and lay him down upon the sand, still fast asleep. Then they took out the presents which Athene had persuaded the Phaeacians to give him when he was setting out on his voyage homewards. They put these all together by the root of the olive tree, away from the road, for fear some passer-by might come and steal them before Odysseus awoke; and then they made the best of their way home again.

But Poseidon did not forget the threats with which he had already threatened Odysseus, so he took counsel with Zeus. "Father Zeus," said he, "I shall no longer be held in any sort of respect among you gods, if mortals like the Phaeacians, who are my own flesh and blood, show such small regard for me. I said I would let Odysseus get home when he had suffered sufficiently. I did not say that he should never get home at all, for I knew you had already nodded your head about it, and promised that he should do so; but now they have brought him in a ship fast asleep and have landed him in Ithaca after loading him with more magnificent presents of bronze, gold, and raiment than he would ever have brought back from Troy, if he had had his share of the spoil and got home without misadventure."

And Zeus answered, "What, O Lord of the earthquake, are you talking about? The gods are by no means wanting in respect for you. It would be monstrous were they to insult one so old and honoured as you are. As regards mortals, however, if any of them is indulging in insolence and treating you disrespectfully, it will always rest with yourself to deal with him as you may think proper, so do just as you please."

"I should have done so at once," replied Poseidon, "if I were not anxious to avoid anything that might displease you; now, therefore, I should like to wreck the Phaeacian ship as it is returning from its escort. This will stop them from escorting people in future; and I should also like to hide their city under a high mountain."

"My good friend," answered Zeus, "I should recommend to you, at the very moment when the people from the city are watching the ship on her way, to turn it into a rock near the land and looking like a ship. This will astonish everybody, and you can then hide their city under a mountain."

When earth-encircling Poseidon heard this, he went to Scheria where the Phaeacians live, and stayed there till the ship, which was making rapid way, had got close in. Then he went up to it, turned it into stone, and drove it down with the flat of his hand so as to root it in the ground. After this he went away.

The Phaeacians then began talking among themselves, and one would turn towards his neighbour, saying, "Bless my heart, who is it that can have rooted the ship in the sea just as she was getting into port? We could see the whole of her only a moment ago."

This was how they talked, but they knew nothing about it; and Alcinous said, "I remember now the old prophecy of my father. He said that Poseidon would be angry with us for taking everyone so safely over the sea, and would one day wreck a Phaeacian ship as it was returning from an escort, and hide our city under a high mountain. This was what my old father used to say, and now it is all coming true. Now, therefore, let us all do as I say; in the first place we must leave off giving people escorts when they come here, and in the next, let us sacrifice twelve picked bulls to Poseidon that he may have mercy upon us, and not hide our city under a high mountain." When the people heard this they were afraid and got ready the bulls.

Thus did the chiefs and rulers of the Phaeacians pray to King Poseidon, standing round his altar; and at the same time Odysseus woke up once more upon his own soil. He had been so long away that he did not know it again; moreover, Zeus's daughter Athene had made it a foggy day, so that people might not know of his having come, and that she might tell him everything without either his wife or his fellow-citizens and friends recognising him until he had taken his revenge upon the wicked suitors. Everything, therefore, seemed quite different to him; the long, straight tracks, the harbours, the precipices, and the goodly trees appeared all changed as he started up and looked upon his native land. So he smote his thighs with the flat of his hands and cried aloud despairingly.

"Alas," he exclaimed, "among what manner of people am I fallen? Are they savage and uncivilised or hospitable and humane? Where shall I put all this treasure, and which way shall I go? I wish I had stayed over there with the Phaeacians; or I could have gone to some other great chief who would have been good to me and given me an escort. As it is, I do not know where to put my treasure, and I cannot leave it here for fear somebody else should get hold of it. In good truth the chiefs and rulers of the Phaeacians have not been dealing fairly by me, and have left me in the wrong country; they said they would take me back to Ithaca and they have not done so: may Zeus, the protector of suppliants, chastise them, for he watches over everybody and punishes those who do wrong. Still, I suppose I must count my goods and see if the crew have gone off with any of them."

He counted his goodly coppers and cauldrons, his gold and all his clothes, but there was nothing missing; still he kept grieving about not being in his own country, and wandered up and down by the shore of the sounding sea bewailing his hard fate. Then Athene came up to him disguised as a young shepherd of delicate and princely mien, with a good cloak folded double about her shoulders; she had sandals on her feet and held a javelin in her hand. Odysseus was glad when he saw her, and went straight up to her.

"My friend," said he, "you are the first person whom I have met with in this country; I salute you, therefore, and beg you to be well disposed towards me. Protect these my goods, and myself too, for I embrace your knees and pray to you as though you were a god. Tell me, then, and tell me truly, what land and country is this? Who are its inhabitants? Am I on an island, or is this the seaboard of some continent?"

Athene answered, "Stranger, you must be very simple, or must have come from somewhere a long way off, not to know what country this is. It is a very celebrated place, and everybody knows it, both east and west. It is rugged and not a good driving country, but it is by no means a bad island for what there is of it. It grows any quantity of corn and also wine, for it is watered both by rain and by dew; it breeds cattle also and goats; all kinds of timber grow here, and there are watering places where the water never runs dry—so, sir, the name of Ithaca is known even as far as Troy, which I understand to be a long way off from this Achaean country."

Odysseus was glad at finding himself, as Athene told him, in his own country, and he began to answer, but he did not speak the truth, and made up a lying story in the instinctive wiliness of his heart.

"I heard of Ithaca," said he, "when I was in Crete, beyond the seas, and now it seems I have reached it with all these treasures. I have left as much more behind me for my children, but am fleeing because I killed Orsilochus, son of Idomeneus, the fleetest runner in Crete. I killed him because he wanted to rob me of the spoils I had got from Troy with so much trouble and danger both on the field of battle and by the waves of the weary sea; he said I had not served his father loyally at Troy as vassal, but had set myself up as an independent ruler, so I lay in wait for him with one of my followers by the roadside, and speared him as he was coming into town from the country. It was a very dark night and nobody saw us; it was not known, therefore, that I had killed him, but as soon as I had done so I went to a ship and besought the owners, who were Phoenicians, to take me on board and set me in Pylos or in Elis, where the Epeans rule, giving them as much spoil as satisfied them. They meant no guile, but the wind drove them off their course, and we sailed on till we came hither by night. It was all we could do to get inside the harbour, and none of us said a word about supper, though we wanted it badly, but we all went on shore and lay down just as we were. I was very tired and fell asleep directly, so they took my goods out of the ship, and placed them beside me where I was lying upon the sand. Then they sailed away to Sidonia, and I was left here in great distress of mind."

Such was his story, but Athene smiled and patted him with her hand. Then she took the form of a woman, fair, stately, and wise. "He must be indeed a shifty, lying fellow," said she, "who could surpass you in all manner of craft even though you had a god for your antagonist. Daredevil that you are, full of guile, unwearying in deceit, can you not drop your tricks and your instinctive falsehood, even now that you are in your own country again? We will say no more, however, about this, for we can both of us deceive upon occasion—you are the most accomplished councillor and orator among all mankind, while I for diplomacy and subtlety have no equal among the gods. Did you not know Zeus's daughter Athene—me, who have been ever with you, who kept watch over you in all your troubles, and who made the Phaeacians take so great a liking to you? And now, again, I am come here to talk things over with you, and help you to hide the treasure I made the Phaeacians give you; I want to tell you about the troubles that await you in your own house; you have got to face them, but tell no one, neither man nor woman, that you have come home again. Bear everything, and put up with every man's insolence, without a word."

And Odysseus answered, "A man, goddess, may know a great deal, but you are so constantly changing your appearance that when he meets you it is a hard matter for him to know whether it is you or not. This much, however, I know exceedingly well; you were very kind to me as long as we

Achaeans were fighting before Troy, but from the day on which we went on board ship after having sacked the city of Priam, and heaven dispersed us—from that day, Athene, I saw no more of you, and cannot ever remember your coming to my ship to help me in a difficulty; I had to wander on, sick and sorry, till the gods delivered me from evil and I reached the city of the Phaeacians, where you encouraged me and took me into the town. And now, I beseech you in your father's name, tell me the truth, for I do not believe I am really back in Ithaca. I am in some other country and you are mocking me and deceiving me in all you have been saying. Tell me then truly, have I really got back to my own country?"

"You are always taking something of that sort in your head," replied Athene, "and that is why I cannot desert you in your afflictions; you are so plausible, shrewd, and shifty. Anyone but yourself on returning from so long a voyage would at once have gone home to see his wife and children, but you do not seem to care about asking after them or hearing any news about them till you have tested your wife, who remains at home vainly grieving for you, and having no peace night or day for the tears she sheds on your behalf. As for my not coming near you, I was never uneasy about you, for I was certain you would get back safely, though you would lose all your men, and I did not wish to quarrel with my uncle Poseidon, who never forgave you for having blinded his son. I will now, however, point out to you the lie of the land, and you will then perhaps believe me. This is the haven of the old merman Phorcys, and here is the olive tree that grows at the head of it; near it is the cave sacred to the Naiads; this is the overarching cavern in which you have offered many an acceptable hecatomb to the nymphs, and this is the wooded mountain Neritum."

As she spoke, the goddess dispersed the mist and the land appeared. Then Odysseus rejoiced at finding himself again in his own land, and kissed the bounteous soil; he lifted up his hands and prayed to the nymphs, saying, "Naiad nymphs, daughters of Zeus, I thought that I was never again to see you; now, therefore, I greet you with all loving salutations, and I will bring you offerings as in the old days, if Zeus's redoubtable daughter will grant me life, and bring my son to manhood."

"Take heart, and do not trouble yourself about that," rejoined Athene. "Let us rather set about stowing your things at once in the cave, where they will be quite safe. Let us see how we can best manage it all."

Therewith she went down into the cave to look for the safest hiding places, while Odysseus brought up all the treasure of gold, bronze, and good clothing which the Phaeacians had given him. He stowed everything carefully away, and Athene set a stone against the door of the cave. Then the two sat down by the root of the great olive, and consulted how to compass the destruction of the wicked suitors.

"Odysseus," said Athene, "noble son of Laertes, think how you can lay hands on these disreputable people who have been lording it in your house these three years, courting your wife and making wedding presents to her, while she does nothing but lament your absence, giving hope and sending encouraging messages to every one of them, but meaning the very opposite of all she says."

And Odysseus answered, "In good truth, goddess, it seems I should have come to much the same bad end in my own house as Agamemnon did, if you had not given me such timely information. Advise me how I shall best avenge myself. Stand by my side and put your courage into my heart as on the day when we loosed Troy's fair diadem from her brow. Help me now as you did then, and I will fight three hundred men, if you, goddess, will be with me."

"Trust me for that," said she. "I will not lose sight of you when once we set about it, and I imagine that some of those who are devouring your substance will then bespatter the pavement with their blood and brains. I will begin by disguising you so that no human being shall know you: I will cover your body with wrinkles; you shall lose all your fair hair; I will clothe you in a garment that shall fill all who see it with loathing; I will blear your fine eyes for you, and make you an unseemly object in the sight of the suitors, of your wife, and of the son whom you left behind you. Then go at once to the swineherd who is in charge of your pigs; he has always been well affected towards you, and is devoted to Penelope and your son; you will find him feeding his pigs near the rock that is called Raven by the fountain Arethusa, where they are fattening on beech mast and spring water after their manner. Stay with him and find out how things are going, while I proceed to Sparta and get your son, who is with Menelaus at Lacedaemon, where he has gone to try and find out whether you are still alive."

"But why," said Odysseus, "did you not tell him, for you knew all about it? Did you want him too to go sailing about amid all kinds of hardship while others are eating up his estate?"

Athene answered, "Never mind about him; I sent him that he might be well spoken of for having gone. He is in no sort of difficulty, but is staying quite comfortably with Menelaus, and is surrounded with abundance of every kind. The suitors have put out to sea and are lying in wait for him, for they mean to kill him before he can get home. I do not think they will succeed, but rather that some of those who are now eating up your estate will first find a grave themselves."

As she spoke, Athene touched him with her wand and covered him with wrinkles, took away all his fair hair, and withered the flesh over his whole body; she bleared his eyes, which were naturally very fine ones; she changed his clothes and threw an old rag of a wrap about him, and a tunic, tattered, filthy, and begrimed with smoke; she also gave him an undressed deerskin as an outer garment, and furnished him with a staff and a wallet all in holes, with a twisted thong for him to sling over his shoulder.

When the pair had thus laid their plans, they **parted**, and the goddess went straight to Lacedaemon to fetch Telemachus.

BOOK XIV

❧

Odysseus in the Hut with Eumaeus

ODYSSEUS NOW left the haven, and took the rough track up through the wooded country and over the crests of the mountain till he reached the place where Athene had said that he would find the swineherd, who was the most loyal servant he had. He found him sitting in front of his hut, which was by the courtyard that he had built on a site which could be seen from far. He had made it spacious and fair to see, with a free run for the pigs all round it; he had built it during his master's absence, of stones which he had gathered out of the ground, without saying anything to Penelope or Laertes, and he had fenced it on top with thorn bushes. Outside the courtyard he had run a strong fence of oaken posts, split, and set pretty close together, while inside he had built twelve stys near one another for the sows to lie in. There were fifty pigs wallowing in each sty, all of them breeding sows; but the boars slept outside and were much fewer in number, for the suitors kept on eating them, and the swineherd had to send them the best he had continually. There were three hundred and sixty boar pigs, and the herdsman's four hounds, which were as fierce as wolves, slept always with them. The swineherd was at that moment cutting out a pair of sandals from a good stout oxhide. Three of his men were out herding the pigs in one place or another, and he had sent the fourth to town with a boar that he had been forced to send the suitors that they might sacrifice it and have their fill of meat.

When the hounds saw Odysseus, they set up a furious barking and flew at him, but Odysseus was cunning enough to sit down and loose his hold of the stick that he had in his hand; still he would have been torn by them in his own homestead had not the swineherd dropped his oxhide, rushed full speed through the gate of the yard, and driven the dogs off by shouting and throwing stones at them. Then he said to Odysseus, "Old man, the dogs were likely to have made short work of you, and then you would have got me into disrepute. The gods have given me quite enough worries without that, for I have lost the best of masters, and am in continual grief on his account. I have to rear swine for other people to eat, while he, if he yet lives to see the light of day, is starving perhaps in some distant land. But come inside, and when you have had your fill of bread and wine, tell me where you come from, and all about your misfortunes."

On this, the swineherd led the way into the hut and bade him sit down. He strewed a good thick bed of rushes upon the floor, and on the top of this he threw the shaggy chamois skin—a great thick one—on which he used to sleep by night. Odysseus was pleased at being made thus welcome, and said, "May Zeus, sir, and the rest of the gods grant you your heart's desire in return for the kind way in which you have received me."

To this the swineherd Eumaeus answered, "Stranger, though a still poorer man should come here, it would not be right for me to insult him, for all strangers and beggars are from Zeus. You must take what you can get and be thankful, for servants live in fear when they have young lords for their masters; and this is my misfortune now, for heaven has hindered the return of him who would have been always good to me and given me something of my own—a house, a piece of land, a good-looking wife, and all else that a liberal master allows a servant who has worked hard for him, and whose labour the gods have prospered as they have mine in the situation which I hold. If my master had grown old here he would have done great things by me, but he is gone, and I wish that Helen's whole race were utterly destroyed, for she has been the death of many a good man. It was this matter that took my master to Ilium, the land of noble steeds, to fight the Trojans in the cause of King Agamemnon."

As he spoke, he bound his tunic round him and went to the stys where the young sucking pigs were penned. He picked out two, which he brought back with him and sacrificed. He singed them, cut them up, and spitted them; when the meat was cooked, he brought it all in and set it before Odysseus, hot and still on the spit, and sprinkled it over with white barley meal. The swineherd then mixed wine in a bowl of ivy wood, and taking a seat opposite Odysseus, told him to begin.

"Fall to, stranger," said he, "on a dish of servant's pork. The fat pigs have to go to the suitors, who eat them up without shame or scruple; but the blessed gods love not such shameful doings, and respect those who do what is lawful and right. Even the fierce pirates who go raiding other people's land, and Zeus gives them their spoil—even they, when they have filled their ships and get home again, live conscience-stricken, and look fearfully for judgement; but some god seems to have told these people that Odysseus is dead and gone; they will not, therefore, go back to their own homes and make their offers of marriage in the usual way, but waste his estate by force, without fear or stint. Not a day or night comes but they sacrifice not one victim nor two only, and they take the run of his wine, for he was exceedingly rich. No other great man either in Ithaca or on the mainland is as rich as he was; he had as much as twenty men put together. I will tell you what he had. There are twelve herds of cattle upon the mainland, and as many flocks of sheep; there are also twelve droves of pigs, while his own men and hired strangers feed him twelve widely spreading herds of goats. Here in Ithaca eleven large flocks of goats feed on the far end of the island, and they are in the charge of excellent goatherds. Each one of these sends the suitors the best goat in the flock every day. As for myself, I am in charge of the pigs that you see here, and I have to keep picking out the best I have and sending it to them."

This was his story, but Odysseus went on eating and drinking ravenously without a word, brooding his revenge. When he had eaten enough and was satisfied, the swineherd took the bowl from which he usually drank, filled it with wine, and gave it to Odysseus, who was pleased, and said as he took it in his hands, "My friend, who was this master of yours that bought you and paid for you, so rich and powerful as you tell me? You say he perished in the cause of King Agamemnon; tell me who he was, in case I may have met with such a person. Zeus and the other gods know if I may be able to give you news of him, for I have travelled much."

Eumaeus answered, "Old man, no traveller who comes here with news will get Odysseus' wife and son to believe his story. Nevertheless, tramps in want of a lodging keep coming with their mouths full of lies, and not a word of truth; everyone who finds his way to Ithaca goes to my mistress and tells her falsehoods, whereon she takes them in, makes much of them, and asks them all manner of questions, crying all the time, as women will when they have lost their husbands. And you too, old man, for a tunic and cloak would doubtless make up a very pretty story. But the wolves and birds of prey have long since torn Odysseus to pieces, or the fishes of the sea have eaten him, and his bones are lying buried deep in sand upon some foreign shore; he is dead and gone, and a bad business it is for all his friends—for me especially; go where I may, I shall never find so good a master, not even if I were to go home to my father and mother where I was born and bred. I do not so much care, however, about my parents now, though I should dearly like to see them again in my own country; it is the loss of Odysseus that grieves me most: I cannot speak of him without reverence, though he is here no longer, for he was very fond of me, and took such care of me that wherever he may be I shall always honour his memory."

"My friend," replied Odysseus, "you are very positive, and very hard of belief about your master's coming home again; nevertheless I will not merely say, but will swear, that he is coming. Do not give me anything for my news till he has actually come; you may then give me a tunic and cloak of good wear if you will. I am in great want, but I will not take anything at all till then, for I hate a man, even as I hate hell-fire, who lets his poverty tempt him into lying. I swear by King Zeus, by the rites of hospitality, and by that hearth of Odysseus to which I have now come, that all will surely happen as I have said it will. Odysseus will return in this selfsame year; with the end of this moon and the beginning of the next he will be here to do vengeance on all those who are ill-treating his wife and son."

To this the swineherd Eumaeus answered, "Old man, you will neither get paid for bringing good news, nor will Odysseus ever come home; drink your wine in peace, and let us talk about something else. Do not keep on reminding me of all this; it always pains me when anyone speaks about my honoured master. As for your oath, we will let it alone, but I only wish he may come, as do Penelope, his old father, Laertes, and his son, Telemachus. I am terribly unhappy too about this same boy of his; he was running up fast into manhood, and bade fair to be no worse man, face and figure, than his father, but someone, either god or man, has been unsettling his mind, so he has gone off to Pylos to try and get news of his father, and the suitors are lying in wait for him as he is coming home, in the hope of leaving the house of Arceisius without a name in Ithaca. But let us say no more about him, and leave him to be taken, or else to escape if the son of Cronus hold his hand over him to protect him. And now, old man, tell me your own story; tell me also, for I want to know, who you are and where you come from. Tell me of your town and parents, what manner of ship you came in, how your crew brought you to Ithaca, and from what country they professed to come—for you cannot have come by land."

And Odysseus answered, "I will tell you all about it. If there were meat and wine enough, and we could stay here in the hut with nothing to do but to eat and drink while the others went to their work, I could easily talk on for a whole twelve months without ever finishing the story of the sorrows with which it has pleased heaven to visit me.

"I am by birth a Cretan; my father was a well-to-do man, who had many sons born in marriage, whereas I was the son of a slave whom he had purchased for a concubine; nevertheless, my father, Castor, son of Hylax (whose lineage I claim, and who was held in the highest honour among the Cretans for his wealth, prosperity, and the valour of his sons), put me on the same level with my brothers who had been born in wedlock. When, however, death took him to the house of Hades, his sons divided his estate and cast lots for their shares, but to me they gave a small house and little else; nevertheless, my valour enabled me to marry into a rich family, for I was not given to bragging, or shirking on the field of battle. It is all over now; still, if you look at the straw you can see what the ear was, for I have had trouble enough and to spare. Ares and Athene made me doughty in war; when I had picked my men to surprise the enemy with an ambush, I never gave death so much as a thought, but was the first to leap forward and spear all whom I could overtake. Such was I in battle, but I did not care about farmwork, nor the frugal home life of those who would bring up children. My delight was in ships, fighting, javelins, and arrows— things that most men shudder to think of; but one man likes one thing and another another, and this was what I was most naturally inclined to. Before the Achaeans went to Troy, nine times was I in command of men and ships on foreign service, and I amassed much wealth. I had my pick of the spoil in the first instance, and much more was allotted to me later on.

"My house grew apace and I became a great man among the Cretans, but when Zeus counselled that terrible expedition in which so many perished, the people required me and Idomeneus to lead their ships to Troy, and there was no way out of it, for they insisted on our doing so. There we fought for nine whole years, and in the tenth we sacked the city of Priam and sailed home again; but heaven dispersed us. Then it was that Zeus devised evil against me. I spent but one month happily with my children, wife, and property, and then I conceived the idea of making a descent on Egypt, so I fitted out a fine fleet and manned it. I had nine ships, and the people flocked to fill them. For six days I and my men made feast, and I found them many victims both for sacrifice to the gods and for themselves, but on the seventh day we went on board and set sail from Crete with a fair north wind behind us as though we were going down a river. Nothing went ill with any of our ships, and we had no sickness on board, but sat where we were and let the ships go as the wind and steersmen took them. On the fifth day we reached the river Aegyptus; there I stationed my ships in the river, bidding my men stay by them and keep guard over them while I sent out scouts to reconnoitre from every point of vantage.

"But the men disobeyed my orders, followed their own desires, and ravaged the land of the Egyptians, killing the men, and taking their wives and children captive. The alarm was soon carried to the city, and when they heard the war cry, the people came out at daybreak till the plain was filled with horsemen and foot soldiers and with the gleam of armour. Then Zeus spread panic among my men, and they would not fight the enemy, for they found themselves surrounded. The Egyptians killed many of us, and took the rest alive to do forced labour for them. Zeus, however, put it in my mind to do thus—and I wish I had died then and there in Egypt instead, for there was much sorrow in store for me: I took off my helmet and shield and dropped my spear from my hand; then I went straight up to the king's chariot, clasped his knees and kissed them, whereon he spared my life, bade me get into his chariot, and took me weeping to his own home. Many made at me with their ashen spears and tried to kill me in their fury, but the king protected me, for he feared the wrath of Zeus, the protector of strangers, who punishes those who do evil.

"I stayed there for seven years, and got together much money among the Egyptians, for they all gave me something; but when it was now going on for eight years, there came a certain Phoenician, a cunning rascal, who had already committed all sorts of villainy, and this man talked me into going with him to Phoenicia, where his house and his possessions lay. I stayed there for a whole twelve months, but at the end of that time, when months and days had gone by till the same season had come round again, he set me on board a ship bound for Libya, on a pretence that I was to take a cargo along with him to that place, but really that he might sell me as a slave and take the money I fetched. I suspected his intention, but went on board with him, for I could not help it.

"The ship ran before a fresh north wind till we had reached the sea that lies between Crete and Libya; there, however, Zeus counselled their destruction, for as soon as we were well out from Crete and could see nothing but sea and sky, he raised a black cloud over our ship and the sea grew dark beneath it. Then Zeus let fly with his thunderbolts and the ship went round and round and was filled with fire and brimstone as the lightning struck it. The men fell all into the sea; they were carried about in the water round the ship looking like so many sea gulls, but the god presently deprived them of all chance of getting home again. I lost all hope; Zeus, however, sent the ship's mast within my reach, which saved my life, for I clung to it, and drifted before the fury of the gale. Nine days did I drift, but in the darkness of the tenth night a great wave bore me onto the Thesprotian coast. There Pheidon, king of the Thesprotians, entertained me hospitably without charging me anything at all—for his son found me when I was nearly dead with cold and fatigue, whereon he raised me by the hand, took me to his father's house, and gave me clothes to wear.

"There it was that I heard news of Odysseus, for the king told me he had entertained him, and shown him much hospitality while he was on his homeward journey. He showed me also the treasure of gold, bronze, and wrought iron that Odysseus had got together. There was enough to keep his family for ten generations, so much had he left in the house of King Pheidon. But the king said Odysseus had gone to Dodona that he might learn Zeus's mind from the god's high oak tree, and know whether after so long an absence he should return to Ithaca openly, or in secret. Moreover, the king swore in my presence, making drink offerings in his own house as he did so, that the ship was by the waterside, and the crew found, that should take him to his own country. He sent me off, however, before Odysseus returned, for there happened to be a Thesprotian ship sailing for the wheat-growing island of Dulichium, and he told those in charge of her to be sure and take me safely to King Acastus.

"These men hatched a plot against me that would have reduced me to the very extreme of misery, for when the ship had got some way out from land they resolved on selling me as a slave. They stripped me of the tunic and cloak that I was wearing, and gave me instead the tattered old clothes in which you now see me; then, towards nightfall, they reached the tilled lands of Ithaca, and there they bound me with a strong rope fast in the ship, while they went on shore to get supper by the seaside. But the gods soon undid my bonds for me, and having drawn my rags over my head, I slid down the rudder into the sea, where I struck out and swam till I was well clear of them, and came ashore near a thick wood, in which I lay concealed. They were very angry at my having escaped and went searching about for me, till at last they thought it was no further use and went back to their ship. The gods, having hidden me thus easily, then took me to a good man's door—for it seems that I am not to die yet awhile."

To this the swineherd Eumaeus answered, "Poor unhappy stranger, I have found the story of your misfortunes extremely interesting, but that part about Odysseus is not right; and you will never get me to believe it. Why should a man like you go about telling lies in this way? I know all about the return of my master. The gods one and all of them detest him, or they would have taken him before Troy, or let him die with friends around him when the days of his fighting were done; for then the Achaeans would have built a mound over his ashes and his son would have been heir to his renown, but now the storm winds have spirited him away we know not where.

"As for me, I live out of the way here with the pigs, and never go to the town except when Penelope sends for me on the arrival of some news about Odysseus. Then they all sit round and ask questions, both those who grieve over the king's absence, and those who rejoice at it because they can eat up his property without paying for it. For my own part I have never cared about asking anyone else since the time when I was taken in by an Aetolian, who had killed a man and come a long way till at last he reached my steading, and I was very kind to him. He said he had seen Odysseus with Idomeneus among the Cretans, refitting his ships, which had been damaged in a gale. He said Odysseus would return in the following summer or autumn with his men, and that he would bring back much wealth. And now you, you unfortunate old man, since fate has brought you to my door, do not try to flatter me in this way with vain hopes. It is not for any such reason that I shall treat you kindly, but only out of respect for Zeus, the god of hospitality, as fearing him and pitying you."

Odysseus answered, "I see that you are of an unbelieving mind; I have given you my oath, and yet you will not credit me; let us then make a bargain, and call all the gods in heaven to witness it. If your master comes home, give me a cloak and

tunic of good wear, and send me to Dulichium, where I want
to go; but if he does not come as I say he will, set your men
onto me, and tell them to throw me from a precipice, as a
warning to tramps not to go about the country telling lies."

"And a pretty figure I should cut then," replied Eumaeus,
"both now and hereafter, if I were to kill you after receiving
you into my hut and showing you hospitality. I should have
to put great effort into my prayers to Zeus after that; but it is
just suppertime and I hope my men will come in directly,
that we may cook something savoury for supper."

Thus they spoke, and presently the swineherds came up
with the pigs, which were then shut up for the night in their
stys, and a tremendous squealing they made as they were
being driven into them. But Eumaeus called to his men and
said, "Bring in the best pig you have, that I may sacrifice him
for this stranger, and we will enjoy him ourselves. We have
had trouble enough this long time feeding pigs, while others
reap the fruit of our labour."

On this, he began chopping firewood, while the others
brought in a fine fat five-year-old boar pig, and set it at the
altar. Eumaeus did not forget the gods, for he was a man of
good principles, so the first thing he did was to cut bristles
from the pig's head and throw them into the fire, praying to all
the gods as he did so that Odysseus might return home again.
Then he clubbed the pig with a billet of oak which he had kept
back when he was chopping the firewood, and stunned it,
while the others slaughtered and singed it. Then they cut it up,
and Eumaeus began by putting raw pieces from each joint in
some of the fat; these he sprinkled with barley meal, and
threw into the fire; they cut the rest of the meat up small, put
the pieces upon the spits, and roasted them till they were
done; when they had taken them off the spits, they threw them
onto the dresser in a heap. The swineherd, who was a most eq-
uitable man, then stood up to give everyone his share. He
made seven portions; one of these he set apart for Hermes, the

son of Maia, and the nymphs, praying to them as he did so; the others he dealt out to the men man by man. He gave Odysseus some slices cut lengthways down the loin as a mark of especial honour, and Odysseus was much pleased. "I hope, Eumaeus," said he, "that Zeus will be as well disposed towards you as I am, for the respect you are showing to an outcast like myself."

To this the swineherd Eumaeus answered, "Eat, my good fellow, and enjoy your supper, such as it is. God grants this, and withholds that, just as he thinks right, for he can do whatever he chooses."

As he spoke, he cut off the first piece and offered it as a burnt sacrifice to the immortal gods; then he made them a drink offering, put the cup in the hands of Odysseus, and sat down to his own portion. Mesaulius brought them their bread; the swineherd had bought this man on his own account from among the Taphians during his master's absence, and had paid for him with his own money without saying anything either to his mistress or to Laertes. They then laid their hands upon the good things that were before them, and when they had had enough to eat and drink, Mesaulius took away what was left of the bread, and they all went to bed after having made a hearty supper.

Now, the night came on stormy and very dark, for there was no moon. It poured without ceasing, and the wind blew strong from the west, which is a wet quarter, so Odysseus thought he would see whether Eumaeus, in the excellent care he took of him, would take off his own cloak and give it him, or make one of his men give him one. "Listen to me," said he, "Eumaeus and the rest of you; although it may seem rather boastful, I will tell you something. It is the wine that makes me talk in this way; wine will make even a wise man fall to singing; it will make him chuckle and dance and say many a word that he had better leave unspoken; still, as I have begun, I will go on. Would that I were still young and strong as when we got up an ambush before Troy. Menelaus and Odysseus were the leaders, but I was in command also, for the other two would have it so. When we had come up to the wall of the city we crouched down beneath our armour and lay there under cover of the reeds and thick brushwood that grew about the swamp. It came on to freeze with a north wind blowing; the snow fell small and fine like hoarfrost, and our shields were coated thick with rime. The others all had cloaks and tunics, and slept comfortably enough with their shields about their shoulders, but I had carelessly left my cloak behind me, not thinking that I should be too cold, and had gone off in nothing but my tunic and shield. When the night was two-thirds through and the stars had shifted their places, I nudged Odysseus, who was close to me, with my elbow, and he at once gave me his ear.

" 'Odysseus,' said I, 'this cold will be the death of me, for I have no cloak; some god fooled me into setting off with nothing on but my tunic, and I do not know what to do.'

"Odysseus, who was as crafty as he was valiant, hit upon the following plan:

" 'Keep quiet,' said he in a low voice, 'or the others will hear you.' Then he raised his head on his elbow.

" 'My friends,' said he, 'I have had a dream from heaven in my sleep. We are a long way from the ships; I wish someone would go down and tell Agamemnon to send us up more men at once.'

"On this, Thoas, son of Andraemon, threw off his cloak and set out running to the ships, whereon I took the cloak and lay in it comfortably enough till morning. Would that I were still young and strong as I was in those days, for then some one of you swineherds would give me a cloak both out of good will and for the respect due to a brave soldier; but now people look down upon me because my clothes are shabby."

And Eumaeus answered, "Old man, you have told us an excellent story, and have said nothing so far but what is proper; for the present, therefore, you shall want neither clothing nor anything else that a stranger in distress may reasonably expect, but tomorrow morning you will have to shake your own old rags about your body again, for we have not many spare cloaks nor tunics up here, but every man has only one. When Odysseus' son comes home again he will give you both cloak and tunic, and send you wherever you may want to go."

With this he got up and made a bed for Odysseus by throwing some goatskins and sheepskins on the ground in front of the fire. Here Odysseus lay down, and Eumaeus covered him over with a great heavy cloak that he kept for a change in case of extraordinarily bad weather.

Thus did Odysseus sleep, and the young men slept beside him. But the swineherd did not like sleeping away from his pigs, so he got ready to go outside, and Odysseus was glad to see that he looked after his property during his master's absence. First he slung his sword over his brawny shoulders and put on a thick cloak to keep out the wind. He also took the skin of a large and well-fed goat, and a javelin in case of attack from men or dogs. Thus equipped, he went to his rest where the pigs were camping under an overhanging rock that gave them shelter from the north wind.

BOOK XV

❧

Athene Summons Telemachus from Lacedaemon—
He Meets Theoclymenus at Pylos and Brings Him to
Ithaca—On Landing He Goes to the Hut of
Eumaeus

BUT ATHENE went to the fair city of Lacedaemon to tell
Odysseus' son that he was to return at once. She found him
and Peisistratus sleeping in the forecourt of Menelaus'
house; Peisistratus was fast asleep, but Telemachus could
get no rest all night for thinking of his unhappy father, so
Athene went close up to him and said:

"Telemachus, you should not remain so far away from
home any longer, nor leave your property with such dangerous people in your house; they will eat up everything you
have among them, and you will have been on a fool's errand.
Ask Menelaus to send you home at once if you wish to find
your excellent mother still there when you get back. Her father and brothers are already urging her to marry Eurymachus, who has given her more than any of the others, and
has been greatly increasing his wedding presents. I hope
nothing valuable may have been taken from the house in
spite of you, but you know what women are—they always
want to do the best they can for the man who marries them,
and never give another thought to the children of their first
husband, nor to their father, either, when he is dead and
done with. Go home, therefore, and put everything in
charge of the most respectable woman servant that you

have, until it shall please heaven to send you a wife of your own. Let me tell you also of another matter which you had better attend to. The chief men among the suitors are lying in wait for you in the strait between Ithaca and Samos, and they mean to kill you before you can reach home. I do not much think they will succeed; it is more likely that some of those who are now eating up your property will find a grave themselves. Sail night and day, and keep your ship well away from the islands; the god who watches over you and protects you will send you a fair wind. As soon as you get to Ithaca, send your ship and men on to the town, but yourself go straight to the swineherd who has charge of your pigs; he is well disposed towards you; stay with him, therefore, for the night, and then send him to Penelope to tell her that you have got back safe from Pylos."

Then she went back to Olympus; but Telemachus stirred Peisistratus with his heel to rouse him, and said, "Wake up, Peisistratus, and yoke the horses to the chariot, for we must get off home."

But Peisistratus said, "No matter what hurry we are in, we cannot drive in the dark. It will be morning soon; wait till Menelaus has brought his presents and put them in the chariot for us; and let him say good-bye to us in the usual way. So long as he lives a guest should never forget a host who has shown him kindness."

As he spoke day began to break, and Menelaus, who had already risen, leaving Helen in bed, came towards them. When Telemachus saw him, he put on his tunic as fast as he could, threw a great cloak over his shoulders, and went out to meet him. "Menelaus," said he, "let me go back now to my own country, for I want to get home."

And Menelaus answered, "Telemachus, if you insist on going I will not detain you. I do not like to see a host either too fond of his guest or too rude to him. Moderation is best in all things, and not letting a man go when he wants to do so is as bad as telling him to go if he would like to stay. One should treat a guest well as long as he is in the house and speed him when he wants to leave it. Wait, then, till I can get your beautiful presents into your chariot, and till you have yourself seen them. I will tell the women to prepare a sufficient dinner for you of what there is in the house; it will be at once more proper and better for you to get your dinner before setting out on such a long journey. If, however, you have a fancy for making a tour in Hellas or in the Peloponnese, I will yoke my horses, and will conduct you myself through all our principal cities. No one will send us away empty-handed; everyone will give us something—a bronze tripod, a couple of mules, or a gold cup."

"Menelaus," replied Telemachus, "I want to go home at once, for when I came away I left my property without protection, and fear that while looking for my father I shall come to ruin myself, or find that something valuable has been stolen during my absence."

When Menelaus heard this, he immediately told his wife and servants to prepare a sufficient dinner from what there was in the house. At this moment Eteoneus joined him, for he lived close by and had just got up; so Menelaus told him to light the fire and cook some meat, which he at once did. Then Menelaus went down into his fragrant storeroom, not alone, but Helen went too, with Megapenthes. When he reached the place where the treasures of his house were kept, he selected a double cup, and told his son Megapenthes to bring also a silver mixing bowl. Meanwhile Helen went to the chests where she kept the lovely dresses which she had made with her own hands, and took out one that was largest and most beautifully enriched with embroidery; it glittered like a star, and lay at the very bottom of the chest. Then they all came back through the house again till they got to Telemachus, and Menelaus said, "Telemachus, may Zeus, the mighty husband of Hera, bring you safely home according to your desire. I will now present you with the finest and most precious piece of plate in all my house. It is a mixing bowl of pure silver, except the rim, which is inlaid with gold, and it is the work of Hephaestus. Phaedimus, king of the Sidonians, made me a present of it in the course of a visit that I paid him while I was on my return home. I should like to give it to you."

With these words he placed the double cup in the hands of Telemachus, while Megapenthes brought the beautiful mixing bowl and set it before him. Hard by stood lovely Helen with the robe ready in her hand.

"I too, my son," said she, "have something for you as a keepsake from the hand of Helen; it is for your bride to wear upon her wedding day. Till then, get your dear mother to keep it for you; thus may you go back rejoicing to your own country and to your home."

So saying, she gave the robe over to him and he received it gladly. Then Peisistratus put the presents into the chariot, and admired them all as he did so. Presently Menelaus took Telemachus and Peisistratus into the house, and they both of them sat down to table. A maidservant brought them water in a beautiful golden ewer, and poured it over a silver basin for them to wash their hands, and she drew a clean table beside them; a housekeeper brought them bread and offered them many good things of what there was in the house. Eteoneus carved the meat and gave them each their portions, while Megapenthes poured out the wine. Then they laid their hands upon the good things that were before them; but as soon as they had had enough to eat and drink, Telemachus and Peisistratus yoked the horses, and took their places in the chariot. They drove out through the inner gateway and under the echoing gatehouse of the outer court, and Menelaus came after them with a golden goblet of wine in his right hand, that they might make a drink offering before they set out. He stood in front of the horses and pledged them, saying, "Farewell to both of you; see that you tell Nestor how I have treated you, for he was as kind to me as any father could be while we Achaeans were fighting before Troy."

"We will be sure, sir," answered Telemachus, "to tell him everything as soon as we see him. I wish I were as certain of finding Odysseus returned when I get back to Ithaca, that I might tell him of the very great kindness you have shown me and of the many beautiful presents I am taking with me."

As he was thus speaking, a bird flew by on his right hand— an eagle with a great white goose in its talons which it had carried off from the farmyard—and all the men and women were running after it and shouting. It came quite close up to them and flew away on their right hands in front of the horses. When they saw it they were glad, and their hearts took comfort within them, whereon Peisistratus said, "Tell me, Menelaus, has heaven sent this omen for us or for you?"

Menelaus was thinking what would be the most proper answer for him to make, but Helen was too quick for him and said, "I will read this matter as heaven has put it in my heart, and as I doubt not that it will come to pass. The eagle came from the mountain where it was bred and has its nest and snatched away the goose that was reared in the house, and in like manner Odysseus, after having travelled far and suffered much, will return to take his revenge—if indeed he is not back already and hatching mischief for the suitors."

"May Zeus so grant it," replied Telemachus. "If it should prove to be so, I will make vows to you as though you were a god, even when I am at home."

As he spoke, he lashed his horses and they started off at full speed through the town towards the open country. They swayed the yoke upon their necks and travelled the whole day long till the sun set and darkness was over all the land. Then they reached Pherae, where Diocles lived, who was son of Ortilochus, the son of Alpheus. There they passed the night and were treated hospitably. When the child of morning, rosy-fingered Dawn, appeared, they again yoked their horses and took their places in the chariot. They drove out through the inner gateway and under the echoing gatehouse of the outer court. Then he lashed his horses on and they flew forward nothing loth; ere long they came to Pylos, and then Telemachus said:

"Peisistratus, I hope you will promise to do what I am going to ask you. You know our fathers were old friends before us; moreover, we are both of an age, and this journey has brought us together still more closely; do not, therefore, take me past my ship, but leave me there, for if I go to your father's house he will try to keep me in the warmth of his good will towards me, and I must go home at once."

Peisistratus thought how he should do as he was asked, and in the end he deemed it best to turn his horses towards the ship, and put Menelaus' beautiful presents of gold and raiment in the stern of the vessel. Then he said, "Go on board at once and tell your men to do so also before I can reach home to tell my father. I know how obstinate he is, and am sure he will not let you go; he will come down here to fetch you, and he will not go back without you. But he will be very angry."

With this he drove his goodly steeds back to the city of the Pylians and soon reached his home, but Telemachus called the men together and gave his orders. "Now, my men," said he, "get everything in order on board the ship, and let us set out home."

Thus he spoke, and they went on board as he had said. But as Telemachus was thus busied, praying also and sacrificing to Athene in the ship's stern, there came to him a man from a distant country, a seer, who was fleeing from Argos because he had killed a man. He was descended from Melampus, who used to live in Pylos, the land of sheep; he was rich and owned a great house, but he was driven into exile by the great and powerful king Neleus. Neleus seized his goods and held them for a whole year, during which he was a close prisoner in the house of King Phylacus, and in much distress of mind both on account of the daughter of Neleus and because he was haunted by a great sorrow that dread Erinyes had laid upon him. In the end, however, he escaped with his life, drove the cattle from Phylace to Pylos, avenged the wrong that had been done him, and gave the daughter of Neleus to his brother. Then he left the country and went to Argos, where it was ordained that he should reign over a large people. There he married, established himself, and had two famous sons, Antiphates and Mantius. Antiphates became father of Oïcles, and Oïcles of Amphiaraus, who was dearly loved both by Zeus and by Apollo, but he did not live to old age, for he was killed in Thebes by reason of a woman's gifts. His sons were Alcmaeon and Amphilochus. Mantius, the other son of Melampus, was father to Polypheides and Cleitus. The Dawn, throned in gold, carried off Cleitus for his beauty's sake, that he might dwell among the immortals, but Apollo made Polypheides the greatest seer in the whole world now that Amphiaraus was dead. He quarrelled with his father and went to live in Hyperesia, where he remained and prophesied for all men.

His son, Theoclymenus, it was who now came up to Telemachus as he was making drink offerings and praying in his ship. "Friend," said he, "now that I find you sacrificing in this place, I beseech you by your sacrifices themselves, and by the god to whom you make them, I pray you also by your own head and by those of your followers, to tell me the truth and nothing but the truth. Who and whence are you? Tell me also of your town and parents."

Telemachus said, "I will answer you quite truly. I am from Ithaca, and my father is Odysseus, unless it has all been a dream. But he has come to some miserable end. Therefore I have taken this ship and got my crew together to see if I can hear any news of him, for he has been away a long time."

"I too," answered Theoclymenus, "am an exile, for I have killed a man of my own race. He has many brothers and kinsmen in Argos, and they have great power among the Argives. I am fleeing to escape death at their hands, and am thus doomed to be a wanderer on the face of the earth. I am your suppliant; take me, therefore, on board your ship that they may not kill me, for I know they are in pursuit."

"I will not refuse you," replied Telemachus, "if you wish to join us. Come, therefore, and in Ithaca we will treat you hospitably according to what we have."

On this, he received Theoclymenus' spear and laid it down on the deck of the ship. He went on board and sat in the stern, bidding Theoclymenus sit beside him; then the men let go the hawsers. Telemachus told them to catch hold of the ropes, and they made all haste to do so. They set the mast in its socket in the cross plank, raised it and made it fast with the forestays, and they hoisted their white sails with ropes of twisted oxhide. Athene sent them a fair wind that blew fresh and strong to take the ship on her course as fast as possible. Thus then they passed by Cruni and Chalcis.

Presently the sun set and darkness was over all the land. The vessel made a quick passage to Pheae and thence on to Elis, where the Epeans rule. Telemachus then headed her for the flying islands, wondering within himself whether he should escape death or should be caught.

Meanwhile Odysseus and the swineherd were eating their supper in the hut, and the men supped with them. As soon as they had had enough to eat and drink, Odysseus began trying to prove the swineherd and see whether he would continue to treat him kindly, and ask him to stay on at the steading or pack him off to the city; so he said:

"Eumaeus, and all of you, tomorrow I want to go away and begin begging about the town, so as to be no more trouble to you or to your men. Give me your advice therefore, and let me have a good guide to go with me and show me the way. I will go the round of the city, begging as I needs must, to see if anyone will give me a drink and a piece of bread. I should like also to go to the house of Odysseus and bring news of her husband to Queen Penelope. I could then go about among the suitors and see if out of all their abundance they will give me a dinner. I should soon make them an excellent servant in all sorts of ways. Listen and believe when I tell you that by the blessing of Hermes, who gives grace and good name to the works of all men, there is no one living who would make a more handy servant than I should—to put fresh wood on the fire, chop fuel, carve, cook, pour out wine, and do all those services that poor men have to do for their betters."

The swineherd was very much disturbed when he heard this. "Heaven help me!" he exclaimed. "Whatever can have put such a notion as that into your head? You are set on self-destruction, if you intend to enter the company of the suitors, for their pride and insolence reach the very heavens. They would never think of taking a man like you for a servant. Their servants are all young men, well-dressed, wearing good cloaks and tunics, with good-looking faces and their hair always tidy; the tables are kept quite clean and are loaded with bread, meat, and wine. Stay where you are, then; you are not in anybody's way; I do not mind your being here, no more do any of the others, and when Telemachus comes home he will give you a tunic and cloak and will send you wherever you want to go."

Odysseus answered, "I hope you may be as dear to the gods as you are to me, for having saved me from going about and getting into trouble; there is nothing worse than being always on the tramp; still, when men have once got low down in the world, they will go through a great deal on behalf of their miserable bellies. Since, however, you press me to stay here and await the return of Telemachus, tell me about Odysseus' mother, and his father, whom he left on the threshold of old age when he set out for Troy. Are they still living or are they already dead and in the house of Hades?"

"I will tell you all about them," replied Eumaeus. "Laertes

is still living and prays heaven to let him depart peacefully in his own house, for he is terribly distressed about the absence of his son, and also about the death of his wife, which grieved him greatly and aged him more than anything else did. She came to an unhappy end through sorrow for her son; may no friend or neighbour who has dealt kindly by me come to such an end as she did. As long as she was still living, though she was always grieving, I used to like seeing her and asking her how she did, for she brought me up along with her daughter Ctimene, the youngest of her children; we were boy and girl together, and she made little difference between us. When, however, we both grew up, they sent Ctimene to Same and received a splendid dowry for her. As for me, my mistress gave me a good tunic and cloak, with a pair of sandals for my feet, and sent me off into the country, but she was just as fond of me as ever. This is all over now. Still it has pleased heaven to prosper my work in the situation which I now hold. I have enough to eat and drink, and can find something for any respectable stranger who comes here; but there is no getting a kind word or deed out of my mistress, for the house has fallen into the hands of wicked people. Servants want sometimes to see their mistress and have a talk with her; they like to have something to eat and drink at the house, and something too to take back with them into the country. This is what will keep servants in a good humour."

Odysseus answered, "Then you must have been a very little fellow, Eumaeus, when you were taken so far away from your home and parents. Tell me, and tell me true, was the city in which your father and mother lived sacked and pillaged, or did some enemies carry you off when you were alone tending sheep or cattle, ship you here, and sell you for whatever your master gave them?"

"Stranger," replied Eumaeus, "as regards your question: sit still, make yourself comfortable, drink your wine, and listen to me. The nights are now at their longest; there is plenty of time both for sleeping and for sitting up talking together; you ought not to go to bed till bedtime; too much sleep is as bad as too little; if any one of the others wishes to go to bed let him leave us and do so; he can then take my master's pigs out when he has done breakfast in the morning. We two will sit here eating and drinking in the hut, and telling one another stories about our misfortunes; for when a man has suffered much, and been buffeted about in the world, he takes pleasure in recalling the memory of sorrows that have long gone by. As regards your question, then, my tale is as follows:

"You may have heard of an island called Syria that lies over above Ortygia, where is the turning point of the sun. It is not very thickly peopled, but the soil is good, with much pasture fit for cattle and sheep, and it abounds with wine and wheat. Famine never comes there, nor are the people plagued by any sickness, but when they grow old, Apollo comes with Artemis and kills them with his painless shafts. It contains two communities, and the whole country is divided between these two. My father, Ctesius, son of Ormenus, a man comparable to the gods, reigned over both.

"Now, to this place there came some cunning traders from Phoenicia (for the Phoenicians are great mariners) in a ship which they had filled with cheap wares of all kinds. There happened to be a Phoenician woman in my father's house, very tall and comely, and an excellent servant; these scoundrels got hold of her one day when she was washing near their ship; one of them seduced her, and lay with her in love, which no woman can resist, no matter how good she may be by nature. The man who had seduced her asked her who she was and where she came from, and on this she told him her father's name. 'I come from Sidon,' said she, 'and am daughter to Arybas, a man rolling in wealth. One day as I was coming into the town from the country, some Taphian pirates seized me and took me here over the sea, where they sold me to the man who owns this house, and he gave them their price for me.'

"The man who had seduced her then said, 'Would you like to come along with us to see the house of your parents and your parents themselves? They are both alive and are said to be well off.'

" 'I will do so gladly,' answered she, 'if you men will first swear me a solemn oath that you will do me no harm by the way.'

"They all swore as she told them, and when they had completed their oath the woman said, 'Hush; and if any of your men meets me in the street or at the well, do not let him speak to me, for fear someone should go and tell my master, in which case he would suspect something. He would put me in prison, and would have all of you killed; keep your own counsel, therefore; buy your merchandise as fast as you can, and send me word when you have done loading. I will bring as much gold as I can lay my hands on, and there is something else also that I can do towards paying my fare. I am nurse to the son of the good man of the house, a funny little fellow just able to run about. I will carry him off to your ship, and you will get a great deal of money for him if you take him and sell him in foreign parts.'

"On this, she went back to the house. The Phoenicians stayed a whole year till they had loaded their ship with much precious merchandise, and then, when they had got freight enough, they sent to tell the woman. Their messenger, a very cunning fellow, came to my father's house bringing a necklace of gold with amber beads strung among it; and while my mother and the servants had it in their hands, admiring it and bargaining about it, he made a sign quickly to the woman and then went back to the ship, whereon she took me by the hand and led me out of the house. In the forepart of the house she saw the tables set with the cups of guests who had been feasting with my father, as being in attendance on him; these were now all gone to a meeting of the public assembly, so she snatched up three cups and carried them off in the bosom of her dress, while I followed her, for I knew no better. The sun was now set, and darkness was over all the land, so we hurried on as fast as we could till we reached the harbour, where the Phoenician ship was lying. When they had got on board, they sailed over the sea, taking us with them, and Zeus sent them a fair wind; six days did we sail both night and day, but on the seventh day Artemis struck the woman and she fell heavily down into the ship's hold as though she were a sea gull diving into the water; so they threw her overboard to the seals and fishes, and I was left all sorrowful and alone. Presently the winds and waves took the ship to Ithaca, where Laertes bought me with his possessions, and thus it was that ever I came to set eyes upon this country."

Odysseus answered, "Eumaeus, I have heard the story of your misfortunes with the most lively interest and pity, but Zeus has given you good as well as evil, for in spite of everything you have a good master, who sees that you always have enough to eat and drink; and you lead a good life, whereas I am still going about begging my way from city to city."

Thus did they converse, and they had only a very little time left for sleep, for it was soon daybreak. In the meantime Telemachus and his crew were nearing land, so they loosed the sails, took down the mast, and rowed the ship into the harbour. They cast out their mooring stones and made fast the hawsers; they then got out upon the seashore, mixed their wine, and got dinner ready. As soon as they had had enough to eat and drink, Telemachus said, "Take the ship on to the town, but leave me here, for I want to look after the herdsmen on one of my farms. In the evening, when I have seen all I want, I will come down to the city, and tomorrow morning in return for your trouble I will give you all a good dinner with meat and wine."

Then Theoclymenus said, 'And what, my dear young friend, is to become of me? To whose house, among all your chief men, am I to repair? Or shall I go straight to your own home and to your mother?"

"At any other time," replied Telemachus, "I should have bidden you go to my own house, for you would find no want of hospitality; at the present moment, however, you would not be comfortable there, for I shall be away, and my mother will not see you; she does not often show herself even to the suitors, but sits at her loom weaving in an upper chamber, out of their way; but I can tell you a man whose house you can go to. I mean Eurymachus, the son of Polybus, who is held in the highest estimation by everyone in Ithaca. He is much the best man and the most persistent wooer, of all those who are paying court to my mother and trying to take Odysseus' place. Zeus, however, in heaven alone knows whether or no they will come to a bad end before the marriage takes place."

As he was speaking, a bird flew by upon his right hand—a hawk, Apollo's messenger. It held a dove in its talons, and the feathers, as it tore them off, fell to the ground midway between Telemachus and the ship. On this Theoclymenus called him apart and caught him by the hand. "Telemachus," said he, "that bird did not fly on your right hand without having been sent there by some god. As soon as I saw it I knew it was an omen; it means that you will remain powerful, and that there will be no house in Ithaca more royal than your own."

"I wish it may prove so," answered Telemachus. "If it does, I will show you so much good will and give you so many presents that all who meet you will congratulate you."

Then he said to his friend Piraeus, "Piraeus, son of Clytius, you have throughout shown yourself the most willing to serve me of all those who have accompanied me to Pylos; I wish you would take this stranger to your own house and entertain him hospitably till I can come for him."

And Piraeus answered, "Telemachus, you may stay away as long as you please, but I will look after him for you, and he shall find no lack of hospitality."

As he spoke he went on board, and bade the others do so also and loose the hawsers, so they took their places in the ship. But Telemachus bound on his sandals, and took a long and doughty spear with a head of sharpened bronze from the deck of the ship. Then they loosed the hawsers, thrust the ship off from land, and made on towards the city as they had been told to do, while Telemachus strode on as fast as he could, till he reached the homestead where his countless herds of swine were feeding, and where dwelt the excellent swineherd who was so devoted a servant to his master.

BOOK XVI

❀

Odysseus Reveals Himself to Telemachus

MEANWHILE ODYSSEUS and the swineherd had lit a fire in the hut and were getting breakfast ready at daybreak, for they had sent the men out with the pigs. When Telemachus came up, the dogs did not bark but fawned upon him, so Odysseus, hearing the sound of feet and noticing that the dogs did not bark, said to Eumaeus:

"Eumaeus, I hear footsteps; I suppose one of your men or someone of your acquaintance is coming here, for the dogs are fawning upon him and not barking."

The words were hardly out of his mouth before his son stood at the door. Eumaeus sprang to his feet, and the bowls in which he was mixing wine fell from his hands, as he made towards his master. He kissed his head and both his eyes, and wept for joy. A father could not be more delighted at the return of an only son, the child of his old age, after ten years' absence in a foreign country, for whom he has suffered much anxiety. He embraced him, kissed him all over as though he had come back from the dead, and spoke fondly to him, saying:

"So you are come, Telemachus, light of my eyes that you are. When I heard you had gone to Pylos I was sure I was never going to see you any more. Come in, my dear child, and sit down, that I may have a good look at you now you are home again; it is not very often you come into the country to see us herdsmen; you stick pretty close to the town generally. I suppose you think it better to keep an eye on what the suitors are doing."

"So be it, old friend," answered Telemachus, "but I am come now because I want to see you, and to learn whether my mother is still at her old home or whether someone else has married her, so that the bed of Odysseus is without bedding and covered with cobwebs."

"She is still at the house," replied Eumaeus, "grieving and breaking her heart, and doing nothing but weep, both night and day continually."

As he spoke, he took Telemachus' spear, whereon he crossed the stone threshold and came inside. Odysseus rose from his seat to give him place as he entered, but Telemachus checked him. "Sit down, stranger," said he. "I can easily find another seat, and there is one here who will lay it for me."

Odysseus went back to his own place, and Eumaeus strewed some green brushwood on the floor and threw a sheepskin on top of it for Telemachus to sit upon. Then the swineherd brought them platters of cold meat, the remains from what they had eaten the day before, and he filled the bread baskets with bread as fast as he could. He mixed wine also in a bowl of ivy wood, and took his seat facing Odysseus. Then they laid their hands on the good things that were before them, and as soon as they had had enough to eat and drink, Telemachus said to Eumaeus, "Old friend, where does this stranger come from? How did his crew bring him to Ithaca, and who were they? For assuredly he did not come here by land."

To this the swineherd Eumaeus answered, "My son, I will tell you the real truth. He says he is a Cretan, and that he has been a great traveller. At this moment he is running away from a Thesprotian ship, and has taken refuge at my steading, so I will put him into your hands. Do whatever you like with him, only remember that he is your suppliant."

"I am very much distressed," said Telemachus, "by what

you have just told me. How can I take this stranger into my house? I am as yet young, and am not strong enough to hold my own if any man attacks me. My mother cannot make up her mind whether to stay where she is and look after the house out of respect for public opinion and the memory of her husband, or whether the time is now come for her to take the best man of those who are wooing her, and the one who will make her the most advantageous offer; still, as the stranger has come to your house, I will find him a cloak and tunic of good wear, with a sword and sandals, and will send him wherever he wants to go. Or if you like, you can keep him here at the steading, and I will send him clothes and food, that he may be no burden on you and on your men; but I will not have him go near the suitors, for they are very insolent, and are sure to ill-treat him in a way that would greatly grieve me; no matter how valiant a man may be, he can do nothing against numbers, for they will be too strong for him."

Then Odysseus said, "Sir, it is right that I should say something myself. I am much shocked by what you have said about the insolent way in which the suitors are behaving in despite of such a man as you are. Tell me, do you submit to such treatment tamely, or has some god set your people against you? Have you reason to complain of your brothers? For it is to these that a man may look for support, however great his quarrel may be. I wish I were as young as you are and in my present mind; if I were the son of Odysseus or, indeed, if Odysseus himself came as a beggar—for there is still some hope of his return—if it were so, a stranger could cut off my head if I did not go to the house and attack every one of these men. If they were too many for me—I being single-handed— I would rather die fighting in my own house than see such disgraceful sights day after day—strangers grossly maltreated, and men dragging the women servants about the house in an unseemly way, wine drawn recklessly, and bread wasted, all to no purpose for an end that shall never be accomplished."

And Telemachus answered, "I will tell you truly every-thing. There is no enmity between me and my people, nor can I complain of brothers, to whom a man may look for sup-port however great his quarrel may be. Zeus has made us a race of only sons. Laertes was the only son of Arceisius, and Odysseus the only son of Laertes. I am myself the only son of Odysseus, who left me behind him when he went away, so that I have never been of any use to him. Hence it comes that my house is in the hands of numberless marauders; for the chiefs from all the neighbouring islands—Dulichium, Same, Zacynthus—as also all the principal men of Ithaca itself, are eating up my house under the pretext of paying court to my mother, who will neither say point-blank that she will not marry, nor yet bring matters to an end, so they are making havoc of my estate, and before long will do so with myself into the bargain. The issue, however, rests with heaven. But do you, old friend Eumaeus, go at once and tell Penelope that I am safe and have returned from Pylos. Tell it to herself alone, and then come back here without letting anyone else know, for there are many who are plotting mischief against me."

"I understand and heed you," replied Eumaeus. "You need instruct me no further, only as I am going that way, say whether I had not better let poor Laertes know that you are returned. He used to superintend the work on his farm in spite of his bitter sorrow about Odysseus, and he would eat and drink at will along with his servants; but they tell me that from the day on which you set out for Pylos he has neither eaten nor drunk as he ought to do, nor does he look after his farm, but sits weeping and wasting the flesh from off his bones."

"More's the pity," answered Telemachus. "I am sorry for him, but we must leave him to himself just now. If people could have everything their own way, the first thing I should choose would be the return of my father; but go, and give your message; then make haste back again, and do not turn out of your way to tell Laertes. Tell my mother to send one of her women secretly with the news at once, and let him hear it from her."

Thus did he urge the swineherd; Eumaeus, therefore, took his sandals, bound them to his feet, and started for the town. Athene watched him well off the steading, and then came up to it in the form of a woman, fair, stately, and wise. She stood against the side of the entry, and revealed herself to Odysseus, but Telemachus could not see her, and knew not that she was there, for the gods do not let themselves be seen by everybody. Odysseus saw her, and so did the dogs, for they did not bark, but went scared and whining off to the other side of the yard. She nodded her head and motioned to Odysseus with her eyebrows; whereon he left the hut and stood before her outside the main wall of the yard. Then she said to him:

"Odysseus, noble son of Laertes, it is now time for you to tell your son: do not keep him in the dark any longer, but lay your plans for the destruction of the suitors, and then make for the town. I will not be long in joining you, for I too am eager for the fray."

As she spoke, she touched him with her golden wand. First she threw a fair clean tunic and cloak about his shoulders; then she made him younger and of more imposing presence; she gave him back his colour, filled out his cheeks, and let his beard become dark again. Then she went away and Odysseus came back inside the hut. His son was astounded when he saw him, and turned his eyes away for fear he might be looking upon a god.

"Stranger," said he, "how suddenly you have changed from what you were a moment or two ago. You are dressed differently and your colour is not the same. Are you some one or other of the gods that live in heaven? If so, be propitious to me till I can make you due sacrifice and offerings of wrought gold. Have mercy upon me."

And Odysseus said, "I am no god; why should you take

me for one? I am your father, on whose account you grieve and suffer so much at the hands of lawless men."

As he spoke, he kissed his son, and a tear fell from his cheek onto the ground, for he had restrained all tears till now. But Telemachus could not yet believe that it was his father, and said:

"You are not my father, but some god is flattering me with vain hopes that I may grieve the more hereafter; no mortal man could of himself contrive to do as you have been doing, and make yourself old and young at a moment's notice, unless a god were with him. A second ago you were old and all in rags, and now you are like some god come down from heaven."

Odysseus answered, "Telemachus, you ought not to be too astonished at my being really here. There is no other Odysseus who will come hereafter. Such as I am, it is I, who after long wandering and much hardship have got home in the twentieth year to my own country. What you wonder at is the work of the redoubtable goddess Athene, who does with me whatever she will, for she can do what she pleases. At one moment she makes me like a beggar, and the next I am a young man with good clothes on my back; it is an easy matter for the gods who live in heaven to make any man look either rich or poor."

As he spoke, he sat down, and Telemachus threw his arms about his father and wept. They were both so much moved that they cried aloud like eagles or vultures with crooked talons that have been robbed of their half-fledged young by peasants. Thus piteously did they weep, and the sun would have gone down upon their lamenting if Telemachus had not suddenly said, "In what ship, my dear father, did your crew bring you to Ithaca? Of what nation did they declare themselves to be? For you cannot have come by land."

"I will tell you the truth, my son," replied Odysseus. "It was the Phaeacians who brought me here. They are great sailors, and are in the habit of giving escorts to anyone who reaches their coasts. They took me over the sea while I was fast asleep, and landed me in Ithaca, after giving me many presents in bronze, gold, and clothing. These things by heaven's mercy are lying concealed in a cave, and I am now come here on the suggestion of Athene, that we may consult about killing our enemies. First, therefore, give me a list of the suitors, with their number, that I may learn who, and how many, they are. I can then turn the matter over in my mind, and see whether we two can fight the whole body of them ourselves, or whether we must find others to help us."

To this Telemachus answered, "Father, I have always heard of your renown both in the field and in council, but the task you talk of is a very great one; I am awed at the mere thought of it; two men cannot stand against many and brave ones. There are not ten suitors only, nor twice ten, but ten many times over; you shall learn their number at once. There are fifty-two chosen youths from Dulichium, and they have six servants; from Same there are twenty-four; twenty young Achaeans from Zacynthus, and twelve from Ithaca itself, all of them well-born. They have with them a servant, Medon, a bard, and two men who can carve at table. If we face such numbers as this, you may have bitter cause to regret your coming, and your revenge. See whether you cannot think of someone who would be willing to come and help us."

"Listen to me," replied Odysseus, "and think whether Athene and her father, Zeus, may seem sufficient, or whether I am to try and find someone else as well."

"Those whom you have named," answered Telemachus, "are a couple of good allies, for though they dwell high up among the clouds they have power over both gods and men."

"These two," continued Odysseus, "will not keep long out of the fray, when the suitors and we join fight in my house. Now, therefore, return home early tomorrow morning, and go about among the suitors as before. Later on the swineherd will bring me to the city disguised as a miserable old beggar. If you see them ill-treating me, steel your heart against my sufferings; even though they drag me feet foremost out of the house, or throw things at me, look on and do nothing, beyond gently trying to make them behave more reasonably; but they will not listen to you, for the day of their reckoning is at hand. Furthermore I say, and you remember my words: when Athene shall put it in my mind, I will nod my head to you, and on seeing me do this, you must collect all the armour that is in the house and hide it in the strong storeroom. Make some excuse when the suitors ask you why you are removing it; say that you have taken it to be out of the way of the smoke, as it is no longer what it was when Odysseus went away, but has become soiled and begrimed with soot. Add to this more particularly that you are afraid Zeus may set them on to quarrel over their wine, and that they may do each other some harm which may disgrace both banquet and wooing, for the sight of arms sometimes tempts people to use them. But leave a sword and a spear apiece for yourself and me, and a couple of oxhide shields, so that we can snatch them up at any moment; Zeus and Athene will then soon bewitch these people. There is also another matter: if you are indeed my son and my blood runs in your veins, let no one know that Odysseus is within the house—neither Laertes, nor yet the swineherd, nor any of the servants, nor even Penelope herself. Let you and me test the women alone, and let us also make trial of some other of the menservants, to see who is on our side and whose hand is against us."

"Father," replied Telemachus, "you will come to know me by and by, and when you do you will find that I can keep your counsel. I do not think, however, the plan you propose will turn out well for either of us. Think it over. It will take us a long time to go the round of the farms and make trial of the men, and all the time the suitors will be wasting your estate with impunity and without compunction. Test the women by all means, to see who are disloyal and who innocent, but I am not in favour of going round and trying the men. We can attend to that later on, if you really have some sign from Zeus that he will support you."

Thus did they converse, and meanwhile the ship which had brought Telemachus and his crew from Pylos had reached the town of Ithaca. When they had come inside the harbour they drew the ship onto the land; their servants came and took their armour from them, and they left all the presents at the house of Clytius. Then they sent a servant to tell Penelope that Telemachus had gone into the country, but had sent the ship to the town to prevent her from being alarmed and made unhappy. This servant and Eumaeus happened to meet when they were both on the same errand of going to tell Penelope. When they reached the house, the servant stood up and said to the queen in the presence of the waiting women, "Your son, Madam, is now returned from Pylos"; but Eumaeus went close up to Penelope, and said privately all that her son had bidden him tell her. When he had given his message, he left the house with its outbuildings and went back to his pigs again.

The suitors were surprised and angry at what had happened, so they went outside the great wall that ran round the outer court, and held a council near the main entrance. Eurymachus, son of Polybus, was the first to speak.

"My friends," said he, "this voyage of Telemachus' is a very serious matter; we were sure that it would come to nothing. Now, however, let us draw a ship into the water, and get a crew together to send after the others and tell them to come back as fast as they can."

He had hardly done speaking when Amphinomus turned in his place and saw the ship inside the harbour, with the crew lowering her sails, and putting by their oars; so he laughed, and said to the others, "We need not send them any message, for they are here. Some god must have told them, or else they saw the ship go by, and could not overtake her."

On this, they rose and went to the waterside. The crew then drew the ship on shore; their servants took their armour from them, and they went up in a body to the place of assembly, but they would not let anyone old or young sit along with them, and Antinous, son of Eupeithes, spoke first.

"See how the gods have saved this man from destruction. We kept a succession of lookouts upon the headlands all day long, and when the sun was down we never went on shore to sleep, but waited in the ship all night till morning in the hope of capturing and killing him; but some god has convoyed him home in spite of us. Let us consider how we can make an end of him. He must not escape us; our affair is never likely to come off while he is alive, for he is very shrewd, and public feeling is by no means all on our side. We must make haste before he can call the Achaeans to assembly; he will lose no time in doing so, for he will be furious with us, and will tell all the world how we plotted to kill him, but failed to take him. The people will not like this when they come to know of it; we must see that they do us no hurt, nor drive us from our own country into exile. Let us try and lay hold of him either on his farm away from the town, or on his road here. Then we can divide up his property amongst us, and let his mother and the man who marries her have the house. If this does not please you, and you wish Telemachus to live on and hold his father's property, then we must not gather here and eat up his goods in this way, but must make our offers to Penelope each from his own house, and she can marry the man who will give the most for her, and whose lot it is to win her."

They all held their peace until Amphinomus rose to speak. He was the son of Nisus, who was son to King Aretias, and he was foremost among all the suitors from the wheat-growing and well-grassed island of Dulichium; his conversation, moreover, was more agreeable to Penelope than that of any of the other suitors, for he was a man of good natural disposition. "My friends," said he, speaking to them plainly and in all honesty, "I am not in favour of killing Telemachus. It is a heinous thing to kill one who is of noble blood. Let us first take counsel of the gods, and if the oracles of Zeus advise it, I will both help to kill him myself, and will urge everyone else to do so; but if they dissuade us, I would have you hold your hands."

Thus did he speak, and his words pleased them well, so they rose forthwith and went to the house of Odysseus, where they took their accustomed seats.

Then Penelope resolved that she would show herself to the suitors. She knew of the plot against Telemachus, for the servant Medon had overheard their counsels and had told her; she went down, therefore, to the court, attended by her maidens, and when she reached the suitors she stood by one of the pillars supporting the roof of the hall, holding a veil before her face, and rebuked Antinous, saying:

"Antinous, insolent and wicked schemer, they say you are the best speaker and councillor of any man your own age in Ithaca, but you are nothing of the kind. Madman, why should you try to compass the death of Telemachus, and take no heed of suppliants, whose witness is Zeus himself. It is not right for you to plot thus against one another. Do you not remember how your father fled to this house in fear of the people, who were enraged against him for having gone with some Taphian pirates and plundered the Thesprotians, who were at peace with us? They wanted to tear him in pieces and eat up everything he had, but Odysseus stayed their hands although they were infuriated, and now you devour his property without paying for it, and break my heart by wooing his wife and trying to kill his son. Leave off doing so, and stop the others also."

To this Eurymachus, son of Polybus, answered, "Take heart, Queen Penelope, daughter of Icarius, and do not trouble yourself about these matters. The man is not yet born, nor ever will be, who shall lay hands upon your son, Telemachus, while I yet live to look upon the face of the earth. I say—and it shall surely be—that my spear shall be reddened with his blood; for many a time has Odysseus taken me on his knees, held wine up to my lips to drink, and put pieces of meat into my hands. Therefore Telemachus is much the dearest friend I have, and has nothing to fear from the hands of us suitors. Of course, if death comes to him from the gods, he cannot escape it." He said this to quiet her, but in reality he was plotting against Telemachus.

Then Penelope went upstairs again and mourned her husband till Athene shed sleep over her eyes. In the evening Eumaeus got back to Odysseus and his son, who had just sacrificed a young pig of a year old and were helping one another to get supper ready; Athene therefore came up to Odysseus, turned him into an old man with a stroke of her wand, and clad him in his old clothes again, for fear that the swineherd might recognise him and not keep the secret, but go and tell Penelope.

Telemachus was the first to speak. "So you have got back, Eumaeus," said he. "What is the news of the town? Have the suitors returned, or are they still waiting for me on my way home?"

"I did not think of asking about that," replied Eumaeus, "when I was in the town. I thought I would give my message and come back as soon as I could. I met a man sent by those who had gone with you to Pylos, and he was the first to tell the news to your mother, but I can say what I saw with my own eyes; I had just got onto the crest of the hill of Hermes above the town when I saw a ship coming into harbour with a number of men in her. They had many shields and spears, and I thought it was the suitors, but I cannot be sure."

On hearing this, Telemachus smiled to his father, but so that Eumaeus could not see him.

Then, when they had finished their work and the meal was ready, they ate it, and every man had his full share so that all were satisfied. As soon as they had had enough to eat and drink, they laid down to rest and were soon asleep.

BOOK XVII

❧

*Telemachus and His Mother Meet—Odysseus and
Eumaeus Come Down to the Town, and Odysseus Is
Insulted by Melanthius—He Is Recognised by the
Dog Argus—He Is Insulted and Presently Struck by
Antinous with a Stool—Penelope Desires that He
Shall Be Sent to Her*

WHEN THE child of morning, rosy-fingered Dawn, appeared, Telemachus bound on his sandals and took a strong
spear that suited his hands, for he wanted to go into the city.
"Old friend," said he to the swineherd, "I will now go to the
town and show myself to my mother, for she will never leave
off weeping till she has seen me. As for this unfortunate
stranger, take him to the town and let him beg there of anyone who will give him a drink and a piece of bread. I have
trouble enough of my own, and cannot be burdened with
other people. If this makes him angry, so much the worse for
him, but I like to say what I mean."

Then Odysseus said, "Sir, I do not want to stay here; a
beggar can always do better in town than in the country, for
anyone who likes can give him something. I am too old to
care about remaining here at the beck and call of a master.
Therefore let this man do as you have just told him, and take
me to the town as soon as I have had a warm by the fire, and
the day has got a little heat in it. My clothes are wretchedly
thin, and this frosty morning I shall be perished with cold,
for you say the city is some way off."

On this, Telemachus strode off through the yard, brooding his revenge upon the suitors. When he reached home, he stood his spear against a pillar threshold, crossed the stone, and went inside.

Nurse Eurycleia saw him long before anyone else did. She was putting the fleeces onto the seats, and she burst out crying as she ran up to him; all the other maids came up too, and covered his head and shoulders with their kisses. Penelope came out of her room looking like Artemis or Aphrodite, and wept as she flung her arms about her son. She kissed his forehead and both his eyes. "Light of my eyes," she cried as she spoke fondly to him, "so you are come home again; I thought I was never going to see you any more. To think of your having gone off to Pylos without saying anything about it or obtaining my consent, to seek news of your father. But come, tell what you saw."

"Do not scold me, Mother," answered Telemachus, "nor vex me, seeing what a narrow escape I have had, but wash your face, change your dress, go upstairs with your maids, and promise full and sufficient hecatombs to all the gods if Zeus will only grant us our revenge upon the suitors. I must now go to the place of assembly to invite a stranger who has come back with me from Pylos. I sent him on with my crew, and told Piraeus to take him home and look after him till I could come for him myself."

She heeded her son's words, washed her face, changed her dress, and vowed full and sufficient hecatombs to all the gods if they would only vouchsafe her revenge upon the suitors.

Telemachus went through, and out of, the hall, spear in hand—not alone, for his two fleet dogs went with him. Athene endowed him with a presence of such divine comeliness that all marvelled at him as he went by, and the suitors gathered round him with fair words in their mouths and malice in their hearts; but he avoided them, and went to sit with Mentor, Antiphus, and Halitherses, old friends of his father's house, and they made him tell them all that had happened to him. Then Piraeus came up with Theoclymenus, whom he had escorted through the town to the place of assembly, whereon Telemachus at once joined them. Piraeus was first to speak. "Telemachus," said he, "I wish you would send some of your women to my house to take away the presents Menelaus gave you."

"We do not know, Piraeus," answered Telemachus, "what may happen. If the suitors kill me in my own house and divide my property among them, I would rather you had the presents than that any of those people should get hold of them. If on the other hand I manage to kill them, I shall be much obliged if you will kindly bring me my presents."

With these words, he took Theoclymenus to his own house. When they got there they laid their cloaks on the benches and seats, went into the baths, and washed themselves. When the maids had washed and anointed them, and had given them cloaks and tunics, they took their seats at table. A maidservant then brought them water in a beautiful golden ewer, and poured it over a silver basin for them to wash their hands; and she drew a clean table beside them. A housekeeper brought them bread and offered them many good things of what there was in the house. Opposite them sat Penelope, reclining on a couch by one of the pillars of the hall, and spinning. Then they laid their hands on the good things that were before them, and as soon as they had had enough to eat and drink, Penelope said:

"Telemachus, I shall go upstairs and lie down on that sad couch which I have not ceased to water with my tears, from the day Odysseus set out for Troy with the sons of Atreus. You failed, however, to make it clear to me, before the suitors came back to the house, whether or no you had been able to hear anything about the return of your father."

"I will tell you the truth," replied her son. "We went to Pylos and saw Nestor, who took me to his house and treated me as hospitably as though I were a son of his own who had just returned after a long absence; his sons were equally friendly; but he said he had not heard a word from any human being about Odysseus, whether he was alive or dead. He sent me, therefore, with a chariot and horses to Menelaus. There I saw Helen, for whose sake so many, both Argives and Trojans, were in heaven's wisdom doomed to suffer. Menelaus asked me what it was that had brought me to Lacedaemon, and I told him the whole truth, whereon he said, 'So then, these cowards would usurp a brave man's bed? A hind might as well lay her newborn young in the lair of a lion, and then go off to feed in the forest or in some grassy dell. The lion, when he comes back to his lair, will make short work of them, and so will Odysseus with these suitors. By Father Zeus, Athene, and Apollo, if Odysseus is still the man that he was when he wrestled with Philomeleides in Lesbos, and threw him so heavily that all the Greeks cheered him—if he is still such, and were to come near these suitors, they would have a short shrift and a sorry wedding. As regards your question, however, I will not prevaricate nor deceive you, but what the old man of the sea told me, so much I will tell you in full. He said he could see Odysseus on an island sorrowing bitterly in the house of the nymph Calypso, who was keeping him prisoner, and he could not reach his home, for he had no ships nor sailors to take him over the sea.' This was what Menelaus told me, and when I had heard his story I came away; the gods then gave me a fair wind and soon brought me safe home again."

With these words he moved the heart of Penelope. Then Theoclymenus said to her:

"Madam, wife of Odysseus, Telemachus does not understand these things; listen therefore to me, for I can divine them surely, and will hide nothing from you. May Zeus, the king of heaven, be my witness, and the rites of hospitality, with that hearth of Odysseus to which I now come, that Odysseus himself is even now in Ithaca, and either going about the country, or staying in one place, is enquiring into all these evil deeds and preparing a day of reckoning for the suitors. I saw an omen when I was on the ship which meant this, and I told Telemachus about it."

"May it be even so," answered Penelope. "If your words come true, you shall have such gifts and such good will from me that all who see you shall congratulate you."

Thus did they converse. Meanwhile the suitors were throwing the discus, or aiming with spears at a mark on the levelled ground in front of the house, and behaving with all their old insolence. But when it was now time for dinner, and the flocks of sheep and goats had come into the town from all the country round with their shepherds, as usual, then Medon, who was their favourite servant, and who waited upon them at table, said, "Now then, my young masters, you have had enough sport, so come inside that we may get dinner ready. Dinner is not a bad thing, at dinnertime."

They left their sports as he told them, and when they were within the house, they laid their cloaks on the benches and seats inside, and then sacrificed some sheep, goats, pigs, and a heifer, all of them fat and well-grown. Thus they made ready for their meal. In the meantime Odysseus and the swineherd were about starting for the town, and the swineherd said, "Stranger, I suppose you still want to go to town today, as my master said you were to do; for my own part I should have liked you to stay here to look after the steading, but I must do as my master tells me, or he will scold me later on, and a scolding from one's master is a very serious thing. Let us then be off, for it is now broad day; it will be night again directly and then you will find it colder."

"I know, and understand you," replied Odysseus. "You need say no more. Let us be going, but if you have a stick ready cut, let me have it to walk with, for you say the road is a very rough one."

As he spoke he put his shabby old tattered wallet over his

shoulders, by the cord from which it hung, and Eumaeus gave him a stick to his liking. The two then started, leaving the steading in charge of the dogs and herdsmen who remained behind; the swineherd led the way and his master followed after, looking like some broken-down old tramp as he leaned upon his staff, and his clothes were all in rags. When they had got over the rough, steep ground and were nearing the city, they reached the fountain from which the citizens drew their water. This had been made by Ithacus, Neritus, and Polyctor. There was a grove of water-loving poplars planted in a circle all round it, and the clear, cold water came down to it from a rock high up, while above the fountain there was an altar to the nymphs, at which all wayfarers used to sacrifice. Here Melanthius, son of Dolius, overtook them as he was driving down some goats, the best in his flock, for the suitors' dinner, and there were two herdsmen with him. When he saw Eumaeus and Odysseus he reviled them with outrageous and unseemly language, which made Odysseus very angry.

"There you go," cried he, "and a precious pair you are. See how heaven brings birds of the same feather to one another. Where, pray, master swineherd, are you taking this poor miserable object? It would make anyone sick to see such a creature at table. A fellow like this never won a prize for anything in his life, but will go about rubbing his shoulders against every man's doorpost, and begging, not for swords and cauldrons, but for a few scraps of food. If you would give him to me for a hand on my steading, he might do to clean out the folds, or bring a bit of sweet feed to the kids, and he could fatten his thighs as much as he pleased on whey; but he has taken to bad ways and will not go about any kind of work; he will do nothing but beg victuals all the town over, to feed his insatiable belly. I say, therefore—and it shall be—if he goes near Odysseus' house he will get his head broken by the stools they will fling at him, till they turn him out."

On this, as he passed, he gave Odysseus a kick on the hip

out of pure wantonness, but Odysseus stood firm, and did not budge from the path. For a moment he wondered whether or not to fly at Melanthius and kill him with his staff, or fling him to the ground and beat his brains out; he resolved, however, to endure it and kept himself in check, but the swineherd looked straight at Melanthius and rebuked him, lifting up his hands and praying to heaven as he did so.

"Fountain nymphs," he cried, "children of Zeus, if ever Odysseus burned you thighbones covered with fat, whether of lambs or kids, grant my prayer that heaven may send him home. He would soon put an end to the swaggering threats with which such men as you go about insulting people— gadding all over the town while your flocks are going to ruin through bad shepherding."

Then Melanthius, the goatherd, answered, "You miserable cur, what are you talking about? Some day or other I will put you on board ship and take you to a foreign country, where I can sell you and pocket the money you will fetch. I wish I were as sure that Apollo would strike Telemachus dead this very day, or that the suitors would kill him, as I am that Odysseus will never come home again."

With this he left them to come on at their leisure, while he went quickly forward and soon reached the house of his master. When he got there he went in and took his seat among the suitors opposite Eurymachus, who liked him better than any of the others. The servants brought him a portion of meat, and a housekeeper set bread before him, that he might eat. Presently Odysseus and the swineherd came up to the house and stood by it, amid a sound of music, for Phemius was just beginning to sing to the suitors. Then Odysseus took hold of the swineherd's hand and said:

"Eumaeus, this house of Odysseus is a very fine place. No matter how far you go, you will find few like it. One building keeps following on after another. The outer court has a wall with battlements all round it; the doors are double-folding, and of good workmanship; it would be a hard matter to take it by force of arms. I perceive too that there are many people banqueting within it, for there is a smell of roast meat, and I hear a sound of music, which the gods have made to go along with feasting."

Then Eumaeus said, "You have perceived aright, as indeed you generally do; but let us think what will be our best course. Will you go inside first and join the suitors, leaving me here behind you, or will you wait here and let me go in first? But do not wait long, or someone may see you loitering about outside, and throw something at you. Consider this matter, I pray you."

And Odysseus answered, "I understand and heed. Go in first and leave me here where I am. I am quite used to being beaten and having things thrown at me. I have been so much buffeted about in war and by sea that I am case-hardened, and this too may go with the rest. But a man cannot hide away the cravings of a hungry belly; this is an enemy which gives much trouble to all men; it is because of this that ships are fitted out to sail the seas, and to make war upon other people."

As they were thus talking, a dog that had been lying asleep raised his head and pricked up his ears. This was Argus, whom Odysseus had bred before setting out for Troy, but he had never had any work out of him. In the old days he used to be taken out by the young men when they went hunting wild goats, or deer, or hares, but now, his master being gone, he was lying neglected on the heaps of mule and cow dung that lay in front of the stable doors till the men should come and draw it away to manure the great estate; and he was full of fleas. As soon as he saw Odysseus standing there, he dropped his ears and wagged his tail, but he could not get close up to his master. When Odysseus saw the dog on the other side of the yard, he dashed a tear from his eyes without Eumaeus seeing it, and said:

"Eumaeus, what a noble hound that is over yonder on the

manure heap; his build is splendid; is he as fine a fellow as he looks, or is he only one of those dogs that come begging about a table, and are kept merely for show?"

"This hound," answered Eumaeus, "belonged to him who has died in a far country. If he were what he was when Odysseus left for Troy, he would soon show you what he could do. There was not a wild beast in the forest that could get away from him when he was once on its tracks. But now he has fallen on evil times, for his master is dead and gone, and the women take no care of him. Servants never do their work when their master's hand is no longer over them, for Zeus takes half the goodness out of a man when he makes a slave of him."

As he spoke, he went inside the buildings to the hall where the suitors were, but Argus died as soon as he had recognised his master after twenty years.

Telemachus saw Eumaeus long before anyone else did, and beckoned him to come and sit beside him; so he looked about and saw a seat lying near where the carver sat serving out their portions to the suitors; he picked it up, brought it to Telemachus' table, and sat down opposite him. Then the servant brought him his portion, and gave him bread from the bread basket.

Immediately afterwards Odysseus came inside, looking like a poor miserable old beggar, leaning on his staff and with his clothes all in rags. He sat down upon the threshold of ashwood just inside the doors, and against a post of cypress wood which the carpenter had skilfully planed, and had made to join truly with rule and line. Telemachus took a whole loaf from the bread basket, with as much meat as he could hold in his two hands, and said to Eumaeus, "Take this to the stranger, and tell him to go the round of the suitors, and beg from them; a beggar must not be shamefaced."

So Eumaeus went up to him and said, "Stranger, Telemachus sends you this, and says you are to go the round of the suitors, begging, for beggars must not be shamefaced."

Odysseus answered, "May King Zeus grant all happiness to Telemachus, and fulfil the desire of his heart."

Then with both hands he took what Telemachus had sent him, and laid it on the dirty old wallet at his feet. He went on eating it while the bard was singing, and had just finished his dinner as he left off. The suitors applauded the bard, whereon Athene went up to Odysseus and prompted him to beg pieces of bread from each one of the suitors, that he might see what kind of people they were, and tell the good from the bad; but come what might, she was not going to save a single one of them. Odysseus, therefore, went on his round, going from left to right, and stretched out his hands to beg as though he were a real beggar. Some of them pitied him, and were curious about him, asking one another who he was and where he came from; whereon the goatherd Melanthius said, "Suitors of my noble mistress, I can tell you something about him, for I have seen him before. The swineherd brought him here, but I know nothing about the man himself, nor where he comes from."

On this, Antinous began to abuse the swineherd. "You precious idiot," he cried, "what have you brought this man to town for? Have we not tramps and beggars enough already to pester us as we sit at meat? Do you think it a small thing that such people gather here to waste your master's property, and must you needs bring this man as well?"

And Eumaeus answered, "Antinous, your birth is good but your words evil. It was no doing of mine that he came here. Who is likely to invite a stranger from a foreign country, unless it be one of those who can do public service as a seer, a healer of hurts, a carpenter, or a bard who can charm us with his singing? Such men are welcome all the world over, but no one is likely to ask a beggar, who will only worry him. You are always harder on Odysseus' servants than any of the other suitors are, and above all on me, but I do not care so long as Telemachus and Penelope are alive and here."

But Telemachus said, "Hush, do not answer him; Antinous has the bitterest tongue of all the suitors, and he makes the others worse."

Then, turning to Antinous, he said, "Antinous, you take as much care of my interests as though I were your son. Why should you want to see this stranger turned out of the house? Heaven forbid; take something and give it to him yourself; I do not grudge it; I bid you take it. Never mind my mother, nor any of the other servants in the house; but I know you will not do what I say, for you are more fond of eating things yourself than of giving them to other people."

"What do you mean, Telemachus," replied Antinous, "by this swaggering talk? If all the suitors were to give him as much as I will, he would not come here again for another three months."

As he spoke, he drew the stool on which he rested his feet from under the table, and made as though he would throw it at Odysseus, but the other suitors all gave him something, and filled his wallet with bread and meat; he was about, therefore, to go back to the threshold and eat what the suitors had given him, but he first went up to Antinous and said:

"Sir, give me something; you are not, surely, the poorest man here; you seem to be a chief, foremost among them all; therefore you should be the better giver, and I will tell far and wide of your bounty. I too was a rich man once, and had a fine house of my own; in those days I gave to many a tramp such as I now am, no matter who he might be or what he wanted. I had any number of servants, and all the other things which people have who live well and are accounted wealthy, but it pleased Zeus to take all away from me. He sent me with a band of roving robbers to Egypt; it was a long voyage and I was undone by it. I stationed my ships in the river Aegyptus, and bade my men stay by them and keep guard over them, while I sent out scouts to reconnoitre from every point of vantage.

"But the men disobeyed my orders, followed their own

desires, and ravaged the land of the Egyptians, killing the men, and taking their wives and children captives. The alarm was soon carried to the city, and when they heard the war cry, the people came out at daybreak till the plain was filled with soldiers, horse and foot, and with the gleam of armour. Then Zeus spread panic among my men, and they would not fight the enemy, for they found themselves surrounded. The Egyptians killed many of us, and took the rest alive to do forced labour for them; as for myself, they gave me to a friend who met them, to take to Cyprus, Dmetor by name, son of Iasus, who was a great man in Cyprus. Thence I am come hither in a state of great misery."

Then Antinous said, "What god can have sent such a pestilence to plague us during our dinner? Get away from my table, into the middle of the hall, or I will give you Egypt and Cyprus over again for your insolence and importunity; you have begged of all the others, and they have given you lavishly, for they have abundance round them, and it is easy to be free with other people's property when there is plenty of it."

On this, Odysseus began to move off, and said, "Your looks, my fine sir, are better than your breeding; if you were in your own house you would not spare a poor man so much as a pinch of salt, for though you are in another man's, and surrounded with abundance, you cannot find it in you to give him even a piece of bread."

This made Antinous very angry, and he scowled at him, saying, "You shall pay for this before you get clear of the hall." With these words, he threw a footstool at him, and hit him on the right shoulder blade near the top of his back. Odysseus stood firm as a rock and the blow did not even stagger him, but he shook his head in silence as he brooded on his revenge. Then he went back to the threshold and sat down there, laying his well-filled wallet at his feet.

"Listen to me," he cried, "you suitors of Queen Penelope, that I may speak as I am minded. A man knows neither ache nor pain if he gets hit while fighting for his money, or for his sheep or his cattle; but Antinous has hit me while in the service of my miserable belly, which is always getting people into trouble. Still, if the poor have gods and avenging deities at all, I pray them that Antinous may come to a bad end before his marriage."

"Sit where you are, and eat your victuals in silence, or be off elsewhere," shouted Antinous. "If you say more I will have you dragged hand and foot through the courts, and the skin will be stripped from your body."

The other suitors were much displeased at this, and one of the young men said, "Antinous, you did ill in striking that poor wretch of a tramp; it will be worse for you if he should turn out to be some god—and we know the gods go about disguised in all sorts of ways as people from foreign countries, and travel about the world to see who do amiss and who righteously."

Thus said the suitors, but Antinous paid them no heed. Meanwhile Telemachus was furious about the blow that had been given to his father, and though no tear fell from him, he shook his head in silence and brooded on his revenge.

Now, when Penelope heard that the beggar had been struck in the banqueting hall, she said before her maids, "Would that Apollo would so strike you, Antinous," and her waiting woman Eurynome answered, "If our prayers were answered, not one of the suitors would ever again see the sun rise." Then Penelope said, "Nurse, I hate every single one of them, for they mean nothing but mischief, but I hate Antinous like the darkness of death itself. A poor unfortunate tramp has come begging about the house for sheer want. Everyone else has given him something to put in his wallet, but Antinous has hit him on the right shoulder blade with a footstool."

Thus did she talk with her maids as she sat in her own room, and in the meantime Odysseus was eating his dinner. Then she called for the swineherd and said, "Eumaeus, go and tell the stranger to come here; I want to see him and ask him some questions. He seems to have travelled much, and he may have seen or heard something of my unhappy husband."

To this the swineherd Eumaeus answered, "If these Achaeans, Madam, would only keep quiet, you would be charmed with the history of his adventures. I had him three days and three nights with me in my hut, which was the first place he reached after running away from his ship, and he has not yet completed the history of his misfortunes. If he had been the most heaven-taught minstrel in the whole world, on whose lips all hearers hang entranced, I could not have been more charmed as I sat in my hut and listened to him. He says there is an old friendship between his house and that of Odysseus, and that he comes from Crete, where the descendants of Minos live, after having been driven hither and thither by every kind of misfortune; he also declares that he has heard of Odysseus as being alive and near at hand among the Thesprotians, and that he is bringing great wealth home with him."

"Call him here then," said Penelope, "that I too may hear his story. As for the suitors, let them enjoy themselves indoors or out as they will, for they have nothing to care about. Their corn and wine remain unwasted in their houses with none but servants to consume them, while they keep hanging about our house day after day, sacrificing our oxen, sheep, and fat goats for their banquets, and never giving so much as a thought to the quantity of wine they drink. No estate can stand such recklessness, for we have now no Odysseus to protect us. If he were to come again, he and his son would soon have their revenge."

As she spoke, Telemachus sneezed so loudly that the whole house resounded with it. Penelope laughed when she heard this, and said to Eumaeus, "Go and call the stranger; did you not hear how my son sneezed just as I was speaking? This can only mean that all the suitors are going to be killed, and that not one of them shall escape. Furthermore I say—

and you remember my words—if I am satisfied that the stranger is speaking the truth, I shall give him a tunic and cloak of good wear."

When Eumaeus heard this he went straight to Odysseus and said, "Father stranger, my mistress Penelope, mother of Telemachus, has sent for you; she is in great grief, but she wishes to hear anything you can tell her about her husband, and if she is satisfied that you are speaking the truth, she will give you a tunic and cloak, which are the very things that you are most in want of. As for bread, you can get enough of that to fill your belly by begging about the town, and letting those give that will."

"I will tell Penelope," answered Odysseus, "nothing but what is strictly true. I know all about her husband, and have been partner with him in affliction, but I am afraid of passing through this crowd of cruel suitors, for their pride and insolence reach heaven. Just now, moreover, as I was going about the house without doing any harm, a man gave me a blow that hurt me very much, but neither Telemachus nor anyone else defended me. Tell Penelope, therefore, to be patient and wait till sundown. Let her give me a seat close up to the fire, for my clothes are worn very thin—you know they are, for you have seen them ever since I first asked you to help me. She can then ask me about the return of her husband."

The swineherd went back when he heard this, and Penelope said as she saw him cross the threshold, "Why do you not bring him here, Eumaeus? Is he afraid that someone will ill-treat him, or is he shy of coming inside the house at all? Beggars should not be shamefaced."

To this the swineherd Eumaeus answered, "The stranger is quite reasonable. He is avoiding the suitors, and is only doing what anyone else would do. He asks you to wait till sundown, and it will be much better, Madam, that you should have him all to yourself, when you can hear him and talk to him as you will."

"The man is no fool," answered Penelope. "It would very likely be as he says, for there are no such abominable people in the whole world as these men are."

When she had done speaking, Eumaeus went back to the suitors, for he had explained everything. Then he went up to Telemachus and said in his ear so that none could overhear him, "My dear sir, I will now go back to the pigs, to see after your property and my own business. You will look to what is going on here, but above all be careful to keep out of danger, for there are many who bear you ill will. May Zeus bring them to a bad end before they do us a mischief."

"Very well," replied Telemachus. "Go home when you have had your dinner, and in the morning come here with the victims we are to sacrifice for the day. Leave the rest to heaven and me."

On this, Eumaeus took his seat again, and when he had finished his dinner he left the courts and the hall with the men at table, and went back to his pigs. As for the suitors, they presently began to amuse themselves with singing and dancing, for it was now getting on towards evening.

BOOK XVIII

❧

*The Fight with Irus—Odysseus Warns
Amphinomus—Penelope Gets Presents
from the Suitors—The Braziers—
Odysseus Rebukes Eurymachus*

Now, THERE came a certain common tramp who used to go
begging all over the city of Ithaca, and was notorious as an
incorrigible glutton and drunkard. This man had no strength
nor might in him, but he was a great hulking fellow to look
at; his real name, the one his mother gave him, was Arnaeus,
but the young men of the place called him Irus, because he
used to run errands for anyone who would send him. As
soon as he came he began to insult Odysseus, and to try and
drive him out of his own house.

"Be off, old man," he cried, "from the doorway, or you
shall be dragged out by your heels. Do you not see that they
are all giving me the wink, and wanting me to turn you out
by force, only I do not like to do so? Get up then, and go of
yourself, or we shall come to blows."

Odysseus frowned on him and said, "My friend, I do you
no harm; people give you a great deal, but I am not jealous.
There is room enough in this doorway for the pair of us, and
you need not grudge me things that are not yours to give.
You seem to be just such another tramp as myself, but perhaps the gods will give us better luck by and by. Do not,
however, talk too much about fighting, or you will annoy me,
and old though I am, I shall cover your mouth and chest

with blood. I shall have more peace tomorrow if I do, for you will not come to the house of Odysseus any more."

Irus was very angry and answered, "You filthy glutton, you run on trippingly like an old fish hag. I have a good mind to lay both hands about you, and knock your teeth out of your head like so many boar's tusks. Get ready, therefore, and let these people here stand by and look on. You will never be able to fight one who is so much younger than yourself."

Thus roundly did they abuse one another on the smooth pavement in front of the doorway, and when Antinous saw what was going on, he laughed heartily and said to the others, "This is the finest sport that you ever saw; heaven never yet sent anything like it into this house. The stranger and Irus have quarrelled and are going to fight; let us set them on to do so at once."

The suitors all came up laughing, and gathered round the two ragged tramps. "Listen to me," said Antinous. "There are some goats' paunches down at the fire, which we have filled with blood and fat, and set aside for supper; he who is victorious and proves himself to be the better man shall have his pick of the lot; he shall be free of our table and we will not allow any other beggar about the house at all."

The others all agreed, but Odysseus, to throw them off the scent, said, "Sirs, an old man like myself, worn out with suffering, cannot hold his own against a young one; but my irrepressible belly urges me on, though I know it can only end in my getting a drubbing. You must swear, however, that none of you will give me a foul blow to favour Irus and secure him the victory."

They swore as he told them, and when they had completed their oath, Telemachus put in a word and said, "Stranger, if you have a mind to settle with this fellow, you need not be afraid of anyone here. Whoever strikes you will have to fight more than one. I am host, and the other chiefs,

Antinous and Eurymachus, both of them men of understanding, are of the same mind as I am."

Everyone assented, and Odysseus girded his old rags
about his loins, thus baring his stalwart thighs, his broad
chest and shoulders, and his mighty arms; but Athene came
up to him and made his limbs stronger still. The suitors were
beyond measure astonished, and one would turn towards his
neighbour, saying, "The stranger has shown such a thigh out
of his old rags that there will soon be nothing left of Irus."

Irus began to be very uneasy as he heard them, but the
servants girded him by force, and brought him forward, in
such a fright that his limbs were all a-tremble. Antinous
scolded him and said, "You swaggering bully, you ought
never to have been born at all if you are afraid of such an old
broken-down creature as this tramp is. I say, therefore—and
it shall surely be—if he beats you and proves himself the
better man, I shall pack you off on board ship to the mainland and send you to King Echetus, who maims everyone
that comes near him. He will cut off your nose and ears, and
draw out your private parts for the dogs to eat."

This frightened Irus still more, but they brought him into
the middle of the court, and the two men raised their hands
to fight. Then Odysseus considered whether he should let
drive so hard at him as to make an end of him on the spot, or
whether he should give him a lighter blow that should only
knock him down; in the end he deemed it best to give the
lighter blow for fear the Achaeans should begin to suspect
who he was. Then they began to fight, and Irus hit Odysseus
on the right shoulder; but Odysseus gave Irus a blow on the
neck under the ear that broke in the bones of his skull, and
the blood came gushing out of his mouth; he fell groaning
in the dust, gnashing his teeth and kicking on the ground, but
the suitors threw up their hands and nearly died of laughter,
as Odysseus caught hold of him by the foot and dragged him
into the outer court as far as the gatehouse. There he

propped him up against the wall and put his staff in his hands. "Sit here," said he, "and keep the dogs and pigs off; you are a pitiful creature, and if you try to make yourself king of the beggars any more you shall fare still worse."

Then he put his dirty old wallet, all tattered and torn, over his shoulder, with the cord by which it hung, and went back to sit down upon the threshold; but the suitors went inside, laughing and congratulating him. "May Zeus and all the other gods," said they, "grant you whatever you want for having put an end to the importunity of this insatiable tramp. We will take him over to the mainland presently, to King Echetus, who maims everyone that comes near him."

Odysseus hailed this as of good omen, and Antinous set a great goat's paunch before him, filled with blood and fat. Amphinomus took two loaves out of the bread basket and brought them to him, pledging him as he did so, in a golden goblet of wine. "Good luck to you," said he, "father stranger; you are very badly off at present, but I hope you will have better times by and by."

To this Odysseus answered, "Amphinomus, you seem to be a man of good understanding, as indeed you may well be, seeing whose son you are. I have heard your father well spoken of; he is Nisus of Dulichium, a man both brave and wealthy. They tell me you are his son, and you appear to be a prudent person; listen, therefore, and take heed to what I am saying. Man is the feeblest of all creatures that have their being upon earth. As long as heaven vouchsafes him health and strength, he thinks that he shall come to no harm hereafter, and even when the blessed gods bring sorrow upon him, he bears it as he needs must, and makes the best of it; for men's attitude of mind varies according to the daily fortune that Zeus sends them. I know all about it, for I was a rich man once, and did much wrong in the stubbornness of my pride, and in the confidence that my father and my brothers would support me; therefore let no man be wholly lawless, but take the good that heaven may see fit to send him without vainglory. Consider the infamy of what these suitors are doing; see how they are wasting the estate, and doing dishonour to the wife, of one who will probably return some day, and that, too, not long hence. Nay, he will be here soon; may heaven send you home quietly first, that you may not meet with him in the day of his coming, for once he is here the suitors and he will not part bloodlessly."

With these words, he made a drink offering, and when he had drunk he put the gold cup again into the hands of Amphinomus, who walked away serious and bowing his head, for he foreboded evil. But even so he did not escape destruction, for Athene had doomed him to fall by the hand of Telemachus. So he took his seat again at the place from which he had come.

Then Athene put it into the mind of Penelope to show herself to the suitors, that she might make them still more enamoured of her, and win still further honour from her son and husband. So she feigned a mocking laugh and said, "Eurynome, I have changed my mind, and have a fancy to show myself to the suitors although I detest them. I should like also to give my son a hint that he had better not have too much to do with them. They speak fairly enough, but they mean mischief."

"My dear child," answered Eurynome, "all that you have said is true; go and tell your son about it, but first wash yourself and anoint your face. Do not go about with your cheeks all covered with tears; it is not right that you should grieve so incessantly; for Telemachus, whom you always prayed that you might live to see with a beard, is already grown up."

"I know, Eurynome," replied Penelope, "that you mean well, but do not try and persuade me to wash and to anoint myself, for heaven robbed me of all my beauty on the day my husband sailed; nevertheless tell Autonoë and Hippodameia that I want them. They must be with me when I am in the hall; I am not going among the men alone; it would not be proper for me to do so."

On this, the old woman went out of the room to bid the maids go to their mistress. In the meantime Athene turned to other thoughts, and sent Penelope off into a sweet slumber; so she lay down on her couch and her limbs became heavy with sleep. Then the goddess shed grace and beauty over her that all the Achaeans might admire her. She washed her face with the ambrosial loveliness that Aphrodite wears when she goes dancing with the Graces; she made her taller and of a more commanding figure, while as for her complexion, it was whiter than sawn ivory. When Athene had done all this, she went away, whereon the maids came in from the women's room and woke Penelope with the sound of their talking.

"What a gentle sleep I have been having," said she, as she passed her hands over her face, "in spite of all my misery. I wish Artemis would let me die so gently now at this very moment, that I might no longer waste in despair for the loss of my dear husband, who possessed every kind of good quality and was the best man among the Achaeans."

With these words, she came down from her upper room, not alone but attended by two of her maidens, and when she reached the suitors she stood by one of the pillars supporting the roof of the hall, holding a veil before her face, and with a demure maidservant on either side of her. As they beheld her, the suitors were so overpowered and became so desperately enamoured of her that each one prayed he might win her for his own bedfellow.

"Telemachus," said she, addressing her son, "I fear you are no longer so discreet and well-conducted as you used to be. When you were younger you had a greater sense of propriety; now, however, that you are grown up, though a stranger, to look at you, would take you for the son of a well-to-do father as far as size and good looks go, your conduct is by no means what it should be. What is all this disturbance that has been going on, and how came you to allow a stranger to be so disgracefully ill-treated? What would have happened if he had suffered serious injury while a suppliant in our house? Surely this would have been very discreditable to you."

"I am not surprised, my dear mother, at your displeasure," replied Telemachus. "I understand all about it and know when things are not as they should be, which I could not do when I was younger; I cannot, however, behave with perfect propriety at all times. First one and then another of these wicked people here keeps driving me astray, and I have no one to stand by me. After all, however, this fight between Irus and the stranger did not turn out as the suitors meant it to do, for the stranger got the best of it. I wish Father Zeus, Athene, and Apollo would see to it that they were all beaten to the ground, these wooers of yours, some inside the house and some out; and I wish they might all be as limp as Irus is over yonder in the gate of the outer court. See how he nods his head like a drunken man; he cannot stand on his feet nor get back to his home, wherever that may be, for he has no strength left in him."

Thus did they converse. Eurymachus then came up and said, "Queen Penelope, daughter of Icarius, if all the Achaeans in Iasian Argos could see you at this moment, you would have still more suitors in your house by tomorrow morning, for you are the most admirable woman in the whole world as regards both personal beauty and strength of understanding."

To this Penelope replied, "Eurymachus, heaven robbed me of all my beauty, whether of face or figure, when the Argives set sail for Troy and my dear husband with them. If he were to return and look after my affairs, I should both be more respected and show a better presence to the world. As it is, I am oppressed with care, and with the afflictions which heaven has seen fit to heap upon me. My husband foresaw it all, and when he was leaving home, he took my right wrist in his hand. 'Wife,' said he, 'we shall not all of us come safe home from Troy, for the Trojans fight well both with bow and with spear. They are excellent also at fighting from chariots, and nothing decides the issue of a fight sooner than this. I know not, therefore, whether heaven will send me back to you, or whether I may not fall over there at Troy. In the meantime do you look after things here. Take care of my father and mother as at present, and even more so during my absence, but when you see our son growing a beard, then marry whom you will, and leave this, your present home.' This is what he said and now it is all coming true. A night will come when I shall have to yield myself to a marriage which I detest, for Zeus has taken from me all hope of happiness. This further grief, moreover, cuts me to the very heart. You suitors are not wooing me after the custom of the country. When men are courting a woman who they think will be a good wife to them and who is of noble birth, and when they are each trying to win her for himself, they usually bring oxen and sheep to feast the relations of the lady, and they make her magnificent presents, instead of eating up other people's property without paying for it."

This was what she said, and Odysseus was glad when he heard her trying to get presents out of the suitors, and flattering them with fair words which he knew she did not mean.

Then Antinous said, "Queen Penelope, daughter of Icarius, take as many presents as you please from anyone who will give them to you; it is not well to refuse a present; but we will not go about our business, nor stir from where we are, till you have married the best man among us, whoever he may be."

The others applauded what Antinous had said, and each one sent his servant to bring his present. Antinous' man returned with a large and lovely dress most exquisitely embroidered. It had twelve beautifully made brooch pins of pure gold with which to fasten it. Eurymachus immediately brought her a magnificent chain of gold and amber beads that gleamed like sunlight. Eurydamas' two men returned with some earrings fashioned into three brilliant pendants, which glistened most beautifully, while King Pisander, son of Polyctor, gave her a necklace of the rarest workmanship, and everyone else brought her a beautiful present of some kind.

Then the queen went back to her room upstairs, and her maids brought the presents after her. Meanwhile the suitors took to singing and dancing, and stayed till evening came. They danced and sang till it grew dark; they then brought in three braziers to give light, and piled them up with chopped firewood, very old and dry, and they lit torches from them, which the maids held up, turn and turn about. Then Odysseus said:

"Maids, servants of Odysseus, who has so long been absent, go to the queen inside the house; sit with her and amuse her, or spin, and pick wool. I will hold the light for all these people. They may stay till morning, but shall not beat me, for I can stand a great deal."

The maids looked at one another and laughed, while pretty Melantho began to gibe at him contemptuously. She was the daughter of Dolius, but had been brought up by Penelope, who used to give her toys to play with, and looked after her when she was a child; but in spite of all this she showed no consideration for the sorrows of Penelope, and was the mistress of Eurymachus.

"Poor wretch," said she, "are you gone clean out of your mind? Go and sleep in some smithy, or place of public gossip, instead of chattering here. Are you not ashamed of opening your mouth before your betters—so many of them, too? Has the wine been getting into your head, or do you always babble in this way? You seem to have lost your wits because you beat the tramp Irus; take care that a better man than he does not come and hit you about the head till he pack you bleeding out of the house."

"Vixen," replied Odysseus, scowling at her. "I will go and tell Telemachus what you have been saying, and he will have you torn limb from limb."

With these words he scared the women, and they went off into the body of the house. They trembled all over, for they thought he would do as he said. But Odysseus took his stand near the burning braziers, holding up torches and looking at the people, brooding the while on things that did in fact come to pass.

But Athene would not let the suitors for one moment cease their insolence, for she wanted Odysseus to become even more bitter against them; she therefore set Eurymachus, son of Polybus, on to gibe at him, which made the others laugh. "Listen to me," said he, "you suitors of Queen Penelope, that I may speak as I am minded. It is not for nothing that this man has come to the house of Odysseus; I believe the light has not been coming from the torches, but from his own head—for his hair is all gone, every bit of it."

Then, turning to Odysseus, he said, "Stranger, will you work as a servant, if I send you to the country and see that you are well paid? Can you build a stone wall, or plant trees? I will have you fed all the year round, and will give you shoes and clothing. Will you go then? Not you; for you have got into bad ways, and do not want to work; you had rather fill your belly by going round the country begging."

"Eurymachus," answered Odysseus, "if you and I were to work one against the other in early summer when the days are at their longest—give me a good scythe, and take another yourself, and let us see which will fast the longer or mow the stronger, from dawn till dark when the mowing grass is about. Or if there were oxen to plough with, a well-fed yoke of tawny oxen, well-mated and of great strength and endurance; and let there be a four-acre field and let the clods of earth break easily beneath the plough—then you would see whether I can drive the furrow straight. If, again, war were to break out this day, give me a shield, a couple of spears, and a helmet fitting well upon my temples—you would find me foremost in the fray, and would cease your gibes about my belly. You are insolent and cruel, and think yourself a great man because you live in a little world, and that a bad one. If Odysseus came to his own again, the doors of his house are wide, but you would find them narrow when you tried to fly through them."

Eurymachus was furious at all this. He scowled at him and cried, "You wretch, I will soon pay you back for daring to say such things to me, and in public, too. Has the wine been getting into your head or do you always babble in this way? You seem to have lost your wits because you beat the tramp Irus." With this, he caught hold of a footstool, but Odysseus sought protection at the knees of Amphinomus of Dulichium, for he was afraid. The stool hit the cupbearer on his right hand and knocked him down; the man fell with a cry flat on his back, and his wine jug fell ringing to the ground. The suitors in the dark hall were now in an uproar, and one would turn towards his neighbour, saying, "I wish the stranger had gone somewhere else, bad luck to him, for all the trouble he gives us. We cannot permit such disturbance about a beggar; if such ill counsels are to prevail, we shall have no more pleasure at our banquet."

On this, Telemachus came forward and said, "Sirs, are you mad? Can you not carry your meat and your liquor decently? Some evil spirit has possessed you. I do not wish to drive any of you away, but you have had your suppers, and the sooner you all go home to bed, the better."

The suitors bit their lips and marvelled at the boldness of his speech; but Amphinomus, the son of Nisus, who was son of Aretias, said, "Do not let us take offence; it is reasonable, so let us make no answer. Neither let us do violence to the stranger nor to any of Odysseus' servants. Let the cupbearer go round with the drink offerings, that we may make them and go home to our rest. As for the stranger, let us leave Telemachus to deal with him, for it is to his house that he has come."

Thus did he speak, and his words pleased them well, so Mulius of Dulichium, servant to Amphinomus, mixed them a bowl of wine and water and handed it round to each of them, man by man, whereon they made their drink offerings to the blessed gods. Then, when they had made their drink offerings and had drunk each one as much as he wished, they took their several ways, each of them to his own abode.

BOOK XIX

❧

*Telemachus and Odysseus Remove the Armour—
Odysseus Interviews Penelope—Eurycleia Washes
His Feet and Recognises the Scar on His Leg—
Penelope Tells Her Dream to Odysseus*

ODYSSEUS WAS left in the hall, pondering on the means whereby with Athene's help he might kill the suitors. Presently he said to Telemachus, "Telemachus, we must get the armour together and take it inside. Make some excuse when the suitors ask you why you have removed it. Say that you have taken it to be out of the way of the smoke, inasmuch as it is no longer what it was when Odysseus went away, but has become soiled and begrimed with soot. Add to this more particularly that you are afraid Zeus may set them on to quarrel over their wine, and that they may do each other some harm which may disgrace both banquet and wooing, for the sight of arms sometimes tempts people to use them."

Telemachus approved of what his father had said, so he called nurse Eurycleia and said, "Nurse, shut the women up in their room, while I put the armour that my father left behind him into the storeroom. No one looks after it now that my father is gone, and it has got all smirched with soot during my own boyhood. I want to put it where the smoke cannot reach it."

"I wish, child," answered Eurycleia, "that you would take the management of the house into your own hands altogether, and look after all the property yourself. But who is to go with you and light you to the storeroom? The maids would have done so, but you do not let them."

"The stranger," said Telemachus, "shall show me a light; when people eat my bread they must earn it, no matter where they come from."

Eurycleia did as she was told, and bolted the women inside their room. Then Odysseus and his son made all haste to take the helmets, shields, and spears inside; and Athene went before them with a gold lamp in her hand that shed a soft and brilliant radiance, whereon Telemachus said, "Father, my eyes behold a great marvel: the walls, with the rafters, crossbeams, and the supports on which they rest, are all aglow as with a flaming fire. Surely there is some god here who has come down from heaven."

"Hush," answered Odysseus. "Hold your peace and ask no questions, for this is the way of the gods. Get you to your bed, and leave me here to talk with your mother and the maids. Your mother in her grief will ask me all sorts of questions."

On this, Telemachus went by torchlight through the hall to the room in which he always slept. There he lay in his bed till morning, while Odysseus was left in the hall pondering on the means whereby with Athene's help he might kill the suitors.

Then Penelope came down from her room looking like Aphrodite or Artemis, and they set her a seat inlaid with scrolls of silver and ivory near the fire in her accustomed place. It had been made by Icmalius and had a footstool all in one piece with the seat itself; and it was covered with a thick fleece. On this she now sat, and the maids came from the women's room to join her. They set about removing the tables at which the wicked suitors had been dining, and took away the bread that was left, with the cups from which they had drunk. They emptied the embers out of the braziers, and heaped wood upon them to give both light and heat; but Melantho began to rail at Odysseus a second time and said, "Stranger, do you mean to plague us by hanging about the house all night and spying upon the women? Be off, you wretch, outside, and eat your supper there, or you shall be driven out with a firebrand."

Odysseus scowled at her and answered, "My good woman, why should you be so angry with me? Is it because I am not clean, and my clothes are all in rags, and because I am obliged to go begging about after the manner of tramps and beggars generally? I too was a rich man once, and had a fine house of my own; in those days I gave to many a tramp such as I now am, no matter who he might be or what he wanted. I had any number of servants, and all the other things which people have who live well and are accounted wealthy, but it pleased Zeus to take all away from me; therefore, woman, beware lest you too come to lose that pride and place in which you now surpass your fellows; have a care lest you get out of favour with your mistress, and lest Odysseus should come home, for there is still a chance that he may do so. Moreover, even if he is dead, as you think he is, yet by Apollo's will he has left a son behind him, Telemachus, who will note anything done amiss by the maids in the house, for he is now no longer a boy."

Penelope heard what he was saying and scolded the maid. "Impudent baggage," said she, "I see how abominably you are behaving, and you shall smart for it. You knew perfectly well, for I told you myself, that I was going to see the stranger and ask him about my husband, for whose sake I am in such continual sorrow."

Then she said to her head waiting woman, Eurynome, "Bring a seat with a fleece upon it, for the stranger to sit upon, while he tells his story, and listens to what I have to say. I wish to ask him some questions."

Eurynome brought the seat at once and set a fleece upon it, and as soon as Odysseus had sat down Penelope began by saying, "Stranger, I shall first ask you who and whence are you? Tell me of your town and parents."

"Madam," answered Odysseus, "who on the face of the

whole earth would criticise you? Your fame reaches the firmament of heaven itself; you are like some blameless king, who upholds righteousness, as the monarch over a great and valiant nation: the earth yields its wheat and barley, the trees are loaded with fruit, the ewes bring forth lambs, and the sea abounds with fish by reason of his virtues, and his people do good deeds under him. Nevertheless, as I sit here in your house, ask me some other question and do not seek to know my race and family, or you will recall memories that will yet more increase my sorrow. I am full of heaviness, but I ought not to sit weeping and wailing in another person's house, nor is it well to be thus grieving continually. I shall have one of the servants or even yourself complaining of me, and saying that my eyes swim with tears because I am heavy with wine."

Then Penelope answered, "Stranger, heaven robbed me of all beauty, whether of face or figure, when the Argives set sail for Troy and my dear husband with them. If he were to return and look after my affairs, I should be both more respected and should show a better presence to the world. As it is, I am oppressed with care, and with the afflictions which heaven has seen fit to heap upon me. The chiefs from all our islands—Dulichium, Same, and Zacynthus, as also from Ithaca itself—are wooing me against my will and are wasting my estate. I can therefore show no attention to strangers, nor to suppliants, nor to heralds, the servants of the people, but am all the time brokenhearted about Odysseus. They want me to marry again at once, and I have to invent stratagems in order to deceive them. In the first place heaven put it in my mind to set up a great tambour frame in my room, and to begin working upon an enormous piece of fine needlework. Then I said to them, 'Young men my suitors, Odysseus is indeed dead; but do not press me to marry again immediately; wait—for I would not have my threads perish unused—till I have finished making a pall for the hero Laertes, to be ready for the time when death shall take him. He is very rich, and the women of the place will talk if he is laid out without a pall.' This was what I said, and they assented; whereon I used to keep working at my great web all day long, but at night I would unpick the stitches again by torchlight. I fooled them in this way for three years without their finding it out, but as time wore on and I was now in my fourth year, as the moons waned and many days had been accomplished, those good-for-nothing hussies, my maids, betrayed me to the suitors, who broke in upon me and caught me; they were very angry with me, so I was forced to finish my work whether I would or no. And now I do not see how I can find any further plan for getting out of this marriage. My parents are putting great pressure upon me, and my son chafes at the ravages the suitors are making upon his estate, for he is now old enough to understand all about it and is perfectly able to look after his own affairs, for heaven has blessed him with excellent sense. Still, notwithstanding all this, tell me who you are and where you come from, for you must have had father and mother of some sort; you cannot be the son of an oak or of a rock."

Then Odysseus answered, "Madam, wife of Odysseus, since you persist in asking me about my family, I will answer, no matter what it costs me; people must expect to be pained when they have been exiles as long as I have, and suffered as much among as many peoples. Nevertheless, as regards your question, I will tell you all you ask. There is a fair and fruitful island in mid-ocean called Crete; it is thickly peopled and there are ninety cities in it; the people speak many different languages, which overlap one another, for there are Achaeans, brave Eteocretans, Cydonians, Dorians of threefold race, and noble Pelasgi. There is a great town there, Cnossus, where Minos reigned, who every nine years had a conference with Zeus himself. Minos was the father of Deucalion, whose son I am, for Deucalion had two sons, Idomeneus and myself. Idomeneus sailed for Troy, and I, who am the younger, am called Aethon; my brother, however, was at once the older and the more valiant of the two; hence it was in Crete that I saw Odysseus and showed him hospitality, for the winds took him there as he was on his way to Troy, carrying him out of his course from Cape Malea and leaving him in Amnisus, where is the cave of Ilithyia, where the harbours are difficult to enter and he could hardly find shelter from the winds that were then raging. As soon as he got there he went into the town and asked for Idomeneus, claiming to be his old and valued friend, but Idomeneus had already set sail for Troy some ten or twelve days earlier, so I took him to my own house and showed him every kind of hospitality, for I had abundance of everything. Moreover, I fed the men who were with him with barley meal from the public store, and got subscriptions of wine and oxen for them to sacrifice to their hearts' content. They stayed with me twelve days, for there was a gale blowing from the north so strong that one could hardly keep one's feet on land. I suppose some unfriendly god had raised it for them, but on the thirteenth day the wind dropped, and they got away."

Many a plausible tale did Odysseus further tell her, and Penelope wept as she listened, for her heart was melted. As the snow wastes upon the mountain tops, snow brought by the west wind, but thawed by the southeast till the rivers run on full with water, even so did her cheeks overflow with tears for the husband who was all the time sitting by her side. Odysseus felt for her and was sorry for her, but he kept his eyes as hard as horn or iron, without letting them so much as quiver, so carefully did he restrain his tears. Then, when she had relieved herself by weeping, she turned to him again and said, "Now, stranger, I shall put you to the test and see whether or no you really did entertain my husband and his men, as you say you did. Tell me, then, how he was dressed, what kind of a man he was to look at, and so also with his companions."

"Madam," answered Odysseus, "it is such a long time ago that I can hardly say. Twenty years are come and gone since he left my home, and went elsewhither; but I will tell you as well as I can recollect. Odysseus wore a mantle of purple wool, folded double, and it was fastened by a gold brooch with two catches for the pin. On the face of this there was a device that showed a dog holding a spotted fawn between his forepaws, and watching it as it lay panting upon the ground. Everyone marvelled at the way these things had been done in gold, the dog looking at the fawn, and strangling it, while the fawn was struggling convulsively to escape. As for the tunic that he wore next to his skin, it was so soft that it fitted him like the skin of an onion, and glistened in the sunlight, to the admiration of all the women who beheld it. But I must add, and please take note of my words, that I do not know whether Odysseus wore these clothes when he left home, or whether one of his companions had given them to him while he was on his voyage; or possibly someone at whose house he was staying made him a present of them, for he was a man of many friends and had few equals among the Achaeans. I myself gave him a sword of bronze and a beautiful purple mantle, folded double, with a tunic that went down to his feet, and I sent him on board his ship with every mark of honour. He had a servant with him, a little older than himself, and I can tell you what he was like: his shoulders were hunched, he was dark, and he had thick, curly hair. His name was Eurybates, and Odysseus treated him with greater familiarity than he did any of the others, as being the most likeminded with himself."

Penelope was moved still more deeply as she heard the indisputable proofs that Odysseus laid before her; and when she had again found relief in tears, she said to him, "Stranger, I was already disposed to pity you, but henceforth you shall be honoured and made welcome in my house. It was I who gave Odysseus the clothes you speak of. I took them out of the storeroom and folded them up myself, and I gave him also the gold brooch to wear as an ornament. Alas! I shall never welcome him home again. It was by an ill fate that he ever set out for that detested city whose very name I cannot bring myself even to mention."

Then Odysseus answered, "Madam, wife of Odysseus, do not disfigure yourself further by grieving thus bitterly for your loss, though I can hardly blame you for doing so. A woman who has loved her husband and borne him children would naturally be grieved at losing him, even though he were a worse man than Odysseus, who they say was like a god. Still, cease your tears and listen to what I can tell you. I will hide nothing from you, and can say with perfect truth that I have lately heard of Odysseus as being alive and on his way home; he is among the Thesprotians, and is bringing back much valuable treasure that he has begged from them; but his ship and all his crew were lost as they were leaving the Thrinacian island, for Zeus and the sun god were angry with him because his men had slaughtered the sun god's cattle, and they were all drowned. But Odysseus clung to the keel of the ship and was drifted onto the land of the Phaeacians, who are near of kin to the immortals, and who treated him as though he were a god, giving him many presents, and wishing to escort him home safe and sound. In fact, Odysseus would have been here long ago, had he not thought better to go from land to land gathering wealth; for there is no man living who is so wily as he is; there is no one can compare with him. Pheidon, king of the Thesprotians, told me all this, and he swore to me— making drink offerings in his house as he did so—that the ship was by the waterside and the crew found who would take Odysseus to his own country. He sent me off first, for there happened to be a Thesprotian ship sailing for the wheat-growing island of Dulichium, but he showed me all the treasure Odysseus had got together, and he had enough lying in the house of King Pheidon to keep his family for ten genera-tions; but the king said Odysseus had gone to Dodona that he might learn Zeus's mind from the high oak tree, and know whether after so long an absence he should return to Ithaca openly or in secret. So you may know he is safe and will be here shortly; he is close at hand and cannot remain away from home much longer; nevertheless I will confirm my words with an oath, and call Zeus, who is the first and mightiest of all gods, to witness, as also that hearth of Odysseus to which I have now come, that all I have spoken shall surely come to pass. Odysseus will return in this selfsame year; with the end of this moon and the beginning of the next he will be here."

"May it be even so," answered Penelope. "If your words come true you shall have such gifts and such good will from me that all who see you shall congratulate you; but I know very well how it will all be. Odysseus will not return, neither will you get your escort hence, for there are now no longer any such masters in the house as Odysseus was (unless it was all a dream), to receive honourable strangers or to further them on their way home. And now, you maids, wash his feet for him, and make him a bed on a couch with rugs and blankets, that he may be warm and quiet till morning. Then, at daybreak, wash him and anoint him again, that he may sit in the hall and take his meals with Telemachus. It shall be the worse for any one of these hateful people who is uncivil to him; like it or not, he will achieve nothing here. For how, Sir, shall you be able to learn whether or no I am superior to others of my sex, both in goodness of heart and understanding, if I let you dine in my house squalid and ill-clad? Men live but for a little season; if they are hard, and deal hardly, people wish them ill so long as they are alive, and speak contemptuously of them when they are dead; but he that is righteous and deals righteously, his guests tell of his praise in all lands, and many speak well of him."

Odysseus answered, "Madam, I have foresworn rugs and blankets from the day that I left the snowy ranges of Crete to go on shipboard. I will lie as I have lain on many a sleepless night hitherto. Night after night have I passed in any rough sleeping place, and waited for morning. Nor, again, do I like having my feet washed; I shall not let any of the young servants about your house touch my feet; but if you have any old and respectable woman who has gone through as much trouble as I have, I will allow her to wash them."

To this Penelope said, "My dear sir, of all the guests who ever yet came to my house there never was one who spoke in all things with such admirable propriety as you do. There happens to be in the house a most respectable old woman— the same who received my poor dear husband in her arms the night he was born, and nursed him in infancy. She is very feeble now, but she shall wash your feet. Come here," said she, "Eurycleia, and wash a contemporary of your master; I suppose Odysseus' hands and feet are very much the same now as his are, for trouble ages all of us dreadfully fast."

On these words, the old woman covered her face with her hands; she began to weep and made lamentation, saying, "My dear child, alas that I can do nothing for you. I am certain no one was ever more god-fearing than yourself, and yet Zeus hated you. No one in the whole world ever burned him more thighbones, nor gave him finer hecatombs when you prayed you might come to a comfortable old age yourself, and see your son grow up to take your place after you; yet see how he has prevented you alone from ever getting back to your own home. Perhaps the women in some foreign palace which Odysseus has got to are gibing at him as all these sluts here have been gibing at you. I do not wonder at your not choosing to let them wash you, after the manner in which they have insulted you; I will wash your feet myself gladly enough, as Penelope has said that I am to do so; I will wash them both for Penelope's sake and for your own, for you have raised the most lively feelings of compassion in my mind; and let me say this, too: we have had all kinds of strangers in distress come here before now, but I make bold to say that no one ever yet came who was so like Odysseus in figure, voice, and feet as you are."

"Those who have seen us both," answered Odysseus,

"have always said we were wonderfully like each other, and now you have noticed it, too."

Then the old woman took the cauldron in which she was going to wash his feet, and poured plenty of cold water into it, adding hot till the bath was warm enough. Odysseus sat by the fire, but ere long he turned away from the light, for it occurred to him that when the old woman had hold of his leg she would recognise a certain scar which it bore, whereon the whole truth would come out. And indeed, as soon as she began washing her master, she at once knew the scar as one that had been given him by a wild boar when he was hunting on Mount Parnassus with his excellent grandfather Autolycus—who was the most accomplished thief and perjurer in the whole world—and with the sons of Autolycus. Hermes himself had endowed him with this gift, for he used to burn the thighbones of goats and kids to him, so he helped him gladly. It happened once that Autolycus had gone to Ithaca and had found the child of his daughter, just born. As soon as he had finished supper Eurycleia set the infant upon his knees and said, "Autolycus, you must find a name for your grandson; you greatly wished that you might have one."

"Son-in-law and daughter," replied Autolycus, "call the child thus: I am highly displeased with a large number of people in one place and another, both men and women; so name the child Odysseus, or the child of anger. When he grows up and comes to visit his mother's family on Mount Parnassus, where my possessions lie, I will make him a present and will send him on his way rejoicing."

Odysseus, therefore, went to Parnassus to get the presents from Autolycus, who with his sons shook hands with him and gave him welcome. His grandmother Amphithea threw her arms about him, and kissed his head and both his eyes, while Autolycus desired his sons to get dinner ready, and they did as he told them. They brought in a five-year-old bull, flayed it, made it ready, and divided it into joints; these they then cut carefully up into smaller pieces and spitted them; they roasted them sufficiently and served the portions round. Thus through the livelong day to the going down of the sun they feasted, and every man had his full share so that all were satisfied; but when the sun set and it became dark, they went to bed and were soon asleep.

When the child of morning, rosy-fingered Dawn, appeared, the sons of Autolycus went out with their hounds hunting, and Odysseus went, too. They climbed the wooded slopes of Parnassus and soon reached its breezy upland valleys; but as the sun was beginning to beat upon the fields, fresh-risen from the slow, still currents of Oceanus, they came to a mountain dell. The dogs were in front, searching for the tracks of the beast they were chasing, and after them came the sons of Autolycus, among whom was Odysseus, close behind the dogs, and he had a long spear in his hand. Here was the lair of a huge boar among some thick brushwood, so dense that the wind and rain could not get through it, nor could the sun's rays pierce it, and the ground underneath lay thick with fallen leaves. The boar heard the noise of the men's feet, and the hounds baying on every side, as the huntsmen came up to him, so he rushed from his lair, raised the bristles on his neck, and stood at bay with fire flashing from his eyes. Odysseus was the first to raise his spear and aim to drive it into the brute, but the boar was too quick for him, and charged him sideways, ripping him above the knee with a gash that tore deep though it did not reach the bone. As for the boar, Odysseus hit him on the right shoulder, and the point of the spear went right through him, so that he fell groaning in the dust until the life went out of him. The sons of Autolycus busied themselves with the carcase of the boar, and bound Odysseus' wound; then, after saying a spell to stop the bleeding, they went home as fast as they could. But when Autolycus and his sons had thoroughly healed Odysseus, they made him some splendid presents, and sent him back to

Ithaca with much mutual good will. When he got back, his father and mother were rejoiced to see him, and asked him all about it, and how he had hurt himself to get the scar; so he told them how the boar had ripped him when he was out hunting with Autolycus and his sons on Mount Parnassus.

As soon as Eurycleia had got the scarred limb in her hands and had well hold of it, she recognised it and dropped the foot at once. The leg fell into the bath, which rang out and was overturned, so that all the water was spilled on the ground; Eurycleia's eyes, between her joy and her grief, filled with tears, and she could not speak, but she caught Odysseus by the beard and said, "My dear child, you are Odysseus himself, only I did not know you till I had actually touched and handled you."

As she spoke, she looked towards Penelope, as though wanting to tell her that her dear husband was in the house, but Penelope was unable to look in that direction and observe what was going on, for Athene had diverted her attention; but Odysseus caught Eurycleia by the throat with his right hand and with his left drew her close to him, and said, "Nurse, do you wish to destroy me, you who nursed me at your own breast, now that after twenty years of wandering I am at last come to my own home again? Since it has been given you by heaven to recognise me, hold your tongue, and do not say a word about it to anyone else in the house, for if you do, I tell you—and it shall surely be—that if heaven grants me to take the lives of these suitors, I will not spare you, though you are my own nurse, when I am killing the other women."

"My child," answered Eurycleia, "what are you talking about? You know very well that nothing can either bend or break me. I will hold my tongue like a stone or a piece of iron; furthermore let me say, and remember my words, when heaven has delivered the suitors into your hand, I will give you a list of the women in the house who have been ill-behaved, and of those who are guiltless."

And Odysseus answered, "Nurse, there is no need for you to tell me about them; I am well able to form my own opinion about one and all of them; hold your tongue and leave everything to heaven."

As he said this, Eurycleia left the hall to fetch some more water, for the first had been all spilled; and when she had washed him and anointed him with oil, Odysseus drew his seat nearer to the fire to warm himself, and hid the scar under his rags. Then Penelope began talking to him and said:

"Stranger, I should like to speak with you briefly about another matter. It is indeed nearly bedtime—for those, at least, who can sleep in spite of sorrow. As for myself, heaven has given me a life of such unmeasurable woe that even by day, when I am attending to my duties and looking after the servants, I am still weeping and lamenting during the whole time; then, when night comes, and we all of us go to bed, I lie awake thinking, and my heart becomes a prey to the most incessant and cruel anxieties. As the dun nightingale, daughter of Pandareus, sings in the early spring from her seat in shadiest covert hid, and with many a plaintive trill pours out the tale how by mishap she killed her own child Iphitus, son of King Zethus, even so does my mind toss and turn in its uncertainty whether I ought to stay with my son here, and safeguard my possessions, my servants, and the greatness of my house, out of regard to public opinion and the memory of my late husband, or whether it is not now time for me to go with the best of these suitors who are wooing me and making me such magnificent presents. As long as my son was still young, and unable to understand, he would not hear of my leaving my husband's house, but now that he is full grown he begs and prays me to do so, being incensed at the way the suitors are eating up his property. Listen, then, to a dream that I have had and interpret it for me if you can. I have twenty geese about the house that eat mash out of a trough, and of which I am exceedingly fond. I dreamed that a great eagle came swooping down from the mountain, and dug his curved beak into the necks of each of them till he had killed them all. Presently he soared off into the sky, and left them lying dead about the yard; whereon I wept in my dream till all my neighbors gathered round me, so piteously was I grieving because the eagle had killed my geese. Then he came back again, and perching on a projecting rafter, spoke to me with human voice, and told me to leave off crying. 'Be of good courage,' he said, 'daughter of Icarius; this is no dream, but a vision of good omen that shall surely come to pass. The geese are the suitors, and I am no longer an eagle, but your own husband, who am come back to you, and who will bring these suitors to a disgraceful end.' On this, I woke, and when I looked out I saw my geese at the trough eating their mash as usual."

"This dream, Madam," replied Odysseus, "can admit but of one interpretation, for has not Odysseus himself told you how it shall be fulfilled? The death of the suitors is portended, and not one single one of them will escape."

And Penelope answered, "Stranger, dreams are very curious and unaccountable things, and they do not by any means invariably come true. There are two gates through which these unsubstantial fancies proceed; the one is of horn, and the other ivory. Those that come through the gate of ivory are deceptive, but those from the gate of horn are true for those that see them. I do not think, however, that my own dream came through the gate of horn, though I and my son should be most thankful if it proves to have done so. Furthermore I say, and remember my words, the coming dawn will usher in the ill-omened day that is to part me from the house of Odysseus, for I am about to hold a tournament of axes. My husband used to set up twelve axes in the hall, one in front of the other, like the stays upon which a ship is built; he would then go back from them and shoot an arrow through the whole twelve. I shall make the suitors try to do the same thing, and whichever of them can string the bow most easily, and send his arrow through all the twelve axes, him will I follow, and quit my lawful husband's house, so goodly and so abounding in wealth. But even so, I doubt not that I shall remember it in my dreams."

Then Odysseus answered, "Madam, wife of Odysseus, you need not defer your tournament, for Odysseus will return before they can string the bow, handle it how they will, and send their arrows through the iron."

To this Penelope said, "As long, Sir, as you will sit here and talk to me, I can have no desire to go to bed. Still, people cannot do permanently without sleep, and heaven has appointed us dwellers on earth a time for all things. I will therefore go upstairs and recline upon that couch which I have never ceased to flood with my tears from the day Odysseus set out for the city with a hateful name. I will lie there; but you must sleep here in the house. Either make your bed upon the floor, or let them put down bedding for you."

She then went upstairs to her own room, not alone, but attended by her maidens, and when there, she lamented her dear husband till Athene shed sweet sleep over her eyelids.

BOOK XX

※

Odysseus Cannot Sleep—Penelope's Prayer to
Artemis—The Two Signs from Heaven—Eumaeus
and Philoetius Arrive—The Suitors Dine—
Ctesippus Throws an Ox's Foot at Odysseus—
Theoclymenus Foretells Disaster and Leaves
the House

ODYSSEUS MADE his bed in the entrance to the hall, with an undressed bullock's hide, on the top of which he threw several skins of the sheep the suitors had eaten, and Eurynome threw a cloak over him after he had laid himself down. There, then, Odysseus lay wakefully brooding upon the way he should kill the suitors; and by and by, the women who had been in the habit of misconducting themselves with them left the house, giggling and laughing with one another. This made Odysseus very angry, and he wondered whether to get up and kill every single one of them then and there, or to let them sleep one more and last time with the suitors. His heart growled within him, and as a bitch with puppies growls and shows her teeth when she sees a stranger, so did his heart growl with anger at the evil deeds that were being done. But he beat his breast and said, "Heart, be still; you had worse than this to bear on the day when the terrible Cyclops ate your brave companions; yet you bore it in silence till your cunning got you safe out of the cave, though you expected to be killed."

Thus he chided his heart, and checked it into endurance, but he tossed about as one who turns a paunch full of blood and fat in front of a hot fire, doing it first on one side and then on the other, that he may get it cooked as soon as possible; even so did he turn himself about from side to side, thinking all the time how, single-handed as he was, he should contrive to kill so large a body of men as the wicked suitors. But by and by Athene came down from heaven in the likeness of a woman, and stood at his head, saying, "My poor unhappy man, why do you lie awake in this way? This is your house; your wife is safe inside it, and so is your son, who is just such a young man as any father may be proud of."

"Goddess," answered Odysseus, "all that you have said is true, but I am in some doubt as to how I shall be able to kill these wicked suitors single-handed, seeing what a number of them there always are. And there is this further difficulty, which is still more considerable: supposing that with Zeus's and your assistance I succeed in killing them, I must ask you to consider where I am to escape to from their avengers when it is all over."

"For shame," replied Athene. "Why, anyone else would trust a worse ally than myself, even though that ally were only a mortal and less wise than I am. Am I not a goddess, and have I not protected you throughout in all your troubles? I tell you plainly that even though there were fifty bands of men surrounding us and eager to kill us, you should take all their sheep and cattle, and drive them away with you. But go to sleep; it is a bad thing to lie awake all night, and you shall be out of your troubles before long."

As she spoke, she shed sleep over his eyes, and then went back to Olympus.

While Odysseus was thus yielding himself to a very deep slumber that eased the burden of his sorrows, his admirable wife awoke, and sitting up in her bed, began to cry. When she had relieved herself by weeping, she prayed to Artemis, saying, "Great goddess Artemis, daughter of Zeus, drive an arrow into my heart and slay me; or let some whirlwind snatch me up and bear me through paths of darkness till it drop me into the mouths of backward-flowing Oceanus, as it did the daughters of Pandareus. The daughters of Pandareus lost their father and mother, for the gods killed them, so they were left orphans. But Aphrodite took care of them, and fed them on cheese, honey, and sweet wine. Hera taught them to excel all women in beauty of form and understanding; Artemis gave them an imposing presence, and Athene endowed them with every kind of accomplishment; but one day when Aphrodite had gone up to Olympus to see Zeus about getting them married (for well does he know both what shall happen and what not happen to everyone), the storm winds came and spirited them away to become handmaids to the dread Erinyes. Even so I wish that the gods who live in heaven would hide me from mortal sight, or that fair Artemis might strike me, for I would fain go even beneath the sad earth if I might do so still looking towards Odysseus only, and without having to yield myself to a worse man than he was. Besides, no matter how much people may grieve by day, they can put up with it so long as they can sleep at night, for when the eyes are closed in slumber people forget good and ill alike; whereas my misery haunts me even in my dreams. This very night methought there was one lying by my side who was like Odysseus as he was when he went away with his host, and I rejoiced, for I believed that it was no dream, but the very truth itself."

On this, the day broke, but Odysseus heard the sound of her weeping, and it puzzled him, for it seemed as though she already knew him and was by his bed. Then he gathered up the cloak and the fleeces on which he had lain, and set them on a seat in the hall, but he took the bullock's hide out into the open. He lifted up his hands to heaven and prayed, saying, "Father Zeus, since you have seen fit to bring me over land and sea to my own home after all the afflictions you have laid upon me, give me a sign out of the mouth of some one or other of those who are now waking within the house, and let me have another sign of some kind from outside."

Thus did he pray. Zeus heard his prayer and forthwith thundered high up among the clouds from the splendour of Olympus, and Odysseus was glad when he heard it. At the same time within the house, a miller woman from hard by in the mill room lifted up her voice and gave him another sign. There were twelve miller women, whose business it was to grind wheat and barley, which are the staff of life. The others had ground their portions and had gone to take their rest, but this one had not yet finished, for she was not so strong as they were, and when she heard the thunder she stopped grinding and gave the sign to her master. "Father Zeus," said she, "you who rule over heaven and earth, you have thundered from a clear sky without so much as a cloud in it, and this means something for somebody; grant the prayer, then, of me, your poor servant who calls upon you, and let this be the very last day that the suitors dine in the house of Odysseus. They have worn me out with the labour of grinding meal for them, and I hope they may never have another dinner anywhere at all."

Odysseus was glad when he heard the omens conveyed to him by the woman's speech and by the thunder, for he knew they meant that he would avenge himself on the suitors.

Then the other maids in the house rose and lit the fire on the hearth; Telemachus also rose and put on his clothes. He girded his sword about his shoulder, bound his sandals onto his feet, and took a doughty spear with a point of sharpened bronze; then he went to the threshold of the hall and said to Eurycleia, "Nurse, did you make the stranger comfortable both as regards bed and food, or did you let him shift for himself? For my mother, good woman though she is, has a way of paying great attention to second-rate people, and of neglecting others who are in reality much better men."

"Do not find fault, child," said Eurycleia, "when there is no one to find fault with. The stranger sat and drank his wine as long as he liked; your mother did ask him if he would take any more bread and he said he would not. When he wanted to go to bed she told the servants to make one for him, but he said he was such a wretched outcast that he would not sleep on a bed and under blankets; he insisted on having an undressed bullock's hide and some sheepskins put for him in the entrance to the hall and we threw a cloak over him."

Then Telemachus went out of the court to the place where the Achaeans met in assembly; he had his spear in his hand, and he was not alone, for his two dogs went with him. But Eurycleia called the maids and said, "Come, wake up; set about sweeping the hall and sprinkling it with water to lay the dust; put the covers on the seats; wipe down the tables, some of you, with a wet sponge; clean out the mixing jugs and the cups, and go for water from the fountain at once; the suitors will be here directly; they will be here early, for it is a feast day."

Thus did she speak, and they did as she had said: twenty of them went to the fountain for water, and the others set themselves busily to work about the house. The men who were in attendance on the suitors also came up and began chopping firewood. By and by the women returned from the fountain, and the swineherd came after them with the three best pigs he could pick out. These he let feed about the premises, and then he said good-humouredly to Odysseus, "Stranger, are the suitors treating you any better now, or are they as insolent as ever?"

"May heaven," answered Odysseus, "requite to them the wickedness with which they deal highhandedly in another man's house without any sense of shame."

Thus did they converse; meanwhile Melanthius, the goatherd, came up, for he too was bringing in his best goats for the suitors' dinner; and he had two herdsmen with him. They tied the goats up under the gatehouse, and then Melanthius began gibing at Odysseus. "Are you still here, stranger," said he, "to pester people by begging about the house? Why can you not go elsewhere? You and I shall not come to an understanding before we have given each other a taste of our fists. You beg without any sense of decency; are there not feasts elsewhere among the Achaeans, as well as here?"

Odysseus made no answer, but shook his head and brooded. Then a third man, Philoetius, joined them, who was bringing in a barren heifer and some goats. These were brought over by the boatmen who are there to take people over when anyone comes to them. So Philoetius made his heifer and his goats secure under the gatehouse, and then went up to the swineherd. "Who, swineherd," said he, "is this stranger that is lately come here? What is his family? Where does he come from? Poor fellow, he looks as if he had been some great man, but the gods give sorrow to whom they will—even to kings if it so pleases them."

As he spoke he went up to Odysseus and saluted him with his right hand. "Good day to you, father stranger," said he. "You seem to be very poorly off now, but I hope you will have better times by and by. Father Zeus, of all gods you are the most malicious. We are your own children, yet you show us no mercy in all our misery and afflictions. A sweat came over me when I saw this man, and my eyes filled with tears, for he reminds me of Odysseus, who I fear is going about in just such rags as this man's are, if indeed he is still among the living. If he is already dead and in the house of Hades, then alas for my good master, who made me his stockman when I was quite young among the Cephallenians, and now his cattle are countless; no one could have done better with them than I have, for they have bred like ears of corn; nevertheless I have to keep bringing them in for others to eat, who take no heed of his son though he is in the house, and fear not the wrath of heaven, but are already eager to divide Odysseus' property among them because he has been away so long. I have often thought—only it would not be right while his son

is living—of going off with the cattle to some foreign country; bad as this would be, it is still harder to stay here and be
ill-treated, watching over cattle that are at the disposal of
strangers. My position is intolerable, and I should long since
have run away and put myself under the protection of some
other chief, only that I believe my poor master will yet return, and send all these suitors flying out of the house."

"Stockman," answered Odysseus, "you seem to be a very
well-disposed person, and I can see that you are a man of
sense. Therefore I will tell you, and will confirm my words
with an oath. By Zeus, the chief of all gods, and by that hearth
of Odysseus to which I am now come, Odysseus shall return
before you leave this place, and if you are so minded, you
shall see him killing the suitors who are now masters here."

"If Zeus were to bring this to pass," replied the stockman,
"you should see how I would do my very utmost to help him."

And in like manner Eumaeus prayed that Odysseus
might return home.

Thus did they converse. Meanwhile the suitors were
hatching a plot to murder Telemachus; but a bird flew near
them on their left hand—an eagle with a dove in its talons. On
this, Amphinomus said, "My friends, this plot of ours to murder Telemachus will not succeed; let us go to dinner instead."

The others assented, so they went inside and laid their
cloaks on the benches and seats. They sacrificed the sheep,
goats, pigs, and the heifer, and when the inner parts were
cooked they served them round. They mixed the wine in the
mixing bowls, and the swineherd gave every man his cup,
while Philoetius handed round the bread in the bread baskets, and Melanthius poured them out their wine. Then they
laid their hands upon the good things that were before them.

Telemachus purposely made Odysseus sit within the hall,
by the stone threshold; he gave him a shabby-looking seat at
a little table to himself, and had his portion of the inner parts
brought to him, with his wine in a gold cup. "Sit there," said

he, "and drink your wine among the great people. I will put a stop to the gibes and blows of the suitors, for this is no public house, but belongs to Odysseus, and has passed from him to me. Therefore, suitors, keep your hands and your tongues to yourselves, or there will be mischief."

The suitors bit their lips, and marvelled at the boldness of his speech; then Antinous said, "We do not like such language but we will put up with it, for Telemachus is threatening us in good earnest. If Zeus had let us, we should have put a stop to his brave talk ere now."

Thus spoke Antinous, but Telemachus heeded him not. Meanwhile the heralds were bringing the holy hecatomb through the city, and the Achaeans gathered in the shady grove of Apollo.

Then they roasted the outer flesh, drew it off the spits, gave every man his portion, and feasted to their hearts' content; those who waited at table gave Odysseus exactly the same portion as the others had, for Telemachus had told them to do so.

But Athene would not let the suitors for one moment drop their insolence, for she wanted Odysseus to become still more bitter against them. Now, there happened to be among them a ribald fellow, whose name was Ctesippus, and who came from Same. This man, confident in his great wealth, was paying court to the wife of Odysseus, and said to the suitors, "Hear what I have to say. The stranger has already had as large a portion as anyone else; this is well, for it is not right nor reasonable to ill-treat any guest of Telemachus who comes here. I will, however, make him a present on my own account, that he may have something to give to the bath woman, or to some other of Odysseus' servants."

As he spoke, he picked up a heifer's foot from the meat basket in which it lay, and threw it at Odysseus, but Odysseus turned his head a little aside, and avoided it, smiling grimly as he did so, and it hit the wall, not him. On this, Telemachus spoke fiercely to Ctesippus. "It is a good thing for you," said he, "that the stranger turned his head so that you missed him. If you had hit him I should have run you through with my spear, and your father would have had to see about getting you buried rather than married in this house. So let me have no more unseemly behaviour from any of you, for I am grown up now to the knowledge of good and evil and understand what is going on, instead of being the child that I have been before. I have long seen you killing my sheep and making free with my corn and wine; I have put up with this, for one man is no match for many, but do me no further violence. If you wish to kill me, kill me; I would far rather die than see such disgraceful scenes day after day—guests insulted, and men dragging the women servants about the house in an unseemly way."

They all held their peace till at last Agelaus, son of Damastor, said, "No one should take offence at what has been said, nor gainsay it, for it is just. Leave off, therefore, ill-treating the stranger, or anyone else of the servants who are about the house; I would say, however, a friendly word to Telemachus and his mother, which I trust may commend itself to both. 'As long,' I would say, 'as you had ground for hoping that Odysseus would one day come home, no one could complain of your waiting and refusing the suitors in your house. It would have been better if he had returned, but it is now sufficiently clear that he will never do so; therefore talk all this quietly over with your mother, and tell her to marry the best man, and the one who makes her the most advantageous offer. Thus you will yourself be able to manage your own inheritance, and eat and drink in peace, while your mother will look after some other man's house, not yours.' "

To this Telemachus answered, "By Zeus, Agelaus, and by the sorrows of my unhappy father, who has either perished far from Ithaca, or is wandering in some distant land, I throw no obstacles in the way of my mother's marriage; on the contrary, I urge her to choose whomsoever she will, and I will give her countless gifts into the bargain, but I dare not insist pointblank that she shall leave the house against her own wishes. Heaven forbid that I should do this."

Athene now made the suitors fall to laughing immoderately, and set their wits wandering; but they were laughing with a forced laughter. Their meat became smeared with blood; their eyes filled with tears, and their hearts were heavy with forebodings. Theoclymenus saw this and said, "Unhappy men, what is it that ails you? There is a shroud of darkness drawn over you from head to foot; your cheeks are wet with tears; the air is alive with wailing voices; the walls and roof beams drip blood; the entrance of the house and the court beyond it are full of ghosts trooping down into the night of hell; the sun is blotted out of heaven, and an evil mist is over all the land."

Thus did he speak, and they all of them laughed heartily. Eurymachus then said, "This stranger who has lately come here has lost his senses. Servants, turn him out into the streets, since he finds it so dark here."

But Theoclymenus said, "Eurymachus, you need not send anyone with me. I have eyes, ears, and a pair of feet of my own, to say nothing of an understanding mind. I will take these out of the house with me, for I see mischief overhanging you, from which not one of you men who are insulting people and plotting ill deeds in the house of Odysseus will be able to escape."

He left the house as he spoke, and went back to Piraeus, who gave him welcome, but the suitors kept looking at one another and provoking Telemachus by laughing at the strangers. One insolent fellow said to him, "Telemachus, you are not happy in your guests; first you have this importunate tramp, who comes begging bread and wine and has no skill for work or for hard fighting, but is perfectly useless; and now here is another fellow, who is setting himself up as a prophet. Let me persuade you; it would be much better to put them on board ship and send them off to the Sicels to sell for what they will bring."

Telemachus gave him no heed, but sat silently watching his father, expecting every moment that he would begin his attack upon the suitors.

Meanwhile the daughter of Icarius, wise Penelope, had had a rich seat placed for her facing the hall, so that she could hear what everyone was saying. The dinner indeed had been prepared amid much merriment; it had been both good and abundant, for they had sacrificed many victims; but the supper was yet to come, and nothing can be conceived more gruesome than the meal which a goddess and a brave man were soon to lay before them—for they had brought their doom upon themselves.

BOOK XXI

❧

The Trial of the Axes, During Which Odysseus
Reveals Himself to Eumaeus and Philoetius

ATHENE NOW put it in Penelope's mind to make the suitors try
their skill with the bow and with the iron axes, in contest
among themselves, as a means of bringing about their destruction. She went upstairs and got the storeroom key, which
was made of bronze and had a handle of ivory; she then went
with her maidens into the storeroom at the end of the house,
where her husband's treasures of gold, bronze, and wrought
iron were kept, and where was also his bow, and the quiver
full of deadly arrows that had been given him by a friend
whom he had met in Lacedaemon, Iphitus, the son of Eurytus. The two fell in with one another in Messene at the house
of Ortilochus, where Odysseus went in order to recover a
debt that was owing from the whole people; for the Messeni-
ans had carried off three hundred sheep from Ithaca, and had
sailed away with them and with their shepherds. In quest of
these Odysseus took a long journey while still quite young,
for his father and the other chieftains sent him on a mission
to recover them. Iphitus had gone there also to try and get
back twelve brood mares that he had lost, and the mule foals
that were running with them. These mares were the death of
him in the end, for when he went to the house of Zeus's son,
mighty Heracles, who performed such prodigies of valour,
Heracles to his shame killed him, though he was his guest, for
he feared not heaven's vengeance, nor yet respected his own

table which he had set before Iphitus, but killed him in spite of everything, and kept the mares himself. It was when looking for these that Iphitus met Odysseus, and gave him the bow which mighty Eurytus had been used to carry, and which on his death had been left by him to his son. Odysseus gave him in return a sword and a spear, and this was the beginning of a firm friendship, although they never visited one another's houses, for Zeus's son Heracles killed Iphitus ere they could do so. This bow, then, given him by Iphitus, had not been taken with him by Odysseus when he sailed for Troy; he had used it so long as he had been at home, but had left it behind him as a keepsake from a valued friend.

Penelope presently reached the oak threshold of the storeroom; the carpenter had planed this duly, and had drawn a line on it so as to get it quite straight; he had then set the doorposts into it and hung the doors. She loosed the strap from the handle of the door, put in the key, and drove it straight home to shoot back the bolts that held the doors; these flew open with a noise like a bull bellowing in a meadow, and Penelope stepped upon the raised platform where the chests stood in which the fair linen and clothes were laid along with fragrant herbs; reaching from there, she took down the bow with its bow case from the peg on which it hung. She sat down with it on her knees, weeping bitterly as she took the bow out of its case, and when her tears had relieved her, she went to the hall where the suitors were, carrying the bow and the quiver, with the many deadly arrows that were inside it. Along with her came her maidens, bearing a chest that contained much iron and bronze which her husband had won as prizes. When she reached the suitors, she stood by one of the pillars supporting the roof, holding a veil before her face, and with a maid on either side of her. Then she said:

"Listen to me, you suitors, who persist in abusing the hospitality of this house because its owner has been long absent, and without other pretext than that you want to marry me;

this, then, being the prize that you are contending for, I will put before you the mighty bow of Odysseus, and whosoever of you shall string it most easily and send his arrow through each one of twelve axes, him will I follow and quit my lawful husband's house, so goodly and so abounding in wealth. But even so, I doubt not that I shall remember it in my dreams."

So she spoke, and told Eumaeus to set the bow and the pieces of iron before the suitors, and Eumaeus wept as he took them to do as she had bidden him. Hard by, the stockman wept also when he saw his master's bow, but Antinous scolded them. "You country louts," said he, "silly simpletons; why should you add to the sorrows of your mistress by crying in this way? She has enough to grieve her in the loss of her husband; sit still, therefore, and eat your dinners in silence, or go outside if you want to cry, and leave the bow behind you. We suitors will have to contend for it with might and main, for we shall find it no easy matter to string such a bow as this is. There is not a man of us all who is such as Odysseus; for I have seen him and remember him, though I was then only a child."

This was what he said, but all the time he was expecting to be able to string the bow and shoot through the iron, whereas in fact he was to be the first that should taste of an arrow from the hands of Odysseus, whom he was dishonouring in his own house, egging the others on to do so also.

Then Telemachus spoke. "Great heavens!" he exclaimed. "Zeus must have robbed me of my senses. Here is my dear and excellent mother saying she will quit this house and marry again, yet I am laughing and enjoying myself as though there were nothing happening. But, suitors, as the contest has been agreed upon, let it go forward. It is for a woman whose equal is not to be found in Pylos, Argos, or Mycenae, nor yet in Ithaca nor on the mainland. You know this as well as I do; what need have I to speak in praise of my mother? Come on then, make no excuses for delay, but let us see whether you can string the bow or no. I too will make trial of it, for if I can string it and shoot through the iron, I should not be so sorry if my mother were to leave this house to go with a stranger, if I myself were left behind capable now of using the fine weapons that belonged to my father."

As he spoke, he sprang from his seat, threw his crimson cloak from him, and took his sword from his shoulder. First he set the axes in a row, in a long groove which he had dug for them, and had made straight by line. Then he stamped the earth tight round them, and everyone was surprised when they saw him set them up so orderly, though he had never seen anything of the kind before. This done, he went on to the threshold to make trial of the bow; thrice did he tug at it, trying with all his might to draw the string, and thrice he had to leave off, though he had hoped to string the bow and shoot through the iron. He was trying for the fourth time, and would have strung it, had not Odysseus shaken his head to check him in spite of his eagerness. So he said:

"Alas! I shall either be always feeble and of no prowess, or I am too young and have not yet reached my full strength so as to be able to hold my own if anyone attacks me. You others, therefore, who are stronger than I, make trial of the bow and get this contest settled."

On this, he put the bow down, letting it lean against the door, with the arrow standing against the top of the bow. Then he sat down on the seat from which he had risen, and Antinous said:

"Come on, each of you in turn, going towards the right from the place at which the cupbearer begins when he is handing round the wine."

The rest agreed, and Leiodes, son of Oenops, was the first to rise. He was sacrificial priest to the suitors, and always sat in the corner near the mixing bowl. He was the only man who hated their evil deeds and was indignant with the others. He was now the first to take the bow and arrow, so he went on to the threshold to make his trial, but he could not string the bow, for his hands were weak and unused to hard work; they therefore soon grew tired, and he said to the suitors, "My friends, I cannot string it; let another have it. This bow shall take the life and soul out of many a chief among us, for it is better to die than to live after having missed the prize that we have so long striven for, and which has brought us so long together. Some one of us is even now hoping and praying that he may marry Penelope, but when he has seen this bow and tried it, let him woo and make bridal offerings to some other woman, and let Penelope marry whoever gives her the most gifts and whose lot it is to win her."

On this, he put the bow down, letting it lean against the door, with the arrow standing against the tip of the bow. Then he took his seat again on the seat from which he had risen; and Antinous rebuked him, saying:

"Leiodes, what are you talking about? Your words are monstrous and intolerable; it makes me angry to listen to you. Shall, then, this bow take the life of many a chief among us, merely because you cannot bend it yourself? True, you were not born to be an archer, but there are others who will soon string it."

Then he said to Melanthius, the goatherd, "Look sharp, light a fire in the court, and set a seat hard by with a sheepskin on it; bring us also a large ball of lard from what they have in the house. Let us warm the bow and grease it; we will then make trial of it again, and bring the contest to an end."

Melanthius lit the fire and set a seat covered with sheepskins beside it. He also brought a great ball of lard from what they had in the house, and the suitors warmed the bow and again made trial of it, but they were none of them nearly strong enough to string it. Nevertheless there still remained Antinous and Eurymachus, who were the ringleaders among the suitors and much the foremost among them all.

Then the swineherd and the stockman left the hall together, and Odysseus followed them. When they had got outside the gates and the outer yard, Odysseus said to them quietly:

"Stockman, and you, swineherd, I have something in my mind which I am in doubt whether to say or no; but I think I will say it. What manner of men would you be to stand by Odysseus, if some god should bring him back here all of a sudden? Say which you are disposed to do—to side with the suitors, or with Odysseus?"

"Father Zeus," answered the stockman, "would indeed that you might so ordain it. If some god were but to bring Odysseus back, you should see with what might I would fight for him."

In like words Eumaeus prayed to all the gods that Odysseus might return; when, therefore, he saw for certain what mind they were of, Odysseus said, "It is I, Odysseus, who am here. I have suffered much, but at last, in the twentieth year, I am come back to my own country. I find that you two alone of all my menservants are glad that I should do so, for I have not heard any of the others praying for my return. To you two, therefore, will I unfold the truth as it shall be. If heaven shall deliver the suitors into my hands, I will find wives for both of you, will give you house and holding close to my own, and you shall be to me as though you were brothers and friends of Telemachus. I will now give you convincing proof, that you may know me and be assured. See, here is the scar from the boar's tooth that ripped me when I was out hunting on Mount Parnassus with the sons of Autolycus."

As he spoke, he drew his rags aside from the great scar, and when they had examined it thoroughly, they both of them wept about Odysseus, threw their arms round him, and kissed his head and shoulders, while Odysseus kissed their hands and faces in return. The sun would have gone down upon their lamenting if Odysseus had not checked them and said:

"Cease your weeping, lest someone should come outside and see us, and tell those who are within. When you go in, do so separately, not both together; I will go first, and do you follow afterwards; let this, moreover, be the token between us: the suitors will all of them try to prevent me from getting hold of the bow and quiver; do you, therefore, Eumaeus, bring it through the hall and place it in my hands, and tell the women to close the doors of their apartment. If they hear any groaning or uproar as of men fighting about the house, they must not come out; they must keep quiet, and stay where they are at their work. And I charge you, Philoetius, to make fast the doors of the outer court, and to bind them securely at once."

When he had thus spoken, he went back to the house and took the seat that he had left. Presently his two servants followed him inside.

At this moment the bow was in the hands of Eurymachus, who was warming it by the fire, but even so he could not string it, and he was greatly grieved. He heaved a deep sigh and said, "I grieve for myself and for us all; I grieve that I shall have to forgo the marriage, but I do not care nearly so much about this, for there are plenty of other women in Ithaca and elsewhere; what I feel most is the fact of our being so inferior to Odysseus in strength that we cannot string his bow. This will disgrace us in the eyes of those who are yet unborn."

"It shall not be so, Eurymachus," said Antinous, "and you know it yourself. Today is the feast of Apollo throughout all the land; who can string a bow on such a day as this? Put it on one side. As for the axes, they can stay where they are, for no one is likely to come to the house and take them away. Let the cupbearer go round the cups, that we may make our drink offerings and drop this matter of the bow; we will tell Melanthius to bring us in some goats tomorrow, the best he has; we can then offer thighbones to Apollo, the mighty archer, and again make trial of the bow, so as to bring the contest to an end."

The rest approved his words, and thereon menservants poured water over the hands of the guests, while pages filled the mixing bowls with wine and water and handed it round after giving every man his drink offering. Then, when they had made their offerings and had drunk each as much as he desired, Odysseus craftily said:

"Suitors of the illustrious queen, listen that I may speak as I am minded. I appeal more especially to Eurymachus, and to Antinous, who has just spoken with so much reason, saying that you should cease shooting for the present and leave the matter to the gods, but in the morning let heaven give victory to whom it will. For the moment, however, give me the bow, that I may test the power of my hands among you all, and see whether I still have as much strength as I used to have, or whether travel and neglect have made an end of it."

This made them all very angry, for they feared he might string the bow. Antinous therefore rebuked him fiercely, saying, "Wretched creature, you have not so much as a grain of sense in your whole body; you ought to think yourself lucky in being allowed to dine unharmed among your betters, without having any smaller portion served you than we others have had, and in being allowed to hear our conversation. No other beggar or stranger is allowed to hear what we say among ourselves; the wine must have been confusing you, as it does with all those who drink immoderately. It was wine that inflamed the centaur Eurytion when he was staying with Peirithous among the Lapiths. When the wine had got into his head, he went mad and did ill deeds about the house of Peirithous; this angered the heroes who were there assembled, so they rushed at him and cut off his ears and nostrils; then they dragged him through the doorway out of the house, so he went away crazed, and bore the marks of his crime, bereft of understanding. Henceforth, therefore, there was war between mankind and the centaurs, but he brought it upon himself through his own drunkenness. In like manner I can tell you that it will go hardly with you if you string the bow: you will find no mercy from anyone here, for we shall at once ship you off to King Echetus, who maims everyone that comes near him—you will never get away alive; so drink and keep quiet without getting into a quarrel with men younger than yourself."

Penelope then spoke to him. "Antinous," said she, "it is not right that you should ill-treat any guest of Telemachus who comes to this house. If the stranger should prove strong enough to string the mighty bow of Odysseus, can you suppose that he would take me home with him and make me his wife? Even the man himself can have no such idea in his mind; none of you need let that disturb his feasting; it would be out of all reason."

"Queen Penelope," answered Eurymachus, "we do not suppose that this man will take you away with him; it is impossible; but we are afraid lest some of the baser sort, men or women among the Achaeans, should go gossiping about and say, 'These suitors are a feeble folk; they are paying court to the wife of a brave man whose bow not one of them was able to string, and yet a beggarly tramp who came to the house strung it at once and sent an arrow through the iron.' This is what will be said, and it will be a scandal against us."

"Eurymachus," Penelope answered, "people who persist in eating up the estate of a great chieftain and dishonouring his house must not expect others to speak well of them. Why then should you mind if men talk as you think they will? This stranger is strong and well-built; he says, moreover, that he is of noble birth. Give him the bow, and let us see whether he can string it or no. I say—and it shall surely be—that if Apollo vouchsafes him the glory of stringing it, I will give him a cloak and tunic of good wear, with a javelin to keep off dogs and robbers, and a sharp sword. I will also give him sandals, and will see him sent safely wherever he wants to go."

Then Telemachus said, "Mother, I am the only man either in Ithaca or in the islands that are over against Elis who has the right to let anyone have the bow or to refuse it. No one shall force me one way or the other, not even though I choose to make the stranger a present of the bow outright, and let him take it away with him. Go, then, within the house and busy yourself with your daily duties, your loom, your distaff, and the ordering of your servants. This bow is a man's matter, and mine above all others, for it is I who am master here."

She went wondering back into the house, and laid her son's words in her heart. Then, going upstairs with her handmaids into her room, she mourned her dear husband till Athene sent sweet sleep over her eyelids.

The swineherd now took up the bow and was taking it to Odysseus, but the suitors shouted at him from all parts of the hall, and one of them said, "You idiot, where are you taking the bow to? Are you out of your wits? If Apollo and the other gods will grant our prayer, your own hounds shall get you into some quiet place, and worry you to death."

Eumaeus was frightened at the outcry they all raised, so he put the bow down there, but Telemachus shouted out at him from the other side of the hall, and threatened him, saying, "Father Eumaeus, bring the bow on in spite of them, or young as I am, I will pelt you with stones back to the country, for I am the better man of the two. I wish I were as much stronger than all the other suitors in the house as I am than you; I would soon send some of them off in poor shape, for they are plotting against me."

Thus did he speak, and they all of them laughed heartily, which put them in a better humour with Telemachus; so Eumaeus brought the bow down the hall and placed it in the hands of Odysseus. When he had done this, he called Eurycleia apart and said to her, "Eurycleia, Telemachus says you are to close the doors of the women's apartments. If they hear any groaning or uproar as of men fighting about the house, they are not to come out, but are to keep quiet and stay where they are at their work."

Eurycleia did as she was told and closed the doors of the women's apartments.

Meanwhile Philoetius slipped quietly out and made fast the gates of the outer court. There was a ship's cable of biblus fibre lying in the gatehouse, so he made the gates fast with it and then came in again, resuming the seat that he had left, and kept an eye on Odysseus, who had now got the bow in his hands, and was turning it every way about, and testing it all over to see whether the worms had been eating into its two horns during his absence. Then would one turn towards his neighbour, saying, "This is some tricky old bow fancier; either he has got one like it at home, or he wants to make one, in such workmanlike style does the old vagabond handle it."

Another said, "I hope he may be no more successful in other things than he is likely to be in stringing this bow."

But Odysseus, when he had taken it up and examined it all over, strung it as easily as a skilled bard strings a new peg of his lyre and makes the twisted gut fast at both ends. Then he took it in his right hand to test the string, and it sang sweetly under his touch like the twittering of a swallow. The suitors were dismayed, and turned colour as they heard it; at that moment, moreover, Zeus thundered loudly as a sign, and the heart of Odysseus rejoiced as he heard the omen that the son of scheming Cronus had sent him.

He took an arrow that was lying upon the table—for those which the Achaeans were so shortly about to taste were all inside the quiver—he laid it on the centre piece of the bow, and drew the notch of the arrow and the string towards him, still seated on his seat. When he had taken aim, he let fly, and his arrow pierced every one of the handle holes of the axes from the first onwards till it had gone right through them, and into the outer courtyard. Then he said to Telemachus:

"Your guest has not disgraced you, Telemachus. I did not miss what I aimed at, and I was not long in stringing my bow. I am still strong, and not as the suitors twit me with being. Now, however, it is time to prepare supper for the Achaeans while

there is still daylight, and then otherwise to disport ourselves
with song and dance, which are the ornaments of a banquet."

As he spoke, he made a sign with his eyebrows, and
Telemachus girded on his sword, grasped his spear, and
stood armed beside his father's seat.

BOOK XXII

❦

*The Killing of the Suitors—The Maids Who Have
Misconducted Themselves Are Made to Cleanse the
Cloisters, and Are Then Hanged*

THEN ODYSSEUS tore off his rags, and sprang onto the broad
threshold with his bow and his quiver full of arrows. He
poured the arrows onto the ground at his feet and said, "The
mighty contest is at an end. I will now see whether Apollo
will vouchsafe it to me to hit another mark which no man
has yet hit."

On this, he aimed a deadly arrow at Antinous, who was
about to take up a two-handled gold cup to drink his wine,
and already had it in his hands. He had no thought of
death—who amongst all the revellers would think that one
man, however brave, would stand alone among so many and
kill him? The arrow struck Antinous in the throat, and the
point went clean through his neck, so that he fell over and
the cup dropped from his hand, while a thick stream of
blood gushed from his nostrils. He kicked the table from
him and upset the things on it, so that the bread and roasted
meats were all soiled as they fell onto the ground. The suitors were in an uproar when they saw that a man had been
hit; they sprang in dismay, one and all of them, from their
seats and looked everywhere towards the walls, but there
was neither shield nor spear, and they rebuked Odysseus
very angrily. "Stranger," said they, "you shall pay for shooting
people in this way: you shall see no other contest; you are a

doomed man; he whom you have slain was the foremost youth in Ithaca, and the vultures shall devour you for having killed him."

Thus they spoke, for they thought that he had killed Antinous by mistake, and did not perceive that death was hanging over every one of them. But Odysseus glared at them and said:

"Dogs, did you think that I should not come back from Troy? You have wasted my substance, have forced my women servants to lie with you, and have wooed my wife while I was still living. You have feared neither god nor man, and now you shall die."

They turned pale with fear as he spoke, and every man looked round about to see whither he might fly for safety, but Eurymachus alone spoke.

"If you are Odysseus," said he, "then what you have said is just. We have done much wrong on your lands and in your house. But Antinous, who was responsible for the offending, lies low already. It was all his doing. It was not that he wanted to marry Penelope; he did not so much care about that; what he wanted was something quite different, and Zeus has not vouchsafed it to him; he wanted to kill your son and to be chief man in Ithaca. Now, therefore, that he has met the death which was his due, spare the lives of your people. We will make everything good among ourselves, and pay you in full for all that we have eaten and drunk. Each one of us shall pay you a fine worth twenty oxen, and we will keep on giving you gold and bronze till your heart is softened. Until we have done this, no one can complain of your being enraged against us."

Odysseus again glared at him and said, "Though you should give me all that you have in the world now and all that you ever shall have, I will not stay my hand till I have paid all of you in full. You must fight, or fly for your lives; and fly not a man of you shall."

Their hearts sank as they heard him, but Eurymachus again spoke, saying:

"My friends, this man will give us no quarter. He will stand where he is and shoot us down till he has killed every man among us. Let us then show fight; draw your swords, and hold up the tables to shield you from his arrows. Let us have at him with a rush, to drive him from the threshold and doorway; we can then get through into the town, and raise such an alarm as shall soon stop his shooting."

As he spoke, he drew his keen blade of bronze, sharpened on both sides, and with a loud cry sprang towards Odysseus, but Odysseus instantly shot an arrow into his breast that caught him by the nipple and fixed itself in his liver. He dropped his sword and fell doubled up over his table. The cup and all the meats went over onto the ground as he smote the earth with his forehead in the agonies of death, and he kicked the stool with his feet until his eyes were closed in darkness.

Then Amphinomus drew his sword and made straight at Odysseus to try and get him away from the door; but Telemachus was too quick for him, and struck him from behind; the spear caught him between the shoulders and went right through his chest, so that he fell heavily to the ground and struck the earth with his forehead. Then Telemachus sprang away from him, leaving his spear still in the body, for he feared that if he stayed to draw it out, some one of the Achaeans might come up and hack at him with his sword, or knock him down, so he set off at a run, and immediately was at his father's side. Then he said:

"Father, let me bring you a shield, two spears, and a brass helmet for your temples. I will arm myself as well, and will bring other armour for the swineherd and the stockman, for we had better be armed."

"Run and fetch them," answered Odysseus, "while my arrows hold out, or when I am alone they may get me away from the door."

Telemachus did as his father said, and went off to the
storeroom where the armour was kept. He chose four
shields, eight spears, and four brass helmets with horsehair
plumes. He brought them with all speed to his father, and
armed himself first, while the stockman and the swineherd
also put on their armour, and took their places near
Odysseus. Meanwhile Odysseus, as long as his arrows lasted,
had been shooting the suitors one by one, and they fell thick
one on another; when his arrows gave out, he leaned the
bow against the end wall of the house by the doorpost, and
hung a shield four hides thick about his shoulders; on his
mighty head he set his helmet, well wrought, with a crest of
horsehair that nodded menacingly above it, and he grasped
two redoubtable bronze-tipped spears.

Now, there was a side door in the wall, where at one end
of the threshold there was an exit leading to a narrow passage, and this exit was closed by a well-made door. Odysseus
told Eumaeus to stand by this door and guard it, for only one
person could attack it at a time. But Agelaus shouted out,
"Cannot someone go up to the side door and tell the people
what is going on? Help would come at once, and we should
soon make an end of this man and his shooting."

"This may not be, Agelaus," answered Melanthius. "The
mouth of the narrow passage is dangerously near the entrance to the outer court. One brave man could prevent any
number from getting out. But I know what I will do; I will
bring you arms from the storeroom, for I am sure it is there
that Odysseus and his son have put them."

On this, the goatherd Melanthius went by back passages
to the storeroom of Odysseus' house. There he chose twelve
shields, with as many helmets and spears, and brought them
back as fast as he could to give them to the suitors.
Odysseus' heart began to fail him when he saw the suitors
putting on their armour and brandishing their spears. He
saw the greatness of the danger, and said to Telemachus,

"Some one of the women inside is helping the suitors against us, or it may be Melanthius."

Telemachus answered, "The fault, Father, is mine, and mine only; I left the storeroom door open, and they have kept a sharper lookout than I have. Go, Eumaeus, put the door to, and see whether it is one of the women who is doing this, or whether, as I suspect, it is Melanthius, the son of Dolius."

Thus did they converse. Meanwhile Melanthius was again going to the storeroom to fetch armour, but the swineherd saw him and said to Odysseus, who was beside him, "Odysseus, noble son of Laertes, it is that scoundrel Melanthius, just as we suspected, who is going to the storeroom. Say, shall I kill him, if I can get the better of him, or shall I bring him here that you may take your own revenge for all the many wrongs that he has done in your house?"

Odysseus answered, "Telemachus and I will hold these suitors in check, no matter what they do; go back, both of you, and bind Melanthius' hands and feet behind him. Throw him into the storeroom and make the door fast behind you; then fasten a noose about his body, and string him close up to the rafters from a high pillar, that he may live on in agony."

Thus did he speak, and they did as he had said; they went to the storeroom, which they entered before Melanthius saw them, for he was busy searching for arms in the innermost part of the room, so the two took their stand on either side of the door and waited. By and by Melanthius came out with a helmet in one hand, and an old dried-up shield in the other, which had been borne by Laertes when he was young, but which had been long since thrown aside, and the straps had become unsewn; the two seized him, dragged him back by the hair, and threw him struggling to the ground. They bent his hands and feet well behind his back, and bound them tight with a painful bond as Odysseus had told them; then they fastened a noose to him and strung him up from a high pillar till he was close up to the rafters, and the swineherd

Eumaeus mocked at him, saying, "Melanthius, you will pass the night on a soft bed as you deserve. You will know very well when morning comes from the streams of Oceanus, and it is time for you to be driving in your goats for the suitors to feast on."

There, then, they left him tied up very painfully, and having put on their armour, they closed the door behind them and went back to take their places by the side of Odysseus; whereon the four men stood on the threshold, fierce and full of fury; nevertheless those who were in the body of the hall were still both brave and many. Then Zeus's daughter Athene came up to them, having assumed the voice and form of Mentor. Odysseus was glad when he saw her, and said, "Mentor, lend me your help, and forget not your old comrade, nor the many good turns he has done you. Besides, you are of the same age as myself."

But all the time he thought it was Athene, and the suitors from the other side raised an uproar when they saw her. Agelaus was the first to reproach her. "Mentor," he cried, "do not let Odysseus beguile you into siding with him and fighting the suitors. This is what we will do: when we have killed these people, father and son, we will kill you, too. You shall pay for it with your head, and when we have killed you, we will take all you have, indoors or out, and add it to Odysseus' property; we will not let your sons live in your house, nor your daughters, nor shall your widow continue to live in the city of Ithaca."

This made Athene still more furious, so she scolded Odysseus angrily. "Odysseus," said she, "your strength and prowess are no longer what they were when you fought for nine long years among the Trojans about the noble lady Helen. You killed many a man in those days, and it was through your stratagem that Priam's city was taken. How comes it that you are so lamentably less valiant now that you are on your own ground, face to face with the suitors in your own house? Come on, my good fellow, stand by my side and

see how Mentor, son of Alcimus, shall fight your foes and requite your kindnesses conferred upon him."

But she would not give him full victory as yet, for she
wished still further to test his own prowess and that of his
brave son, so she flew up to one of the rafters in the roof of
the hall and sat upon it in the form of a swallow.

Meanwhile Agelaus, son of Damastor, Amphimedon, Demoptolemus, Pisander, and Polybus, son of Polyctor, bore
the brunt of the fight upon the suitors' side; of all those who
were still fighting for their lives, they were by far the most
valiant, for the others had already fallen under the arrows of
Odysseus. Agelaus shouted to them and said, "My friends,
he will soon have to leave off, for Mentor has gone away
after having done nothing for him but brag. They are standing at the doors unsupported. Do not aim at him all at once,
but six of you throw your spears first, and see if you cannot
cover yourselves with glory by killing him. When he has
fallen, we need not be uneasy about the others."

They threw their spears as he bade them, but Athene
made them all of no effect. One hit a pillar of the hall; another went against the door; the pointed shaft of another
struck the wall; and as soon as they had avoided all the spears
of the suitors, Odysseus said to his own men, "My friends, we
too had better let drive into the middle of them, or they will
crown all the harm they have done us by killing us outright."

They therefore aimed straight in front of them and threw
their spears. Odysseus killed Demoptolemus, Telemachus
Euryades, Eumaeus Elatus, while the stockman killed
Pisander. These all bit the dust, and as the others drew back
into a corner, Odysseus and his men rushed forward and re-
gained their spears by drawing them from the bodies of the
dead.

The suitors now aimed a second time, but again Athene
made their weapons for the most part without effect. One
hit a pillar of the hall; another went against the door; while

the pointed shaft of another struck the wall. Still, Amphimedon just took a piece of the top skin from off Telemachus' wrist, and Ctesippus managed to graze Eumaeus' shoulder above his shield; but the spear went on and fell to the ground. Then Odysseus and his men let drive again into the crowd of suitors. Odysseus hit Eurydamas, Telemachus Amphimedon, and Eumaeus Polybus. After this the stockman hit Ctesippus in the breast, and taunted him, saying, "Foul-mouthed son of Polytherses, do not be so foolish as to talk wickedly another time, but let heaven direct your speech, for the gods are far stronger than men. I make you a present of this advice to repay you for the foot which you gave Odysseus when he was begging about in his own house."

Thus spoke the stockman, and Odysseus struck the son of Damastor with a spear in close fight, while Telemachus hit Leocritus, son of Evenor, in the belly, and the dart went clean through him, so that he fell forward full on his face upon the ground. Then Athene from her seat on the rafter held up her deadly aegis, and the hearts of the suitors quailed. They fled to the other end of the hall like a herd of cattle maddened by the gadfly in early summer, when the days are at their longest. As eagle-beaked, crook-taloned vultures from the mountains swoop down on the smaller birds that cower in flocks upon the ground, and kill them, for they can neither fight nor fly, and onlookers enjoy the sport—even so did Odysseus and his men fall upon the suitors and smite them on every side. They made a horrible groaning as their brains were being battered in, and the ground ran with their blood.

Leiodes then caught the knees of Odysseus and said, "Odysseus, I beseech you, have mercy upon me and spare me. I never wronged any of the women in your house either in word or in deed, and I tried to stop the others. I saw them, but they would not listen, and now they are paying for their folly. I was their sacrificing priest; if you kill me, I shall die without having done anything to deserve it, and shall have got no thanks for all the good that I did."

Odysseus looked sternly at him and answered, "If you were their sacrificing priest, you must have prayed many a time that it might be long before I got home again, and that you might marry my wife and have children by her. Therefore you shall die."

With these words he picked up the sword that Agelaus had dropped when he was being killed, and which was lying upon the ground. Then he struck Leiodes on the back of his neck, so that his head fell rolling in the dust while he was yet speaking.

The minstrel Phemius, son of Terpes—he who had been forced by the suitors to sing to them—now tried to save his life. He was standing near the side door, and held his lyre in his hand. He did not know whether to fly out of the hall and sit down by the altar of Zeus that was in the outer court, and on which both Laertes and Odysseus had offered up the thighbones of many an ox, or whether to go straight up to Odysseus and clasp his knees, but in the end he deemed it best to clasp Odysseus' knees. So he laid his lyre on the ground between the mixing bowl and the silver-studded seat; then, going up to Odysseus, he caught hold of his knees and said, "Odysseus, I beseech you, have mercy on me and spare me. You will be sorry for it afterwards if you kill a bard who can sing both for gods and men as I can. I make all my lays myself, and heaven visits me with every kind of inspiration. I would sing to you as though you were a god; do not therefore be in such a hurry to cut my head off. Your own son, Telemachus, will tell you that I did not want to frequent your house and sing to the suitors after their meals, but they were too many and too strong for me, so they made me."

Telemachus heard him, and at once went up to his father. "Hold!" he cried. "The man is guiltless, do him no hurt; and we will spare Medon too, who was always good to me when I was a boy, unless Philoetius or Eumaeus has already killed him, or he has fallen in your way when you were raging about the court."

Medon caught these words of Telemachus, for he was crouching under a seat, beneath which he had hidden by covering himself up with a freshly flayed heifer's hide; so he threw off the hide, went up to Telemachus, and laid hold of his knees.

"Here I am, my dear sir," said he. "Stay your hand, therefore, and tell your father, or he will kill me in his rage against the suitors for having wasted his substance and been so foolishly disrespectful to yourself."

Odysseus smiled at him and answered, "Fear not; Telemachus has saved your life, that you may know in future, and tell other people, how much better good deeds prosper than evil ones. Go, therefore, outside the hall into the outer court, and be out of the way of the slaughter—you and the bard—while I finish my work here inside."

The pair went into the outer court as fast as they could, and sat down by Zeus's great altar, looking fearfully round, and still expecting that they would be killed. Then Odysseus looked the whole house carefully over, to see if anyone had managed to hide himself and was still living, but he found them all lying in the dust and weltering in their blood. They were like fishes which fishermen have netted out of the sea, and thrown upon the beach to lie gasping for water till the heat of the sun makes an end of them. Even so were the suitors lying all huddled up, one against the other.

Then Odysseus said to Telemachus, "Call nurse Eurycleia; I have something to say to her."

Telemachus went and knocked at the door of the women's room. "Make haste," said he, "you old woman who have been set over all the other women in the house. Come outside; my father wishes to speak to you."

When Eurycleia heard this, she unfastened the door of the women's room and came out, following Telemachus. She found Odysseus among the corpses, bespattered with blood and filth like a lion that has just been devouring an ox, and his breast and both his cheeks are all bloody, so that he is a fearful sight; even so was Odysseus besmirched from head to foot with gore. When she saw all the corpses and such a quantity of blood, she was beginning to cry out for joy, for she saw that a great deed had been done; but Odysseus checked her. "Old woman," said he, "rejoice in silence; restrain yourself, and do not make any noise about it; it is an unholy thing to vaunt over dead men. Heaven's doom and their own evil deeds have brought these men to destruction, for they respected no man in the whole world, neither rich nor poor, who came near them, and they have come to a bad end as a punishment for their wickedness and folly. Now, however, tell me which of the women in the house have misconducted themselves, and who are innocent."

"I will tell you the truth, my son," answered Eurycleia. "There are fifty women in the house whom we have taught to do things, such as carding wool, and all kinds of household work. Of these, twelve in all have misbehaved, and have been wanting in respect to me, and also to Penelope. They showed no disrespect to Telemachus, for he has only lately grown up, and his mother never permitted him to give orders to the female servants; but let me go upstairs and tell your wife all that has happened, for some god has sent her to sleep."

"Do not wake her yet," answered Odysseus, "but tell the women who have misconducted themselves to come to me."

Eurycleia left the hall to tell the women, and make them come to Odysseus; in the meantime he called Telemachus, the stockman, and the swineherd. "Begin," said he, "to remove the dead, and make the women help you. Then get sponges and clean water to swill down the tables and seats. When you have thoroughly cleansed the whole house, take the women into the space between the domed room and the wall of the outer court, and run them through with your swords till they are quite dead, and have forgotten all about love and the way in which they used to lie in secret with the suitors."

On this, the women came down in a body, weeping and wailing bitterly. First they carried the dead bodies out, and propped them up against one another in the gatehouse. Odysseus himself ordered them about and made them do their work quickly, so they had to carry the bodies out. When they had done this, they cleaned all the tables and seats with sponges and water, while Telemachus and the two others shovelled up the blood and dirt from the ground, and the women carried it all away and put it out of doors. Then, when they had made the whole place quite clean and orderly, they took the women out and hemmed them in the narrow space between the wall of the domed room and that of the yard, so that they could not get away; and Telemachus said to the other two, "I shall not let these women die a clean death, for they were insolent to me and my mother, and used to sleep with the suitors."

So saying, he made a ship's cable fast to a great pillar and attached it to the top of the domed room, at a good height, lest any of the women's feet should touch the ground; and as thrushes or doves beat against a net that has been set for them in a thicket just as they were getting to their nests, and an unwished-for sleep awaits them, even so did the women have to put their heads in nooses one after the other and die most miserably. Their feet moved convulsively for a while, but not for very long.

As for Melanthius, they took him through the hall into the inner court. There they cut off his nose and his ears; they drew out his private parts and gave them to the dogs raw, and then in their fury they cut off his hands and his feet.

When they had done this, they washed their hands and feet and went back into the house, for all was now over; and Odysseus said to the dear old nurse Eurycleia, "Bring me sulphur, which cleanses all pollution, and fetch fire also, that

I may burn it, and purify the hall. Go, moreover, and tell Penelope to come here with her attendants, and also all the maidservants that are in the house."

"All that you have said is wise," answered Eurycleia, "but let me bring you some clean clothes—a tunic and cloak. Do not keep these rags on your back any longer. It is not right."

"First light me a fire," replied Odysseus.

She brought the fire and sulphur, as he had bidden her, and Odysseus thoroughly purified the hall and both the inner and outer courts. Then she went inside to call the women and tell them what had happened; whereon they came from their apartment with torches in their hands, and pressed round Odysseus to embrace him, kissing his head and shoulders and taking hold of his hands. It made him feel as if he should like to weep, for he remembered every one of them.

BOOK XXIII

❖

Penelope Eventually Recognises Her Husband—
Early in the Morning Odysseus, Telemachus,
Eumaeus, and Philoetius Leave the Town

EURYCLEIA NOW went upstairs laughing to tell her mistress that her dear husband had come home. Her aged knees became young again and her feet were nimble for joy as she went up to her mistress and bent over her head to speak to her. "Wake up, Penelope, my dear child," she exclaimed, "and see with your own eyes something that you have been wanting this long time past. Odysseus has at last come home again, and has killed the suitors who were giving so much trouble in his house, eating up his estate and ill-treating his son."

"My good nurse," answered Penelope, "you must be mad. The gods sometimes send some very sensible people out of their minds, and make foolish people become sensible. This is what they must have been doing to you; for you always used to be a reasonable person. Why should you thus mock me when I have trouble enough already—talking such nonsense, and waking me up out of a sweet sleep that had taken possession of my eyes and closed them? I have never slept so soundly from the day my poor husband went to that city with the ill-omened name. Go back again into the women's room; if it had been anyone else who had woken me up to bring me such absurd news, I should have sent her away with a severe scolding. As it is, your age shall protect you."

"My dear child," answered Eurycleia, "I am not mocking you. It is quite true, as I tell you, that Odysseus is come home again. He was the stranger whom they all kept on treating so badly in the hall. Telemachus knew all the time that he was come back, but kept his father's secret that he might have his revenge on all those wicked people."

Then Penelope sprang up from her couch, threw her arms round Eurycleia, and wept for joy. "But, my dear nurse," said she, "explain this to me; if he has really come home, as you say, how did he manage to overcome the wicked suitors single-handed, seeing what a number of them there always were?"

"I was not there," answered Eurycleia, "and do not know; I only heard them groaning while they were being killed. We sat crouching and huddled up in a corner of the women's room with the doors closed, till your son came to fetch me because his father sent him. Then I found Odysseus standing over the corpses that were lying on the ground all round him, one on top of the other. You would have enjoyed it if you could have seen him standing there all bespattered with blood and filth, and looking just like a lion. But the corpses are now all piled up in the gatehouse that is in the outer court, and Odysseus has lit a great fire to purify the house with sulphur. He has sent me to call you, so come with me, that you may both be happy together after all; for now at last the desire of your heart has been fulfilled; your husband is come home to find both wife and son alive and well, and to take his revenge in his own house on the suitors who behaved so badly to him."

"My dear nurse," said Penelope, "do not exult too confidently over all this. You know how delighted everyone would be to see Odysseus come home—most particularly myself, and the son who has been born to both of us; but what you tell me cannot be really true. It is some god who is angry with the suitors for their great wickedness, and has made an end of them; for they respected no man in the whole world, neither rich nor poor, who came near them, and they have come to a bad end in consequence of their iniquity; Odysseus is dead, far away from the Achaean land; he will never return home again."

Then nurse Eurycleia said, "My child, what are you talking about? But you were always unbelieving, and have made up your mind that your husband is never coming, although he is in this house and by his own fireside at this very moment. Besides, I can give you another proof; when I was washing him I perceived the scar which the wild boar gave him, and I wanted to tell you about it, but in his wisdom he would not let me, and clapped his hands over my mouth; so come with me and I will make this bargain with you: if I am deceiving you, you may have me killed by the most cruel death you can think of."

"My dear nurse," said Penelope, "however wise you may be, you can hardly fathom the counsels of the gods. Nevertheless we will go in search of my son, that I may see the corpses of the suitors, and the man who has killed them."

On this, she came down from her upper room, and while doing so, she considered whether she should keep at a distance from her husband and question him, or whether she should at once go up to him and embrace him. When, however, she had crossed the stone threshold, she sat down opposite Odysseus by the fire, against the other wall, while Odysseus sat near one of the pillars, looking upon the ground, and waiting to see what his brave wife would say to him when she saw him. For a long time she sat silent and as one lost in amazement. At one moment she looked him full in the face, but then again directly; she was misled by his shabby clothes and failed to recognise him till Telemachus began to reproach her and said:

"Mother—but you are so hard that I cannot call you by such a name—why do you keep away from my father in this way? Why do you not sit by his side and begin talking to him and asking him questions? No other woman could bear to keep away from her husband when he had come back to her after twenty years of absence, and after having gone through so much; but your heart always was as hard as a stone."

Penelope answered, "My son, I am so lost in astonishment that I can find no words in which either to ask questions or to answer them. I cannot even look him straight in the face. Still, if he really is Odysseus come back to his own home again, we shall get to understand one another better by and by, for there are tokens with which we two alone are acquainted, and which are hidden from all others."

Odysseus smiled at this, and said to Telemachus, "Let your mother put me to any proof she likes; she will make up her mind about it presently. She rejects me for the moment and believes me to be somebody else, because I am covered with dirt and have such bad clothes on; let us, however, consider what we had better do next. When someone has killed one man, even though he was not one who would leave many friends to take up his quarrel, the man who has killed him must still say goodbye to his friends and flee the country; whereas we have killed the most powerful men in the city, and all the picked youth of Ithaca. I would have you consider this matter."

"Look to it yourself, Father," answered Telemachus, "for they say you are the wisest councillor in the world, and that there is no other mortal man who can compare with you. We will follow you with right good will, nor shall you find us to fail you in so far as our strength holds out."

"I will say what I think will be best," answered Odysseus. "First wash and put your tunics on; tell the maids also to dress; Phemius shall then strike up a dance tune on his lyre, so that if people outside hear, or any of the neighbours or someone going along the street happens to notice it, they may think there is a wedding in the house, and no rumours about the death of the suitors will get about in the town, before we can escape to the woods upon my own land. Once there, we will settle which of the courses heaven vouchsafes us shall seem wisest."

Thus did he speak, and they did as he had said. First they washed and put their tunics on, while the women got ready. Then Phemius took his lyre and set them all longing for sweet song and stately dance. The house re-echoed with the sound of men and women dancing, and the people outside said, "I suppose the queen has been married at last. She ought to be ashamed of herself for not continuing to protect her husband's property until he comes home."

This was what they said, but they did not know what it was that had been happening. The housekeeper Eurynome washed and anointed Odysseus in his own house and gave him a tunic and cloak, while Athene made him look taller and stronger than before; she also made the hair grow thick on the top of his head, and flow down in curls like hyacinth blossoms; she beautified him about the head and shoulders just as a skilful workman who has studied art of all kinds under Hephaetus or Athene—and his work is full of beauty—enriches a piece of silver plate by gilding it. He came from the bath looking like one of the immortals, and sat down opposite his wife on the seat he had left. "My dear," said he, "heaven has endowed you with a heart more unyielding than woman ever yet had. No other woman could bear to keep away from her husband when he had come back to her after twenty years of absence, and after having gone through so much. But come, nurse, get a bed ready for me; I will sleep alone, for this woman has a heart as hard as iron."

"My dear," answered Penelope, "I have no wish to set myself up, nor to depreciate you; nor am I overcome by wonder, but I remember very well what kind of a man you were when you set sail from Ithaca. Nevertheless, Eurycleia, take his bed outside the bedchamber that he himself built. Bring the bed outside this room, and put bedding upon it with fleeces, good coverlets, and blankets."

She said this to try him, but Odysseus was very angry and said, "Wife, I am much displeased at what you have just been saying. Who has been taking my bed from the place in which I left it? He must have found it a hard task, no matter how skilled a workman he was, unless some god came and helped him to shift it. There is no man living, however strong and in his prime, who could move it from its place, for it is a marvellous curiosity which I made with my very own hands. There was a young olive growing within the precincts of the house, in full vigour, and about as thick as a pillar. I built my room round this with strong walls of stone and a roof to cover them, and I made the doors strong and well-fitting. Then I cut off the top boughs of the olive tree and left the stump standing. This I dressed roughly from the root upwards and then worked with carpenter's tools well and skilfully, straightening my work by drawing a line on the wood, and making it into a bedpost. I bored holes in it, and made it the first post of my bed, at which I worked till I had finished it, inlaying it with gold, silver, and ivory; after this I stretched a hide of crimson leather from one side of it to the other. So you see I know all about it, but I do not know whether it is still there, or whether anyone has been removing it by cutting down the olive tree at its roots."

When she heard the sure proofs Odysseus now gave her, she broke down. She flew weeping to his side, flung her arms about his neck, and kissed him. "Do not be angry with me, Odysseus," she cried, "you, who are the wisest of mankind. We have suffered, both of us. Heaven has grudged us the happiness of spending our youth and growing old together; do not then be aggrieved or take it amiss that I did not embrace you thus as soon as I saw you. I have been shuddering all the time through fear that someone might come here and deceive me with a lying story; for there are many very wicked people going about. Zeus's daughter Helen would never have slept with a man from a foreign country, if she had known that the sons of Achaeans would come after her and bring her back. Heaven put it in her heart to do wrong, and she gave no thought to that sin, which has been the source of all our sorrows. Now, however, that you have convinced me by showing that you know all about our bed (which no human being has even seen but you and I and a single maidservant, the daughter of Actor, who was given me by my father on my marriage, and who keeps the doors of our room), unbelieving though I have been, I can mistrust no longer."

Then Odysseus in his turn melted, and wept as he clasped his dear and faithful wife to his bosom. As the sight of land is welcome to men who are swimming towards the shore, when Poseidon has wrecked their ship with the fury of his winds and waves; a few alone reach the land, and these, covered with brine, are thankful when they find themselves on firm ground and out of danger—even so was her husband welcome to her as she looked upon him, and she could not tear her two fair arms from about his neck. Indeed they would have gone on indulging their sorrow till rosy-fingered morn appeared, had not Athene determined otherwise, and held night back in the far west, while she would not suffer Dawn to leave Oceanus, nor to yoke the two steeds Lampus and Phaethon that bear her onward to bring the day to mankind.

At last, however, Odysseus said, "Wife, we have not yet reached the end of our troubles. I have an unknown amount of toil still to undergo. It is long and difficult, but I must go through with it, for thus the shade of Teiresias prophesied concerning me, on the day when I went down into Hades to ask about my return and that of my companions. But now let us go to bed, that we may lie down and enjoy the blessed boon of sleep."

"You shall go to bed as soon as you please," replied Penelope, "now that the gods have sent you home to your own good house and to your country. But as heaven has put it in your mind to speak of it, tell me about the task that lies before you. I shall have to hear about it later, so it is better that I should be told at once."

"My dear," answered Odysseus, "why should you press me to tell you? Still I will not conceal it from you, though you will not like it. I do not like it myself, for Teiresias bade me travel far and wide, carrying an oar, till I came to a country where the people have never heard of the sea, and do not even mix salt with their food. They know nothing about ships, nor oars that are as the wings of a ship. He gave me this certain token, which I will not hide from you. He said that a wayfarer should meet me and ask me whether it was a winnowing shovel that I had on my shoulder. On this, I was to fix my oar in the ground and sacrifice a ram, a bull, and a boar to Poseidon; after which I was to go home and offer hecatombs to all the gods in heaven, one after the other. As for myself, he said that death should come to me from the sea, a very gentle death when I was full of years and peace of mind, and my people happy around me. All this, he said, should surely come to pass."

And Penelope said, "If the gods are going to vouchsafe you a happier time in your old age, you may hope then to have some respite from misfortune."

Thus did they converse. Meanwhile Eurynome and the nurse took torches and made the bed ready with soft coverlets; as soon as they had laid them, the nurse went back into the house to go to her rest, leaving the bedchamber woman, Eurynome, to show Odysseus and Penelope to bed by torchlight. When she had conducted them to their room, she went back, and they then came joyfully to the rites of their own old bed. Telemachus, Philoetius, and the swineherd now left off dancing, and made the women leave off also. They then laid themselves down to sleep in the hall.

When Odysseus and Penelope had had their fill of love, they fell talking with one another. She told him how much she had had to bear in seeing the house filled with a crowd of wicked suitors who had killed so many sheep and oxen on her account, and had drunk so many casks of wine. Odysseus in his turn told her what he had suffered, and how much trouble he had himself given to other people. He told her everything, and she was so delighted to listen that she never went to sleep till he had ended his whole story.

He began with his victory over the Cicones, and how he thence reached the fertile land of the lotus-eaters. He told her all about the Cyclops and how he had punished him for having so ruthlessly eaten his brave comrades; how he then went on to Aeolus, who received him hospitably and furthered him on his way, but even so he was not to reach home, for to his great grief, a hurricane carried him out to sea again; how he went on to the Laestrygonian city Telepylos, where the people destroyed all his ships with their crews, save himself and his own ship only. Then he told of cunning Circe and her craft, and how he sailed to the chill house of Hades, to consult the ghost of the Theban prophet Teiresias, and how he saw his old comrades in arms, and his mother, who bore him and brought him up when he was a child; how he then heard the wondrous singing of the Sirens, and went on to the wandering rocks and terrible Charybdis and to Scylla, whom no man had ever yet passed in safety; how his men then ate the cattle of the sun god, and how Zeus therefore struck the ship with his thunderbolts, so that all his men perished together, himself alone being left alive; how at last he reached the Ogygian island and the nymph Calypso, who kept him there in a cave, and fed him, and wanted him to marry her, in which case she intended making him immortal so that he should never grow old, but she could not persuade him to let her do so; and how after much suffering he had found his way to the Phaeacians, who had treated him as though he had been a god, and sent him back in a ship to his own country after having given him gold, bronze, and clothing in great abundance. This was the last thing about which he told her, for here a deep sleep took hold upon him and eased the burden of his sorrows.

Then Athene turned to other thoughts. When she deemed that Odysseus had had enough both of love and of sleep, she bade golden-throned Dawn rise out of Oceanus, that she might shed light upon mankind. On this, Odysseus rose from his comfortable bed and said to Penelope, "Wife, we have both of us had our full share of troubles—you here, in lamenting my absence, and I in being prevented from getting home though I was longing all the time to do so. Now, however, that we have at last come together, take care of the property that is in the house. As for the sheep and goats which the wicked suitors have eaten, I will take many myself by force from other people, and will compel the Achaeans to make good the rest till they shall have filled all my folds. I am now going to the wooded lands out in the country to see my father, who has so long grieved on my account, and to yourself I will give these instructions, though you have little need of them. At sunrise it will at once get abroad that I have killed the suitors; go upstairs, therefore, and stay there with your women. See nobody and ask no questions."

As he spoke, he girded on his armour. Then he roused Telemachus, Philoetius, and Eumaeus, and told them all to put on their armour also. This they did, and armed themselves. When they had done so, they opened the gates and sallied forth, Odysseus leading the way. It was now daylight, but Athene nevertheless concealed them in darkness and led them quickly out of the town.

BOOK XXIV

---❧---

*The Ghosts of the Suitors in Hades—Odysseus and
His Men Go to the House of Laertes—The People of
Ithaca Come Out to Attack Odysseus, but Athene
Concludes a Peace*

THEN HERMES of Cyllene summoned the ghosts of the suitors, and in his hand he held the fair golden wand with which
he seals men's eyes in sleep or wakes them, just as he
pleases; with this he roused the ghosts and led them, while
they followed whining and gibbering behind him. As bats fly
squealing in the hollow of some great cave, when one of
them has fallen out of the cluster in which they hang, even
so did the ghosts whine and squeal as Hermes, the helper,
led them down into the dark abode of death. When they had
passed the waters of Oceanus and the rock Leucas, they
came to the gates of the sun and the land of dreams,
whereon they reached the meadow of asphodel where dwell
the souls and shadows of them that can labour no more.

Here they found the ghost of Achilles, son of Peleus, with
those of Patroclus, Antilochus, and Ajax, who was the finest
and handsomest man of all the Danaans after the son of
Peleus himself.

They were gathered round the ghost of the son of Peleus,
and the ghost of Agamemnon joined them, sorrowing bitterly. Round him were gathered also the ghosts of those who
had perished with him in the house of Aegisthus; and the
ghost of Achilles spoke first.

"Son of Atreus," it said, "we used to say that Zeus loved you better from first to last than any other hero, for you were captain over many and brave men when we were all fighting together before Troy; yet the hand of death, which no mortal can escape, was laid upon you all too early. Better for you had you fallen at Troy in the heyday of your renown, for the Achaeans would have built a mound over your ashes, and your son would have been heir to your good name, whereas it has now been your lot to come to a most miserable end."

"Happy son of Peleus," answered the ghost of Agamemnon, "for having died at Troy, far from Argos, while the bravest of the Trojans and the Achaeans fell round you fighting for your body. There you lay in the whirling clouds of dust, a vast figure covering a vast expanse of ground, heedless now of your horsemanship. We fought the whole of the day, nor should we ever have left off if Zeus had not sent a hurricane to stay us. Then, when we had borne you to the ships out of the fray, we laid you on your bed and cleansed your fair skin with warm water and with ointments. The Danaans tore their hair and wept bitterly round about you. Your mother, when she heard, came with her immortal nymphs from out of the sea, and the sound of a great wailing went forth over the waters so that the Achaeans quaked for fear. They would have fled panic-stricken to their ships had not wise old Nestor, whose counsel was ever truest, checked them, saying, 'Hold, Argives, fly not, sons of the Achaeans; this is his mother coming from the sea with her immortal nymphs to view the body of her son.'

"Thus he spoke, and the Achaeans feared no more. The daughters of the old man of the sea stood round you weeping bitterly, and clothed you in immortal raiment. The nine Muses also came and lifted up their sweet voices in lament, calling and answering one another; there was not an Argive but wept for pity at the dirge they sang. Days and nights seven and ten we mourned you, mortals and immortals, but on the eighteenth day we gave you to the flames, and many a fat sheep with many an ox did we slay in sacrifice around you. You were burnt in raiment of the gods, with rich ointment and with honey, while heroes, horse and foot, clashed their armour round the pile as you were burning, with the tramp as of a great multitude. But when the flames of heaven had done their work, we gathered your white bones at daybreak and laid them in ointments and in pure wine. Your mother brought us a golden urn to hold them, gift of Dionysus, and work of Hephaestus himself; in this we mingled your bleached bones with those of Patroclus, who had gone before you, and separate we enclosed also those of Antilochus, who had been closer to you than any other of your comrades now that Patroclus was no more.

"Over these the host of the Argives built a noble tomb, on a point jutting out over the open Hellespont, that it might be seen from far out upon the sea by those now living and by those that shall be born hereafter. Your mother begged prizes from the gods, and offered them to be contended for by the noblest of the Achaeans. You must have been present at the funeral of many a hero, when the young men gird themselves and make ready to contend for prizes on the death of some great chieftain, but you never saw such prizes as silver-footed Thetis offered in your honour; for the gods loved you well. Thus even in death your fame, Achilles, has not been lost, and your name will live evermore among all mankind. But as for me, what solace had I when the days of my fighting were done? For Zeus willed my destruction on my return, by the hands of Aegisthus and those of my wicked wife."

Thus did they converse, and presently Hermes came up to them with the ghosts of the suitors who had been killed by Odysseus. The ghosts of Agamemnon and Achilles were astonished at seeing them, and went up to them at once. The ghost of Agamemnon recognised Amphimedon, son of Melaneus, who lived in Ithaca and had been his host, so it began to talk to him.

"Amphimedon," it said, "what has happened to all you fine young men—all of an age, too—that you are come down here under the ground? One could pick no finer body of men from any city. Did Poseidon raise his winds and waves against you when you were at sea, or did your enemies make an end of you on the mainland when you were cattle-lifting or sheep-stealing, or while fighting in defence of their wives and city? Answer my question, for I have been your guest. Do you not remember how I came to your house with Menelaus, to persuade Odysseus to join us with his ships against Troy? It was a whole month ere we could resume our voyage, for we had hard work to persuade Odysseus to come with us."

And the ghost of Amphimedon answered, "Agamemnon, son of Atreus, king of men, I remember everything that you have said, and will tell you accurately about the way our end was brought about. Odysseus had been long gone, and we were courting his wife, who did not say point-blank that she would not marry, nor yet bring matters to an end, for she meant to bring about our destruction: this, then, was the trick she played us. She set up a great tambour frame in her room and began to work on an enormous piece of fine needlework. 'Young men my suitors,' said she, 'Odysseus is indeed dead, but do not press me to marry again immediately; wait—for I would not have my threads perish unused—till I have completed a pall for the hero Laertes, against the time when death shall take him. He is very rich, and the women of the place will talk if he is laid out without a pall.' This is what she said, and we assented; whereupon we could see her working upon her great web all day long, but at night she would unpick the stitches again by torchlight. She fooled us in this way for three years without our finding it out, but as time wore on and she was now in her fourth year, as the moons waned and many days had been accomplished, one of her maids, who knew what she was doing, told us, and we caught her in the act of undoing her work, so she had to finish it whether she would or no; and when she showed us the robe she had made, after she had had it washed, its splendour was as that of the sun or moon.

"At that very time some malicious god conveyed Odysseus to the upland farm where his swineherd lives. Thither presently came also his son, returning from a voyage to Pylos, and the two came to the town when they had hatched their plot for our destruction. Telemachus came first, and then after him, accompanied by the swineherd, came Odysseus, clad in rags and leaning on a staff as though he were some miserable old beggar. He came so unexpectedly that none of us knew him, not even the older ones among us, and we reviled him and threw things at him. He endured being both struck and insulted without a word, though he was in his own house; but when the will of aegis-bearing Zeus inspired him, he and Telemachus took the armour and hid it in an inner chamber, bolting the doors behind them. Then he cunningly made his wife offer his bow and a quantity of iron to be a contest for us ill-fated suitors; and this was the beginning of our end, for not one of us could string the bow—nor nearly do so. When it was about to reach the hands of Odysseus, we all of us shouted out that it should not be given him, no matter what he might say, but Telemachus insisted on his having it. When he had got it in his hands, he strung it with ease and sent his arrow through the iron. Then he stood on the floor of the cloister and poured his arrows on the ground, glaring fiercely about him. First he killed Antinous, and then, aiming straight before him, he let fly his deadly darts and they fell thick on one another. It was plain that some one of the gods was helping them, for they fell upon us with might and main throughout the hall, and there was a hideous sound of groaning as our brains were being battered in, and the ground ran with our blood. This, Agamemnon, is how we came by our end, and our bodies are lying still uncared for in the house of Odysseus, for our friends at home do not yet know what has happened, so that they cannot lay us out and wash the black blood from our wounds, making moan over us according to the offices due to the departed."

"Happy Odysseus, son of Laertes," replied the ghost of Agamemnon. "You are indeed blessed in the possession of a wife endowed with such rare excellence of understanding, and so faithful to her wedded lord, as Penelope, the daughter of Icarius. The fame, therefore, of her virtue shall never die, and the immortals shall compose a song that shall be welcome to all mankind in honour of the constancy of Penelope. How far otherwise was the wickedness of the daughter of Tyndareus, who killed her lawful husband; her song shall be hateful among men, for she has brought disgrace on all womankind, even on the good ones."

Thus did they converse in the house of Hades, deep down within the bowels of the earth. Meanwhile Odysseus and the others passed out of the town and soon reached the fair and well-tilled farm of Laertes, which he had reclaimed with infinite labour. Here was his house, with a lean-to running all round it, where the slaves who worked for him slept and sat and ate, while inside the house there was an old Sicel woman, who looked after him in this, his country farm. When Odysseus got there, he said to his son and to the other two:

"Go to the house, and kill the best pig that you can find for dinner. Meanwhile I want to see whether my father will know me, or fail to recognise me after so long an absence."

He then took off his armour and gave it to Eumaeus and Philoetius, who went straight on to the house, while he turned off into the vineyard to make trial of his father. As he went down into the great orchard, he did not see Dolius, nor any of his sons nor of the other bondsmen, for they were all gathering stones to make a wall for the vineyard, at the place where the old man had told them; he therefore found his father alone, hoeing a vine. He had on a dirty old tunic, patched and very shabby; his legs were bound round with thongs of oxhide to save him from the brambles, and he also wore sleeves of leather; he had a goatskin cap on his head, and was looking very woebegone. When Odysseus saw him so worn, so old and full of sorrow, he stood still under a tall pear tree and began to weep. He wondered whether to embrace him, kiss him, and tell him all about his having come home, or whether he should first question him and see what he would say. In the end he deemed it best to make trial of him with mocking words, so in this mind he went up to his father, who was bending down and digging about a plant.

"I see, sir," said Odysseus, "that you are an excellent gardener: what pains you take with it to be sure. There is not a single plant, not a fig tree, vine, olive, pear, nor flower bed, but bears the traces of your attention. I trust, however, that you will not be offended if I say that you take better care of your garden than of yourself. You are old, dirty, and very meanly clad. It cannot be because you are idle that your master takes such poor care of you; indeed your face and figure have nothing of the slave about them, and proclaim you of noble birth. I should have said that you were one of those who should wash well, eat well, and lie soft at night as old men have a right to do; but tell me, and tell me true, whose bondman are you, and in whose garden are you working? Tell me also about another matter. Is this place that I have come to really Ithaca? I met a man just now who said so, but he was a dull fellow, and had not the patience to hear my story out when I was asking him about an old friend of mine, whether he was still living, or was already dead and in the house of Hades. Believe me when I tell you that this man came to my house once when I was in my own country and never yet did any stranger come to me whom I liked better. He said that his family came from Ithaca and that his father was Laertes, son of Arceisius. I received him hospitably, making him welcome to all the abundance of my house, and when he went away I gave him all customary presents. I gave him seven talents of fine gold, and a cup of solid silver with flowers chased upon it. I also gave him twelve cloaks of single fold, twelve rugs, twelve fair cloaks, and an equal number of tunics. To all this I added four good-looking women skilled in all useful arts, and I let him take his choice."

His father shed tears and answered, "Sir, you have indeed come to the country that you have named, but it is fallen into the hands of wicked people. All this wealth of presents has been given to no purpose. If you could have found your friend here alive in Ithaca, he would have entertained you hospitably and would have requited your presents amply when you left him—as would have been only right considering what you had given him. But tell me, and tell me true, how many years is it since you entertained this guest—my unhappy son, if he ever was? Alas! He has perished far from his own country; the fishes of the sea have eaten him, or he has fallen a prey to the birds and wild beasts of some continent. Neither his mother nor I his father, who were his parents, could throw our arms about him and wrap him in his shroud, nor could his excellent and richly dowered wife, Penelope, bewail her husband, as was fitting, upon his deathbed, and close his eyes according to the offices due to the departed. But now tell me truly, for I want to know. Who and whence are you; tell me of your town and parents. Where is the ship lying that has brought you and your men to Ithaca? Or were you a passenger on some other man's ship, and those who brought you here have gone on their way and left you?"

"I will tell you everything," answered Odysseus, "truly. I came from Alybas, where I have a fine house. I am the son of King Apheidas, who is the son of Polypemon. My own name is Eperitus; heaven drove me off my course as I was leaving Sicania, and I have been carried here against my will. As for my ship, it is lying over yonder, off the open country outside the town, and this is the fifth year since Odysseus left my country. Poor fellow; yet the omens were good for him when he left me. The birds all flew on our right hands, and both he and I rejoiced to see them as we parted, for we had every hope that we should have another friendly meeting and exchange presents."

A dark cloud of sorrow fell upon Laertes as he listened. He filled both hands with the dust from off the ground and poured it over his grey head, groaning heavily as he did so. The heart of Odysseus was touched, and his nostrils quivered as he looked upon his father; then he sprang towards him, flung his arms about him, and kissed him, saying, "I am he, Father, about whom you are asking—I have returned after having been away for twenty years. But cease your weeping and lamentation; we have no time to lose, for I should tell you that I have killed the suitors in my house, to punish them for their insolence and crimes."

"If you really are my son Odysseus," replied Laertes, "and have come back again, you must give me such manifest proof of your identity as shall convince me."

"First observe this scar," answered Odysseus, "which I got from a boar's tusk when I was hunting on Mount Parnassus. You and my mother had sent me to Autolycus, my mother's father, to receive the presents which when he was over here he had promised to give me. Furthermore I will point out to you the trees in the vineyard which you gave me when I was small, and I asked you all about them as I followed you round the garden. We went over them all, and you told me their names and what they all were. You gave me thirteen pear trees, ten apple trees, and forty fig trees; you also said you would give me fifty rows of vines, rows that ripen successively, and they yield grapes of every kind when the heat of heaven has been laid heavy upon them."

Laertes' strength failed him when he heard the convincing proofs which his son had given him. He threw his arms about him, and Odysseus had to support him, for he fainted; but as soon as he came to, and was beginning to recover his senses, he said, "O Father Zeus, then you gods are still in Olympus after all, if the suitors have really been punished for their insolence and folly. Nevertheless I am much afraid that we shall have all the townspeople of Ithaca up here directly, and they will be sending messengers everywhere throughout the cities of the Cephallenians."

Odysseus answered, "Take heart and do not trouble yourself about that, but let us go into the house hard by your garden. I have already told Telemachus, Philoetius, and Eumaeus to go on there and get dinner ready as soon as possible."

Thus conversing, the two made their way towards the house. When they got there they found Telemachus with the stockman and the swineherd, cutting up meat and mixing wine with water. Then the old Sicel woman took Laertes inside and washed him and anointed him with oil. She put on him a good cloak, and Athene came up to him and gave him a more imposing presence, making him taller and stouter than before. When he came back, his son was surprised to see him looking so like an immortal, and said to him, "My dear father, some one of the gods has been making you much taller and better-looking."

Laertes answered, "Would, by Father Zeus, Athene, and Apollo, that I were the man I was when I ruled among the Cephallenians, and took Nericum, that strong fortress on the shore. If I were still what I then was, and had been in our house yesterday with my armour on, I should have been able to stand by you and help you against the suitors. I should have killed a great many of them, and you would have rejoiced to see it."

Thus did they converse; but the others, when they had finished their work and the meal was ready, took each his place on the benches and seats. Then they began eating; by and by old Dolius and his sons left their work and came up, for their mother, the Sicel woman who looked after Laertes now that he was growing old, had been to fetch them. When they saw Odysseus and were certain it was he, they stood there lost in astonishment; but Odysseus scolded them good-naturedly and said, "Sit down to your dinner, old man, and never mind about your surprise; we have been wanting to begin for some time and have been waiting for you."

Then Dolius put out both his hands and went up to Odysseus. "Sir," said he, seizing his master's hand and kissing it at the wrist, "we have long been wishing you home; and now heaven has restored you to us after we had given up hoping. All hail, therefore, and may the gods prosper you. But tell me, does Penelope already know of your return, or shall we send someone to tell her?"

"Old man," answered Odysseus, "she knows already, so you need not trouble about that." On this, he took his seat, and the sons of Dolius gathered round Odysseus to give him greeting and embrace him one after the other; then they took their seats in due order near Dolius, their father.

While they were thus busy getting their dinner ready, Rumour went round the town, and noised abroad the terrible fate that had befallen the suitors; as soon, therefore, as the people heard of it, they gathered from every quarter, groaning and hooting before the house of Odysseus. They took the dead away, buried every man his own, and put the bodies of those who came from elsewhere on board the fishing vessels, for the fishermen to take, each of them to his own place. They then met angrily in the place of assembly, and when they were got together, Eupeithes rose to speak. He was overwhelmed with grief for the death of his son Antinous, who had been the first man killed by Odysseus, so he said, weeping bitterly, "My friends, this man has done the Achaeans great wrong. He took many of our best men away with him in his fleet, and he has lost both ships and men; now, moreover, on his return he has killed all the foremost men among the Cephallenians. Let us be up and doing before he can get away to Pylos or to Elis, where the Epeans rule, or we shall be ashamed of ourselves forever afterwards. It will be an everlasting disgrace to us if we do not avenge the murder of our sons and brothers. For my own part, I should have no more pleasure in life, but had rather die at once. Let us be up then, and after them, before they can cross over to the mainland."

He wept as he spoke and everyone pitied him. But Medon and the bard Phemius had now woken up, and came to them from the house of Odysseus. Everyone was astonished at seeing them, but they stood in the middle of the assembly, and Medon said, "Hear me, men of Ithaca. Odysseus did not do these things against the will of heaven. I myself saw an immortal god take the form of Mentor and stand beside him. This god appeared, now in front of him encouraging him, and now going furiously about the hall and attacking the suitors, whereon they fell thick on one another."

On this, pale fear laid hold of them, and old Halitherses, son of Mastor, rose to speak, for he was the only man among them who knew both past and future; so he spoke to them plainly and in all honesty, saying:

"Men of Ithaca, it is all your own fault that things have turned out as they have; you would not listen to me, nor yet to Mentor, when we bade you check the folly of your sons, who were doing much wrong in the wantonness of their hearts, wasting the substance and dishonouring the wife of a chieftain who they thought would not return. Now, however, let it be as I say, and do as I tell you. Do not go out against Odysseus, or you may find that you have brought down evil on your own heads."

This was what he said, and more than half raised a loud shout, and at once left the assembly. But the rest stayed where they were, for the speech of Halitherses displeased them, and they sided with Eupeithes; they therefore hurried off for their armour, and when they had armed themselves, they met together in front of the city, and Eupeithes led them on in his folly. He thought he was going to avenge the murder of his son, whereas in truth he was never to return, but was himself to perish in his attempt.

Then Athene said to Zeus, "Father, son of Cronus, king of kings, answer me this question: What do you propose to do? Will you set them fighting still further, or will you make peace between them?"

And Zeus answered, "My child, why should you ask me? Was it not by your own arrangement that Odysseus came home and took his revenge upon the suitors? Do whatever you like, but I will tell you what I think will be the most reasonable arrangement. Now that Odysseus is revenged, let them swear to a solemn covenant, in virtue of which he shall continue to rule, while we cause the others to forgive and forget the massacre of their sons and brothers. Let them then all become friends as heretofore, and let peace and plenty reign."

This was what Athene was already eager to bring about, so down she darted from the topmost summits of Olympus.

Now, when Laertes and the others had done dinner, Odysseus began by saying, "Some of you go out and see if they are not getting close up to us." So one of Dolius' sons went as he was bid. Standing on the threshold, he could see them all quite near, and said to Odysseus, "Here they are; let us put on our armour at once."

They put on their armour as fast as they could—that is to say, Odysseus, his three men, and the six sons of Dolius. Laertes also and Dolius did the same—warriors by necessity in spite of their grey hair. When they had all put on their armour, they opened the gate and sallied forth, Odysseus leading the way.

Then Zeus' daughter Athene came up to them, having assumed the form and voice of Mentor. Odysseus was glad when he saw her, and said to his son, Telemachus, "Telemachus, now that you are about to fight in an engagement which will show every man's mettle, be sure not to disgrace your father's house, men who have been eminent for our strength and courage all the world over."

"You say truly, my dear father," answered Telemachus, "and you shall see, if you will, that I am in no mind to disgrace your family."

Laertes was delighted when he heard this. "Good heavens," he exclaimed, "what a day I am enjoying. I do indeed rejoice at it. My son and grandson are vying with one another in the matter of valour."

On this, Athene came close up to him and said, "Son of Arceisius—best friend I have in the world—pray to the grey-eyed maiden, and to Zeus, her father; then poise your spear and hurl it."

As she spoke, she infused fresh vigour into him, and when he had prayed to her, he poised his spear and hurled it. He hit Eupeithes' helmet, and the spear went right through it, for the helmet stayed it not, and his armour rang rattling round him as he fell heavily to the ground. Meantime Odysseus and his son fell upon the front line of the foe and smote them with their swords and spears; indeed they would have killed every one of them, and prevented them from ever getting home again, only Athene raised her voice aloud, and made everyone pause. "Men of Ithaca," she cried, "cease this dreadful war, and settle the matter at once without further bloodshed."

On this, pale fear seized everyone; they were so frightened that their arms dropped from their hands and fell upon the ground at the sound of the goddess' voice, and they fled back to the city for their lives. But Odysseus gave a great cry, and gathering himself together, swooped down like a soaring eagle. Then the son of Cronus sent a thunderbolt of fire that fell just in front of Athene, so she said to Odysseus, "Odysseus, noble son of Laertes, stop this battle, or Zeus will be angry with you."

Thus spoke Athene, and Odysseus obeyed her gladly. Then Athene, in the form and with the voice of Mentor, presently made a covenant of peace between the two parties.

PRONOUNCING GUIDE
AND INDEX

❦

EACH ENTRY in this index of personages and places includes the following items:

1) The Homeric form of the name in capital letters;
2) The Latin or Roman version of the name, if any, in parentheses and italics;
3) A simple respelling to suggest a suitable English pronunciation of the Homeric form based on traditional practices, and variant forms in fairly common usage, which are likely to be closer to the classical pronunciation;
4) A brief explanation, where pertinent, of the name's significance in Greek mythology, in *The Iliad* and *The Odyssey*, and in modern culture;
5) Page or book references to the text, where applicable.

It can be assumed that a name not included here has been adequately explained in the original context or is without sufficient interest to justify separate notice.

APHRODITE (*Venus*) / AF—ro—DYE—tee

Goddess of love, fertility, beauty; daughter of Zeus and Dione; wife of Hephaestus; mother of Eros (*Cupid*); lover of Ares; 38, 98–100, 262; *Introduction*, IB3.

APOLLO / a—POL—low

God of prophecy, music, medicine, archery; son of Zeus and Leto; attributes: lyre, bow and arrow; 32, 46, 93, 111, 200, 203, 267, 277.

ARCEISIUS / ar—SEE—see—us / ar—SAY—see—us

A son of Zeus who founded the royal house of Ithaca; father of Laertes; grandfather of Odysseus; great-grandfather of Telemachus; 56–57, 180.

ARES (*Mars*) / AIR—ees / AH—rays

God of offensive war; son of Zeus and Hera; attributes: weapons of destruction; in Homer, often a ridiculous character; 97–100, 149; *Introduction*, IB3.

ARETE / a—RAY—ta / ah—RAY—tay

Queen of Phaeacians; wife of Alcinous; mother of Nausicaa; 73–74, 81, Book VII, 101–02, 165.

ARTEMIS (*Diana*) / AHR—te—mis

Goddess of hunting, wild animals, moon, childbirth; daughter of Zeus and Leto; twin sister of Apollo, attributes: bow and arrow, hind; 41, 76, 144, 200, 202, 238, 261–62.

ATHENE (*Minerva*) / a—THEE—nee / ah—thay—NIGH—a

Goddess of wisdom, defensive war, arts of peace; daughter of Zeus (according to Homer, Trito-born, *i.e.*, born of water; later believed to have sprung from Zeus' head); patron goddess of Odysseus; attributes: owl, olive tree, aegis; Books I–III, V, 73–74, 82–84, 96, XIII, 190–91, 209, XXII, XXIV; *Introduction*, IB3.

ATLAS / AT—las

One of the Titans, an earlier group of divinities who ruled the earth until overthrown by the Olympian gods; Zeus then assigned Atlas the eternal task of holding the heavens on his shoulders; 88; *Introduction,* IB3.

CADMUS / CAD—mus

Slew a dragon, sowed the earth with its teeth; from the furrows there sprang up armed men, some of whom helped Cadmus found Thebes; one of his daughters, Ino, became a sea nymph, charged with aiding men in peril on the sea; 68.

CALYPSO / ka—LIP—so

Sea nymph of Ogygian isle; daughter of Atlas; 3, 52, Book V, 88, 102; *Introduction,* ID.

CASSANDRA / ka—SAN—dra / kah—SAHN—drah

A princess of Troy; prophetess whose predictions were never believed; became slave of Agamemnon; killed by his wife on arrival at Mycenae; 146; *Introduction,* IB.

CENTAUR / SEN—torr

A monster with a man's head, trunk, and arms, and with a horse's body and legs; 278.

CHARYBDIS / ka—RIB—dis

Powerful, destructive whirlpool, supposedly located in the Straits of Messina, opposite Scylla; the Mediterranean equivalent of the Maelstrom of the Northern Seas; 154, 158, 163; *Introduction,* ID.

CICONES or CICONIANS / si—CONE—ees

Thracian allies of Troy; see ISMARUS; Book IX.

CIRCE / SIR—see / KEER—kay

Nymph of Aeaea; daughter of Helios; bewitched men and turned them into wild beasts; 102, 107, Books X, XII.

his name became a byword for cruel, sadistic torture; 235–36, 278.

EREBUS / ERR—i—bus
Dark place under the earth through which the dead passed before entering the Kingdom of Hades; 137.

ERINYES (*Furies*) / e—RIN—yes
Goddesses who avenged transgressions of the natural order, pursued criminals, drove them insane; 17, 196, 262; *Introduction*, IB3.

EUMAEUS / you—ME—us / you—MY—us
Prince, kidnaped as child, sold into slavery; faithful swineherd of Odysseus; slept with his master's pigs; helped slay the suitors; Books XIV–XVI, XX–XXIV.

EURYCLEIA / you—ri—CLAY—a
Faithful old nurse of Odysseus, twice entrusted with explosive information; 13, 22–23, Books XIX, XXII, 300.

EURYLOCHUS / you—RILE—o—kus
Relative of Odysseus, leading member of the crew, whose poor judgment (in Odysseus' opinion) brings disaster; 131–32, 159–61.

EURYMACHUS / you—RIME—a—kus
A leading suitor of Penelope, "much the best man and the most persistent wooer"; 12, 18–19, 203, 215, 239, 241–42, 284–85.

GAIA or GE (*Tellus*) / GAY—er or GAY / GUY—er
Goddess of the earth (Mother Earth), whence our names for *geo*graphy, *geo*logy, *geo*physics, etc.; mother of the Titans; giver and receiver of life; 90, 150.

GORGON / GORE—gun
Horrible creature who turned men into stone when they

looked at her; daughter of Phorcys; slain and beheaded by Perseus; 151; *Introduction*, IB3.

HADES or PLUTO (*Orcus*) / HAY—dees
God of the underworld, which was located in the western end of the Mediterranean and also known as Hades; brother of Zeus; captor-husband of Persephone; 135, Book XI, 152, Book XXIV.

HELEN / HELL—in
Demigoddess, beautiful daughter of Zeus and the mortal woman Leda; sister of Clytemnestra; wife of Menelaus; abducted by Paris of Troy, recaptured by the Greeks; Books IV, XV, 301; *Introduction*, IB.

HELIOS HYPERION / HEEL—i—us high—PEER—i—on
Hyperion was the Titan sun god; his son Helios, from whose name we derive our name for the element *helium*, is known in Homer either by the father's name or as the son of Hyperion; his sacred cattle could not be eaten because any diminution in their number would upset the lunar calendar (350 nights, 350 days); 3, 98, Book XII; *Introduction*, IB3.

HEPHAESTUS (*Vulcan*) / he—FESS—tus / hay—FIGH—stus
God of fire, forge, and handicrafts; lame son of Zeus and Hera; husband of Aphrodite; attributes: anvil and forge; all great works of craftsmanship were attributed to his influence; 53, 84, 98–100, 193.

HERA (Juno) / HERE—a
Wife of Zeus, queen of gods; patron deity of women and marriage; 50, 102, 150, 154, 262; *Introduction*, IB3.

HERACLES (*Hercules*) / HER—a—klees
Demigod; son of Zeus and Alcmene; the strong man of ancient legend, famous for his twelve labors; 150–51; *Introduction*, IB3.

HERMES (*Mercury*) / HERM—ees
Official messenger of Olympian gods; son of Zeus and nymph Maia; slayer of hundred-eyed Monster Argus; 4, 61–63, 85, 128, 186–87, 306.

HYPERION (see HELIOS HYPERION)

INO / EYE—no
Daughter of mortal Cadmus; made a marine goddess; aided men in peril on the sea; 68.

ISMARUS / is—MAR—us
A city on the coast of Thrace; inhabited by Cicones, allies of Troy; first stop in Odysseus' postwar adventures; first indication that past glory does not guarantee permanent success; Book IX.

ITHACA / ITH—a—ka / EE—thah—kah
Island in Ionian Sea, usually associated with modern Thiaki; ruled for three generations by House of Arceisius; main scene of Homer's *The Odyssey*, described 53, 106, 169–70, 172.

LAERTES / lay—AIR—tees / lah—AIR—tays
Retired king of Ithaca; son of Arceisius, hence grandson of Zeus; husband of Anticleia; father of Odysseus, grandfather of Telemachus; 13, 208–09, Book XXIV.

LAESTRYGONIANS / LESS—tri—JOE—nians / LIE—stry—GO—nians
Race of giant cannibals dwelling in the far north, where nights are very short; 123–24.

LETO (*Latona*) / LEE—to / LAY—to
Daughter of a Titan; a lover of Zeus; mother of Artemis and Apollo; 75, 150.

LOTOPHAGI / LOW—toe—FOG—gy
Literally, lotus-eaters; inhabitants of land supposedly off

North Africa; fruit of lotus plant was believed to cause amnesia; Book IX; *Introduction*, ID.

MAIA / MAY—a / MY—a
Daughter of Atlas; mother of Hermes by Zeus; 187.

MELANTHIUS / Me—LAN—thee—us / May—LAHN—thee—us
Traitorous, surly, but brave goatherd of Odysseus; mutilated and slain by Telemachus for aiding the suitors; 222–23, 286–88, 294; *Introduction*, IIC.

MEMNON / MEM—nun
Beautiful demigod; son of goddess Eos (Dawn) and mortal Tithonus; nephew of Priam, fought on Trojan side, killed Nestor's son; 43.

MENELAUS / men—e—LAY—us / men—e—LAH—os
King of Sparta; brother of Agamemnon; husband of Helen, hence son-in-law of Zeus; as host to Telemachus, tells famous stories of Proteus and Troy; Books IV, XV; *Introduction*, ID.

MINOS / MY—nos
Powerful king of Crete; son of Zeus and Europa; supposedly conferred every nine years with Zeus before decreeing new laws; in Hades, therefore, a judge of the dead; 143, 149, 248; *Introduction*, IB1, IB3.

MUSE / MEWS
Homer is referring to the goddess of epic poetry, Calliope, one of the nine Muses, all daughters of Zeus and Mnemosyne (Memory, whence our word *mnemonic*); patrons of the various arts and sciences; 3, 103; *Introduction*, IA, IB3.

MYCENAE / my—SEE—knee
City-state, center of Mycenaean culture that overthrew Minoan culture; 32; *Introduction*, IB.

ORESTES /oh—RES—tees
Son of Agamemnon and Clytemnestra; avenged the murder of his father; held up to Telemachus as shining example of son's assumption of responsibility; 4, 10, 30, 33, 51, 147; *Introduction*, IC.

PAEËON / PEE—ee—on / pie—AY—ee—on
Physician to the Olympian gods; from his name we derive the word *paean*, for a solemn hymn of thanksgiving to the gods, especially to Apollo, god of medicine; 44.

PENELOPE / pe—NELL—oh—pee
Daughter of Icarius and the nymph Periboea; fair and faithful wife of Odysseus; mother of Telemachus; by series of stratagems, postponed choice of one of 108 exploitative suitors as her second husband until Odysseus could return and destroy them all; her most famous action is described indirectly in Book II; she appears actively in Books I, IV, XVII–XXI, XXIII; *Introduction*, IB2, ID, IIC.

PERSEPHONE (*Proserpina*) / per—SEFF—oh—knee
Daughter of Demeter; wife of Hades, queen of the underworld; 133, Book XI; *Introduction*, IB3.

PHAEACIANS / fee—AY—shuns / fie—AH—kee—ans
Mythical people inhabiting island of Scheria, ruled by King Alcinous and Queen Arete; somewhat utopian; did not practice arts of war, concentrated on arts of peace, most notably developing superships; Books V–XIII.

PHORCYS / FOR—kiss
Greek sea god; father of Gorgons, Sirens, Thoösa, Scylla; 5, 166.

POLYPHEMUS / polly—FEE—mus
King of the Cyclopes; son of Poseidon and Thoösa; Odysseus

blinded and derided him, bringing upon himself the wrath of Poseidon; 5, Book IX.

POSEIDON (*Neptune*) / poh—SIGH—don
God of sea, hurricane, earthquake, horses; brother of Zeus; attribute: the trident, or three-pronged spear; 3, 25, 50, 68–70, 138–39, 141–42, 143, 168; *Introduction*, IB3.

PROTEUS / PRO—tee—us / PRO—tyoos
Immortal old man of the sea; Egyptian subject of Poseidon; tended the flocks of seals belonging to Amphitrite; father of Idothea, who helped Menelaus; can change shape at will (whence we get our word *protean*); 47–52.

RHADAMANTHUS / rad—a—MAN—thus
Son of Zeus and Europa; brother of Minos; famous as wise judge during lifetime on earth; made ruler of Elysian fields in afterworld; 52, 90.

SCHERIA / SHEER—y—a / SKER—ee—a
Mythical Mediterranean isle, assumed to be in Ionian Sea north of Ithaca; usually identified with modern Corcyra; home of Phaeacians; Odysseus' last steppingstone in his odyssey; Books V–XIII.

SCYLLA / SILL—a
Doglike female monster on rock in Straits of Messina, opposite Charybdis; six-headed, could seize six men at a time; 154–55, 157–58.

SIREN / SIGH—ren
A mermaid, or sea nymph, whose singing supposedly lured sailors to their death on rocky island; 153, 156.

TANTALUS / TAN—ta—lus
Son of Zeus, originally a favorite of the gods; punished in Hades for his crimes (including cannibalism) by being *tanta-*

lized: i.e., made to stand in a pool of water that drained when he wanted to drink, under a tree whose fruits moved away when he wanted to eat; 150.

TEIRESIAS / tie—REES—i—as
Blind soothsayer of Thebes, appearing in many works of ancient and modern literature; in Homer, carries golden scepter of prophecy even in Hades; of all the ghosts, he alone is allowed by Persephone to keep his wisdom and memory intact; 133, 138–40.

TELEMACHUS / te—LEM—a—kus
Son of Odysseus and Penelope, who arrives at man's estate under difficult and distressing circumstances; proves himself worthy to vie with father and grandfather "in the matter of arms"; especially active in Books I–IV, XV–XXIV; see also *Introduction,* ID.

THEMIS / THEME—is
Goddess who, with Zeus, presided over law and justice; attribute: a set of scales; 15; *Introduction,* IB3.

THETIS / THEE—tis
Sea nymph; mother of Achilles; 149.

TITHONUS / ti—THO—nus
Beautiful brother of King Priam of Troy; carried off by Eos (Dawn) to be her consort; sired Memnon; 60.

TITYUS / TIT—yus / TIT—ee—us
Giant son of Gaia; molested Zeus' lover Leto; was killed by her children, Apollo and Artemis; punished in Hades by having his liver (believed to be seat of passions) pecked at by vultures; 90, 150.

TROY or ILIUM / ILL—ee—um / ILL—yum
Ancient city in northwestern Asia Minor, three miles from

SUGGESTIONS FOR FURTHER READING

---※---

TRANSLATIONS

Cook, Albert, trans. *The "Odyssey": A Verse Translation*, second edition. New York: W. W. Norton & Co., 1993.

Fagles, Robert, trans. *The Odyssey*. Introduction and notes by Bernard Knox. New York: The Viking Press, 1996.

Fitzgerald, Robert, trans. *The Odyssey*. Introduction by Seamus Heaney. New York: Everyman's Library, 1992.

Lawrence, T. E., trans. *The Odyssey*. Introduction by Bernard Knox. New York: Oxford University Press, 1991.

Lombardo, Stanley, trans. *The Odyssey*. Introduction by Sheila Murnaghan. Indianapolis: Hackett Publishing Company, 2000.

Lattimore, Richard, trans. *The "Odyssey" of Homer*. New York: Harper and Row, 1965.

Rieu, E. V., trans. *The Odyssey*. New York: Penguin, 1946.

COMMENTARIES AND MONOGRAPHS

Ahl, Frederick, and Hanna M. Roisman. *The "Odyssey" Reformed*. Ithaca: Cornell University Press, 1996.

Arnold, Matthew. *On Translating Homer*. 1861.

Austin, N. *Archery at the Dark of the Moon: Poetic Problems in Homer's "Odyssey."* Berkeley: University of California Press, 1975.

Bloom, Harold, ed. *Homer.* New York: Chelsea House, 1986.

———. *The Odyssey.* New York: Chelsea House, 1988.

Clarke, Howard, ed. *Twentieth-Century Interpretations of the "Odyssey."* Englewood Cliffs, NJ: Prentice-Hall, 1967.

Cohen, Beth, ed. *The Distaff Side: Representing the Female in Homer's "Odyssey."* New York: Oxford University Press, 1995.

Camps, W. A. *An Introduction to Homer.* Oxford: The Clarendon Press, 1980.

Carpenter, Rhys. *Folk Tale: Fiction and Saga in the Homeric Epics.* Berkeley: University of California Press, 1958.

Clarke, Howard W. *The Art of the "Odyssey."* Englewood Cliffs, NJ: Prentice Hall, 1967.

Clay, Jenny Strauss. *The Wrath of Athena: Gods and Men in the "Odyssey."* Princeton: Princeton University Press, 1983.

Cook, Irwin F. *The "Odyssey" in Athens: Myths of Cultural Origins.* Ithaca: Cornell University Press, 1995.

Dimock, George E. *The Unity of the "Odyssey."* Amherst: University of Massachusetts Press, 1989.

Dodds, E. R. *The Greeks and the Irrational.* Berkeley: University of California Press, 1951.

Doherty, Lilian Eileen. *Siren Songs: Gender, Audiences and Narrators in the "Odyssey."* Ann Arbor: University of Michigan Press, 1996.

Finley, M. I. *The World of Odysseus.* New York: The Viking Press, 1954. Revised edition, 1965.

Ford, Andrew. *Homer: The Poetry of the Past.* Ithaca: Cornell University Press, 1992.

Graves, Robert. *The Greek Myths.* London: Penguin, 1955.

Griffin, Jasper. *Homer: The "Odyssey."* Cambridge: Cambridge University Press, 1987.

Hexter, Ralph. *A Guide to the "Odyssey": A Commentary on the English Translation of Robert Fitzgerald.* New York: Vintage, 1993.

Huebeck, Alfred, Stephanie West, and J. B. Hainsworth. *A Commentary on the "Odyssey."* Oxford: Oxford University Press, 1988.

Katz, Marilyn A. *Penelope's Renown: Meaning and Interdeterminacy in the "Odyssey."* Princeton: Princeton University Press, 1991.

Lord, Albert B. *The Singer of Tales,* second edition. Stephen Mitchell and Gregory Nagy, editors. Cambridge: Harvard University Press, 2000.

Myrsiades Kostas, ed. *Approaches to Teaching Homer's "Illiad" and "Odyssey."* Modern Languages Association, 1993.

Nilsson, Martin Persson. *Homer and Mycenae.* London: Methuen, 1933.

Page, Denys Lionel. *The Homeric "Odyssey."* Westport, CT: The Greenwood Press, 1976.

Parry, Milman. *The Making of Homeric Verse.* Oxford: The Clarendon Press, 1971.

Peradotto, John. *Man in the Middle: Voice, Name, and Narration in the "Odyssey."* Martin Classical Lectures, New Series, Volume I. Princeton: Princeton University Press, 1990.

Schein, Seth L., ed. *Reading the "Odyssey": Selective Interpretive Essays.* Princeton: Princeton University Press, 1995.

Segal, Charles. *Singers, Heroes, and Gods in the "Odyssey."* Ithaca: Cornell University Press, 1994.

Taylor, Charles H. *Essays on the "Odyssey."* Bloomington: Indiana University Press, 1963.

Thornton, Agathe. *People and Themes in Homer's "Odyssey."* London: Methuen, 1970.

Tracy, Stephen V. *The Story of the "Odyssey."* Princeton: Princeton University Press, 1990.

Wace, A.J.B., and F. H. Stubbings. *A Companion to Homer.* New York: Macmillan, 1962.

Whitman, Cedric H. *Homer and the Heroic Tradition.* New York: Norton, 1965.

Woodhouse, W. J. *The Composition of Homer's "Odyssey."* Oxford: The Clarendon Press, 1969.